Spark

Book Three in Red-Line: The Fletcher Family Saga
J. T. Bishop

Eudoran Press LLC

J. T. Bishop/Eudoran Press LLC

6009 Parker Rd. Suite 149 #205

Plano, TX 75093

www.jtbishopauthor.com

Updated Cover by J.T. Bishop

Author Photos by Mayza Clark Photography

Book Editing by Amie McCracken

Spark/ J. T. Bishop. -- 1st ed.

ISBN 978-1-7325531-0-1

To Julia and Sarah.
I knew one of you well and the other not at all, but your examples of courage and strength epitomize all I strive to be.
I am honored to be called your granddaughter.

Other Books by J. T. Bishop

The Red-Line Trilogy
Red-Line: The Shift
Red-Line: Mirrors
Red-Line: Trust Destiny
The Red-Line Trilogy Boxed Set

Red-Line: The Fletcher Family Saga
Curse Breaker
High Child
Spark
Forged Lines
The Fletcher Family Boxed Set

The Family or Foe Saga with Detectives Daniels and Remalla
First Cut
Second Slice
Third Blow
Fourth Strike
The Family or Foe Saga Boxed Set

<u>Detectives Daniels and Remalla standalones/novellas</u>
The Girl and the Gunshot (subscribers only)
A Hamburger Christmas
The Magic of Murder (subscribers only)
Murder Unveiled—a prequel to Haunted River

<u>Detectives Daniels and Remalla</u>
Haunted River
Of Breath and Blood
Of Body and Bone
Of Mind and Madness
Of Power and Pain
Of Love and Loss
Dominion
Illusions
Vendetta

<u>The Redstone Chronicles</u>
Lost Souls
Lost Dreams
Lost Chances
Lost Hope
Lost Lives
Lost Time
Lost Love

Chapter One

"How much longer is this going to take?"

Adam leaned back against a scrubby tree and stared at the ground. "I don't know."

Tezik walked up and grabbed his shoulder. "We've been here two months."

Adam pulled away from Tezik's grasp. "Neither one of us knew what to expect when we got here. We were aware of the unknowns."

"There weren't that many unknowns." He pointed a finger. "All we had to do was get close and figure out where her brother was. How hard is it?"

"How the hell would you know?" Adam kicked at the leafy dirt. "You're sitting here in a cushy craft while I have to live among them. Every day. Trying to wade through all that chaotic energy is torture. You should see some of the people she works with. Not to mention being able to feel all of them. The pure exertion of trying to protect myself is exhausting."

"Hanging out and getting close to a beautiful woman must be traumatic."

"You don't understand, Tez..."

"Tell me what I don't understand. You know this woman by now. You and I both know her track record. She likes men. You need to use that. That was the plan all along."

"I know," yelled Adam. He swiped at one of the brushy trees that muffled their conversation. He'd driven outside of the city and into the wooded acreage that bordered the road to meet his partner and friend, Tezik.

"You don't have to marry her. Sleep with her, yes. Get her to talk. Then, when she trusts you, she tells you what we need to know. What is wrong with that plan?"

Adam sighed. "I can't—"

Tez's eyes widened. "Don't tell me you're getting a conscious. Since when have you ever hesitated to bed a gorgeous woman? I don't have enough fingers to count your conquests. And this one isn't even looking for a commitment." He shook his head. "You know what we have at stake here. What we promised. We agreed to come here and get this information. It's what we do. We get well paid for it."

"You don't have to tell me what we do."

"Apparently I do."

Adam knew his friend was fighting to hold his temper. "I'll get it."

Tez set his jaw. "Listen. Roma will only wait so long. You know how she works. It wouldn't surprise me in the least if she sent somebody else as a backup, in case we fail."

"She's never done that before. Why would she start now?"

"We're overdue, and she hasn't heard from us. I can't initiate a signal from here. If she thinks we failed, she'll send another team. She doesn't care about us. She just wants the information. You and I both have family back home. If we come back with nothing, you know what could happen."

Adam scoffed. "Family? I have a sister married to one of the Council's goons. And parents I barely talk to. They're too busy playing suck-up at their master's feet."

"What do you think we're doing?" asked Tez. "We suck up to the Red-Lines for a living. Would you rather live in a slum, living day to day doing menial tasks?"

Adam frowned. "I am not like my parents."

Tez smirked. "I've got news for you. Yes, you are. We get hired to do the dirty work. We do it so we don't live in poverty. It's what Grays have been reduced to. I think your parents see it the same way."

Adam pushed off the tree. "My parents sold me to the highest bidder."

"Your parents offered your services to Galen. Just like mine. It put food in our mouths."

"And money in their pockets."

"You could have left a long time ago. We haven't seen Galen in almost two seasons. You were offered a job, which you accepted. We both did."

Adam crossed his arms. "We didn't have much of a choice."

Tez groaned and rubbed his head. "This is not the time for a philosophical discussion about our life choices. As they say down here, this is the hand we've been dealt. Now, if you want to live in a fantasy world and hope and pray that one day things will change, and suddenly Grays will have equal standing, then go ahead. But in the meantime, you still have work to do."

The breeze brushed against Adam's face. He looked up at the blue, cloudless sky. It was one of the things he liked about Earth. Outside of the highly populated areas, it was beautiful. The woods reminded him of his parent's home before he was given away. "Why do you think they want him?"

"It doesn't matter."

"Word is, he's the High Child."

"Who cares?"

"The man's on another planet. He shouldn't be that big of a threat."

Tez walked up and poked Adam in the chest. "Listen to me. That's not your concern. You've got one week. You either get what we came for, or we're pulling up stakes. And if that happens, she'll assign someone else and never use us again. We'll be sent to the hills to mine old Kista fields, and we'll die years from now from lung waste."

Adam didn't respond.

"Get your act together," said Tez. "Maybe you don't care about your family, but I have a wife back home. And I'd like to get back to her." He stepped back. "My parents groveled at the Red-Lines' feet and barely got by. But not me. I won't live like that again. We're going to finish this job and get our payday. What happens after that is not my business, nor yours."

Adam started to speak, but Tez held up his palm. "Maybe there was a time where the Reds and Grays were unified. Maybe there was a time when we were given freedom to do and go where we wished. But that's been over for a long time. And it's not coming back. So, do me a favor and pull yourself together. If this fails, it's on you, not on me. And I'm not going down because you suddenly feel guilty."

The men held each other's gaze.

"How long have we known each other?" asked Adam.

"Since we worked in Galen's fields when we were kids." He paused. "A long time."

Adam stood solemnly. Tez took a deep breath and released it. Adam could relate to Tez's anger. A memory flashed of the two of them as children, their faces encrusted with dirt and their clothes tattered and worn, working on Galen's property. "I won't let you down, Tez." His friend nodded. "I'll find him. I promise. By the end of this week, I'll find Royce Fletcher."

Chapter Two

EVE FLETCHER WALKED INTO Benny's Juke Joint. The usually crowded bar was quiet, and the stage from which she sang her ballads was dark. The crimson curtains were pulled back in their usual place. Benny never closed them. The smell of stale cigarettes still hung in the air. It seemed to have permeated the walls after years of puffing patrons had come and gone. The chairs hung upside down on tables and the floor was clean, but Eve pictured the spilled drinks, dirty napkins, and cigarette stubs that would litter the ground a mere three hours from now. The bar and lounge would be humming with customers, and she would be thirty minutes into her first set. The crowd would be boisterous but respectful. The rowdy ones wouldn't come out until her second set, after the haze of several rounds of drinks and whatever fashionable drug people were trying these days, settled in. By the second set, inhibitions were lost, and Benny posted bouncers at the sides of the stage to keep the loons at bay. Crazy as it was, it was that set that Eve enjoyed the most. There was something about the energy of the crowd during that time that gave her a thrill. Or it was the element of risk. She always sang better than too.

She headed backstage toward her dressing room. The hall was quiet. She'd agreed to come early to practice. Although she knew the songs well, her most recent piano man, Richie, had asked for the time. They worked well together, but there were still some areas that needed polishing. She glanced at her watch. Richie would be there in fifteen minutes.

Walking down the hall, she flipped a switch and illuminated the small corridor. A drawer slammed nearby, and she jumped. She walked across the hall to Benny's office. "Benny?" she asked, heading toward the door. "Is that you?"

Eve pushed the door open to reveal a small, cramped work area. One window with partially opened blinds allowed enough light for her to see the wooden desk piled with folders, books, and papers. A laptop sat precariously on top of the mound. The room had dark paneled walls and the only picture displayed was a black-and-white photo of a young man and woman. The woman wore a wedding dress and held a small bouquet. The man wore a tux and had his arm around her.

Benny sat in the desk chair. His thinning gray hair, narrow frame, striped pants, and orange shirt gave him the appearance of a retiree on a golf course in Florida.

"Spark?" he asked when she walked in. He pushed his glasses up on his nose. "What are you doing here so early?"

"Hey, Benny," said Eve, walking into the small space. "I'm practicing with Richie. I could ask you the same question. Why are you here?" She looked over his clothes. "Shouldn't you be playing golf?"

"I hate that game." He opened another drawer and closed it again. "I had business crap to deal with." He eyed her outfit. "You look beautiful, as usual."

Eve glanced down at her slim jeans, red low-cut blouse, and red heels. "This?" she asked. "I just threw this on."

"Babe, you could wear a pillowcase and look good." He glanced at the picture on the wall. "You remind me of my Maggie." He made a sign of the cross. "God bless her."

Eve looked at the framed photo. "She was more beautiful than me."

Benny smiled. "Not by much."

Eve eyed his desk. "When are you going to clean this so called desk of yours?"

"This?" He waved a hand. "I know exactly where everything is. If I cleaned it, I'd be lost." He dug through some papers and pulled out a folder.

"You okay?" she asked.

Benny stopped rifling. "Sure, babe. Why wouldn't I be?"

A blur of orange jumped out from behind the desk, and Eve startled. "Jeez," she said, holding her hand to her chest. Benny's cat sauntered to the worn brown couch that sat against the wall. "Louis, you scared me."

Louis made himself comfortable on the sofa, and Eve walked up to pet him. Holding her hand on the animal's head, she stilled for a moment, then she turned and faced Benny. "What's going on?"

Benny looked at her as if she'd asked him why he was wearing shoes. "Wrong?" He placed the folder on his cluttered desk. "Nothing's wrong."

"Something's going on."

Benny narrowed his eyes. "You and that spidey sense of yours. It never ceases to amaze me."

"I've known you a long time. I can tell when you're stressed."

"You've known me three years. But my own kid doesn't get me like you do. How is that possible?"

"Vince is an idiot."

Benny chuckled. "So why'd you date him?"

She shrugged. "I had a less discriminating filter at the time."

"Not anymore, you don't."

"Things change."

He raised a brow. "What about your latest? Jerry is it?"

She tilted her head. "Yes."

"He's an idiot."

"You're changing the subject."

"You're the one that brought up idiots."

Eve scratched Louis's ears. "He's not an idiot. He owns Barwells."

"A retail store?" Benny waved a hand. "Big deal. He's a suit. He's worse than an idiot. He's boring. You don't belong with a suit. You need someone who brightens the stage, not dims the lights."

Eve sighed. This was not the first time they'd had this conversation. "Who do I belong with then?"

Benny hesitated, and Eve waited. "Somebody who makes you laugh."

"I laugh."

"Not near enough. And not with him."

Eve stopped petting Louis. "How did we go from talking about you to my love life?"

"Because I'm boring too. Don't worry about me, kid. Just take care of yourself. You understand? If something happens to me, stay out of it."

Eve stiffened. "What would happen to you?"

"Nothing. Forget I said anything."

"No. What is it? What's wrong?"

Benny sighed and tapped on his desk. "I've owned this place for years. Problems are second nature to me. I've dealt with robbers, liars, and thieves my whole life. And I've always managed to survive. This is no different."

Eve crossed her arms and studied him. She had her suspicions, but she'd never voiced them. "Does this have to do with the mob?"

Benny winced. He pushed up from his seat and walked around the desk. "Listen, Spark. You and I are close. You're my best singer, and you draw the biggest crowds." He reached out and took her hand. "I love you like my own. You're a daughter to me. You know that?"

Eve squeezed his fingers. "I know that. You're like a father to me."

He nodded. "Despite that, if there's one thing I need you to do, it's to stay out of this part of my life."

"Benny—"

He held up a finger. "Don't argue with me. Don't mention that word again. You know nothing. You see nothing. And don't you ever get mixed up with my boy Vinny again. You got that?"

His anger surprised her. She'd never seen him like this. "What's Vinny got to do with the mob?"

Benny shook his head. "Stay out of it. It's not your business."

"But—"

Benny waved his hand. "End of discussion." He walked back to his desk. "Don't you have to meet with Richie?" His tone told her everything.

"I don't want anything to happen to you."

He sat. "Nothing's going to happen to me." He rubbed his eyes. "I think you're just picking up on my fatigue. That's all it is."

She knew it was more. "Sure." She fiddled with the edge of his desk.

"You like Richie?" he asked.

"What?"

"The new guy. The piano man. He working out?"

She tried to focus. "I like him. We just need to get our timing down."

"He likes you, too. He's got that puppy dog look in his eyes."

She rolled her eyes. "He's got a girlfriend."

"So what? You have that effect. That sparkle. Men can't take their eyes off of you."

"You're exaggerating."

"What about that new guy? The bartender. Adam, is it? I see him watching you."

"Adam?"

"Yes. Good-looking guy. Been here what? Two months now?"

"I know who he is."

"You like him?"

"I'm seeing Jerry."

Benny laughed. "Babe, that's never stopped you before."

She almost argued with him, but realized it was pointless. "He's cute, but he barely speaks to me."

"The kid's tongue-tied around you. I've seen him with the patrons, though. He's good with the customers. They like him."

She picked up a paper from Benny's desk. "Good for him."

Benny took the paper out of her hand. "You should talk to him. Make an effort. Help him open up. Be approachable. Besides, if you two got together, you'd be Adam and Eve. Sounds destined to me."

"You think Adam is the man for me? You barely know him."

He leaned forward in his seat. "You're not the only one with a good sense of people."

She couldn't deny that. She glanced at the clock on the wall. "I should go. Richie will be waiting."

"Knock 'em dead tonight."

"I always do." She turned to walk away.

"Hey."

Reaching the threshold, she looked back. "What?"

"Thanks for checking in on me. I appreciate it."

She nodded. "You're welcome."

He paused. "You're my sparkler, kid. Have been since I've known you." She smiled. "And one day, I want you to meet your own sparkler. Someone who lights you up." He glanced at the wall. "Like me and my Maggie."

A lump welled in her throat. "I love you, Benny."

He winked at her. "I love you too." He sat back in his seat and grabbed the folder. Eve saw and felt his gruffness return. "So go teach Richie who's boss."

She laughed softly. "I will."

Chapter Three

THE BAR HUMMED WITH activity. Customers waited at the counter as last call approached. Adam felt the sweat drip down his back as he filled a glass with beer from the tap. He slid the drink to a customer as another ordered a rum and coke. The room was filled with a haze of smoke, and the steady beat of conversation carried among the low lit tables. Eve's set had just ended and now that the music was over, the atmosphere had changed from the sexy and enchanting feel of a jazz ballad to the harsh reality of drunkenness and an impending hangover.

Adam rang up a tab and took a credit card payment. A man in a blue suit, with salt-and-pepper hair, talked on a cell phone at the bar. Adam knew who he was. His name was Jerry—the man Eve was dating.

"Here you go," said Adam, as he slid a receipt to a customer who stood beside Jerry.

"Hey, sweetie," said Jerry into his phone. Adam listened as he rang up another tab. As a bartender, Adam heard all sorts of conversations, perhaps better left unheard. "I'm sorry," said Jerry. "Something came up."

A man in a purple striped suit and bowtie signed his bill and added a tip.

"Sure," said Jerry. "Okay. I'll come over. Just give me an hour." He paused and looked at his watch. "I know. It's late." He smiled and laughed. "But we can sleep in."

Adam shook his head as he listened. A customer approached the bar, but Adam waved him off. "Sorry. The bar just closed."

Jerry hung up his phone. He glanced at Adam. "Any chance I can get one for the road?"

Adam wished he could give him something entirely different. "Sorry. We're closed." He felt Jerry's stare as he wiped the sink and counter.

"What if it was Eve asking?" asked Jerry. "Would you give her a drink?"

Adam opened his mouth but didn't get the chance to respond because Eve walked up. "Did I hear my name?" she asked. She put her arm around Jerry, and he pulled her close.

"Hi, baby," he said. "You sang great tonight." He nuzzled her neck. "But you always do."

Eve kissed him, and Adam fought the urge to tell her exactly what he thought of Jerry, but he bit his tongue. He couldn't help but let his eyes wander, though. She still wore her stage attire—a black satin dress that hugged her fantastic hourglass frame. The slit in her skirt exposed her long smooth thigh, and the front was cut just as deep, revealing the ample cleavage of her perfect breasts. Her auburn hair was as voluptuous as her body, and it was pulled up tonight, revealing a long, curved neck framed by soft tendrils of hair left hanging. Adam didn't think he'd ever seen a more perfect woman.

"You gettin' a good view?" asked Jerry.

Adam felt his cheeks burn as Eve glanced at him. Despite his desire to get to know her, he'd found it difficult to speak in her presence. He doubted he was the first man who'd felt that way.

"How was business tonight?" she asked Adam.

He appreciated her intention to save him some embarrassment. "Great," he said. "But it always is when you sing."

"Bar's closed, honey," Jerry said. "Our boy here won't break the rules." Jerry threw Adam an annoyed stare.

"Good thing," Eve said. "Benny doesn't break the rules, either. It's how he trains the staff." She ran a hand through Jerry's hair. "I might have a secret stash in my dressing room." She turned in his arms to face him. "If you're good, I might invite you back there."

Jerry hugged her close. "About that..." Adam waited for the lie. "I better call it a night. I've got an early meeting tomorrow."

Eve pulled back. "Tomorrow is Saturday."

Adam tensed. He'd never liked Jerry. Not from the first moment he'd met him. Although they'd never been formerly introduced.

Eve was like a disco ball in a nightclub. Bits of light emitted from her that ignited the room in splashes of sparkling reflections. Benny always called her "Spark," and Adam knew why. It was as if every man in a fifty-foot radius was drawn to her like a gambler to money.

"I know, hon," said Jerry. "But we've got that huge convention coming up, and we've got to prepare."

Adam felt the bile rise in his throat. He stifled it. He was getting good at it.

"How come you didn't mention this before?" asked Eve. Adam picked up on her tension and looked away. He had to be careful not to reveal what he knew.

But the tension only grew, and then he sensed eyes on him. He glanced back as he replaced a bottle of bourbon on a shelf. Eve was staring right at him.

He felt her then, probing at him, and he closed up, intent on keeping her out, but he knew he'd only been partially successful.

Eve's stare returned to Jerry. "You're lying to me."

Jerry dropped his hands and held them up. "Whoa. Wait a minute. What are you talking about?"

"You don't have a meeting, do you?"

"Yes. I do."

"No, he doesn't." Adam almost dropped the wine he was holding. He had no idea why he'd just spoken.

Jerry glared at him. "Mind your own business."

"Then maybe you should take your cell conversations outside." He looked at Eve. "He's meeting someone tonight." He chuckled and glanced at Jerry. "Someone he'll be 'sleeping in' with tomorrow."

Jerry stood. "You son-of-a bitch." He faced Eve. "He's lying."

Eve stood unfazed. "No, he's not. You are."

Jerry's mouth dropped. "Come on, honey. I'm telling you. I have a meeting."

Eve stepped away from the bar. "Goodbye, Jerry. Enjoy whoever she is."

Jerry threw out his hands. "There is no 'she.' I swear."

Eve put a hand on her hip. "Then 'he.' Which is fine, either way."

She turned to leave, but Jerry took her arm. "Come on, baby. What's the big deal?" He smirked. "Were we really exclusive?"

Eve didn't move, and Adam anticipated her response, certain it would be worth the wait. "It's not that, Jerry."

"Then what?"

Eve shrugged out of his grasp. "You're boring."

Jerry's jaw dropped. "I'm what?"

"And you don't make me laugh."

Jerry stood there, mouth open, as Eve walked away. She opened a door marked *Employees only* and disappeared behind it.

Jerry's frame slouched, and Adam went back to cleaning the counter, mumbling to himself about intervening. After a few seconds, Jerry turned and looked at him. "Women," was all he said, then he left the bar.

Adam stopped wiping, but held the dish towel in his hand. His heart was racing. What had just happened? He'd been trying his damnedest to keep his thoughts to himself, and up until then, he'd succeeded. But now, Eve had just read him with ease. Then he'd opened his mouth. He knew it was because he'd become emotional, which had made it harder for him, but now he realized his mistake. If he'd allowed her to read more than just what he knew about Jerry, then his whole cover could be blown. This mission would end in failure.

Adam stared at the door through which Eve had just left. He sighed and moaned. Now he knew he had no choice. What happened tonight would either open the door to Eve and her secrets, or close it forever.

· · • • • • • • • · ·

Eve felt the warm breeze ruffle her hair as she took a sip of her scotch. She closed her eyes, took a deep breath, and let it out, allowing herself to relax. The night was quiet, and all she could hear was the distant sound of cars from below. Benny's Juke Joint sat in the middle of the city's nightlife. And even though it was 3:30 a.m., people were still out. It was Saturday, and the night owls were going strong. Tuning out the distant noise, she felt the alcohol soothe her, and she looked up at the night sky. A few stars twinkled through the sparse clouds, and the moon was high in the sky.

She shifted in the lounge chair. Benny had placed a couple of them out on the roof, and had told only Eve where the key was to access this area. It was a private spot where either of them could go to get away. Sitting there now, Eve thought of her father. Her eyes scanned the sky, and she wondered from which bright star he had come. Many years ago, when Eve was still a child, he'd pointed in a certain direction up at one of the constellations, and he'd told her he'd come from far away. At the time, she'd thought he was teasing, but she'd learned long after that he was not.

It had been several years since she'd seen him. The last time had been when he'd arrived to help her and her siblings, Gillian and Royce, through their Shifts. It had been a difficult time for each of them, and just as they had begun to get their bearings, her father had left again. Eve recalled all that had happened since then. The changes they'd all experienced. The gifts they'd developed, and the tragedies they'd endured. She smiled, thinking of

Gillian, recently married. The path had been hard for her sister, but Gillian seemed to have found the light at the end of the tunnel.

The road had not been so easy for her brother Royce. Eve took another swallow as she thought of him and grimaced. Reflecting on her brother made her heart hurt, so she turned her attention to something else.

Her mind wandered back to Jerry, and then Adam, the new bartender. Her earlier encounter with the two men had surprised her. Not because of Jerry's lie, but because of Adam's revelation.

Although Eve's sister Gillian had inherited most of the intuitive gifts, Eve had some ability to sense dishonesty. She was still working on honing the skill that came naturally to her sister. She found it fascinating that those who lied with ease were harder to read. Eve could only assume they were so used to doing it that they didn't give off the usual signals. She supposed that was the case with Jerry. Eve would have figured it out soon enough, but what took her by surprise was that she'd picked up on Adam's signals far quicker than Jerry's.

Prickles on her skin made her tune in and reveal Adam's distaste for the man, and then it didn't take much after that to recognize he was angry. And a little more probing revealed why. Eve took another sip of her scotch. It wasn't the end of her relationship with Jerry that had her out on the roof, enjoying a drink. Instead, it was the vibe of Adam. That little peek of insight made him feel entirely different to her. And when he'd closed up on her, she'd realized that he'd known she was reading him. A shooting star streaked the sky, and she shook her head. She knew there were humans who were gifted with advanced intuition and higher sensitivities, and she felt fairly certain that Adam was one of them.

A door opened and closed behind her. Eve turned, expecting to see Benny, but raised an eyebrow when she saw the man she had been pondering instead. Adam stood outside the roof entrance with his hands in his pockets, and Eve admired his rugged appeal. He had sandy, almost blonde hair with a shadow of stubble on his jaw. His tall frame showcased his broad shoulders and narrow waist. Eve imagined a muscled chest and arms beneath his white shirt and black pants. He was not hard to look at, and Eve didn't hide her appraisal.

Adam approached the empty chair beside her. He looked like a nervous kid who was about to ask the prettiest girl in school for a date. "Hi," was all he said.

"Hi," she answered. She noticed his own appraisal of her. Although she'd changed out of her black dress into jeans and a T-shirt, he looked at her as if she still wore the outfit.

"How'd you find me?" she asked.

"Benny told me I might find you up here."

She smiled. Benny was indeed playing matchmaker. He'd never allowed anyone else on the roof. "Ah," she said. "I see."

"You want me to leave? I don't want to interrupt."

She waved a hand. "No. Not at all." She gestured at the seat beside her. "Sit." She picked up the bottle of scotch that Benny had given her for her birthday. She kept it in her dressing room for occasions such as these. Pouring more in her glass, she said, "Want some?" She put the bottle down and held out the glass.

Adam hesitated, but then walked slowly to the chair and sat. "What is it?"

"Scotch. Have a sip." He stared at the glass. "Sorry. It's the only cup I have." She leaned closer to him. "I promise. I don't have any cooties."

He reached for the beverage and took it from her, his finger touching hers briefly. He sniffed at the drink and grimaced.

"Go ahead," she said. "It will put some hair on your chest."

His eyebrows furrowed, and he pulled at his shirt and looked below it. "Do I need more?"

Eve grinned. "I don't know. Do you?"

The side of his mouth rose, and he lifted the glass and took a healthy sip. The reaction was immediate. His lips blanched, his jaw set, and he coughed. He held the glass at arm's length. "God," he sputtered, "what is that?" He choked again as his face turned red.

Amused, Eve took the glass from him. "Only the best scotch you can buy. Smooth, isn't it?" She took another swallow.

"I think my guts are melting." He cleared his throat and held his chest. "How do you drink that stuff?"

"Very easily." She cocked her head at him. "Scotch is for those with more discerning taste." She narrowed eyes. "Don't tell me. You're a Tequila man. Am I right?"

He managed to stop coughing long enough to answer. "Actually, I'm not much of a drinker."

"Really? A bartender?"

He nodded. "I may know my drinks, but that doesn't mean I indulge in them."

"AA?" she asked.

He frowned. "AA?"

"Yes. Are you a member?"

He shook his head. "Of what?"

"AA?" When it was clear he was confused, she added. "You know, Alcoholics Anonymous?"

"Alcoholics...what? Who's that?"

She quirked up a brow. "Seriously?"

For a moment, he looked stricken, but then his eyes widened. "Oh, you're asking if I'm an alcoholic?" He smiled. "No. I'm not. Just don't drink much. Maybe the occasional glass of wine. That's all."

She wasn't sure what to think. Maybe he wasn't as smart as he was good looking. "Wine, huh?"

His knee bounced. "Yes."

She studied him as he looked everywhere else but at her. "Were you looking for me?"

He glanced over. "Huh?"

"Benny never tells people about this place. Obviously, you asked where I was."

"I did. Yes."

"So, here I am."

"Yes. There you are." His knee kept bouncing.

"Well?" She sat back in her chair and waited.

"I guess I just wanted to apologize."

"For what?"

"For tonight. For what happened with Jerry."

She shifted sideways. "Really? Why?"

He finally glanced briefly at her. "I should have minded my own business."

"You wouldn't have said anything if I hadn't figured it out?"

His mouth dropped open, but he didn't speak.

"You don't really mean your apology, do you?"

Then he did make eye contact with her. "I'm sorry you two broke up."

She smiled. "You're a worse liar than he is."

He groaned. "Sorry. I guess I'm not explaining myself very well."

She took a sip of her drink. "No. You're not." She thought back to their earlier encounter. "How about I take a shot?" She sat straight, swiveled her legs to the side, and faced him. "I knew he was lying because I felt it from you. Before you said anything. And you're wondering how I did that. Is that it?"

He studied her, this time with no nervousness. "You get to the point, don't you?"

"It saves a lot of time."

"I suppose it does."

"Well," she said, resting her elbows on her knees. "I could tell you I just guessed, but then that would make us both liars. The fact is that I read people pretty easily. And when you're in my business, and you look like this, and you deal with the people I deal with, you better learn to read between the lines, or you're going to get screwed, literally and figuratively."

"And you could read me?"

She nodded. "It wasn't hard. Your body language said it all. It was obvious Jerry was hiding something, and you knew it. You wanted to say it, but you held back. That's hard for people to conceal. Their facial expressions and body postures automatically tense. The guessing part came in with his so called 'meeting,' but it was the logical conclusion." Her explanation was as close to the truth as she could offer, without sounding like a mental patient.

"That's amazing."

She sipped her scotch, and her body warmed from the alcohol. She was going to have to slow down if she expected to walk off this roof unassisted. But since she was up here with Adam, she couldn't help but have some fun. She smiled seductively. "It's one of my many talents."

He didn't look away. For a moment, the barrier dropped and Eve felt an intense heat bloom in her core, and she knew intuitively that he was feeling the same. Just as quickly, though, the shield returned, and he swallowed. "I'll think I'll have another sip of that drink, if you don't mind."

She grinned and held the glass out to him. "I think I'm getting to you."

He took the scotch and drank some more. His face tightened, but his reaction was less volatile. "If you're reading my body language, then you already know the answer."

Smiling, she sat back in her seat. "We drink much more and you might be reading me." She glanced at him. "But not with your mind." His blush made her laugh. "I like you Adam. You're like the handsome football player who wants to run off with the sexy cheerleader but can't figure out how to leave the game." She leaned closer to him. "You want to go make out under the bleachers?"

His knee bounced much faster. "I don't see any bleachers."

She shrugged. "We can improvise."

He took another sip of her drink and handed it back to her. "Can't."

Eve took the glass. "Why not?"

He eyed her. "Like you said. Game's not over. Coach will kill me."

Eve raised her drink. "Your loss."

His foot stopped bouncing, and he looked her way. "But believe me, after that last second ticks off the clock, and I've won the game, I may take you up on that offer."

Eve figured the alcohol was making him bolder. She eyed him back. "That's assuming the offer still stands." She leaned back and looked up at the stars. "I wait for no man."

She heard him chuckle. "No," he said. "I can see that." He paused. "But there's an exception to every rule."

She giggled, and she knew she'd had too much to drink. She never giggled. "I think the scotch is helping you relax."

"It's helping with a lot of things."

She giggled again and picked up the bottle. Sitting up, she said, "You're right. It is." She handed the scotch to him. "Which is probably why we should go."

Taking the bottle, Adam stared up at her as she stood. "Go?"

"Yes," she said. "It's late."

"You mean early," he said, standing with her. He looked at his watch. "It's almost four o'clock."

"I need my beauty sleep."

"I think you've had plenty of that." He blushed again.

Eve liked his shyness. It was refreshing to see it in a man. "Walk me down the stairs?"

"Sure."

They headed to the roof access. After walking back in, Adam ensured the door was locked, and the key returned to its hiding place. They took the stairs carefully and descended to the ground floor. The halls were quiet and dark as Eve headed back to her dressing room, where she returned the half-full bottle of scotch.

"You okay to get home?" asked Adam.

Eve checked her reflection in the mirror. Her cheeks were flushed, and her lips were dry. She reapplied some lipstick and fluffed her hair. "Yes. I'm fine." She turned from the mirror. "I'll probably just walk. I don't live far from here."

"Walk?" he asked. "At this hour?"

"Sure. Why not? It's a nice night."

"No way. We'll share a cab."

She turned from the mirror. "What for? It's Saturday. There are people out."

"Drunk and high people."

"My kind of people."

He shook his head. "The exact opposite of your kind of people."

"Really?" she asked. "And how do you know what kind of people I am?"

The question seemed to take him off guard. His mouth opened, but he didn't speak. She was about to say something when a loud crash traveled from down the hall. It sounded as if a piece of furniture had overturned. They both jumped at the noise.

"What was that?" asked Adam. "I didn't think anyone else was here."

"I don't know." Eve moved to the door of her dressing room. She edged it open and looked down the corridor. There was another adjacent dressing room that was dark and empty. The stage access was closed, as was the stairwell to the roof. The only other room was Benny's office. The door was slightly ajar and a faint light emitted from the room.

"Benny?" asked Eve. She walked into the hall, and Adam followed. Reaching the entrance, she pushed on the door. It swiveled open. She saw his cluttered desk, but his file cabinet was overturned. Benny was lying on the floor.

Eve gasped. "Benny. Oh, my god." She ran over to him. He was pale, and his eyes were closed. Eve patted his cheeks. "Benny. Can you hear me?"

His eyelids fluttered. "Spark?" He spoke so quietly, Eve had to lean close.

"Benny? What's wrong? What happened?" She looked at Adam. "Call an ambulance." Patting at Benny's chest, she looked for injuries. Her heart thumped with fear. Benny wore a dark jacket, and she stopped when she felt something warm and sticky. Her fingers turned red. Pushing the jacket back, she saw the red spreading over his shirt. "Oh god. No." Her fingers trembled.

"Spark," he said. "It's..." His lips were white.

"Shh, Benny. Don't talk. We're getting you some help." She took his hand, and he squeezed it gently.

Benny whispered. "It's all for you, kid."

"Benny, please..."

"I love you like my own."

Tears welled up and spilled over her lashes. She grasped his hand tightly. "I love you too." His eyes closed, and his straining eased. "Benny. Don't." A tear dropped on his shirt. "Please stay with me." But as soon as she said it, she felt his life force ebb, then fade completely. His eyes parted slightly, and he released one last breath, and Eve knew he was gone.

"No!" She tugged on his jacket. "No. Don't go." Her stomach flipped, and she shook her head. The tears fell fast. "Benny?" She rubbed his cheek.

"Eve."

She barely heard Adam. Everything seemed to spin around her. What had happened? Why was Benny bleeding? Why hadn't Adam called for help?"

She whirled on him. "Get some help, damn it." She wiped at her face. "Why are just standing there?"

"Eve..."

Eve wiped her bloody hand on her jeans. "Adam...please..."

"He can't help you Eve."

The words came from nowhere. Eve fought to focus. She recognized the voice. It was then that she noticed the man in the corner of the room. In her haste to get to Benny, she'd never seen him. She blinked, trying to clear her head and get a good look at him. He stepped out of the shadows, and Eve sucked in a breath. "Vince."

"Hey, babe," he said. "Long time, no see." He raised a hand and waved, and Eve froze when she saw the gun.

Chapter Four

Up until then, Adam had been pleased with his progress. He'd found work at Benny's, met Eve, and had finally engaged with her. His preparations had paid off since she appeared to accept him as the easy-to-read, shy bartender. The movies and TV shows Tez had told him to watch must have helped, but he hoped it would be enough. Not knowing about the group of alcoholics Eve had mentioned was the kind of blunder he needed to avoid.

As a Gray-Line, he didn't have the advanced skills of Red-Lines. He couldn't move objects with his mind, read thoughts, cloak himself, or heal anyone, but he was highly intuitive, sensitive, and skilled in energy manipulation. All Gray-Lines were, but to varying degrees. And his were exceptional. He and Tez were both gifted Grays. Adam could read a situation and determine the best approach within minutes. And handling Eve was no different. The moment he'd met her, he'd known she was special. This was not a woman you took for granted. And since her father was a powerful Red-Line, Adam knew her gifts would be formidable. He wondered if she even knew what she could do. Most Red-Lines, once their Shift ended, cultivated and developed their talents, which grew over time. But on Earth, Eve and her siblings had only each other to rely on for guidance. He knew from speaking with her that she was sensitive and intuitive, but what her specific abilities were, he wasn't sure. Because of that, he'd trained himself to hide his thoughts and emotions, otherwise this gig would have been over before pouring his first drink.

Walking into Benny's office, he'd been wondering how far this evening could go, when everything took a dramatic turn.

Benny was lying on the ground, and Eve had rushed to his side. Adam could do nothing. The moment he'd turned to find the phone was when he'd seen the man in the corner, holding the gun. The man had shaken his head at him. All he could do was watch the scene unfold.

"What are you doing here, Vince?" asked Eve. She'd frozen momentarily when she'd seen the weapon and wiped her bloody fingers on her pants.

Vince smiled. "You look just as good as ever." He looked her over. "Mm...Mm...Mm. God. Why'd we ever break up?"

Eve slowly stood. "I left you. You were an asshole."

Adam swallowed, and Vince's expression didn't change. "You haven't changed a bit."

Tears ran down her face. "Benny. What happened to Benny?"

Vince's face hardened. "The old man wouldn't listen to reason. I had my associates talk to him, but he was a stubborn bastard." He pointed the gun at the dead man, his father. "He should have done what I asked." His jaw set. But then Vince stopped staring and looked at Eve. "It wasn't personal, sweetheart. Just business."

"He was your dad," she yelled. Another tear trickled down her cheek. "And I loved him. Didn't you?"

Vince walked up to her, the gun pointing at the floor. Eve didn't move. "That man never gave a shit about me. You think he loved you back?"

"He did."

"Then he fooled you, too."

"He loved you, Vince. You were just too stupid to know it."

Vince grabbed her by the face, and Eve winced. Adam took a step, but Vince held the gun to Eve's side. "Step back pretty boy," said Vince, looking at Adam. "This ain't none of your concern."

Adam's mind rushed. How were they going to get out of this situation without one of them being hurt or killed? If he could get close enough to

Vince, he could hit him with a heat flare. That might immobilize him long enough for him and Eve to get out of there. But Vince was too cautious for that.

"Don't tell me what I know, Eve," said Vince, squeezing Eve's jaw. "I grew up with him. You've known him, what, three years? He may have liked watching you walk away, but he never loved anyone. The only thing he loved was himself." He let go of her face.

"He loved your mother," she said. "And he was kind to me. He gave me this job. And we talked all the time. He knew my faults, and I knew his, but he was a good and kind man."

"Well, yippee. Let's throw a party."

Adam debated jumping in while Vince was distracted, but another man walked into the room. He was the opposite of Vince. Where Vince was tall and soft, with a round face, this man was small and hard, and his face looked like it was cut from a tree trunk.

"Vinny?" he said, looking around the room.

Vinny held his stare with Eve. "What, Saul?"

"Car's out front." His eyes shifted between Adam and Eve. "What do you want to do?"

A few seconds of silence passed. Adam caught a glance from Eve and wondered what would happen if he opened up his thoughts to her. Would she be able to read him?

"What's your name?" asked Vince, looking at Adam. "Adam? Is that what she called you?" He chuckled and stepped back from Eve. "You gotta be kidding me. Adam and Eve?" He stood next to Saul and elbowed the small man. "You believe that, Saul?"

"No," said Saul. The man did not look like conversation was his strong suit.

"That's funny," said Vince. "Don't you think that's funny?"

"No," said Saul.

"Shit. You're always so damn serious."

Saul looked at Eve and then at Adam. "We can't leave them here."

Adam caught Eve's eye. He didn't know if she was reading him, but he was reading her. Her mind was working as fast as his.

"I know we can't," said Vince. "Hell. What a mess."

"Vince," said Eve. "You can't possibly kill us too."

Vince grinned. "I can do whatever I want, babe." He nudged Saul. "You thinking what I'm thinking?"

Saul glanced at Benny's remains. "Sure." He pointed at Benny. "He's sleeping with the help. They have an argument. She shoots him. Her jealous lover interrupts, sees it, and she shoots him too. Then she turns the gun on herself."

Adam's stomach flipped.

"Vince, no," said Eve. "That story will never work. Nobody will believe it."

"Sure they will." Vince pulled out a cloth from his pocket and wiped down his gun. "We'll make it look convincing. Plus, the drugs they'll find in your system will help, along with the alcohol." He smiled. "You two been drinking tonight?"

Eve's face paled. Adam tried to think. If they were going to do something, they were going to have to do it fast.

"Sorry, pretty boy," said Vince, holding the gun on Adam. "Like I said, nothing personal."

"Louis Armstrong," said Eve.

Both men paused. Adam kept an eye on the gun.

"Excuse me?" asked Vince. "Louis who?"

"The musician, you idiot," said Saul. "What about him?" he asked Eve.

"Louis Armstrong," she said, more loudly.

"You goin' stupid, babe?" asked Vince. He waved the gun. "Last I heard, he was dead, just like you're about to be."

The gun swiveled back toward Adam just as a black shadow emerged from above with a screech. It launched itself at Vince. Adam watched in shock as it locked onto Vince's face. Vince shrieked and fell back against Saul. What felt like slow motion to Adam took mere microseconds as the black shadow shrieked again and swiped at the big man's cheeks. Vince flailed, trying to get it off.

Adam made himself move at the same time as Eve. He drove himself into the smaller man, knocking him backwards into a set of shelves. The shelves collapsed, and books and magazines rained down. Saul struggled, trying to right himself, but Adam placed both palms against him and sent a powerful surge of heat through them. Saul stilled, made a muffled grunt, and froze, unable to move. Adam took the opportunity to rise up and slug the man hard across the jaw. Saul slumped against the floor, unconscious.

Reeling, Adam gained his footing and stood. He caught sight of Eve standing over Vince, holding a baseball bat. The big man's head sported a large gash, and he lay unmoving on the floor, his face bleeding from numerous cuts.

Something moved across the floor, and Adam jumped. His heart was racing so fast, he was surprised he hadn't had a heart attack. He calmed when he saw it was a cat. The animal jumped up on the couch, and to Adam's surprise, started purring.

Eve dropped the baseball bat. She was breathing hard, and her face was white. She looked around the room.

Adam struggled to make his voice work. "Where'd you get the bat?"

Eve's jaw moved as if she also struggled to speak. "The door," she said breathlessly. "Benny kept it behind the door."

Adam nodded.

After a few seconds of collecting themselves, Eve walked over to the cat and patted its head. "Good job, Louis." Her fingers shook.

Adam stepped closer to look at the animal, which was now licking its fur. "Louis?" he asked. "Louis Armstrong, I take it?"

"Yes. Benny's cat."

Adam starred in surprise. They'd been saved by Benny's cat? He found that hard to believe. He raised a brow at Eve. She'd called the cat and he'd come. Something clicked, and Adam knew what had occurred. Some Red-Lines could communicate with animals, and now he realized Eve was one of them.

Eve seemed to shake off her shock. She picked up the cat. "Come on. We have to get out of here."

"Out of here?" he asked. "Shouldn't we call the police?" He followed her out of the office and picked up his pace when he heard a moan from one of the men. He didn't look back to see which one.

"We will. But not from here." She raced into her dressing room and grabbed her purse. "If I know Vince, there could be others. We have to leave." She raced out the back door into the alley with Adam close behind as they walked toward the street. Eve stopped at the corner and peered around the brick wall.

"You see anything?" asked Adam. It was still dark outside, but it would be dawn soon. The streets were quiet now, as most of the weekend night owls were on their way home.

Eve turned back. "There's a car out front. Black. There's a driver, staring at himself in the rear-view mirror." She pulled on Adam's arm. "Come on."

"Where are we going?"

"Shh," she said. "Be quiet."

She jogged down the alley, holding the cat and her purse. Adam stayed close behind. At the other end of the street they crossed over, passing dumpsters and trash, and emerged onto another street that ran parallel to the road they were avoiding.

Eve stepped out and raised a hand, whistling. Adam looked to see a cab parked across the road in front of a small hotel. Its engine fired up, and a few seconds later, it pulled up to the curb in front of them.

"How'd you do that?" asked Adam. Finding a cab at four o'clock in the morning while holding a cat would have been a long shot at best in Adam's mind, but apparently Eve made it easy.

Eve didn't answer though as she pulled the door open and got in. Adam slid in next to her. Louis didn't seem fazed. He sat in her lap and licked his hindquarters.

The cabbie looked back. "You're out late tonight, Eve."

"Hey, Charlie," she said. "So are you."

"Ah. Supposed to pick up some drunk business guy an hour ago. He never showed. I was about to call it a night."

"I'm glad you didn't."

"Back to the apartment?" asked Charlie.

"Yes. Thanks."

Eve glanced at Adam. "Charlie here has driven me home a few times."

"I guessed that." He made eye contact with the driver through the rear-view mirror. The man winked at him. He could only assume that he was not the first man to go home with Eve in Charlie's cab. He spoke low and pulled out his cell phone. "Don't you think we should call the police?"

Eve pushed his phone down. "Not yet."

"Why not?"

"You two been out on the town tonight?" asked Charlie.

"You could say that," said Adam.

"Because," said Eve, almost whispering. "Once we do that, we open a very big can of worms. And we can't go back."

"What do you mean?"

"How are the wife and kids, Charlie?" asked Eve. "Everyone okay?"

"Just great. Little Nora's getting bigger every day."

"That's great."

"Eve?" asked Adam.

"As soon as we make that phone call, all hell breaks loose."

"I think that's already happened," said Adam. "How much worse can this get?"

"Keep your voice down."

Adam looked forward again and knew Charlie was listening. He tapped at his phone. "How far is your place?"

"Not far. Just another block."

"Then can we call?"

"Once we get inside."

"Don't you think they'll come looking for us? Your place is the where they'll come first."

"That's why we have to move fast."

"Eve..."

"Just trust me."

Adam sat back, frustrated. This was not a situation for which he had planned. All he'd wanted was to find Eve's brother, but instead he was running for his life. Tez was waiting for answers, but now Adam wondered how long his friend would wait if Adam never returned.

Chapter Five

EVE RACED UP THE stairs to her second-floor apartment. She handed Louis to Adam and dug for the keys in her purse. Unlocking the door, she hurried inside and threw her purse on the small dining table cluttered with unopened mail. She glanced at the pile of dishes in the sink and the newspapers on the coffee table. There would be no point in cleaning now.

"Eve, what is the plan here?" asked Adam, releasing the cat to the floor.

"I need to get a few things." She headed into her room, grabbed a small suitcase, and started throwing clothes and toiletries into it.

"What are you doing?" asked Adam. He stood at the open doorway.

"Listen," she said. "The moment we make that phone call is the moment everything changes. The police will want to talk to us, get our statements, go down to the station." She opened a drawer and grabbed a couple of bras. "But what happened tonight was not just about a son killing his father." She felt a lump rise in her throat, thinking of Benny, but she pushed it back. "This was a mob hit."

"A what?"

She grabbed her toothbrush and toothpaste and put them in a small bag. "A mob hit." She added some cosmetics to the bag and closed it. "You know? Like *The Godfather*?"

"Oh, yeah," said Adam. "*The Godfather*." His tone sounded reflective, and Eve glanced at him. "I saw that one," he said and his face turned serious. "Are you kidding me?"

"No. I am not kidding you." She threw the small bag into her suitcase. "They'll want to take us into protective custody. We'll be expected to testify against Vince and his goon."

Adam raised a palm. "Wait a minute. The police will want to hide us?"

"Yes. That's what protective custody is." She shook her head. "Honestly. Where are you from? Some remote farm? Are you Amish or something?" She snapped the suitcase shut.

"No," he said. "Not Amish, but definitely remote."

"Come on." She grabbed the suitcase and walked into the living room.

"Where are we going?" asked Adam. "Are we calling the police or not?"

She turned and faced him. "This is my plan. We call and tell them, but anonymously. We tell them who did it, but then we disappear. You go one way, I'll go the other."

"What?" He looked like she'd asked him to jump off Benny's roof. "That's crazy."

"It is. I don't like it either, but I don't think we have a choice. Vince will come looking for us. If he's mixed up in the mob, and I think his friend Saul was confirmation of that, then we have to get lost. I don't trust the police either. The mob has connections everywhere."

"What about your job? Your home?"

"I'm a lounge singer at a bar whose owner was just murdered. I think my job security just took a radical nose dive. So did yours."

"Where will we go?"

She pointed at him. "You will go back to your farm, or wherever you came from. I will go...somewhere. I haven't figured that part out yet."

His jaw dropped. "You mean we're splitting up?"

Eve squinted. "This isn't a movie, Adam. We are not two misfits on the run who end up stuck together in some faraway location and fall in love and get the bad guys. This is real life, and we are in trouble."

"I kind of prefer the whole movie scenario."

"So does Steven Spielberg, but he's not here at the moment."

A knock on the door made them both freeze. Eve held her breath. Had Vince and his men already arrived? A high-pitched voice sounded from behind the door. "Eve, is that you?"

Eve released her held breath. She walked over, peered through the peephole, and unlocked the door.

"What are you doing?" asked Adam.

"Hi, Dixie," said Eve, opening the door. She eyed her neighbor, who stood six feet, wearing heavy make-up. Her blonde wig dusted her shoulders, and she placed a hand with bedazzled fingernails on her hip. The pink feathers on her pink robe fluttered.

"Evie, where have you been?" she asked. "Fred and Ginger have been waiting for you." She eyed Adam and raised an eyebrow. "I see," she said. "And who is this handsome fellow?"

Eve glanced back at Adam. "Just a friend." She pointed. "Grab my suitcase." She found her purse and picked up Louis. "Come on."

"Where are we going?" he asked.

"Next door."

"Next door?" said Dixie. "Oh, honey. At this hour?" She bustled to the side as Eve walked past. "You're lucky I don't have a gentleman caller."

"Sorry, Dixie. We're in a bit of a bind. We need to go to your place." She closed the door to her apartment and locked it after Adam walked out.

"You have a cat now, too?" asked Dixie. "Since when?"

"It's Benny's cat. His name is Louis."

"You and animals," Dixie sighed. "I hope you don't mind my mess." Adam followed them into Dixie's apartment, which looked far different from Eve's. It was much cleaner. A leopard spotted couch and matching chairs were in the living area and the bright yellow paint showcased a variety of photographs on the walls, each one of Dixie in a variety of outfits and hairstyles, usually standing with a celebrity. The mantel sported two lit candles, and the room smelled like fresh flowers.

Barking sounded the moment they walked in, and two small black and white dogs with wiry hair ran into the room. Louis sprang to the ground, and Eve stooped to greet her pets. They bounced up and down, eager to be held. Louis ignored them and sauntered into another room.

"Hey, Ginger. Hi, Fred." Eve petted and gave them the attention they demanded. "How were they Dixie? Did they behave?"

"Little Fred peed on my shoe. I don't think he likes my blue pumps."

"Oh. I'm sorry, Dix. I'll pay for new ones."

"That's okay, hon. I don't like them either."

Eve stood once the dogs had settled down. She saw Adam perusing the photos on the wall, and Dixie perusing Adam.

"Friend, huh?" her neighbor asked. She crossed her arms, and her nails reflected the light.

"Yes," said Eve. "This is Adam. He's a bartender at Benny's. Adam, this is my neighbor and friend, Dixie Royal."

Dixie raised an eyebrow. "Adam and Eve?" She cocked her head at Adam. "She offered you the forbidden apple yet, sugar?"

Adam's brow furrowed. "The what?" He picked up a snow globe on a shelf and shook it. White flakes fluttered over a cityscape.

Dixie paused. "Oh, dear," she said, looking at Eve. "He's slow, isn't he?" She glanced back at Adam. "Good thing you're cute, honey."

Adam's face dropped.

"You like my gift?" asked Dixie. Adam shook the globe again. "My new suitor gave it to me. We've only just met, and he's already giving me gifts." She lowered her voice. "I think he likes me, but don't they all?" She winked.

"We need your help, Dix."

"Of course, honey. What is it?" She scratched at her head and scrunched her face. "You don't mind, do you?" She reached up and pulled off her wig, revealing short, dark hair beneath. "I threw this on, but it's making my head itch." She scratched her scalp. Eve watched Adam and almost chuckled at his reaction.

Dixie saw it too. "Oh, my," she said. "He is sheltered, isn't he?" She stepped closer to Adam, who couldn't stop looking at Dixie.

Dixie put a hand on her hip. "Poor thing. I've seen that look before, but not in a long time." She reached out and touched his shoulder. "Let me help you. Yes, I am a man," she rolled her eyes, "but I identify as a woman. Have since I was thirteen years old. I sing and entertain at the Blue Parrot Lounge. I'm sort of a big name there. I've met lots of famous people." She leaned closer and spoke low. "And slept with several of them, too." She winked and fiddled with the wig in her hand. "I wear wigs to change up my look." She touched her dark hair. "Natural gets so boring." She glanced back at Eve. "Except for Evie here. She always looks gorgeous."

Eve smiled. "Thanks, Dix." She glanced at the clock. "Sorry to rush you, but we don't have a lot of time here. I have a big favor to ask."

Adam didn't move. Dixie poked his arm a couple of times. "I think I may have broken him." She put the wig back on and adjusted it. "There, sugar. Does that help?"

Adam finally shook his head. "Sorry. I just...I wasn't...you just took me by surprise."

Dixie smiled. "I take 'em all by surprise, sweetheart."

"Dixie..." said Eve.

"Sorry, hon," she turned from Adam. "How can I help?"

"Benny, he," she swallowed. "We...um...Adam and I saw..." She cleared her throat.

"Benny was murdered tonight at the bar by his son Vince," said Adam. "Eve and I walked in on it, and now we think the killers are coming after us."

Dixie looked between the two of them, wide eyed. Her face relaxed, and she smiled. "Did Leonardo put you two up to this? That bitch. He's been trying to get back at me..."

"Dixie..." Eve shook her head. Her eyes welled up. She hated getting emotional. "It's true."

Dixie's jaw dropped. "No. Benny's dead?"

Eve nodded. "Yes. And Vince is looking for us. It's only a matter of time before he comes here."

"Vince? Benny's son? Is he the one you dated for a while? The idiot?"

Eve nodded.

"Oh, honey. Come here." Dixie walked over and wrapped her arms around Eve. Eve brushed feathers out of her face, but accepted the hug. She wiped away a tear.

"I'm okay."

"The hell you are. I know how close you were to him." Dixie's voice sounded shaky.

Eve pulled back and saw Dixie's own tears. "I'm sorry. I didn't mean to upset you."

Dixie wiped her eyes. Mascara blotted her cheek. "I'm fine, honey."

Eve squeezed Dixie's wrist in comfort. She saw Adam staring. "Dixie lost her father a month ago," she explained. "It's been hard for her."

Dixie sniffed. "Never mind me. We have to worry about you." She found a tissue and wiped her eyes. "What do you want me to do?"

"I'm going to call the cops and tell them what happened. But anonymously. Then we have to get out of here."

"But if you call, they'll have your cell number."

"Hell," Eve thought about it. "I'll use the phone outside the drugstore. They still have a phone booth."

"You should call Tony."

"No," said Eve, shaking her head. "Not Tony."

"Why not, sugar?"

"I don't want him involved."

"Evie, he's a good man. You can trust him."

"No, Dix. It took us a long time to sort things out between us. And we've finally managed to go our separate ways. Plus, this could be dangerous for him."

"Sugar, he's a police officer. That's his job."

"Who's Tony?" asked Adam.

"He lives in the building. He and Eve dated after he moved in. It was serious."

Eve grunted. "No, it wasn't."

Dixie threw out her hands and the pink feathers fluttered. "He wanted to marry you."

"They all say that."

"Not in my experience, honey."

"Or mine," said Adam. "If he's a cop and you trust him, why not call him?"

"Because I know him. He'll make this personal. And that could get him killed."

"Evie, honey..."

"No, Dixie. No Tony." She glanced at Adam. "We'll stop at the drugstore and call."

"I can do it," said Dixie. She put a hand on her chest. "I'll make the call."

Eve studied her. "You sure? The police? Not Tony?"

She raised her hand. "I will not call Tony. I promise." Her eyes softened. "But what about you? Your place? Your dogs?" Dixie shook her head. "Where will you go? How long will you be gone?" Eve didn't answer, and Dixie's face froze. "You're not leaving for good, are you?"

"We have no choice. I think Vince is mixed up with the mob. They'll be looking for us. We know what he did."

"But...but..." Her eyes shined in the light.

"I know. I know." Eve hugged her friend. "I'll be in touch, though. As soon as I figure out where I'm headed, I'll contact you. I'll make arrangements for the animals. I promise. We'll see each other again."

Dixie sniffed. "First dad, and now you. Oh, sugar. This is hard to take."

"I'm sorry." Eve searched for her own tissue and dabbed her eyes. "Do you mind looking after Fred, Ginger, and Louis? I promise I'll come pick them up as soon as I can."

Dixie nodded. "Sure." She wiped away a tear. Her mascara was running down her face.

"Please don't cry," said Eve.

"Once I call, you can't come around here. It will be too dangerous."

Eve sniffed. "The heat will die down after a while."

"Will it?" asked Adam.

Eve glanced at him. He was standing with his hands in his pockets, looking like he'd just stepped off a plane, but no one was there to greet him. "Yes. It will." She shifted her eyes toward Dixie.

He seemed to get the message and nodded. "Maybe it will. They'll get bored chasing us after a while."

"Exactly," said Eve. "But it's important that you say nothing about us, Dixie. They may come here looking."

Dixie cleared her throat and appeared to collect herself. "Does Vince know where you live?"

"No. I don't think so. But he'll find me soon enough. And if he comes here..."

"I don't know a thing, sugar," said Dixie. "He'll just think I'm some crazy drag queen in high heels whose apartment smells like cat pee. He won't hang around long."

"Maybe we shouldn't call the police," said Adam.

"What?" asked Eve.

"Don't call them. Don't put the heat on Vince. Maybe that will help him to back off."

"No." Eve shook her head. "I have to tell them what happened to Benny."

"What will it matter?" asked Adam. "Without us to testify, they can't prove anything."

Eve hesitated. "You don't know that. Maybe somebody else will talk. Maybe the police know something we don't."

"You said yourself," said Adam. "You don't trust the police."

"I have to say something," said Eve. "I owe Benny that much. And if there are no other options, I'll come forward and testify."

Adam sighed. "You'd never make it to the witness stand."

Eve knew that was true. Could she risk her life for a dead man? If something happened to her, her family would be devastated. "I can't think about that right now. All I know is that we need to leave, find a place to hide for a while, and then figure out what to do next."

"We should stick together."

"Why? It's better if we separated."

He stepped away from the wall. "Because we're in this together. We have nowhere else to go. We can rely on each other until we decide what to do."

"He's right, sugar," said Dixie. "I don't want you to be alone. You need to look out for one another."

Eve tensed. "I don't need any help."

"Yes, you do," said Adam. "We both do." He pulled out a wallet. "How much money have you got?" he asked, counting his bills. "I have a hundred and twenty bucks. What do you have?"

Eve paused. "Maybe twenty dollars. I don't carry much cash."

"I have some," said Dixie. She reached for a purse and pulled out some bills. "Here. It's my emergency stash. It's three hundred dollars."

Eve pushed it back. "Dixie. I can't take that."

"Shut up, hon. Yes, you can. If this isn't an emergency, I don't know what is." She held out the money to Eve.

Eve took it and squeezed Dixie's fingers. "I'll pay you back. I promise."

Dixie nodded. "Just come home. That's all I want."

"I know." She felt the tears well up again. "I promise as soon as..."

A knock sounded at the door. Eve went quiet.

The knock sounded again. Then a deep voice responded. "Anybody home?"

Eve froze. It was Vince.

Chapter Six

"G ET IN THE BEDROOM ," whispered Dixie. "Hurry."

Eve picked up her suitcase, grabbed her purse, and Adam followed her into the bedroom. The dogs trotted behind them. The first thing Adam saw was a large fourposter bed covered by a zebra patterned bed spread. Silky pink fabric edged in feathers adorned the lamp shades and lacy undergarments hung from the bathroom door.

They moved to the closet, but when Eve opened it, it was stuffed with clothes. "Oh, honey," said Dixie in a whisper, "I couldn't put a handkerchief in there." She guided them back into the corner of the room. "Just stay here. There's no point in hiding. If they search, they'd find you."

Adam eyed the window and staircase beyond. "What about there?"

Dixie shook her head. "Not enough time. That window is stuck shut, and it would make too much noise besides." She studied herself in the mirror situated over a vanity table covered with jars and bottles of all shapes and sizes. Eying herself, she dabbed at her runny mascara, patted on some powder, and poked at her wig. "Just let me handle this."

The knock came again. "Maybe you shouldn't answer it," said Adam.

"I have to. They probably heard talking." She turned, her face looking fresh again. "Keep your ears peeled, in case I need you."

"What?" asked Adam. "Keep my ears what?"

"Just stay alert," said Eve.

Dixie left the room but left the door cracked. Eve and Adam waited. Adam could see Dixie flip on the television, but she kept the volume low.

Dixie's voice carried. "Well, hello gentlemen. To what do I owe this unexpected early morning visit?"

There was a pause. Adam could picture the man at the door eyeing Dixie. Then a man's voice. "Sorry to bother you, but we're looking for your neighbor." It was Vince.

"My neighbor?"

"Yes. She lives in apartment two-ten. Have you seen her?"

"That bitch?" They heard Dixie laugh. "If you see her, tell her she owes me three hundred bucks."

"Excuse me?"

"She owes me money, sugar. I'm quite sure she's avoiding me."

"So you know her?"

Eve stilled, and Adam felt her worry. "Just relax," he whispered.

Her eyes widened. "The cat," she said. "Where's Louis?"

Fred and Ginger were laying quietly at Eve's feet, but Louis wasn't around. Adam's heart thudded. "If he walks through the room..."

"I know." She went quiet and closed her eyes.

Dixie spoke. "If you're looking for her, you might check with any of the men around here." Adam heard her scoff. "She doesn't sleep alone often, sugar, if you get what I mean."

Adam heard another deep voice. It was the goon he'd knocked into the shelves. "Do you know when she'll be back?"

Dixie chuckled. "Certainly not. She's up at crazy hours, keeps to herself, and dates idiots." Dixie's voice lowered. "I'm sure you gentleman would never date a woman like that. Would you?"

Adam almost smiled. He saw Eve open her eyes as Louis walked into the bedroom. He breathed a sigh of relief.

"Pardon me," said Vince, "but we thought we heard voices through the door. Are you alone?"

Adam held his breath again. He glanced at Eve, who looked just as tense.

"You may have heard the TV," said Dixie. "Or..."

"Or what?" asked the other man.

"Well, gentlemen, I have a suitor. My neighbor is not the only one who entertains gentlemen callers." There was a pause. "Perhaps you heard us?"

"Where is he?"

"You two seem awfully nosy, but he's in the bedroom." Another pause. "Eagerly awaiting my return."

Eve nudged Adam, who grunted. "Say something," she said.

"What?" he asked.

"You sure about that?" asked the voice from the other room.

"I should know," said Dixie. "He's been here all night." Her voice rose. "Right, honey?"

Eve nudged Adam again.

Adam's brain fought the urge to go blank, but he deepened his voice and answered. "Hey, baby. The sheets are gettin' cold. Either tell 'em to join us or get lost and get your pretty ass back here."

The room was quiet, and Adam didn't breathe. Eve looked pale in the dark room.

"You heard him," said Dixie. Her voice turned low. "You two care to join us?"

Adam could imagine her staring at the two men the way she'd stared at him, looking them up and down, her eyes suggesting much more than conversation.

He heard a throat clear. "That's fine. You mind calling us though, if you see her? Here's a card."

"Sure, honey. You gonna give me my three hundred bucks if I do?"

"How about this?" asked Vince. "I'll give you five hundred if we find her. Deal?"

"Oh, sugar. You sure you don't want to join me and my friend? We could have some fun."

"I'll pass, thanks."

"Your loss."

"Just call us if you see her."

"I will. Good morning."

"Right."

The door closed, and Adam let go of his breath. He and Eve stayed put until the bedroom door swung open and Dixie walked in. "You two okay?"

"Dixie, you're amazing," said Eve.

"Me? That was nothing. You, however," she pinched Adam's arm, "surprised me." She fanned her face. "Got me all hot and bothered."

Adam felt his own face flush. "I had no idea what to say."

"Well, you figured it out, sugar. It was perfect."

"We have to go," said Eve. "I'm so sorry I got you mixed up in this."

"Don't worry about me, sweetie. This is the most fun I've had since last Saturday night." She stared off. "And that was a hell of a Saturday."

Eve started to leave the room. "Oh, honey. Not that way," said Dixie. "They'll be watching. Take the fire escape." She pointed toward the bedroom window. "That will take you to the alley. Then you can find a place to..." Her eyes widened. "Wait a minute." She hurried to her nightstand and opened a drawer. "What am I thinking?" She pulled out a card. "Here, take this. Mike can help. He owns a motel on the east side. Tell him I sent you. He'll give you a cheaper rate. He owes me. You two can stay there a few days until you figure out what's next."

"You're sure?" asked Eve. She took the card. "You can trust him?"

"Don't give him your real names, but he'll take cash and won't ask any questions."

"Okay," said Eve. "Thanks, Dix." Her eyes watered.

"Oh, honey. Don't do that," said Dixie, fanning her face. "You'll make my mascara run again."

The two hugged warmly. "You'll call the cops after we leave?" asked Eve. She pulled back from the hug. "Tell them you know Benny was murdered by his son Vince at the bar. Tell them to go check on Benny."

Dixie nodded and dabbed her eyes. Despite her efforts, her mascara was running again. "I will, sweetheart. I'll go down to the corner store and contact them."

"You can't leave now," said Adam. "If they're watching…"

Dixie tipped her head. "You're so cute," said Dixie. "Worrying about me." She fluffed the feathers on her robe. "No. I'll change first. Then I'll go. I'll look just as butch as the two of them. They'll have no idea it's me. It's almost too fun. Being in disguise. It's almost like *La Cage aux Folles*."

"La what?" asked Adam.

"Oh sweetie, never mind. I'm so glad you're pretty." She leaned in. "Now give me a hug."

Adam stepped close, and Dixie wrapped her arms around him and squeezed. "You take care of my girl, okay?" She said into his ear. "I'm counting on you. She's my best friend."

Adam nodded. "I will."

Dixie pulled back, dabbed her eyes, and pulled the curtains back. "You ready?"

Eve unlocked the window and, after several hard shoves, it opened with a loud creak. She stepped out. "I'll be in touch."

"You just keep yourself safe. That's all I want."

"Thanks, Dixie," said Adam.

She narrowed her eyes. "You remember what I said."

"I will."

"Good. Now get going."

"Love you, Dix," said Eve.

"Love you, too, Evie."

Eve headed down the stairs, and Adam followed, wondering what in the hell would happen next.

· · · · ● · ● · · ·

They made it down to the alley and headed in the opposite direction of the street where Vince was likely watching. Eve hailed a cab and gave the cabbie the motel address. Little was said in the car, as the night's events and lack of sleep began to take their toll.

"We need food," said Adam.

"I know." She looked at him. "And you need a change of clothes."

"And a toothbrush would be nice."

"We'll stop and find a store once we get there."

Twenty minutes later, the cab pulled up in front of an older building. The sign blinked *The West Hotel*. There was trash out front and a homeless man sat on the curb, staring into space.

"It's not fancy," said Adam, getting out of the car.

"We don't need the Waldorf," said Eve. "Just a place to stay for a day or two until we get our bearings." She looked around the area. "There," she said, pointing at a small restaurant. "It's open. Let's get some breakfast."

They walked across the street and spent the next thirty minutes eating eggs and bacon. They had turned off their phones in case Vince had connections and could trace where they were, but that prevented them from connecting with the outside world. Eve asked the waitress where to find a drugstore, and thirty minutes after that, they had purchased clothes for Adam and a few toiletries.

Adam carried his purchases as they walked into the hotel. The trash that littered the street also seemed to have traveled into the dark-paneled, low-lit lobby. There were a couple of chairs with ripped fabric, and it smelled like Benny's Bar after a busy night.

"I'm looking for Mike," said Eve, approaching the counter.

A man, smoking a cigarette, looked up from his magazine, which Eve saw was *Better Homes and Gardens*. His blue sweater sat loosely on his body.

"I'm Mike," he said, stubbing out his cigarette. His voice was as grave as his face. He perused Eve and then Adam. "What can I do for you?"

"Dixie Royal sent us." She glanced at Adam. "We need two rooms."

"Dixie?" asked Mike. "Really?" His eyes widened, and he dropped his magazine. "She's some dame."

Eve smiled. "Yes, she is."

"I go see her show whenever I can." He leaned in close. "Don't tell the wife, though." He pointed at his wedding ring. "She thinks I'm here all the time." He snickered.

"I won't say a word."

"I can't believe she mentioned me," said Mike. "What did she say?"

"She said you could help us out," said Eve. "We need a place to stay for a couple of days. Said you owed her one. That you could give us a deal."

"She did? That little minx." He smiled. "I'd give her a deal anytime." He looked between Adam and Eve. "But I don't know you two. How do I know she sent you?"

"Get many people coming through here using Dixie as a referral?" asked Adam.

Eve nudged him as Mike frowned. She pulled out the card Dixie had given her. "I have this."

Mike took the card. "Yup. That's my card all right." He flipped it over and back again, then eyed Eve and Adam again. "Okay. I'll give you one room. Fifty bucks a night."

"But we need two rooms," said Eve.

"We'll take it," said Adam.

Mike grinned. "I figured you would." He winked at Adam.

"Does it at least have twin beds?" asked Eve.

"Queen," said Mike.

"That's fine," said Adam. He pulled out some cash. "Here's for the next two nights. Plus a little extra to keep quiet that we're here."

"Keeping a low profile, huh?" asked Mike, taking the cash. He pulled out a book and picked up a pen. "Should I say who's here?"

"Kate and Spencer Tracy," said Adam.

Eve raised a brow at him. She took the key from Mike.

"Room four-one-two."

"Thanks," said Adam.

"The elevator's out. You'll need to use the stairs."

Eve eyed the staircase. It had a dirty carpet and a rickety handrail. "Terrific."

They walked up the four flights and found their room. Once inside, Eve was pleased to see that at the least the room looked cleaner than the lobby. The furniture was dinged, but usable, and the bed looked comfortable, although the pillows looked lumpy.

"You realize you're sleeping on the ground," she said, dropping her suitcase.

"I'd rather sleep on the bottom of a birdcage," said Adam.

She sighed. The carpet resembled the floor of a movie house. "I see your point." She sat on the bed. "We should have gotten two rooms."

"No," he said, pulling his toothbrush out of the bag. "We shouldn't. We need to stick together. Plus, it looks suspicious. A man and a woman check in and get two separate rooms?"

"Suspicious? How about the Spencer and Kate thing?"

"What?" he asked. "I saw their movies."

She bounced on the mattress. "I didn't realize you liked old cinema."

"There's a lot you don't know about me."

"Really?" She shifted to look at him. "Like what?"

"Like I'm dying to take a shower. I feel like something that lives in that carpet."

"I'm after you. Don't use all the hot water."

"Be out in a sec." He disappeared into the bathroom.

Eve heard the spray come on. She sat on the bed and began to lean back, but stopped. Thinking about what was likely on the bedspread, she rose and pulled the heavy covering off the bed and threw it over the worn chair.

Regarding the sheets, she was pleased to note that they looked washed, as did the pillowcases, although the lumpy pillows were confirmed.

She considered lying down, but knew if she did, she'd never get up. Spying her suitcase, she picked it up and laid it on the bed. She flipped it open and perused her belongings. She hadn't brought much. Just something to sleep in and a couple of changes of clothes. There was one other item she had grabbed, and she picked it up. It was a small, framed picture of her and her siblings. Royce and Gili stood on either side of her. Bits of confetti rested in their hair and Royce had a paper blower in his mouth. It was the last New Year's they had spent together, before their dad had shown up and everything had changed.

Eve thought back on those days. They had been happy ones. She and her brother and sister were very close. They'd lived with their mother in a typical suburb in a typical house. They'd had an uneventful upbringing, other than their absent dad. Since their father was a rare visitor, they all took comfort in each other, relying on one another in times of trouble. But Dad's last visit had interrupted that. That's when they'd learned who they were, where Dad came from, and why he was gone so often. She and Royce and Gillian had begun their Shifts not long after, and since then, out of necessity, they'd all gone their separate ways.

It had been hell, but Eve saw it as an opportunity. As much as she loved her family, the urge to make her own way, figure out who she was, and what she wanted, especially after Dad's revelations, made the break more bearable for her. She'd moved to the city, found odd jobs, lived in scary places, dated lousy men, did stupid things, but ultimately, had found her way to Benny's. He'd taken her in, nurtured her, believed in her, and made her his star performer, all without asking for anything in return. He'd become the father she so rarely had.

She stared at the picture. Her body warmed at the thought of picking up the phone and calling, but she knew she couldn't. She couldn't take the risk.

The spray turned off, and Eve placed the photo on the bedside table. A lump in her throat blossomed, but she pushed it back. Sitting on the bed, she thought of Benny. The lump returned. Thinking of him, and her current situation, she wondered what to do next, but her brain wouldn't form a response.

The bathroom door opened, and Adam emerged from the steamy room with a towel wrapped around his narrow waist. Eve admired his muscular arms and chest. Normally, she'd make a suggestive comment, but the shower beckoned. She picked up a t-shirt and shorts from her suitcase. "I'm next," she said, and headed into the foggy room.

· · · · ● · ● · · · ·

Adam ruffled his hair with his towel and threw it on the bed. He pulled out a pair of boxers and a shirt from his purchases and put them on. Hearing the shower run from the other room, he picked up his phone and hit a button. He heard the ringing over the line.

Although his cell looked like any other cell, it was actually a communicator he could use to contact Tez at any time. It was untraceable by anyone on this planet.

He heard Tez pick up. "Where are you?"

"Tez. Listen. I've got a problem."

"You're right about that. You've got a list of them."

"No. It's more than that."

"Listen," said Tez. "Unless you tell me you've found her brother, then there's not much to say."

"Shut up, will you? I'm with her now."

There was a pause. "Finally."

"You don't understand. We're on the run. We saw Benny murdered. Now we're being chased by the men who did it."

Another pause. "I don't have time for this."

"I'm serious. If they find us, they'll kill us."

He heard a sigh. "Where are you now?"

"We found an old hotel to stay in until we figure out what's next and what to do." There was no response. "Are you there?"

"That's perfect. I couldn't have written this better. You two are on the run and you're holed up in a hotel? It's the opportunity you've been waiting for."

"What are you talking about?"

"Use your head. She's vulnerable. Get her talking. Ask about her family. Be persuasive."

"Damn it. This is serious."

"And you think our situation isn't?" His voice rose. "I don't care who's chasing you or what happened to some guy named Benny. We need information, and we need it now. Screw the bad guys. You get what we need and you get it tonight. Then you leave her behind tomorrow, get your ass back here, and we go home."

"I can't leave her alone with this mess."

Tez yelled. "You can and you will. You're not here to court her. You came to do a job. Now do it and stop whining about what happens to her. That's not your concern."

Adam set his jaw. "We're in trouble."

"No, you're not. Do what you came to do and don't come back until you have what we need. You've got forty-eight hours."

"What?"

"You heard me. Find out where he is, or I'm leaving you behind."

"Tez..."

The line went dead.

The shower turned off, and the curtain slid open. He dropped his cell into his shopping bag. Spying the picture on the nightstand, he picked it up and stared at it.

Chapter Seven

Eve opened the bathroom door and stepped out.

"Feel better?" asked Adam, sitting on the bed.

"Much." She dumped her dirty clothes in her suitcase. A wet ringlet hung in her face and she pushed it back. From her peripheral vision, she saw Adam staring at her. "What?"

A blush colored his cheeks. "Sorry. It's just..."

"Just what?"

"You're not wearing make-up."

She smiled. "I know. I look like a twelve-year-old."

His eyes moved over her. "Uh, no. That's not the comparison I would make."

"No?"

"No," he said. "You look...softer. Almost innocent."

She glanced at him. "That's not the comparison I would use."

He kept staring. "You look beautiful."

She closed her suitcase and pushed it out of the way. "Listen, Adam. Just because we're sharing the same bed tonight doesn't mean you get privileges."

His face scrunched. "Privileges?" His eyes widened. "You think I'm telling you that, hoping you'll sleep with me?"

"That's been my experience."

He sat up. "Well, here's a news flash. I'm telling you because it's true. That's it. Nothing more. Besides..."

She walked to the opposite of the bed. "Besides what?"

"If I wanted to sleep with you, I'd just take off my shirt."

Eve narrowed her eyes. "Really? Does that work?"

Adam flexed. "Absolutely. No woman can resist me. My muscles are magnetic."

She pulled back the sheets and sat on the bed, facing him. "I had no idea."

"I know. Few know of my powers."

She nodded. "I see. And what happens to those who do?"

"They leave with a smile."

Eve grinned. "I didn't know you were gifted with such abilities."

He leaned in. "It's an enormous responsibility." He pulled on the sleeve of his T-shirt. "I have to keep my shirt on, or I never get any rest."

She stuck out her bottom lip. "Poor guy. That must be hard for you."

"It's very stressful."

She pulled the sheet up. "Well, don't let me tax you. Feel free to keep your shirt on around me."

He nodded. "I will. But feel free if you'd like to remove yours."

Eve laughed and some of the heaviness she'd been carrying seemed to lift. "If the mood strikes me, I'm glad to hear you won't be offended."

"Not at all."

"Of course..." she added.

He pushed back and sat beside her. "Of course what?"

"I have the same powers. All women do."

He sighed and threw out his hand. "I've been wondering why you always keep your shirt on. Now I know."

Knowing she was tired because she giggled, Eve scooted down under the sheet. "Go to sleep." She rolled over on her side, away from him. There was rustling, and Eve assumed he'd laid down next to her.

"It's eight o'clock in the morning," he said.

"I know."

The bed jostled as he got comfortable. "Good morning, Eve."

"Good morning, Adam."

· · · · • • · • • · ·

Two hours later, Eve stared at the ceiling. She'd expected to fall asleep the moment her head hit the pillow, but instead, everything turned on. Her mind replayed the events of the morning. Seeing Benny wounded on the ground. Watching him die. Vince and his counterpart with guns in their hands. Getting away and finding Dixie. Lying in bed next to a bartender she barely knew. She blinked and rubbed her eyes.

"Can't sleep?" said Adam's groggy voice.

She glanced over at him. He was turned away, but he shifted and faced the ceiling. "Can't you?"

"I'm trying."

"I think that's the problem."

"I keep thinking about it," he said.

"Me too."

He scratched his forehead. "I mean, how in the hell did this happen?"

"I don't know."

He let out a deep breath. "We need to think of something else, or we'll never rest."

Eve stared at a small bug as it walked across the ceiling. "Like what?"

He glanced at her. "Tell me something about yourself."

"I'm not that interesting."

"I doubt that." He turned on his side and faced her. "Tell me about your family." Even though his eyes were heavy with fatigue, he appeared boyish with his head on the pillow.

"My family?"

He yawned. "Yes. You have one, don't you?"

Eve shifted toward him. "Yes, I do."

"Great. Tell me about your mom." His brown eyes twinkled from the yawn.

"She's a strong woman. Took good care of us growing up."

"Us? You have siblings?"

"Yes. Gillian and Royce." She shifted in the bed. "We're actually triplets."

His eyes widened. "See. Now that's interesting." He paused. "Don't tell me there's two more people out there who look like you."

"No." She smiled. "I'm the only one. We're fraternal."

"Tell me about them. Are you close?"

She nodded. "Very. We always have been. We were inseparable growing up. Mom always said we were glued together." She thought back. "Royce was born first. I was second, and Gillian third."

"Where are they now? You still close?"

She hesitated. "We are. It's just...it's complicated."

"What is?"

"It's hard to explain."

"You still see them?"

"Yes, sort of."

"When's the last time you saw your sister?"

Eve smiled at the memory. "Her wedding. A few months ago. It was beautiful."

"Sounds nice."

"It was. I'm happy she's happy."

"What about Royce?"

She picked at her pillowcase. "He wasn't there."

"Why not?"

Eve tensed and her belly constricted. "He couldn't make it."

"You look sad. Did something happen?"

She stared at the ceiling. "He...He'd been through a lot...before the wedding. He needed time."

"Time for what?"

She released an audible moan. "Can we talk about something else?"

Adam raised his torso and rested his head on his hand. "Sure. Tell me about your dad. Where's he?"

She couldn't stifle a humorless laugh. "That subject isn't much better."

"Why not?"

"Because." she pulled the sheets up to her chin. "I haven't seen him in years."

"Where is he?"

"Far away."

"Do you know where?"

"Vaguely."

"You can't visit?"

She snorted. "No."

"What does he do?"

"That's a good question. I think he's a leader of some sort. He's always been sort of hush-hush about the whole thing."

"A leader? Of what?"

"I suspect a group of people."

He frowned. "Smart ass."

Eve shook her head. "I don't know. He never told us. I know he had his reasons. I suspect it was to keep us safe."

"Safe from what?"

"I don't know that either. I think it has something to do with 'the less we know, the better.' Or something like that."

Adam was quiet for a moment. "Do you know if he'll come back?"

"I have no idea. I could see him tomorrow, or never again."

He watched her, and she felt a wave of something emit from him. It felt like sympathy. "You don't have to feel sorry for me."

His face dropped, and she felt him pull back, like he'd just hit a bracing wind after a hot shower. "Will you see your brother again?"

Her stomach clenched again. "One day," she said. She studied his face and let her guard down. She was so used to keeping it up that it felt strange to feel exposed. Opening up, she allowed her energy to probe him. He felt warm and soothing, but that was as far as she got. The man was good at keeping his feelings to himself. "Now it's your turn," she said. "Tell me about you."

His face flattened, but just as quickly relaxed. "There's not much to tell."

"Oh, I'm sure you have a few secrets lurking in there." His jaw clenched. "Come on," she said. "I showed you mine. Now you show me yours."

His breathing slowed, and he seemed to think about what to say. "My parents are alive and well, although we're not very close."

She snuggled into the covers. "Why not?"

He shrugged. "We're...different, you could say. My family comes from the wrong side of the tracks. We didn't have much growing up."

"Was it just you?"

"No," he said. "I have a sister."

"What's her name?"

"Mirana."

"Are you close?"

"Not like your family. We were growing up, but things changed."

"Why?"

He hesitated. "My parents..." He pursed his lips. "Like I said, we didn't have much, so my parents sent me away when I was a child."

She pulled on the sheets. "Sent you where?"

"To another family. And I use the term 'family' loosely."

Eve wondered what to say. "I'm sorry to hear that."

"Me too."

"Your sister too?"

"Not at first. She was older than me, but I guess as the male, I was expected to make the sacrifice. She left after her...when she was a teenager."

"Where did she go?"

"She went to work for someone, as a live in assistant, or something like that."

"What about you?"

"Me? I pretty much did the same. I was fed, clothed, and schooled, and outside of that, worked whatever odd jobs were assigned."

"And your parents were okay with that?"

"I don't think they really cared."

"Didn't they check in on you?"

"Once or twice. They didn't seem overly concerned."

Eve rarely probed anyone without permission, save the occasional date who may have had ulterior motives, but without thinking, she allowed her energy to multiply and pushed a little harder toward Adam. Pain and betrayal were the first things she felt, and then something else. Something familiar, before the door slammed shut. She almost physically moved back in the bed.

Adam glanced at her before turning and facing the ceiling. Eve retracted her energy and wondered about Adam's unique ability to shut her out.

"I'm sorry," she said.

He shifted his eyes toward her. "You don't have to feel sorry for me."

She chuckled as she heard her own words mirrored back. "Where are they now?"

He seemed to relax in the bed, his posture less rigid. "Who?"

Eve punched him lightly in the arm. "Your parents? Your sister?"

"Oh. Mirana married her employer's son, who's a loser. And my parents live on their farm but still socialize with the people who raised me. We barely speak."

"Who? Your parents or the people who raised you?"

"Both," he said.

Eve raised her head. "That sucks."

"Yeah. It does." He shifted back toward her. "At least you have siblings you can talk to." She nodded. "Have you considered contacting them?"

She shook her head. "No. That's not an option. I won't get them involved."

"They might be able to help. Give you a place to stay."

"No, Adam."

"But what if something happens?" He sat up. "We're in a precarious situation here. We're being chased by the mob. If they catch up to us, and God help us, succeed in getting rid of us, then your family needs to know."

"You think the mob is going to find us?"

"I hope not. But what if they do?"

She pushed up next to him. "I thought this conversation was supposed to help us sleep?"

His shoulders slumped. "You're right." He rubbed his face. "I'm trying to get your mind off things, and instead I wind up right back where we started." He looked at her with weary eyes. "Sorry."

Eve felt her own fatigue, but knew sleep would remain elusive. He was only asking the questions she'd been asking herself. And she had no answers. "God. We need to rest."

"Agreed."

Eve watched as he kneaded his muscles. His shirt raised, and she noticed the ridges beneath. Something fired through her belly. The idea of seducing him flickered, but she ignored it. It would only complicate matters. But the more she thought about it, the more it gained strength. What could it hurt? It wasn't like they were a couple. Or even planned to be. Why not consider it?

"Adam?"

He stretched and groaned. "Yes?"

"I have an idea about how we might relax." She reached out and touched his knee under the sheet.

His reaction was immediate. There were some things that were too hard to hide. He locked eyes with her. "Excuse me?"

Her hand moved up his leg, and she felt him respond. "I mean, why not? We're in this bed together. We're both stressed out. We could use a little relaxation. It'll get our mind off things."

He put his hand over hers to stop her advancing fingers. His jaw dropped. "Are you serious?"

She let her thumb tickle his skin. "It doesn't mean we're engaged. We're just two people who need to take the edge off."

"But you said—"

"Adam," she said, her heart beginning to race, "I know what I said. But that was then, and this is now. I'm just saying I'm open to it if you are." He swallowed. His breathing had picked up, and he looked a little pale.

He cleared his throat. "I need a glass of water."

"There's some bottled water in the shopping bag. Do you want it?"

"No." He let out a breath. "I don't think I can move."

She smiled. "I'll get it." She slid off the mattress, feeling his eyes on her. The bag was at the foot of the bed, and she dug through it, finding the bottle of water. "Here." She held it out to him.

He reached out with shaky fingers. "Thanks." He took a hasty drink and put the bottle on the nightstand.

"Well?" she asked.

Taking a deep breath, he studied her. "You're sure?"

"I wouldn't have made the offer if I wasn't."

Groaning, he ran a hand through his hair. "I'll be honest. This may not last long."

Chuckling, she said, "It probably won't. That's the point. We'll both have a pleasant moment, and then we'll sleep like babies." She cocked her head at him. "But I state we *both* have a pleasant moment. Not just you."

He shook his head at her. "Don't worry," he said. "I'll see to that."

Her body warmed considerably at his words, and the intensity surprised her, but she didn't stop to think about it. She slid back into the bed and sat facing him. Adam watched her like he was starving and she was the first food he'd seen in days. The look made her pulse race. She had no doubt that he would honor his word.

Eve pulled off her shirt and threw it to the ground. His eyes took her in, and she heard him suck in a breath. "You're right," he said.

"About what?"

"Your superpowers far exceed mine."

She laughed and reached for his leg again. She trailed her fingers up his thigh. "Your turn."

He didn't hesitate. His shirt came off, and he tossed it aside. She admired him in the dusky light. "Nice," she said. "Very nice."

He reached for her. He brought his hand up to her face and cupped her jaw. He let his other hand find her hip, and his fingers caressed her thigh under her shorts. Her breath caught, and it felt like a taut rubber band suddenly released inside her.

He brought his face next to hers, and his lips lingered near hers. Their breath intermingled.

She put her other hand against his chest. "Wait," she said. "No kissing."

He scowled. "What?"

"We shouldn't kiss. It's too personal."

He stared at her. "Are you crazy?"

"No. It confuses things." Her own breath was coming fast, and she was finding it hard to think. Normally, she took the lead when it came to sex, but this time felt different. She fought to gain control. "I think..."

He moved in before she could answer. "That's the problem," he said. His arm wrapped around her and pulled her close. "No more thinking. If we're gonna do this, then we're gonna do it right." He brought his lips down to graze over hers. Their noses touched and his fingers trailed over her back and into her shorts, where he cupped her bottom.

In one movement, he pulled her forward and rested her against his lap, where she felt the intensity of his desire for her.

She instinctively rocked against him, and he moaned. Her own groan of need escaped her, and she couldn't believe how quickly this had escalated. She thought this would be a quick roll in the hay that would help her insomnia, but it was becoming much more. Something about Adam was triggering a greater hunger than she knew existed.

Staring into his eyes and feeling his body against hers, she let her hands travel down his back as she moved against him. Her heart pounding, she touched her forehead to his and gave in to her need. "Don't say I didn't warn you," she whispered. She nibbled at his lips and then covered his hungry mouth with her own.

·· • • • • • • • · ·

Eve blinked and stared into the dark room. Adam slept beside her. The sex had been wild and tempestuous. Eve was not a stranger in the bedroom. She'd been with a myriad of men with a range of tastes. She knew what she liked, and she could give as good as she got, but her encounter with Adam had been altogether different. They didn't even have to speak. Adam met her every move with an intensity and desire that matched her own. They moved in perfect unison together, every touch building on the previous one, until a crescendo was reached that even Eve had never experienced. And then when it ended, they started again, until fatigue eventually won over and they succumbed to sleep.

Eve listened to Adam's soft sounds of breathing as she thought back. They'd finally closed their eyes sometime after noon and had slept the rest of the day. Her internal clock sensed it was somewhere around three am. They had slept past dinner and into the night, but considering their previous day, Eve figured the rest was needed. She was still tired, but her mind raced. What had happened with Adam was sensational, and her body responded again to the thought of reaching over and waking him, but she held back. Something about the encounter troubled her.

She recalled her sister Gillian's words when she'd met her husband, Grayson. Unexpected intensity and attraction. Powerful desire. The inability to stop touching. Wanting to be with him. Twenty-four hours of pure lust before it was unintentionally interrupted. The need and longing which ultimately revealed what had happened between them. They had Binded.

Eve swallowed. Binding. It was what happened with females such as her when they found a potential mate. It was powerful and instinctual. And if allowed to proceed, would end with her pregnant. It was the natural conclusion to a Binding. Her father had told her a little about it. It was normal for all female Red-Lines to experience it. The only unknown was that Eve was half human. He wasn't sure how that would affect the process. Eve hadn't worried about it too much until it had happened with Gilli. After that, she'd paid more attention. But none of her suitors had fit the bill. They were kind and attentive, and sometimes a little kinky, but none of them had elicited the response from Eve that Adam had. And now she couldn't stop thinking about it. Had she initiated the Binding process with him?

She rubbed her forehead. How could that be possible? She barely knew him. And why him? He was a bartender, and there was nothing overtly special about him. Eve had wanted men before, but once she got them, the thrill was gone. She may have hung around for a little while and had some serious relationships, but nothing that matched this.

She rolled on her side and faced his back. Her mind replayed their bodies moving together. But she held back. If this truly was the start of a Binding, she had to keep her distance. The power of the Binding was its momentum. If the energy was allowed to build and grow, then at some point, a connection was secured. And pregnancy would result, regardless of any birth control methods being used. And once that happened, there was no turning back. The power of the connection was so strong that if something were to sever the energy between the couple, then it could affect the health of the man and woman, and could also affect the pregnancy.

Eve couldn't let that happen. Now was not the time to Bind with anyone, and she sure as hell didn't want to get pregnant. She blinked her tired eyes and yawned. If this truly was the beginning of a Binding, then she had to do everything in her power not to touch Adam again. She would make that very clear in the morning.

Making her decision, and feeling somewhat relieved, she closed her eyes and fell back to sleep.

Chapter Eight

Soft light pierced the dirty blinds, and the room lost its murky bleakness. Although the light didn't help much to cheer the room.

Adam stirred in the bed. He punched the pillow and tried to get comfortable. Although the mattress was lumpy, he'd managed a fitful sleep. That he'd slept at all surprised him. He'd expected after... His eyes shot open, and he went rigid in the bed. Everything went rigid. His whole body became a tuning fork that someone had just whacked against a table top. Moving slowly, he glanced behind him. Eve slept on her side, facing him, looking peaceful.

He turned back and tried to breathe. The memory of his time with her came racing back. Every touch, kiss, and stroke felt like it had just happened. His desire for her made him ache to roll over, take her in his arms, and make love to her over and over again. He could still hear her moans and feel her body rock against his, and he almost audibly groaned. What the hell had happened between them?

Trying not to think about her, he focused on his current situation. He believed he was close to getting the information he needed. Although being chased by mobsters was less than ideal, it certainly proved helpful in the getting-to-know-Eve department. She'd opened up about her brother, and Adam thought with a bit more cajoling, he might determine her brother's location. But then she'd made the offer to sleep with him. Some part of his subconscious had told him no, but he'd ignored it. Tez's words reverberated. Forty-eight hours. And twenty-four were already gone.

He wondered if she might tell him more after yesterday. If she did, maybe he could suggest she at least try to get a message to Royce. Adam could volunteer to contact him. He would have to use Eve's protective urge to his advantage. Maybe suggest Vince might start looking for her brother and sister in order to find her and she should warn them.

Once he had the information, then he could suggest going their separate ways. Eve had already proposed the idea, and it would be the best way to end this and go home.

But the memory of kissing her made it hard to breathe. Her soft lips moving over his, their tongues probing and intertwining. Despite his plans, he knew everything had changed. His reaction to her had been passionate and ravenous. The more he'd touched her, the more he'd wanted her. Her body had responded to his with equal intensity and what he thought would be a ten-minute moment had turned into a lust fest. She was magnificent. Her energy was electric, and he was entranced by her. Just lying next to her now, he could almost see the tendrils of light connecting the two of them.

He rolled to face her and watched her sleep. A soft shoulder peeked out from under the covers, and he reached to touch it. Her skin was softer than a butterfly's wing, or at least how he imagined a butterfly's wing would feel. She sighed softly, and her eyes opened. Her lids blinked the sleep away, and she focused on him. They stared at each other. Adam's heart instantly thumped faster. Without thinking, he leaned in and met her lips with his own. She met his kiss and kissed him back, when she suddenly stopped. She pushed against his chest and sat up, holding the sheet against her breasts.

"No. Wait," she said breathlessly.

Adam tried to catch his own breath. "What?" he asked. "What is it?"

"We can't." She ran a hand through her hair.

He smiled and sat next to her. "I think after yesterday, we proved that we can."

She bit her lip. "Listen, Adam. What happened yesterday..."

"Was amazing," he said. "You know it, and I know it. And I want to do it again. Don't you?"

She blinked and glanced at his bare chest and his barely covered lower body. She took a deep breath and let it out. "I...I did enjoy it."

"So." He reached for the sheet to pull it away, but she yanked it back.

"I can't." She dropped the sheet, and he got a brief glimpse of her naked as she jumped out of the bed, grabbed her clothes, and raced into the bathroom.

"Eve."

The door closed, and every part of him hurt. His body wanted her, and not being able to have her made him physically ache. He was going to have to take one hell of a cold shower, which in this place would not be difficult.

Struggling to understand, he got out of bed and put on his own clothes. Maybe once she saw he was backing off, she might relax a little. But something nagged at him. This was not the fear of a scared woman. Men did not intimidate Eve. This was something different. He listened as the shower ran and debated calling Tez. Should Adam inform him of his progress? He shook his head, trying to clear the sexual haze. What was going on? What was the big deal if Eve said no? It wasn't like they planned to be a couple. It was just sex. Physically uncomfortable, maybe, but not the end of the world.

So why was this different?

The shower turned off a few minutes later. By then, Adam had composed himself. He needed a shower himself, and once she stepped out, he figured he'd just walk in behind her, acting confident in his control.

But when she did step out, all of that so-called control almost crumbled. Her hair was up, with damp tendrils framing her face. She wore jeans and a t-shirt, and her face looked fresh and clean. It took the will of a stubborn two-year-old for him to walk by her. He almost spoke, but stopped himself, knowing if he did, he might relent. She gave him no signs she'd changed her mind, so he entered the bathroom and flipped on the shower to the coldest setting.

Fifteen minutes later, despite the frigid water, he still felt aroused, but he felt like he could walk out of the bathroom without acting like he was still naked beside her. He opened the door and stepped out. She was sitting on the bed, staring at the wall, her closed suitcase beside her. He didn't speak. Just walked past her. He'd thrown on a navy T-shirt, his pair of jeans, and tennis shoes, and he put the rest of his few belongings into his shopping bag. The bed had been somewhat made. The bedspread was still in the chair, but the sheets had been smoothed and the pillows arranged.

He didn't know what to say.

A few seconds passed, and she stood, facing him, looking like it was an effort to do it. "I figured we could go get some breakfast, and then..."

He cleared his throat. "And then what?"

She shifted from foot to foot and stared at the floor. "Go our separate ways."

He was disappointed she didn't say, "And come back here and screw our brains out."

He groaned inwardly. What was the matter with him? He didn't trust his voice, so he just said, "Okay."

She nodded. "Okay." She reached for her suitcase.

"Let me help you with that," he said, reaching for it at the same time. Their fingers touched, and the spark became an inferno.

Their eyes met.

"Shit," he said, and he let go of the suitcase, dropped his bag, and pulled her into his arms. A low moan escaped her, and she wrapped around him. Her lips covered his, and their tongues met. Adam thought his heart was going to break out of his chest. She was fire, and he was the match. They fell back into the bed, touching, kissing, and stroking again, as if for the first time. Her nails raked against the back of his shirt, her legs encircled him, and her hips arched against him. He couldn't wait to get her clothes off.

Then came the knock on the door.

·········

They froze. Adam pulled back. Eve's heart hammered, but for a different reason other than Adam. "Who's that?" she whispered.

Adam sat up. "I don't know. No one knows we're here."

Eve rose and stood. "Mike in the lobby does. So does Dixie."

"Should we answer?"

"Just wait," said Eve, speaking low.

A few seconds passed before the knock came again. "Eve?" asked a man from the other side of the door. "Are you in there?"

Eve sucked in a lungful of air. "Shit," she said. "Damn it, Dixie."

"What?" asked Adam. "Who is it?"

Eve shook her head. "It's Tony."

"Tony?"

"He's the policeman. He lives in my building."

Adam blinked. "The one Dixie mentioned. The one you dated?"

Eve nodded. "Yes."

Another knock, this time louder. "Eve, please. Open the door."

"Can you trust him?" asked Adam.

Eve sighed. "He's one of the few people I do. He's a straight up guy."

"So why not ask him for help?"

"Because I don't want him to get involved. It could put him at risk. Besides, I'm still not sure about going to the police."

"I think that decision has just been taken out of your hands."

"Come on, Eve," said Tony through the door. "I can hear talking. Open the door."

"Damn it," said Eve. She walked to the door and looked out the peephole. After a second, she unlocked the door. The door creaked open. Tony stared back at her.

"Let me in," said Tony. "I talked to Dixie."

Eve moved back, and he stepped inside. Seeing Adam, he stopped. The two men sized each other up. Adam's tall frame matched Tony's, but Tony's barrel chest and bulky shoulders gave him the appearance of a seasoned wrestler that could clock Adam in under ten seconds.

"What are you doing here?" She shut the door behind her.

"Dixie told me what was going on. She's scared to death." He scowled. "What the hell do you think you're doing?" He pointed a thumb at Adam. "And what are you doing here with this loser?"

"Wait a minute..." said Adam.

Tony raised a palm. "You'll have your say, boy toy."

"Boy toy?"

"Tony, stop it," said Eve.

"Damn it, Eve. You get involved in something like this and you don't come to me?" He raised a hand. "I can live with you not wanting to get married. But, Jesus. You don't ask me for help when you see Benny killed?" He shook his head. "I don't understand." He patted his chest. "I'm a cop and your friend." He glanced back at Adam. "But you go to him? Some bartender? A pretty boy? How long have you known him? Five minutes?"

"Excuse me?" asked Adam.

"Adam..." said Eve, waving at him. "Just..."

"Just what, Eve?" asked Tony. "There is nothing to say. You need to get your stuff and come with me. We're going to the precinct to report this." He reached for her arm, but she pulled away.

"No. We're not," she said.

"Yes, we are."

Eve moved past him and stood next to Adam. "You don't understand. He and I know who killed Benny. It was Vince. And Vince is mixed up with the mob. You bring us in, and we're both dead."

Tony grimaced. "No. *You* don't understand. They're looking for you."

"I know. Why do you think we're hiding?" said Eve.

"I'm not talking about Vince," said Tony. "The police. They want to talk to you about Benny. There are reports that you and pretty boy here left the scene of the crime."

"What?" asked Eve.

"We didn't do anything," said Adam. "They were going to kill us."

"Are you saying we're suspects?" asked Eve.

"We can still get out ahead of this," said Tony. "Right now, they just want to talk with you. But you stay on the run, it just looks like you're guilty. You come in and tell your story, then we can handle it."

Eve rubbed her arms. "You bring us in, and we're dead. Benny will never get justice."

Tony squared his shoulders. "You don't come in, then they can create whatever story they want. Suddenly, it looks like you murdered him. There are already whispers that you two were close."

"Close?" asked Eve. "He was like a father to me. You know that."

"I know that, but you know how the story will turn if you don't come forward. It will become some sort of sordid affair gone bad. And you're not there to defend yourself."

"They don't have proof of that," said Adam.

Tony's voice boomed. "Did I ask you a question?"

"Hey," said Adam, angrily. "I was there."

"And you did a hell of a job. You got Eve here in a world of trouble. Did you tell her to run?"

"Stop it, Tony," said Eve, stepping forward. "I don't need you to come in here and solve all my problems and tell me what to do. If I'd wanted that, I would have married you."

Tony set his jaw. "Eve..."

"No," she said. "I'm the one that ran. Adam wanted to go to the police. I've been trying ever since to convince him we need to separate, but he won't go."

Tony sneered. "He's just a regular Prince Charming."

Eve sighed. "Listen. I know what you're trying to do."

"I'm trying to protect you."

"Bring us in, and we'll never make it to any trial."

"We'll keep you safe."

"Sure you will," said Adam.

Tony glowered. "Then let me clarify, Paul Newman." He patted his chest. "I'll keep her safe."

"Where?" asked Adam. "In the privacy of your bedroom?"

Tony's face froze. "You son of a bitch." He stepped forward. "Who the hell do you think you are?"

Eve stepped between them. "Stop it."

"Paul Newman. Remember?" asked Adam. Tony sneered at him, but Adam didn't back down. "And who are you? One of those thugs from *The Godfather*?"

Tony pointed again. "Are you saying I'm crooked? I'll kick your ass."

Adam tried to move closer, but Eve blocked him. "Whenever you're ready," said Adam.

"Oh, for god's sake," said Eve. "Why does testosterone make you boys so stupid?" She put a hand on Tony's chest to hold him back. "Both of you need to shut up. We've got bigger problems than your egos."

Tony's snarl dropped. "I don't care about this guy. What I care about is you. I don't want to see you accused of a crime you didn't commit. If you come in, we'll put you in protective custody."

"You know as well as I do the police can't be trusted," said Eve. "Somebody will be on the take. They'll give us up. Plus, it puts my family at risk."

Tony backed up and gave Eve some space. "I don't want you out there hiding. Where will you go? It makes you look guilty."

"I know how it looks," said Eve. "But Adam's right. There isn't any evidence linking us to Benny's death. They just know we were there."

"Vince could come forward and accuse you."

Eve shook her head. "He won't do that. That puts him out in the open. He doesn't want that. And he certainly doesn't want to place himself at the scene. He might talk a lot, but he can't prove anything."

"He can make it look bad," said Adam.

"He might, but don't forget. Benny had a lot of friends and loyal employees. They'll defend him against any lies Vince may try to spread."

Adam put his hand on the wall. "I think you're underestimating Vince."

"No," said Eve. "I know Vince. He'll wait me out. He wants me to come out in the open. Go to the police. It's what he's waiting for."

"How do you know that?" asked Adam.

"Because he knows that Benny's death will eat at me. He knows I want justice for him. He expects me to accuse him."

"So we'll keep an eye on him," said Tony.

"You can't keep your eye on everyone."

"You can't stay here," said Tony. He glared at Adam. "You expect this guy to take care of you?"

"I just need time to think." Eve rubbed her head. She sighed, stepped back, and leaned against the wall. "I know I should go to the police. I want Vince to pay for his crimes. But I don't think turning myself in will do it."

"What will do it?" asked Adam.

She tried to think. "Vince killed his father. That's what I don't understand."

"What do you mean?" asked Tony. "Domestic violence isn't uncommon."

"Between a father and son?" asked Eve. "I remember Vince worshipping his dad."

"That was a long time ago," said Tony. "Things change."

"But what changed?" asked Eve. "What made Vince homicidal? What did he want?"

"If he's mixed up in the mob," said Tony, "it could be anything."

"Well, if we could find out what it is," said Eve, "maybe that could help us get the evidence we need against Vince."

"How do we do that?" asked Adam. "It's not like we can ask him."

"No, we can't," said Eve. She held Tony's gaze. "But you could."

Tony's jaw dropped. "What are you saying?"

"I'm saying you could do a little digging. See what you can find out. Vince's father was just murdered," said Eve. "It's a good reason to go talk to Vince. Dig into his background. Find out any reason why he might want to kill Benny."

Tony stared at her. "You want me to investigate Vince?"

"Yes."

"That's crazy."

"Why is that crazy?" asked Adam.

Tony glared again. "I'm not talking to you."

Adam's eyes narrowed. "It seems you are. And she's got a point. Vince wants something. If I were you, I'd check out Benny's club."

"What about it?"

Adam snorted. "I worked there. That place brought in plenty of money. It's also sitting on a valuable piece of real estate. Maybe somebody wanted Benny to sell, but he wasn't going for it."

Tony snickered. "Now you're a private dick?"

"He's got a point," said Eve. "The club was Benny's baby. It's all he had. He'd never sell that place."

"With Benny dead, Vince is the logical choice to inherit," said Adam.

"Exactly," said Eve.

Tony crossed his arms. "And what are you supposed to do while I'm checking into this theory of yours?"

"We stay in hiding until you can get some more information. Maybe we can get Vince without us ever having to testify."

"This is a long shot at best," said Tony.

"I know it is. But we have to try. I'd rather walk into that police station at the last possible moment. Hopefully after Vince is already under suspicion."

"If Vinny inherits the bar," said Adam, "then I'll be curious to see what he does with it."

"If Benny left it to him," said Tony, "then Vince can do whatever he wants. We can't stop that."

"I know," said Eve. "But Vince is not the brightest guy. If he's involved in something, then he'll likely leave a bread crumb trail a mile wide."

Tony hesitated. "I don't like this, Eve."

"I don't like it either. But to be honest, I feel safer on my own."

"You mean with him?" He eyed Adam.

"With him or without him, I still feel safer."

Tony sighed. "How will I get in touch with you?"

"You won't. I'll get in touch with you."

"Eve..."

"It's better you don't know where we are."

"You have your phone?"

"It's turned off."

"That's not good enough. Take the battery out, too."

"Really?"

"Yes." He studied Eve. "You sure about this? It's a big risk."

"It's a risk for you, too. But I trust you."

He paused. "I care about you. If this turns ugly, I won't hesitate to bring in the cavalry."

"If we get to that point, then by all means, I'll welcome your assistance."

"I think we may already be at that point."

"Not yet," said Eve. "Not unless Vince finds us. And there's no reason he should."

Tony set his jaw. "You keep saying 'us.'"

Eve huffed and felt the beginnings of a headache. "Adam is stuck in this, just like I am."

Tony tipped his head at Eve. "I know you, Eve." He squinted at Adam. "But I don't know a damn thing about him."

"He's a bartender."

"Exactly. How do I know he won't leave you to fend for yourself? He could give you up to Vince, for all you know."

"You know, I am standing here," said Adam, waving a hand.

Eve rolled her eyes at Tony. "I've been trying to get him to leave me since this started. I still think it's a good idea if we separate."

"Yeah," said Tony. He glanced at the crumpled bed. "I can tell he's dying to leave."

Eve ignored Tony's innuendo. "And he wouldn't turn me in without risking himself."

"I'm not going anywhere," said Adam. He put an arm around Eve. "She and I make a good team." He pulled her closer, but Eve pushed away. Tony gritted his teeth.

"Stop it, Adam." Eve stepped closer to Tony and put a hand on his forearm. "Listen. Please don't let what happened between you and me affect your judgment. Adam and I are just friends."

"Friends, huh?" Tony scoffed.

"Friends?" asked Adam.

Eve patted Tony's arm. "You know me. You know I'm right about this. I just need a little time. Can you give me that?"

Tony paused. "How much time?"

"A week."

Tony's eyebrow rose. "Two days."

"Five days."

"Three."

"Four."

Tony hesitated. "Eve..."

"Four days. Give me four days. Go check out Vince. Get more information on Benny and his business dealings. I'll hang low. Let's wait it out. See what happens."

"Where will you go?"

"You let me worry about that. The less you know, the better."

Tony looked around the room. "You won't stay here, I hope."

"No," said Eve. "We won't. We'll leave today."

"I'll make sure she's safe," said Adam.

Eve glanced at him. "No. You and I should part. We draw attention together."

"I disagree," said Adam. "We need to look out for each other."

"Adam..."

"He's right," said Tony. Adam's eyes narrowed. "That's right, Paul Newman," said Tony. "It doesn't mean I like it. But sadly, I think you two are safer together. And I'll feel better knowing you're not alone." He grimaced at Adam. "Even if you are just a bartender." He looked back at Eve. "But I suggest you work on a disguise." He touched an auburn ringlet. "You tend to stand out in a crowd, my dear."

Eve nodded, and Tony dropped his hand. "We will." She squeezed his arm. "Thank you."

Tony sighed. "You're damn lucky I like you." He pointed. "Four days. That's it. Then you call me and you come in."

Eve relaxed. "I promise. Four days."

"You go somewhere safe, and don't come out until you contact me. Got it?"

"Got it," said Eve.

Tony faced Adam, his face stony. "And I swear to God, anything happens to her and I'll turn you into fertilizer. You understand?"

"I think that's pretty clear," said Adam. He nodded at Eve. "We'll be okay."

Eve was relieved they'd come to an agreement, although she wished Tony would have supported her about separating from Adam. "You be careful too."

Tony stepped to the door and opened it. "Don't worry about me. You just take care of yourself." He shook his head. "I can't believe I'm agreeing to this."

"Talk to Dixie too," said Eve. "Tell her I'm okay and not to worry."

"You know Dix," said Tony. "She's gonna worry no matter what I say. Between this and her dad, she's an emotional mess."

Eve sighed. "I know. Just make sure she stays safe. I don't want her in danger because of us."

"I'll keep an eye on her."

"Thank you, Tony. I appreciate this."

Tony held her gaze. He seemed to consider what to say next. "I...I still care about you."

Eve smiled softly. "I know you do."

"I always will."

"I know," she said.

He held still for a moment, glanced at Adam, and then left, closing the door behind him.

Eve stared out the peephole for a few seconds, then returned to her suitcase and picked it up.

Adam hesitated. "What? Are we leaving right now?"

Eve nodded. "Yes. I think we should. The sooner, the better."

"But..."

"But, what?"

Adam glanced at the bed. "You and I were engaged a few minutes ago before we were rudely interrupted."

The heat returned, but Eve pushed it back. Her earlier response to Adam resulting from the mere grazing of their fingers told her that a Binding was imminent if she didn't keep her distance.

"Listen, Adam," she said. "What happened between us was a mistake. It's a good thing we stopped. Now is not the time for us to get distracted."

"Distracted?" asked Adam. "Considering what we're dealing with, I'd say a distraction is exactly what we need."

He moved closer, but Eve stepped back. "No." He stopped and stared, and for one second, she reconsidered. The thought of kissing and falling back into bed with him was alluring. But then she thought of the repercussions.

He stared at her, as if he only waited long enough, she'd cave. "You're sure?"

"I am."

"I could take my shirt off."

"Please don't."

"You could take yours off, too, if you feel like it."

"I don't."

Watching her, he nodded. "Fine. But if you change your mind..."

"I'll let you know." She gripped her suitcase and pointed at his shopping bag. "Don't forget that."

Sighing, he nodded. He leaned low and reached for her case. "Here. Let me take that."

She pulled her hand back and leaned away. "Nice try." Even though he hadn't touched her, he was close enough to smell. The scent of soap and what Eve could only describe as sexual heat almost made her waver, but then he stepped back and Eve kept her composure.

He groaned, and his face dropped. "Okay. You win," he said. "Just know that I am very uncomfortable right now."

She almost smiled. "Sorry about that."

He grabbed his shopping bag. "Where do you want to go next?"

"I think we need to get something to eat and then figure it out."

"Our budget is tight."

"I know." She walked away and gripped the knob. "You got everything?"

Adam lifted his bag. "There isn't much to leave behind."

Eve nodded. "Let's go."

She opened the door and walked straight into Vince.

Chapter Nine

"HEY, BABY," SAID VINCE. His cheeks sported red scratches from his encounter with Louis. He glanced at her suitcase. "Going somewhere?"

"Shit," said Adam.

Eve stepped back, and Vince advanced into the room. He pulled a gun from his waistband. "Fancy seeing you here."

"Vince..." said Eve.

Adam took in the scene and tried to think. Vince was just inside the entry and the door was open. Where was Saul? Had Vince brought his goon?

In answer to his question, Vince glanced out the open door. "Keep an eye on the hallway."

Adam saw a brief shadow in the door frame and knew that there was a second gunman. He could only assume it was Saul. His mind raced as to how to escape without revealing his origins.

"Vince, listen..." Eve held out a shaky hand.

Vince chuckled. "No, babe. You listen. Who do you think you are? You think you can just walk away from this? You think I couldn't find you?" He rubbed the back of his scalp with his free hand. "And you're gonna pay for the whack on the head."

Adam fought to buy time. "How did you find us?"

Vince shifted his eyes toward him. "I have connections."

Eve scoffed. "You mean the mob?"

Vince waved the gun at her. "You really want to irritate me right now?"

"Is it the mob?" asked Adam.

Vince looked between the two of them and shrugged.

"Why, Vinny?" asked Eve.

Vince lifted a brow. "Why? Because they show me some respect."

"Respect? That's what you want?" asked Eve.

"Damn straight it is."

"I don't believe that," said Eve.

"I don't give a damn what you believe."

"Why kill your dad? What did he do to you to deserve that?"

Vince paused, and he set his jaw. "He didn't respect me."

"That's crap, Vince. He loved you."

Vince's voice rose. "No, he didn't."

Eve stepped farther back. Adam watched, wondering if there was a way to get to Vince's gun. If Adam could deliver another heat flare, he could incapacitate Vince. But how to deal with the man in the hall?

Eve spoke calmly. "That's not true." A stir of emotions seemed to play across Vince's face. "And I think you know that."

Vince cleared his throat. "He wouldn't listen to me."

"About what?" asked Eve.

Vince shook his head. "He should have just listened to me."

"What happened, Vinny?"

Adam kept an eye on the door, waiting for the mystery man to show his face. Considering the timing of Vince's visit, he had the sinking feeling that perhaps Tony wasn't as stand up as Eve believed.

Vince stared off, looking lost, but he still held his gun on Eve. "I'm in too deep."

Eve spoke softly. "Why?"

His stony glare softened. "Money. It's all about money. It always is."

"You can get out."

"No, I can't."

"Yes. You can. There's always a way. My friend Tony. He can help."

Vince's eyes widened. "Tony? Your ex? The cop?" He chuckled. "He's the one who led us here."

Eve's jaw dropped, and she straightened. "That's not true. He'd never betray me."

Vince waved the gun. "Oh, he didn't realize it. We had some people on the inside. They told us about your history with him. Said he lived in your building and to keep an eye out. And lo-and-behold, two of my guys see your sweet Tony leave early this morning. They followed him here. One quick phone call and a few minutes later, Saul and I are at your door." He fixed the gun back on Eve. "Not that hard, really."

Adam was glad the man outside was not Tony. Saul was a smaller man and would be easier to confront.

"You can't really want to kill me," said Eve.

Tony snorted. "I don't want to," said Vince. "I mean, you and I have some fond memories." He looked her up and down.

"They were good memories," she said. "We had fun together."

"For a while." His face darkened. "But then you left." The side of his mouth raised. "Dad called me an idiot for letting you get away." He paused. "Honestly, I think he loved you more than me."

Eve shook her head. "That's not true."

He lifted a brow. "I think he was in love with you."

"No, he wasn't."

"I think you loved him back, too."

Eve's eyes widened. "What are you saying?"

"I'm saying you two were having an affair. He tried to break it off, maybe wanted to fire you, and you were about to lose your meal ticket. You went crazy. Found the gun he kept in the desk, and shot him."

"Vince..."

Adam watched the hall. The shadow moved and stuck his head in. It was Saul. He looked around the room. "What's taking so long?"

Adam focused his energy. Since he was only a Gray-Line, his abilities were limited, but that didn't mean he was defenseless. He kept an eye on Eve. Knowing she was a Red-Line, he waited to see how she would react. Her talents would be much more effective. It would have to be soon, though, because they were running out of time.

"You're going to kill me? Is that it? And then shoot him?" Eve pointed at Adam. "How do you propose to walk out of this building without being seen or heard?"

Vince smiled. "Where do you think we are? The Ritz? People around here don't see or hear anything. And they sure as hell aren't going to testify against us."

"You don't know that," said Eve. "The police will find us dead. There will be a million questions. Most of them directed at you."

"Let them ask," said Vince. "I already have an alibi. I'm eating lunch with an associate right about now." He checked his watch.

Adam waited. As soon as he suspected an opening, he would move.

"There's something else," said Eve.

Vince cocked his gun. "Sorry, sweetheart, but we're out of time."

"Papers," she said. "That Benny gave me."

Adam perked up.

Vince paused. "What are you talking about?" His smile slipped.

"Benny gave me papers. Documents. In a sealed envelope. He told me not to open them and to put them in a safe deposit box. Said if anything happened to him, to give them to the cops."

Vinny's hard stare returned. "You're lying."

"I'm not." Eve padded her purse. "I've got the key."

Vince paused. "So, I kill you and get the key."

Eve shook her head. "Doesn't work like that. You can't get into the box without me."

Vince shrugged. "So the papers sit forever in a box. Who cares?" He snickered at his deduction.

"Someone else has the key."

Vince's face dropped. "Who?"

"Someone important. Someone who will take everything to the police. And you can't stop him."

"Him, huh?" asked Vince. "Don't tell me it's your lovebird, Tony?"

Eve's eyes didn't stray. "No. Not him. Someone you don't know."

Adam held his breath. If something was going to happen, it would be now.

Vince sneered. "You lying bitch."

Saul stepped to the threshold. "What's going on? Do it already."

Vince lunged for Eve's purse. Adam focused on the door and, directing his energy with his mind, slammed it shut in Saul's face. Eve grabbed at the gun in Vince's hand and pushed it away as Adam jumped forward. There was a soft *thunk* as the weapon discharged. Adam's adrenaline surged, and he slammed himself against Vince. They fell back into the entry. The door started to open, but in the small space, Adam and Vince's bodies prevented Saul from entering.

Vince dropped the gun, and it skittered across the dirty carpet as Adam mustered more energy and sent a powerful jolt into Vince, who immediately stilled, just as Eve brought the old rotary phone in the room down on his head.

With Vince still, the door opened more easily and half of Saul's body appeared through the door. Adam had just enough time to reach for the man's arm and yank him into the room. Saul's other hand held a gun, and Adam grabbed his wrist and pushed Saul against the wall. They struggled as Adam tried to keep Saul pinned and the gun directed away from Eve.

Adam heard another whack of the phone against Vince's head just as Adam brought his knee directly into Saul's groin. Saul heaved and released a breathless grunt. His hold on his gun went limp. It dropped to the ground. Adam placed a free hand against Saul's midsection and sent a jolt, just as Eve slammed the phone onto Saul's head. The man went down faster than the Titanic.

Breathless, Eve and Adam didn't waste time. Eve picked up Vince's gun, and Adam picked up Saul's. They threw them in Adam's bag, grabbed her suitcase, walked into the hallway, and closed the door behind them. Trying to act casual, they walked to the top of the stairs and began to walk down when Adam suddenly felt lightheaded. He grabbed at the wall to support himself.

"Adam?" asked Eve. "What's wrong?" She came around to help him when her eyes widened and she stared at his shirt. "Oh my god. You're bleeding."

The mere mention of blood sent a surge of pain through Adam. He glanced at his left shoulder and saw the spreading patch of darkness travel down his navy shirt. The light-headedness grew, and he blinked. Eve grabbed him around the waist and helped him to sit on the top stair. She pulled on the neckline of his shirt to look beneath it and surveyed his wound. Her eyes rounded. "You've been shot." She met his gaze. "Adam?" She patted his face. "Talk to me."

Adam shook his head. The effects of the attack and the swings of adrenaline were making him shake. "I'm okay. Help me get back up."

"You need a doctor."

"I can't. They'll find us. It's not that bad." He grimaced when he tried to move his arm. The dark patch on his shirt was getting darker.

"Hell," said Eve, looking back toward the door.

"Just go. Leave me here."

"No way." She stared at the suitcase as if considering her options. She reached for it and flipped it open. She pulled out a shirt, balled it up, and stuck it under Adam's shirt to staunch the blood. "Here. Hold this against it."

Adam did as he was told.

"Where's your bag?" She found it and pulled it closer. They'd bought him a windbreaker, and she pulled it out. He moaned and felt the sweat pop out on his skin as she eased the jacket on him. "That will help hide the blood until we get where we're going."

She closed her case and the bag. "Lean on me." Getting herself under his unwounded shoulder, she helped lift him to a standing position.

A wave of nausea hit him, and he had to brace himself against the wall as he fought not to vomit on the ugly orange carpet.

"Come on," she said, "we've got to get downstairs." She helped him take a step down.

"You need to go. They could wake up at any time. Just leave me."

"No," she said. "Now shut up and walk."

He grimaced as another wave of pain moved down his arm, but he made it down the stairs with Eve's help. "Where are we going?" he whispered. "And more importantly, how are we going to get there?" His back was sticky with sweat.

They reached a landing, and Eve guided him down to the next story. "You let me worry about that."

They made it to the ground floor after what felt like hours. Adam let Eve guide him to a scarred wooden chair in the lobby. Mike, the owner, wasn't there, but once Eve got Adam settled, she walked to the counter and rang the bell several times.

"Mike!" she yelled. "Where the hell are you?"

Adam watched the staircase, expecting at any moment to see Vince and Saul racing down it. He hoped his heat flares and Eve's phone whacks would keep them out a little longer.

Eve kept dinging the bell and finally, a door that led to a back room opened and Mike stepped out. Adam could hear what sounded like more than one phone ringing, as well as the soft drone of a TV in the background. "Keep your shorts on," he said. "What's the big hurry?" He eyed Eve. "Oh, it's you. What do you want? Did your friends find you?"

Eve looked like she wanted to strangle him, and Adam figured if there wasn't a counter separating them, she might have.

"What part of 'we're keeping a low profile' was confusing to you?" she asked.

His jaw dropped. "Excuse me? You didn't tell me you didn't want visitors."

"You told a police officer and two gangsters where we were."

His eyes widened. "I did?" He looked at Adam and knitted his brows. "Your friend over there doesn't look too good."

Eve's eyes went dark. "Listen, you idiot. I need a car, and I need it now."

"A car?" asked Mike. "What do I look like? A dealership?"

"I know exactly what you look like. This whole innocence game is bullshit." She glanced at Adam. "He's hurt. He needs medical assistance, and you've got two mob hitmen lying in a room upstairs."

"I do?" He grinned. "Maybe we should call the cops."

"Go right ahead," said Eve. "And I'll be glad to tell them how you led them to us. How you knew exactly who they were. That you asked them for money, they gave it to you, and you turned a blind eye to everything else."

Mike stared at her. "I don't know what you're talking about."

"I suspect there're a few other tasty issues I might mention as well. Like maybe the illegal gambling business you're running behind that door?"

Adam perked his head up at that. So did Mike.

"How in the hell..." Mike glanced back at the closed door and surveyed his countertops, looking for clues that were giving him away.

Adam was alert enough to realize what Eve was revealing. Not only could she read animals, but she was adept at reading people, too.

"I need a car," she said. "Now."

Mike continued to stare, but then his frame relaxed, and he smiled. "Go ahead and call 'em." He glanced at Adam and then back at her. "I suspect I'm not the only one keeping secrets."

Eve seemed to deflate. Mike had called her bluff, but then she pushed her shoulders back. "It's a pity."

Mike frowned. "What is?"

Eve sighed. "Dixie's new shows. Sad you'll have to miss them."

"Miss them?"

"Yes. Didn't you know? Dixie's ramping up some new songs. Got a whole new gig. She's thrilled. Can't wait to share it with her fans. I hear she's throwing a huge party to celebrate. Maybe even offering backstage passes."

Adam held back a chuckle. Backstage passes at a bar? The maintenance guy could get back there.

Mike stilled. "I didn't know that. When?"

Eve shrugged. "Doesn't matter, because you're not invited." Mike opened his mouth, but then closed it. Eve leaned over the counter. "Because the moment I leave here, I'm calling Dixie. And by the time I fill her ear, you'll be lucky if you can see her from a distance."

"You wouldn't," said Mike.

"I would." She peered at him as he stood there, looking perplexed. "A car, Mike."

Mike stood still for a moment, then looking defeated. He opened a drawer and pulled out a set of keys. He threw them on the counter. "White Caddy. Out back in the alley. I usually take the subway, but I drove today. Just bring her back when you're done with her."

Eve snatched the keys. "And don't you breathe a word of this to anyone. Those goons find us, and I promise you, you'll never see, hear, or talk to Dixie Royal again. You understand?"

"Just get out of here," said Mike. He waved her off as he disappeared behind the closed door.

Eve ran over to Adam, got up under his shoulder, and helped him stand. "Come on," she said. "We're almost there."

Adam stood and almost fell. The blood was soaked through the T-shirt now and round speckles were forming on the windbreaker.

They walked to the back of the motel and found the emergency exit. Stepping out into the alley, Adam saw the Cadillac, just where Mike said it would be. It was an older model, and likely had a lot of miles, but as long as it ran, it was fine.

Eve got him settled in the front seat, and Adam groaned when his shoulder pulled. Eve grabbed his shopping bag, walked to a dumpster, and dropped the guns into it. Still holding his bag, she ran around to the driver's side and got in. She put the keys in the ignition, and Adam breathed a sigh of relief when the engine roared to life. At least something had gone their way.

"We got gas?" he asked.

"Full tank."

"Good," he said. "Where are we going?" he asked. His vision blurred.

Eve pulled out of the alley. "Some place safe where I can get you help. Just rest for now."

Adam nodded, closed his eyes, and let himself drift away.

Chapter Ten

JOHN RAMSEY HAMMERED THE nail into the board. After a few hard knocks, the nail head was flush with the wood. He heard the saw blade run and turned to pick up another piece of lumber. He raised and placed it next to the piece he'd just attached and nailed it to the crossbeam. The electric saw stopped whirring, and a piece of wood fell to the ground.

After securing the board, he stopped and wiped his brow. It was a cool day, but he was warm. He and his step-brother Declan had been working since dawn on the new addition to his house. The frame was finally up, and they'd made good progress. He watched Declan add a new piece of wood to the pile.

"Take a break. Get some water," he said.

Declan took off his safety goggles. He picked up a bottled water and took a drink. Looking at the structure, he said. "It's coming together."

"Yeah. I told Sarah I'd get it done before the weather turns."

"You've got plenty of time." Declan sat on one of the two plastic chairs in the room. Ramsey took the other.

"The sooner, the better. The twins need the space." He drank from his own water. "So do we."

"It should be a nice playroom for them."

"Plus an extra room if we need it."

"That too. And maybe, when they're grown, you can have a man cave."

Ramsey chuckled. "I don't see that in my foreseeable future."

"You could sell the place. Get something bigger."

Ramsey shook his head. "Nah. You know Grandma Rose left it to me. I don't plan on selling it."

Declan looked around. "Holds good memories."

"It sure does." He glanced at Declan. "It was the one place I could go to get away from you."

Declan widened his eyes. "Me? I was the perfect brother."

"I can think of other adjectives."

"You weren't exactly an angel."

Ramsey opened his mouth to reply when he heard the soft ring of the doorbell from the other room. He looked at his watch. "Who's that?"

"It's not Hannah and Sarah."

"No. They won't be back for a couple of hours." Ramsey stood and put down his water. He stepped over some wood and headed into the back of his house, went through the kitchen and living area to the front. The doorbell rang again.

"I'm coming." He opened the door and stopped. The woman on his doorstep was familiar. "Eve?"

He'd met her brother Royce a year ago, and not long after, Royce had brought his sisters, Gillian and Eve, over to meet him, Sarah, and the twins. They'd had an interesting night full of eye-opening discussion.

Eve was wide-eyed and pale. There was blood on her shirt and fingers. "Ramsey." She called him by his last name, which most people did. She looked to be in shock.

Ramsey scanned the area. There was no one else around and the only thing out of place was a white Caddy parked in his driveway. "What's wrong?" He stepped outside.

"In the car," she said. "Sarah, is she here?" She gripped her fingers.

"Eve, you're not making sense." He took her elbow. "Come inside. Tell me what's wrong."

She pulled away and took his arm. "No. In the car. Adam is in the car. He needs help."

Ramsey glanced at the Caddy. "There's someone in the car?"

Declan appeared at the doorway. "What's going on?" He looked at Eve and narrowed his eyes. "Is that blood?"

Ramsey nodded. "Appears so. She says there's someone in the car."

"Who is she?"

"Adam," said Eve. "Adam is in the car."

"Who's Adam?" asked Declan.

"Got me," said Ramsey. He gestured at Declan. "Eve, this is Declan, my step-brother. Declan, this is Eve. Royce's sister."

Eve shook her shaking hands. "He needs help."

"Come on," said Ramsey to Declan. "Eve, why don't you wait inside?"

"No. I'm coming with you."

Ramsey didn't argue and walked down the side of the house to the driveway. Declan followed. They approached the car and Ramsey went around to the side. He saw the blood on the passenger door and a slumped figure in the seat. Ramsey wasn't sure what to make of it. "Declan?"

Declan paused. "It's safe. Open it."

Ramsey popped the door open and squatted. The man in the seat was partially slumped, but Ramsey could make out the dark patch of blood on his shirt and jacket. He looked back at an anxious Eve. "What happened?"

"Shot. He's been shot."

"He needs to go to a hospital."

Eve shook her head. "Can't. No hospital."

"Eve...he's losing blood. He needs medical attention."

Eve shook her head. "I know. But they're looking for us. They'll kill us if they find us."

Ramsey shot a look at Declan.

"I didn't know where else to go. The only thing I could think of was Sarah. She can help him."

Ramsey looked at the bleeding man. "You said his name was Adam?"

"Yes."

Adam opened his eyes and blinked. Ramsey leaned farther into the car. "Adam, can you hear me?"

Adam blinked again, and shifted his gaze toward Ramsey. Ramsey heard a faint "Yes."

Ramsey regarded Declan for a few seconds before Declan nodded at him. Ramsey poked his head back into the car.

"Adam. My name's John Ramsey. My brother, Declan, and I are going to pull you out and get you inside, okay?"

He heard a quiet moan of agreement.

"C'mon." Ramsey reached in and pulled on Adam's elbow to get him to move. Adam grunted, but managed to swivel his legs out of the vehicle. Declan and Ramsey each grabbed an arm and helped him stand. His legs buckled briefly but then engaged, and Adam was able to walk under his own power with Ramsey and Declan's assistance.

"We got you," said Ramsey. "Let's go inside."

Eve followed.

"Eve," said Ramsey. "Run into the house. In the second bedroom is the kid's room. There's a futon. Open it up. We'll put him in there."

"What about the kids?" asked Declan.

"They're at Mom's for the rest of the day. This will do for now."

They got Adam inside the house and into the second bedroom just as his legs gave way. Ramsey and Declan lowered him onto the bed before he lost consciousness.

"Eve," said Ramsey. "There's a blanket in the closet. Get it."

Eve retrieved a heavy blanket dotted with images of Winnie the Pooh and handed it to Ramsey. He opened the blanket and covered Adam.

Declan pulled back the covering and checked the wound. "You got some old rags or towels?"

Ramsey nodded. "In the hall closet."

"I'll get them," said Eve, running out of the room.

Declan eyed Ramsey. "You sure about this?"

Ramsey glowered. "You got any better ideas?"

"Yes. Call the cops."

Ramsey studied Adam, whose eyes were closed. His face was almost white. "What's your feel on him?"

Declan studied the injured man. "Nothing good...but nothing bad, either."

Eve ran back into the room. "Here." She handed the towels to Declan, who took them.

"Thanks."

"Eve," said Ramsey, looking back. "You need to sit. You look like you're about to pass out on me."

"I'm fine."

"No, you're not. Go into the kitchen, clean your hands, get some water, and take a breath."

"Ramsey..."

"Go. Now."

Eve stood for a second, then nodded and left the room.

Declan removed the soiled cloth from beneath Adam's shirt and replaced it with a fresh towel. "He's losing a lot of blood."

"I know."

Declan pressed against the wound, and Adam moaned, but didn't open his eyes. "Your call. Sarah or an ambulance."

Ramsey looked at Declan, then back toward the door. "Damn it." He patted his back pocket and pulled out a phone. He punched a number and put the phone to his ear. A few seconds passed. "Sarah..." He talked to his wife and explained the situation. She listened and, without hesitating, said she and Hannah would be home within the hour. Ramsey hung up and put the phone back in his pocket.

"You sure?" asked Declan.

Ramsey grabbed a rag, stood, and went into the adjacent bathroom. He wet it and returned to the bedside, where he placed the wet cloth over Adam's sweaty forehead. "Well, we've been in a few sticky situations ourselves where we needed a little extra help. Maybe it's time to return the favor."

Declan added a second towel under the jacket. "You got a belt?"

Ramsey tipped his head toward the closet. "Got a couple of suits in the closet I rarely wear. Should be a belt in there."

Declan stood and retrieved what he needed. He sat back down on the bed and maneuvered the belt behind and around Adam's shoulder, where he pulled it tight over the towels and hooked it together. "That ought to slow the blood loss. At least until Sarah and Hannah get here."

Ramsey nodded.

Declan prodded him. "How about we go talk to Eve?"

Ramsey pulled Adam's covers up. "That's a good idea."

They found Eve sitting at the kitchen table. Her hands were clean and a little shaky, but she wasn't drinking any water.

Ramsey walked to the cabinets and opened a lower one. He pulled out a bottle of bourbon and set it on the table. He pulled out three glasses, put them down on the table, and put a small amount of liquor in each.

"It's a little early, don't you think?" asked Declan.

Eve took hers and shot it back in one gulp.

"I think that answers your question." Ramsey gave her a touch more and put the bottle away.

Declan took a sip of his as Ramsey sat down and picked up his glass. "Okay. Tell me what's going on."

Eve bit her lip and put her glass down. "Where's Sarah? Is she coming?"

"She's on her way."

Eve nodded and studied her glass.

Declan and Ramsey waited, but Eve sat quietly. Declan reached over and touched her arm, and Eve jumped.

"Eve?"

Even though Declan was only a Gray-Line, he possessed the unique ability to read and manipulate energy. It had come in handy on more than one occasion. A few seconds passed with nothing happening until Eve finally offered a weary smile.

"You're good." She took a shaky breath and let it out. "Are you a Red-Line, too?"

Ramsey snorted. "He wishes."

Declan shook his head. "No. Just a Gray."

"Just?" asked Ramsey.

Eve nodded. "You're strong. Thanks for the pick-me-up."

Declan pulled his hand back. "You looked like you needed it."

Ramsey sat forward. "Now that you're feeling a little more grounded, why don't you tell us what happened? Who is Adam?"

Eve made a soft chuckle. "He's a bartender." The chuckle became a giggle, and then the giggle became full-on laughter as Eve grabbed her belly and tears sprang into her eyes. She wiped at them. "I'm sorry. I'm losing it."

Ramsey thought back to a similar situation with Sarah over two years earlier. "You're not losing it. Just take some deep breaths."

She nodded and dabbed at her eyes with a napkin on the table. She took a lungful of air and let it go. "Adam and I saw a murder." She chuckled again.

Ramsey wasn't sure he heard right.

"What?" asked Declan.

Her anxious laughter stopped. "My boss, Benny," said Eve. "He was killed by his son Vince at the bar." She looked between Declan and Ramsey. "I'm a singer." She tapped her finger on the table. "Adam and I walked in on it. We got away, but they've been chasing us ever since. We holed up in a motel last night, but they found us this morning. We fought them, but Adam was shot. I couldn't take him to a hospital, or they'd find us."

"Why not call the police?" asked Ramsey.

She pushed back her hair. "Vince, Benny's son, is mixed up with a bad bunch. I think it's the mob. He's in deep. If I call the cops, I suspect Adam and I'd be dead within twenty-four hours."

"Crap," said Ramsey, sitting back in his seat.

Eve slumped in her seat. "I'm sorry. I didn't want to get you mixed up in this, but I know Sarah can heal Adam. She helped Royce last year when he needed it."

"I know," said Ramsey.

"As soon as he's better, we'll leave. I promise." Eve bounced her knee and played with her glass.

Ramsey made eye contact with Declan. "We could call Leroy," said Declan. "See what he can find out."

Ramsey thought about contacting his best friend who worked for the Council. "Not just yet. I'd rather keep this as low profile as possible while we can." He glanced at Eve. "No one else knows you're here?"

Eve shook her head. "No one."

Declan raised a brow. "Cell phones. Do you have them?"

"Turned off," said Eve. "And the batteries are out."

"Nobody followed you?"

"No."

Declan went to the front window. He scanned the area for a second, then closed his eyes.

Ramsey watched. "Anything?"

Declan opened his eyes. "Nothing."

Ramsey tapped at his drink, then shot it back in one gulp. He put the glass down. "Looks like the new addition will have to wait."

Declan came back to the table and finished his drink. "You were never going to finish it in time, anyway."

· · · · · ● · · · ·

Thirty minutes later, a car pulled up in the driveway.

"They're here," said Ramsey. He opened the front door as Sarah parked behind the Caddy and she and Hannah got out of the car. Sarah ran up and gave him a quick kiss.

"You okay?" she asked.

"I'm great, but I can't say the same for our guest."

"Where is he?" asked Hannah.

"Kid's room," said Ramsey.

Hannah walked past Sarah, and Ramsey and Sarah followed.

They walked in to see Eve sitting on the side of the bed, attempting to get Adam to drink some water. He made a feeble attempt, but much of the water dribbled down his chin. Declan greeted them and gave Hannah a hug. "Hey, babe."

Hannah squeezed his hand. "How is he?" She let go of his fingers and dropped a bag and her purse on a side chair.

"It's a shoulder wound. He's lost a lot of blood. He's in and out of consciousness."

Hannah walked to the side of the bed. Eve looked up. "I'm trying to give him fluids."

"Let me look at him."

Eve looked back with wary eyes.

"She's a nurse," said Declan. "It's okay."

Eve stood and gave Hannah room. Hannah sat beside him and checked his vitals, then pulled the covers back and checked the wound. Sarah walked up beside her. "What can I do?"

Hannah probed the injury, and Adam moaned. "His name's Adam?" she asked.

"Yes," said Ramsey.

Hannah leaned low. "Adam, I'm going to sit you up and take your jacket off."

Adam didn't answer.

Declan went to the opposite side of the bed and helped Hannah lift him as she and Sarah pulled his windbreaker off. Adam groaned with the effort.

"Ramsey, I need my bag."

They laid Adam back as Ramsey handed Hannah her medical bag. She opened it and pulled out some scissors. "I'm going to cut off your shirt, Adam."

Adam barely grunted in response. A trickle of sweat ran down his face from the effort of removing the jacket. Sarah wiped it with a wet cloth.

Hannah cut the shirt off and removed it. Adam was sweaty and shaky. Hannah took his temperature. "Wipe down his neck and chest," she said. "He's burning up."

Eve stood in the corner, wringing her hands.

Sarah re-wet the cloth in the bathroom sink and took Declan's place on the other side of the bed. She moved the rag over his damp skin.

"Why don't we wait in the kitchen," said Ramsey, eyeing Eve.

"No, I'm fine."

Hannah checked the shoulder again. "The bullet's still in him."

"What?" said Eve.

"There's no exit wound."

"Terrific," said Ramsey.

Eve hugged herself and closed her eyes.

Hannah looked at Ramsey and Declan. "How do you want to handle this?"

Ramsey looked at his wife, who looked at Eve. "Who is he?" asked Sarah.

"He's a bartender," said Ramsey.

Eve bit her lip and nodded.

Declan spoke up. "Adam and Eve..." He stopped when he realized what he'd said. He softly chuckled and shook his head. "Our friends here witnessed a murder. Now they're on the run."

"Why not go to..." she started.

"It's a mob hit. They don't trust the police," answered Ramsey.

"A mob hit?" asked Hannah. "Are you kidding me?"

"No. I'm not kidding," said Eve, dropping her arms. "I didn't know where else to go." She looked at Sarah. "You helped Royce. I thought, if you could help him." Her face fell. "I promise. I don't want to make trouble. I'll leave as soon—" She pursed her lips as she tried to control her emotions.

Sarah turned toward Hannah. "Can you get the bullet out?"

Hannah probed some more. "I'll need more supplies." She looked at Declan. "Can you drive to the office?"

Declan straightened. "Just tell me what you need."

"How long will it take to get what Hannah needs?" Sarah asked.

"Thirty minutes, tops." He stepped away from the wall.

Sarah spoke to Hannah. "If you can extract the bullet, then I can do the rest."

Hannah covered Adam with the blanket. "I'll write down a list of what to get."

Sarah stood and walked over to Eve. "Let's go sit." Eve nodded and left the room with Sarah.

Sarah gestured toward the table, and Eve took a seat. Sarah sat beside her. Ramsey walked in and grabbed a glass. "Anybody else like some water?"

"Please," said Sarah.

"Thanks," said Eve.

Sarah watched as he placed the filled glasses in front of them. When he began to sit, she made eye contact with him. He stopped in mid-crouch, and Sarah raised a brow. He glanced at Eve. "On second thought, maybe I'll go work in the man-cave." He straightened and took his glass.

"The what?" asked Sarah.

"My man-cave. In eighteen years, it's going to be all mine."

Sarah smiled. "Whatever you say, hon. Have fun."

Declan appeared from the hallway, holding a piece of paper. "I'll be back as soon as I can."

Ramsey swiveled mid-step. "You want some company?"

Declan glanced at the two women. "Sure."

"Great. I'm right behind you." He waved. "Back soon."

"Okay." Sarah took a sip of her water as her husband and Declan left the house. She studied Eve as Eve played with the rim of her cup.

"So," she said. "Tell me the details."

Eve glanced up. "The details? You mean how I saw my boss murdered by his own son, who used to be my boyfriend, and who has now tried to kill me twice, and almost succeeded with Adam?" She put her face in her palm. "How did I get myself into this mess?"

"You don't think the police can help?"

Eve shook her head. "I know a police officer. He's doing some digging for me. Right now, the police want to talk to me and Adam. They know we were there. I'm trying to wait and see what Tony finds out first."

"Tony is your policeman friend?"

"Yes. I asked him to give us four days. I'm hoping that's enough time for Tony to shake something from the tree before Adam and I have to go in."

"Tell me exactly what happened."

Eve sighed and relayed the story to Sarah, all the way up to where she'd ended up on Sarah's doorstep, minus the personal details between her and Adam.

Sarah sat back. "Sounds like Adam can take care of himself." She tapped her glass. "And he's certainly loyal to you."

"I tried to get him to leave, but he wouldn't do it. Said it would be safer to stay together."

"What do you know about him?"

"Not much. He's a bartender at Benny's. Fairly new. Quiet. Barely spoke to me until last night on the roof. He's not from around here, and he's pretty sheltered. He's trusting me to do the right thing."

Sarah shrugged. "That's a lot of faith to have in someone."

"It's a scary situation. He should have left when he had the chance."

"Is that what you wanted?"

Eve straightened. "I didn't want any of this. I sure as hell didn't want Benny dead. He... he..." She looked away.

"You were close?"

Eve sniffed. "He was like a father to me."

Sarah nodded. "You talk to your family? Tell them you're okay?"

Eve waved her hand. "No. I don't want them to worry, or get them involved. It's too dangerous." Her face fell and paled. "Not that I want you to be in danger, either. I didn't mean to jeopardize you..." She shook her head, her face pinched.

Sarah reached over and took Eve's hand. "I know what you mean. I've been in a similar situation. You don't want anyone to get hurt, especially the ones you love."

Eve closed her eyes. "I don't know what I would do if that happened."

Sarah patted her wrist. "Don't worry. We'll figure it out." Eve opened her eyes and cleared her throat. "We'll get Adam back on his feet first."

"I want justice for Benny."

"I'm sure you do. How will you get in touch with your friend?"

"I told him I'd call after four days."

"So we have some time."

Eve sat back and took a shaky breath. "I didn't plan on staying here the entire time. As soon as Adam is up and around, we'll go."

"Eve, it's going to take a few days for him to recover. Even with my help."

"But once the bullet's out...I figured we could leave by tomorrow."

Sarah shook her head. "Everyone's different. Judging by his condition right now, he's feverish and in shock. Once we get the bullet out, I can ensure he'll heal, but he's probably not going to be back up to full speed as quickly as you think."

"But you healed Jasper."

Sarah recalled helping Royce's half-brother. "Jasper was a full-blooded Red-Line. They heal quickly. It won't be the same with Adam. He'll need more time."

"But you can heal him, right? You can still help him? He saved my life."

Sarah picked up on something else from Eve besides worry. She leaned in. "He do anything else?"

Eve uncharacteristically blushed.

Sarah got her answer. "I see."

Eve squirmed. "It's not what you think."

"It's not what I think that matters. It's what you think."

"What happened between us..." Eve played with the edge of the tablecloth. "It didn't mean anything."

"Okay."

"I mean, it was just a temporary distraction. We couldn't sleep." She rubbed her forehead. "I mean, you know how it is. You just need to take the edge off."

"Sure."

"It was just that. Nothing more. We had a moment, that's all."

"Great."

Eve fiddled with her glass, then clicked her nails against it. "Except that it was a mind-blowing moment. I was shocked by the power of it. I mean, I've had great sex before, but this..."

Sarah tipped her head. "Totally exceeded your wildest expectations?"

"Yes. I..."

Sarah waited, but Eve sat there with her mouth open. Sarah spoke for her. "You couldn't believe it. It was totally unexpected."

Eve nodded in agreement. "Yes. He did everything right. I didn't have to say a word. It was like..."

Sarah gripped her glass. "The two hands of a clock, each clicking together, perfectly in sync."

Eve groaned. "Exactly." She dropped her hand and looked up. "Wait a minute."

Sarah smiled. "How do I know?"

Eve's face went from curiosity to despair. "Oh no. Nope. It's not what you're going to say. Just stop right there. It's not that." She waved a finger and stood.

Sarah kept a straight face. "You mean a Binding?"

Eve put her hands over her ears. "I'm not listening. I didn't hear it, so it's like you never said it. La, la, la, laaa." She made odd noises until she looked over at Sarah, who sat quietly at the table. She dropped her hands. "We're not saying that word."

Sarah couldn't help herself. "You mean the Binding word?"

Eve's face fell. "Oh, hell." She dropped into her seat and stared at the floor. "Is it too late?"

"Is what too late?"

"In nine months, will I be singing a lullaby, ready to pull my hair out?"

Sarah chuckled. "I don't know. Will you?"

Eve frowned. "I could really use some help here. Now is not the time to be cryptic."

Sarah sipped from her water and considered her answer. "You two had that one moment together?"

Eve nodded with vigor. "Yes. That's it. But it's taken every ounce of strength I have not to jump his bones again. Well, at least until he got shot. That sort of killed the mood."

Sarah rested her elbow on the back of the chair. "That's not long enough for a pregnancy to occur. From what I understand, it's a twenty-four-hour marathon, at least."

Eve sighed with what sounded like relief and rested her head in her hands. "Sounds like a lot of fun if it doesn't result in procreation." She raised her hand. "No offense."

"None taken." Sarah stared off, her own memories surfacing. "And it is a lot of fun." She smiled, thinking of earlier that morning when she'd rolled over and awakened John. "Still is."

Eve waited. "Sarah? You there?"

Sarah brought herself back to the present moment. "Sorry. I got distracted." Warming, she drank some water. "Anyway, my point here is that a pregnancy is completely up to you."

Eve looked baffled. "What do you mean? You got pregnant. So did Gilli."

"That was our path. We didn't take the precautions to stop it."

"What precautions? I didn't think there were any."

Sarah sighed. "There are. There always are."

"But you didn't take them." She grimaced. "Sorry. I don't mean to insinuate you didn't want children."

Sarah shook her head. "Don't worry. I know what you mean." She thought back to that time in her life and her first romantic moments with her husband. "It was different for me. Just like it was for Gillian. We knew what we needed to know at the time. But I firmly believe that if I wasn't ready to have children, I would have not become pregnant. Same for your sister.

"Gilli miscarried though."

"That's the tricky part. The power of the Binding can result in unfortunate circumstances if interrupted. But she's okay?"

"She's better. She's a happy newlywed."

"I suspect it won't be long before she'll be pregnant again, if that's what she wants."

Eve blinked. "So you're saying that I don't have to worry?"

Sarah rested her elbows on the table. "You forget who you are, Eve. You can speak with animals, read objects, and probably a myriad of other things. What makes you think you don't have control over your own body?"

Eve's jaw dropped. "I won't get pregnant?"

"Do you want to get pregnant?"

Eve sat back, looking dumbfounded. "No, I don't."

"Good. Then you won't." Sarah raised her hand. "Doesn't mean you're not Binded to Adam, though."

Eve crossed her arms. "I'm confused. I thought this child thing was a done deal. No exceptions."

Water dropped from her glass, and Sarah wiped at it with a napkin. "Not at all. You just need to make a decision and stick to it. If I had to go back and make a different choice, I would have made the same one. John and I were destined to have children. Maybe if you'd asked me at the time, I would have hesitated, but I doubt I would have done anything differently. I'm sure if you asked your sister, she'd feel the same."

"I don't believe this. So I could have..." She stopped and stared off. "Damn."

Sarah smiled. "Don't worry. I think you'll have ample opportunities to express your interest to Adam."

Eve frowned. "Does this mean we're married or something?"

Sarah put down the napkin. "No. But I think you'll find being separated from him will be difficult. A Binding is intense. It combines the energy of two people in such a way that it makes it hard to be apart. It's a powerful force not easily ended." She sighed. "Breaking from that energy likely caused your sister's miscarriage."

Eve rubbed her temples and groaned. "I just never thought this would happen to me, and certainly not with a shy, sheltered bartender. I would have never considered him to be my...Bindee, or whatever you call it."

"Life is full of surprises."

"Especially considering my unique situation."

"Indeed."

Hannah walked into the room.

"How is he?" asked Eve.

Hannah went to the sink and washed her hands. "Hanging in there, but I'll feel better when I can give him some fluids and get that bullet out of him."

Eve stood. "What can I do?"

Hannah turned off the sink and dried her hands on a towel. "Go sit with him until Declan gets back. I think he'd prefer your company."

Eve nodded. "I will."

"Keep him cool. We need to keep his fever down."

"Okay." Pausing, she looked back at Sarah. "Thank you."

Sarah pushed back her empty glass. "You're welcome. And don't worry. You two will get through this."

Eve smiled softly, leaving the room.

Hannah joined Sarah at the table. She watched Eve step out and then turned a worried eye on Sarah.

Sarah noticed. "What is it?"

"We may be dealing with more than we bargained for."

Sarah tensed. "What do you mean?"

"He mumbled in his sleep."

"So? He's feverish."

"He said, 'Call Tez. Tell Tez where I am.'"

"Who's Tez?"

"I guess a friend."

"What's wrong with that?"

Hannah crossed her arms. "He said he had to find Royce. Find Royce and tell Tez."

Chapter Eleven

ADAM BLINKED, OR AT least he thought he did. He couldn't be certain of anything. In one moment, he was lying back, warm and still. In another, he was in a car, sitting upright, with what felt like a white-hot poker grinding into his arm. Then he was back in a bed, in a home he didn't recognize, with a woman with long russet-colored hair and pretty eyes telling him to be still while she probed his shoulder. He wanted to get up and leave, but she wouldn't let him. Talking didn't seem to be an option, either. His throat was dry, and anything he said only came out as a croak or groan. It seemed each time he blinked, he was somewhere else. The woman disappeared and then he was back on the ship. Tez was going over the plan: get to Earth, meet Eve, find Royce, and then leave. Adam tried to reach out to Tez, to tell his friend where he was, but Tez couldn't hear him.

Another blink, and Eve was there. He was hot, sweaty, and shivering, although he was covered in blankets. "Shhh," she said, wiping his forehead. "You're going to be all right."

He opened his mouth to speak, to tell her to leave him. That he was not worth the effort, but she was so beautiful. Her auburn hair was down, and she pushed a ringlet off her face. All he wanted to do was to hold her close, but another shiver ran through him and he moaned. A searing flare of pain traveled down his arm. He cursed. Looking around, he tried to make sense of his surroundings. With monumental effort, he managed to say the word, "Where?"

Eve understood. "I brought you to a friend's house. They're going to help you. She wiped his neck. "Here. I have some ice." She reached and brought back a cup. "You want some?"

If he'd been offered all the Eudoran gold in the universe, he would have turned it down for that one cube. He nodded, and she put it on his tongue. The cold felt like sunshine after a month of rain. He let it melt, and the coolness in his throat made him want to launch into song, like one of those musicals Tez had made him watch.

He coughed, and the pain ripped through him. Eve's face turned worried, and she put her hand on his chest. "Easy," she said. "Not much longer."

Adam blinked again, and that's all he remembered.

·•·•••·••••·

Eve paced in the kitchen. Declan and Ramsey had returned an hour ago with Hannah's supplies. Hannah had quickly prepared the room, sterilizing everything she could. After giving Adam an IV to get some fluids into him, she'd told Eve she was welcome to stay and watch, but Eve chose to wait outside.

Sarah and Declan had remained to help Hannah, and Ramsey sat with Eve at the kitchen table. He'd offered her something to eat, but she'd declined. She felt sick to her stomach, as if she herself were undergoing the procedure, and she didn't understand why she felt so anxious.

Ramsey tapped the table. It was apparent the lack of conversation, along with the waiting, unnerved him as well. "So, Sarah tells me you and Adam Binded."

Eve stopped pacing and stared at Ramsey.

His face fell. "Sorry. Too soon?"

Eve picked up her pacing.

He sighed. "How's Gillian?"

Eve crossed her arms and leaned against a counter. "She's fine."

"Married?"

Eve nodded.

"Some tech guy, right? Entrepreneur?"

She nodded again and stared at the back bedroom door.

"You like him?"

"Yes. I do."

Ramsey settled back in his seat. "Good."

Eve wondered what was taking so long. "Shouldn't they be done now?"

Ramsey glanced at the door. "I don't know. In my vast experience of bullet removals being performed by my wife and sister-in-law in my kid's room, I'd say we're right on schedule."

Eve pushed off the counter. "Don't do much of these, then?"

"This would be our first."

Eve rubbed her shoulders. "Mine too."

"Lucky us."

A few more minutes passed. Ramsey helped himself to some juice and made a sandwich but didn't eat it. Eve continued to pace.

Finally, the door opened and Hannah stepped out. She held a towel and was drying her hands. Eve stepped forward. "How is he?"

Hannah dropped the towel on the counter. "Doing okay. His vitals are strong. I got the bullet out and sewed him up. Now it's up to Sarah."

"She's with him?"

"You can go in. You won't disturb her."

Declan walked out carrying a plastic bag. Eve could see red streaked cloths through the material. "I'm going to dump this in your bins out back."

Ramsey waved a hand. "By all means."

Eve headed to the bedroom and poked her head in. Adam was covered up to his neck in blankets, looking peaceful and warm. Sarah sat beside him. Her hands were lightly placed on his shoulder and her eyes were closed.

"Come in," she said without opening her eyes.

Eve stepped in and walked to the bedside. She chewed her lip.

"He's doing fine," said Sarah, answering Eve's unspoken question.

Eve nodded. "You're sure?"

"He feels great." She moved her hands to his chest. "I'm working on the infection." She took a breath. "Trying to bring the fever down." She stilled, and Eve saw her eyes clench and relax.

"What? Something wrong?"

Sarah shook her head. "No. Nothing is wrong. Just sorting some things out."

Eve continued to watch Sarah work.

· · · · ● · ● · · · ·

Adam was floating. At some point, the woman with the russet hair had returned, and she'd poked and prodded him some more, but then the pain eased and disappeared, and he felt as if he slept on a cloud, a warm wind soothing him. He was grateful to be pain free. Then another woman appeared. He could see her in his head. Her chestnut wavy hair brushed her shoulders, but her eyes were closed. Adam settled into the puffy cloud, feeling comfortable and relaxed. His arm stopped throbbing, and his chest felt infused with light. Heat spread through him, but not the type that came with chills. This felt energized, like he'd just come from a morning run. If he hadn't been so at ease on his cloud, he might have been tempted to wake, find Eve, and do all sorts of fun things with her. Thinking of her made the heat bloom, and his whole body buzzed.

The sensation reminded him of home. When he was young, he'd had a toothache and his mother, before she'd abandoned him, had taken him to a Red-Line healer. The mystic woman had put her hands on him and he'd felt the warmth of her energy flood through him.

He felt the same way now. It was almost as if he was back on Eud—he jolted on the cloud. In his mind, he came awake. Someone was working on him, sending a healing force through him. The energy moved and settled into his bones and joints. Then it shifted. His head pulsed, and he felt the healing fuel engage, but he realized the risk. Whoever was doing this would read him and know who he was. He instantly shut down and closed himself off from the flow.

· · · · ● · ● · · · ·

Sarah sucked in a breath and opened her eyes. Eve jumped. "What's wrong?"

Sarah blinked and shook out her hands.

"Sarah, what's wrong?"

Sarah looked up. "It's okay, Eve. He's fine. I'm all done." She stood and walked to the foot of the bed, watching Adam.

"You don't look like you're happy," said Eve. "Did you find something? Is he still sick?"

Sarah pulled herself out of her reverie and smiled. "No. Not at all. Just reviewing my process, making sure I didn't miss anything." She put a hand on Eve's shoulder. "Sit with him. He'll probably sleep for a while, but he should come around soon."

Eve nodded, and Sarah left the room.

His earlier discomfort now gone, Adam looked peaceful, like a child sleeping after a busy day with no nap. She brushed a tendril of hair off his forehead. Now that her initial fear and worry were waning, her fatigue grew. Her muscles felt heavy, and she yawned. Her relief was now translating into exhaustion. Seeing him sleep, she envied his rest, and took advantage of the quiet. She pulled off her shoes and pushed back on the bed. Stretching beside him, she moved against him and put her arm across his midsection. She was careful to avoid his shoulder. Resting her head in the crook of his neck and feeling his body heat warm her, she closed her eyes, and within minutes, was sound asleep.

Chapter Twelve

"SOMETHING'S NOT RIGHT." SARAH sat at the breakfast table. She'd warmed some soup and Ramsey, Declan, and Hannah all sat with her.

Ramsey rubbed his eyes. "There are several things not right."

The day was turning to night, and all of them were weary after the afternoon's events. Sarah played with her spoon. Sighing, she put it down.

"Did you say anything to Eve about what Adam said?" asked Hannah. She pulled apart of piece of bread and put it beside her soup bowl.

Sarah shook her head. "No. Not yet."

"Could mean nothing," said Declan. "It's likely Eve mentioned she had a brother, Royce, to Adam. And in his feverish state, Adam somehow put Royce and whoever Tez is together."

"Or it could mean that Adam wants to know where Royce is," said Ramsey. "And if that's true, then Eve needs to know." He looked at Sarah, who picked up her spoon again and continued to fiddle with it. "But that's not what's bothering you, is it?"

Sarah stared at her bowl, recalling the healing session with Adam. In her mind's eye, she retraced her steps, remembering how she'd worked on his shoulder, moved up to his head, and how he'd pulled back from her. "When I was working on him, he felt..." She put the spoon on the table.

"What?" asked Declan.

"The shoulder went fine, but when I moved up and worked on his whole body, he sensed me. He cut me off."

"Really?" asked Declan.

"Is that unusual?" asked Ramsey.

Sarah sat back. "In my experience, yes. That's never happened before."

"That doesn't mean it couldn't," said Hannah.

"He may be a highly sensitive human, and in his unconscious state, may have been able to access reserves he wouldn't normally be aware of when he's conscious. Maybe he sensed an unfamiliar presence and naturally pulled back," said Declan.

"Or there's more to the story," said Ramsey. "And what he did with you along with the Royce thing means something." He squinted at her. "What are you not telling us?"

Sarah glanced at her husband. He could always read her with ease. "I'm not sure, but it's something." She rubbed her forehead. "The answer is probably staring me in the face."

Ramsey stirred his soup. "This is one of those times where I'm happy I'm not a Red-Line."

Declan chortled. "I think we're all happy with that." Ramsey scowled at him. "But I agree. Gray-Line problems are enough for me." He took a sip of his soup.

Sarah sucked in a breath and put her hands on the table.

"What?" asked Ramsey.

She thought back, again reviewing her time with Adam, remembering the feel of him.

"Sarah?" asked Hannah.

"What's wrong?" asked Declan.

Sarah stood, her mind racing. "I know what it is. What I felt. Now I know why he pushed me back." She grabbed the back of the chair. "He was so strong."

"Sarah?" asked Ramsey. "What is it?"

Sarah stared back at him. "He's not human. He's a Gray-Line."

· • · • • · • • · ·

Eve snuggled into Adam. Her dreams had been active. Visions played in her mind—chasing her siblings among the trees around their house and playing hide and seek, her dad laughing during his last visit, sharing dinner with Benny on the roof after a busy night at the club, in Adam's arms during their stay in the motel.

She blinked and came awake fully. Looking around, she saw the small room with the two empty cribs pushed against the wall. Adam slept beside her. She remembered the previous day, bringing Adam here, removing the bullet, Sarah working on him.

After Eve had fallen asleep beside him, Hannah had woken her not long after. They roused Adam enough to check on him, get him to eat some soup, drink some water, and use the bathroom, but then he'd collapsed back into bed, exhausted by the activity.

Eve had tried some soup as well. She'd eaten nothing all day. Hannah advised her to keep up her strength so Hannah didn't end up with two patients. Eve complied and finished most of her dinner. But she felt weary, as if her worry for Adam had sapped all her strength, and as night fell and Hannah left the room to eat her own dinner, Eve fell asleep again next to Adam, and didn't awake until the sun was breaking through the blinds.

Sitting up, she looked over at her sleeping companion. He was still out, but his color was better. His shoulder was wrapped. From what she could tell, it looked fine to her. She breathed a sigh of relief, finally feeling confident that Adam would recover. Hopefully, he would be up more today and possibly they could leave tomorrow.

Eve leaned back against the wall, considering her options. What would they do next? Where would they go? Tony would expect to hear from her in two days. She wondered if he'd been able to talk to Vince. The worry for Adam now returned to worry about her future. Should she go to the police? What about her and Adam? Did she really expect to have a future with him? The Binding between them was not complete. Would it be better to separate now, before their relationship became even more complicated?

Eve pushed the hair off her face. What she needed was a long, hot shower. She eyed the adjacent bathroom and wondered where her suitcase was. Probably still in the car.

Adam stirred and made a soft groan. His eyes fluttered.

"Adam?" she whispered.

He cleared his throat.

"You awake?"

His eyes opened. He looked around groggily. "Where am I?" His voice was raspy.

She shifted beside him. 'You're at a friend's house. You were shot. Do you remember?"

He moved and grimaced. He pushed the covers off him with his good arm. "The pain is a good reminder."

She picked up the glass with a straw on the nightstand. "Here. Drink some." He took a sip and swallowed. "You need something? Hannah has some pain pills. She gave you one last night."

"Hannah? Is she the one who kept poking at me?"

Eve smiled, glad to see his personality return. "That would be her."

Adam took a breath and closed his eyes, as if still half asleep. After a second, his eyes opened wide. "Who was the other one?"

"Other one? Oh, you mean Sarah." She couldn't tell Adam that Sarah was a Red-Line, and she'd helped to heal him, but she did her best to explain. "She assisted Hannah."

Adam blinked and stared at the ceiling. "Is that all she did?"

Eve considered how to answer. Had Adam been aware of Sarah working on him? "She's also a Reiki practitioner. She worked on you while you were out."

Adam narrowed his eyes. "What's that?"

"Someone who works with energy. They use it and direct it in order to enable healing."

Adam looked dubious. "Does it work?"

"I don't know. How do you feel?"

Adam rubbed his face. "Wiped, but at least I'm not shivering."

"You were feverish." She put a palm on his forehead. "You feel much better today."

"I could go for a hot shower."

"You and me both."

He raised his head, and despite his weariness, she swore he was leering at her. "You want to take one together?"

Heat bloomed. She wished they could. "Why don't you just focus on getting well? We can talk about future showers later."

"A shower with you might work a lot better than Reili, or whatever it is."

She laughed. "It's Reiki. And, let's be honest, a shower with me would sap any remaining strength you have."

He sighed. "I'd probably lapse into a coma."

"And I'd have to find some way to wake you."

He grinned. "I could think of one way."

She was sure she was blushing, which surprised her. She rarely blushed. "Come here," he said.

"I'm sitting right beside you. Where else would you like me to go?"

He touched her arm and tugged on it. "I want to kiss you."

Her belly swirled, and she wondered how she could be so attracted to this man. They barely knew each other. "I have morning breath."

His fingers trailed down her arm and over her hand. "So do I."

Although her brain told her to hold back, that it was better to stop this Binding before it took hold, she listened to the pull, shifted in the bed, and leaned over him. He brought his hand up and ran it through her hair, pulling her closer.

"But I'm willing to risk it," he said, before raising his head and pressing his lips against hers. She moved closer, allowing him to fall back against the pillow. The kiss was slow and deliberate before the energy began to build and deepen. She slanted her lips over his and wanted to wrap herself around him. His hand slid behind her neck. Their chests touched, and he reached with his other hand to touch her when he moaned, but not with pleasure.

Eve pulled back, breathless. "You okay?"

He tried to catch his own breath. "I'm fine. Just pulled my shoulder. No big deal." He reached out for her, but she sat back.

"Hold on there. Let's not start something we can't finish."

He wiggled his brows. "I can make sure you finish." He rubbed her thigh.

White heat surged through her midsection. She considered taking him up on his offer when there was a soft knock on the door. She moved off the bed and smoothed her clothes. She'd slept in her jeans and shirt. "Come in."

Sarah poked her head in. "You're awake?"

"Yes," said Eve.

Sarah stepped into the room, freshly showered, wearing jeans and an oversized sweatshirt. "How'd you sleep?"

Eve moved away from the bed. "Pretty good. Better than I expected."

"How's Adam?"

"Much better. He's..." She turned toward the bed, but was surprised to see Adam's eyes were closed. "Well, he was awake."

"He needs the rest, I'm sure." Sarah pointed toward the corner of the room. "John brought your bag in from the car. I'm sure you'd like to shower."

"That sounds like heaven."

"There's toothpaste, shampoo, and soap in the bathroom. Help yourself."

"Thank you."

"Hannah will be over soon. She'll want to check on him. See how he's doing."

"Okay."

"And there's coffee in the kitchen, and I pulled out a coffee cake for breakfast."

Eve nodded. "Listen, what you and John have done for us...I don't know how to thank you."

Sarah waved her off. "Don't worry about it. I'm glad we could help. I just want to be sure you're okay. You two aren't out of the woods yet."

"No. I know." Eve rubbed her head. She didn't want to think about it.

"Go take your shower." She glanced back at the bed. "Then we'll talk."

Eve sighed. Her mother had always told her that a good hot shower always helped to sort things out. She'd found that to be true. "I'll be out soon."

"Take your time." Sarah walked to the door and left.

· · · · • · • · · ·

Thirty minutes later, Eve emerged from the bedroom, clean and refreshed. Hannah had arrived a few minutes before and was checking on Adam, who appeared to have fallen back to sleep. The thought of a hot cup of coffee spurred Eve to leave Adam for a bit and let him rest. She walked into the kitchen and spied the half-filled pot.

"Cups are in the cabinet above." She turned to see Ramsey sitting at the breakfast table, looking relaxed, with a mug in his hand. "Cream's in the fridge."

"Thanks." She reached for a cup and helped herself to the coffee.

"There's coffee cake on the counter. Help yourself."

Eve took a sip of the hot liquid and sighed. "I'm fine. This is all I need."

He nodded and took a sip from his own cup. "How'd you sleep?"

"Pretty good, considering. You?"

"Fine, considering."

Eve looked around the house. "Where are your kids? Shouldn't they be here?"

He scratched his jaw. "We keep them in the basement." He checked his watch. "It's almost time for their feeding."

Eve cocked her head.

"Just kidding. My mom's got them. They stayed with her last night."

Eve felt a twinge of guilt. "Sorry. I guess my arrival has upset everyone, hasn't it?"

He studied her. "I can't judge you. I've been in a few scrapes myself and had to rely on friends and family. I wasn't exactly endearing either."

"I want to thank you for helping us out. I don't know what we would have done otherwise."

"You're welcome."

The front door opened and Declan walked in. "Good morning."

"Morning," said Ramsey. "You make your phone call?"

Declan glanced at Eve. "Sure did."

"Everything good?"

"Where's Sarah?"

"In the bedroom. She'll be out in a sec."

"Hannah with Adam?"

"She is."

They shared a look.

"Everything okay?" asked Eve.

The bedroom door opened, and Sarah stepped out and greeted Declan, who helped himself to the coffee.

Eve sipped from her mug and felt strangely uncomfortable, as if she'd walked in late to a party. She walked to the table and put her cup down. "Something wrong?"

Sarah glanced at Ramsey, who nodded. Sarah gestured toward her. "Why don't you have a seat?"

Alarm bells went off in Eve's head. She watched Declan come over with his mug and sit at the table, his expression unreadable. Before Eve could respond, the bedroom door opened and Hannah stepped out, closing the door behind her. "He's healing nicely. Should be up and around in no time." She stepped up to the table and looked at the group. "Are we about to have this conversation?" She pulled out a chair and sat.

Icy fear crept up Eve's spine. "You're kicking me out, aren't you?" She clenched her hands. "I'm so sorry. We'll leave now." She turned, but Sarah stopped her.

"That's not it. We're not kicking you out." She sat at the table. "Have a seat and we'll explain."

Eve stared in confusion. What was going on? She slowly sat.

Sarah paused. "How well do you know Adam?"

Eve thought that was an odd question. "How long have I known him?"

"Yes," said Ramsey.

Sarah reached over and touched her arm. "There's a reason we're asking, trust me."

Eve tried not to overreact. "Well, not long. Just a few days."

"That's when he first showed up?" asked Declan.

Eve shook her head. "No. He started working at Benny's a couple of months ago, I think."

"So not long," said Ramsey.

"No," said Eve. "Why?" Eve watched as the other four at the table looked at each other. "What is going on?"

"Eve," said Sarah. "There's something you need to know."

Eve felt a chill move through her and crossed her arms. "What?"

"Adam's not who you think he is," said Sarah.

·•·•••·•··

Adam opened his eyes. Hannah had just left. He had feigned sleepiness in order to prevent having to talk to her any more than he needed to. She'd checked his wound and his vitals and told him to get some rest. He blinked and stared up at the ceiling. The memory of being read by the other woman, Sarah, still lingered. Something about her felt different, as if he knew she could see all his secrets. If he'd been home, he'd swear she was a Red-Line. That couldn't be possible, though. Even if she was proficient in what Eve called Reiki, he doubted as a human that she'd be able to sense who he was. Still, her skills were impressive, so when she'd entered the room earlier, he'd closed his eyes to avoid talking with her.

Eve had not returned, and Adam felt his stomach rumble. Hannah had told him she'd bring him something to eat soon. He'd acted weaker than he actually was. As a Gray-Line, his recovery would be quicker than a human's, but he didn't want to alert them or make them suspicious. He sat up in the bed with a grimace. His shoulder pulled, but the pain was subsiding. He rubbed it and tried to move his arm, but sucked in a breath. He wasn't quite healed yet.

On shaky legs, he pushed himself up and stood. He managed to use the restroom without falling over and stared at himself in the mirror. His hair was askew, and he had stubble on his jaw. His eyes were puffy, but his skin had a healthy color. He eyed the shower, wishing he could take one. He wasn't sure how he could though with his bad arm.

Spying a washcloth and soap, he figured he could adequately clean himself up a little. It wasn't a shower, but it would still feel better than his present state. Smiling in the mirror, he knew he needed to brush his teeth too.

Stepping out of the bathroom, he saw his shopping bag on the floor near the entrance to the room. Gingerly, he walked over to pick it up. As he passed the door, though, he heard voices. Curious, he listened closely. Thinking he heard his name, he took hold of the knob, turned it, and silently opened the door. The voices from the other room traveled easily. As the conversation continued, he heard his name again.

········

"What are you talking about?" asked Eve. "Who exactly is he?" Her mind whirled with possibilities.

Ramsey sat forward. "He's a Gray-Line."

Eve was grateful she had not sipped her coffee because she would have spit it out. "A what? A Gray-Line? Are you serious?"

"It's true," said Sarah. "I felt it when I worked on him yesterday."

Eve could only sit with her mouth open.

"I wasn't sure at first. He's good at keeping himself cloaked. But he sensed me too and pulled away. That's what triggered it, and I knew."

Eve stood. "Knew what? He'd been shot. He was feverish. There could be any number of reasons he pulled back from you. I mean, you're a Red-Line. I'm sure that kind of energy coursing through anyone could make them pull back." She shook her head. "But that doesn't mean he's a Gray-Line." She ran a hand through her hair. "That's ridiculous. Why would a Gray-Line..." She stopped.

The rest of the group waited. She thought of her brother.

"Listen," said Sarah. "This doesn't necessarily mean anything bad."

"That depends," said Hannah. "Don't forget what he said."

Eve was trying to get her bearings. Adam was a *Gray-Line*? If that were true, then how had she missed it? She dropped her head, still not understanding. "I don't know what to say." She looked at Sarah. "If he is, how come I couldn't tell?"

Sarah's eyes softened. "He's very good at hiding his identity. That's why it took me a while to figure it out. If he'd walked in here uninjured, I'm not sure I would have even noticed."

Eve squinted. "But the rest of you are Gray-Lines. Wouldn't you know?"

"It's not like we have a badge on our arm," said Ramsey. "And we don't have the sensitivities of you and Sarah, so no. We wouldn't know."

Eve paced. "I can't believe this." Her mind was still trying to understand. "Who is he then? He's not a member of your group? Some long-lost cousin or something?"

"No," said Declan. "I checked."

"He came down here from...wherever," said Ramsey. "That's the only explanation."

A shockwave rocked her as her suspicions were being confirmed. "He came down here for me? Right? I mean," she made a sad chuckle, "some random Gray-Line walking around Earth just happens to meet one of only four half Red-Lines on the planet?"

"I think it would be safe to assume it's not a coincidence," said Declan.

Eve set her jaw. Memories of her morning with Adam raced through her head. Now her attraction to him made more sense. Sucking in a breath, she could still feel his pull on her, and she remembered how good he felt. *God*, she thought, *I'm Binding to a Gray-Line.* She closed her eyes.

"Eve." Sarah stood. "There may be a perfectly good explanation for this."

Eve opened her eyes. She looked at Hannah. "What did he say to you?"

Hannah looked conflicted. "When he was feverish, he mumbled something about a man named Tez."

"You know who that is?" asked Declan.

Eve shook her head.

Hannah hesitated. "He said, 'Find Royce and tell Tez.'"

Eve froze and felt the color drain from her face.

· · · • · • · · ·

Adam cursed. He slowly closed the door. Grabbing the bag, he sat on the edge of the bed and pulled out his phone. Although Eve thought it could not be used, he hovered his hand over it and it buzzed and came to life. Adam quickly punched a button and listened as the call beeped and clicked. Then silence.

"Damn it, Tez. Answer."

Although he knew his twenty-four-hour window had long since ended, he had to believe that Tez wouldn't actually leave without him. They'd known each other too long. He listened as the silence continued, and then he heard a double beep. That was his prompt to leave a message.

"Tez," he said. "It's me. Listen. I know you're wondering where I am. It's a long story. I got shot. By a gun. Eve brought me to a house and there are people here who helped me. I've been out of it since yesterday, but I'm better now." He paused, unsure of what he wanted to say. "I'm in a bind here, buddy. I still don't know where Royce is, but I'm close. The problem is..." He rubbed his head. "You're not gonna believe this. I've been outed. My cover's blown. Eve knows who I am." He paused again, trying to sort out his jumbled thoughts. "There are others like us here. In this house. Other Grays. There must be a community here. But there's something else you're not going to believe. One of them is a Red-Line like Eve and her siblings. She healed me and discovered who I was." He shook his head, shocked at his own words. "I'm completely baffled, and I'm not sure how to handle this."

He tried to think. He was rambling, but he sensed he was running out of time. He thought of Eve. His desire for her was real, and he didn't want to lose her, but he had to be realistic. He couldn't stay here. His shoulder, and his heart, ached. "I'm coming in. This job is over. There's no way she's going to trust me now. I'll find a way to get to the ship by tonight. And then we'll leave. Just wait for me, okay?"

There was no answer. Sighing, he hung up.

·•·•●·•●·•·

"Eve?" asked Sarah.

"He said 'Royce'?" asked Eve. "You're sure?"

"Had you mentioned Royce to him before?" asked Ramsey.

Eve thought back through her muddled thoughts. "Yes. I told him I had a brother and sister."

"That may be all it is then," said Hannah. "In his fevered state, he may have just been muttering rubbish. It probably didn't mean anything."

Eve looked around the table. "Do you all believe that?"

Nobody answered.

Eve turned and headed for the bedroom door.

"Eve, wait," said Sarah.

"Oh, boy," said Ramsey.

Eve threw open the bedroom door. Adam was sitting on the bed, his shopping bag in his hand.

"Well," she said, "look who's up."

He put the bag down. "Eve..."

"Eve what?"

His face was flat. "I know you know."

"So you're not going to deny it?"

He shook his head. "No."

"You're a Gray-Line?"

"I am."

Sarah stepped inside, with Ramsey behind her. Declan and Hannah stood at the door.

Adam regarded them. "You're Grays too?"

"We are," said Ramsey.

He looked at Sarah. "You're obviously a Red-Line."

"Half-Red-Line," she answered.

He flexed his arm. "You did a nice job."

Ramsey stepped forward. "Before Miss Eve here unleashes her fury and contemplates your demise, I'd like to know if your presence here puts my family at risk, because if it does, I'm going to kill you first, and Eve can have the scraps."

Adam raised a palm. "No. Your family is not at risk."

Ramsey glowered at him and then looked at Declan. Declan nodded. Ramsey stepped back and took Sarah's hand. "Eve. He's all yours. We'll let you two talk."

Chapter Thirteen

ADAM DIDN'T KNOW WHAT to say. Eve glared at him as if he was refusing her food after a week-long fast.

"Why?" she finally asked. "Who are you?"

"Eve...I..."

She cocked her head. "You what? Please think about what you're about to say. Don't sit there and lie to me. I think I've had enough of that."

Adam shifted on the bed. He put the shopping bag down. "There's a reason I'm here."

"Enlighten me."

"I came to meet you."

She crossed her arms.

He tried to think of how to explain. "I'll start from the beginning. I came with my friend Tez a few months ago. My mission was to get employed, blend in, and meet you. I already knew you worked at Benny's. I practiced some bartending skills and got the job."

"Mission? Did you say mission?"

Adam held his breath. This would be the hard part. "Yes. I did. I was assigned."

She paced, her feet stomping. "I can't believe this. That whole time at Benny's, you were there because of me? Watching me?"

"Yes." Adam saw no point in denying it.

"And the night up on the roof?" She sucked in a breath. "Wait a minute. That's how I read you? That's how you knew about Jerry, isn't it? That he was seeing someone else?"

"Well, that had more to do with hearing him on the phone, but the part about you picking it up from me? Yes. I was pissed and my guard slipped a bit."

"Son-of-a..."

"I went up to the roof to meet you because I finally got up the nerve to talk to you. I could never do it before." He chuckled. "You intimidated me."

Eve didn't smile.

Adam's face dropped. "Then Benny happened...and you know the rest."

She waved a hand. "Whoa. Wait one second. I know the rest? How about the huge missing piece you conveniently left out? Why? What did you hope to gain by meeting me?"

Adam hesitated. "I needed to know a few things."

She squinted. "Like what? My favorite food? What I like to wear at night?"

Adam thought of their time at the motel. Despite the situation, heat bloomed in his gut.

Eve straightened and spoke softly. "Don't you dare even go there."

"Eve, I'm limited to what I can say..."

Her eyes widened. "You're what? You're limited?" She put her hands on her hips. "How about the fact that I'm Royce's sister? Would that have anything to do with it?"

Adam tensed.

"Yes. You got a little mouthy when you were out of it. Told Hannah you needed to find Royce and tell Tez." Adam didn't respond, and she pushed further. "Why, Adam? Why do you need to find Royce? And think very carefully before you answer."

"I don't have to think carefully because I can't tell you why."

"What do you mean?"

"I wasn't told why. All I was supposed to do was secure his location and report back."

Eve studied him, nodding. "I see. You're supposed to hook up with sister Eve, get cozy, get in her pants, and make her spill the location of her brother to the sexy bartender who's made her swoon with desire. Then, once you have what you want, dump her and leave. Then tell some elusive leader where Royce is so they can do who knows what to him. Is that it?"

Adam opened his mouth, but couldn't deny it. He shook his head, knowing how it looked. "It's close enough."

Eve set her jaw. She turned away, and he thought he heard her mumble. "And to think I was Binding with you." She hung her head. "I'm so stupid."

Adam sat straight. "What did you say? You thought what?" His stomach flipped. "Did you say Binding?"

She turned back. "It doesn't matter. It's over now."

"Eve..."

"So, this whole thing with Vince, how'd you plan on dealing with that?"

He wanted to talk about the Binding part, but she'd moved on. "Vince was a shock to me, just like it was to you. I've just been trying to stay alive."

"Gave you a great opportunity to get to me, didn't it? Bed the poor, scared sister?"

He shook his head. "What happened between us..."

She waved. "Spare me the 'it meant something' talk. You and I both know it was just sex. I wanted it just as much as you did. I just wish I'd known I was sleeping with a two-faced liar."

Adam groaned. "Maybe this sounds bad right now, but I like you. I like being with you. The sex was great, and I'll admit, at the time, I'd hoped to learn Royce's location. I was...am...very conflicted. At this point, I don't know what I want. Right now, I just want us to get out of this and make sure you're safe."

She pointed. "You're conflicted?"

He ran a hand through his hair and closed his eyes. "This is a mess."

She paused. "You closed the door."

He opened his eyes. "What?"

"On Saul. In the room at the motel. It just hit me. It distracted Vince. It's how we got the upper hand."

He struggled to keep up with the change in subject. He thought back. "Yes. I find that under certain circumstances, I can summon the energy required to get out of a tight spot."

She nodded and narrowed her eyes. "How's that working for you right now?"

He sighed. "Not very well."

"No kidding."

"Eve, please...I'm sorry."

She squared her shoulders. "Forget it. I'll make this simple for you. Get up, get clean, and get your stuff. We're leaving. We've put these people through enough. And now they're worried about you and your presence here. And I'm the one who brought you. We've all had experiences with others like us that have not been positive and now they have to worry about mobsters on top of that. They don't need any more upheaval."

"Where will we go?"

"*We're* not going anywhere. I'm dropping you off at the nearest bus station. Then you can find your way back to your ship and get the hell out of here. You can report back to your cronies that you failed in your mission. After that, who cares?"

Adam wanted to argue with her. "What about you?"

"I'll do what I always do. Take care of myself." Her face went dark. "It appears that's the one thing we have in common. We're both good at it."

"Eve..."

She walked to the door. "I'm leaving in fifteen minutes. Be ready." She opened the door and slammed it behind her.

• • • • • • • • • •

"Here, take this," said Declan.

Eve raised her head. Feeling sick, she'd sat the table and put her head in her hands. She expected to see a shot of some liquor similar to the one Ramsey had given her yesterday, but it was a phone. She took it.

"It's a burner phone, with a few tweaks. You can use it without fear of being tracked." He reached into a pocket and pulled out his card. "This is how you can reach me. Use it if you need to."

She held the card. "Thank you, but I think I've asked enough of you."

"Don't be afraid to request help," said Sarah.

"I already did. You were all there for me and I appreciate it, but it's time for us to go."

"There's something else you need to be aware of," said Declan.

Eve couldn't imagine what else.

Declan opened a newspaper on the table. He turned a few pages and pointed to a small article on the bottom corner. "They're looking for you."

Eve scanned the headline: "Couple Sought in Death of Bar Owner."

Her shoulders dropped. "Hell."

"It says you're suspects in his death. The police are looking for both of you."

Eve groaned. What Tony had warned her about had come true. She realized that despite the risks, she was going to have to turn herself in. If Tony had learned nothing from Vince, then it would be the only way to get this straightened out. She thought of her brother and wished he were there. God, she missed him.

Taking a deep breath, she sat up. She pushed her hair back. "Okay."

"What are you going to do?" asked Sarah.

"I'm going to drop off Adam and then I'm going to the police."

"You're sure?" asked Ramsey.

"I don't think I have a choice."

"You want us to do some digging?" asked Declan. "In my line of work, I might be able to help."

Eve played with the tip of the card. "Sorry if I should know this, but what exactly is your line of work?"

"I've managed the security of the Council for a while now," said Declan.

"He's good in a crisis," said Ramsey. "He can be trusted."

Eve nodded and put the card in her pocket. "You don't need to do any digging. That's the last thing I want. You've risked enough with us being in this house. I'll be fine. I always am."

"What about him?" Ramsey tilted his head at the bedroom door. "You gonna let him fly away and you take all the heat?"

She laughed softly. "Maybe I'll blame him for the whole thing. He'll be long gone, so what will it matter?"

There was a pause. "It's not a bad idea," said Declan.

"I'm kidding."

"He deserves it for lying to you," said Ramsey.

"Maybe so, but I can't lie about what happened. Vince is the one who needs to be punished. Adam didn't kill Benny. And he helped save my life. I can't deny that."

"You get any indication of why he wants to find Royce?" asked Ramsey.

"No." Eve shook her head. She looked at Sarah. "Did you?"

"No," said Sarah. "I couldn't read that from him."

"He says he doesn't know. Just that he was told to get his location."

"If he's lower on the chain, he probably isn't privy to that information," said Declan.

"My fear is," she started. "Well, you know what my fear is."

Ramsey agreed. "The whole High Child thing. Royce would be next in line. He's considered a threat."

"Yes."

"Well, Adam's mission failed. He can't tell them anything," said Eve.

"I know, but what happens after that?" asked Ramsey. "I don't think the people who want Royce will give up so easily."

No one said anything, and before anyone could, the bedroom door opened and Adam stepped out. He'd cleaned himself up and wore a fresh set of clothes. He favored his wounded arm and held it against his torso.

The conversation ended. Hannah opened a bag and pulled something out. She walked over to Adam. "Here. It's a sling. You can wear it till your shoulder's better."

He let her slide the sling over his neck and around his shoulder. "Thanks," he said, relaxing his arm. He looked around the room, his face flat. "Listen. I'm sorry about lying. I know how this may look. I just want you all to know I don't mean you any harm. I was supposed to be long gone by now."

"With my brother's location snug in your pocket," said Eve.

"How much were you going to get for the information?" asked Ramsey. "I assume this is a paid gig."

Adam's face fell. "A lot."

"I bet," said Declan.

"You know who Royce is? Why he's important?" asked Ramsey.

Adam shrugged. "I don't know anything, other than Eve is his sister, and she would be the most likely to know something."

"What happens if you don't find him?" asked Declan.

"I don't know that either."

"It means no paycheck," said Eve. She stood. "I'll get my suitcase." She walked by him without making eye contact. She grabbed her bag and purse and stood by the door.

Sarah retrieved two plastic bags from the kitchen. "Here. It's not much, but I packed some food."

Eve took a bag, and so did Adam. "Thank you," said Eve. After a brief hesitation, she gave Sarah a hug.

Sarah spoke in her ear. "Please be careful."

Eve's chest constricted. Leaving the warmth and safety of a kind home was harder than she expected. "I will. Don't worry."

"Use Declan's card if you need to. He can help."

Eve gave her a squeeze. "I will."

They let go and said their goodbyes to the rest of the group. Five minutes later, they were on the road. Adam sat beside her as she drove.

"You going to talk to me?" he asked.

She studied the road. "Nothing to talk about."

"Where are we going?"

"Like I said, to the nearest bus station."

"What happens after that?"

Eve shifted in her seat. Adam's nearness was making her uncomfortable. That damn attraction to him would not go away. She forced herself to focus. "You go home, and I go to the police."

"Let me go with you."

She looked over at him. "Don't be stupid. What are you going to do when they ask for your personal details? Huh? You going to give them your home address?"

"I'm staying in an apartment. I accomplished that much."

"Don't be naïve. They're going to check back all the way to your childhood. They'll want to know everything. After they talk to you, you'll become their prime suspect." She swung into a gas station. "We need some gas."

"What about Tony? Shouldn't you talk to him first? You told him you would. What if he found out something important?"

Eve considered that. She had the burner phone Declan had given her. Maybe it wasn't a bad idea.

Adam popped the door open. "I'll get the gas. You call him." He stepped out and closed the door.

Eve dug through her purse and found the phone. Thankfully, she and her siblings were good with numbers. She recalled his contact information and dialed. Tony picked up on the second ring.

· · · ·•· •· · · ·

Adam hopped back in the car. After pumping the gas, he had bought bottled water for the two of them. He felt the need to do something. The guilt ate at him and now that the time was nearing for him to go, he dreaded it. The thought of leaving Eve and never seeing her again made his stomach hurt. He didn't even know if Tez was still here.

He put the water by his feet. Despite everything, he still felt himself react to her. Obviously, his body had other plans than his brain. He remembered what she'd said. Had she actually started to Bind with him? His heart thumped at the thought, but he realized the implications. Maybe it was better to end this before it got started.

"Eve, before you drop me off, I need to say something. I know you don't believe me, but I care about you. Maybe more than I planned to. And I want to be sure you're okay. If I could, I'd stay and take the heat with you. I just want to be sure Vince won't get near you."

He waited for her to answer, but she just stared through the windshield. Looking closer, he noticed she was pale. She held the burner phone in her lap.

"Eve? What's wrong? Did you talk to Tony?" He waited. "Eve?" He touched her arm.

That roused her. She looked over at him, her face sullen. She started the car. "I'm going to drop you off." She pulled away from the pump.

"What did Tony say?" asked Adam.

"Nothing," she said quietly.

He knew that wasn't true. "Damn it. What's going on?"

She was quiet until she pulled up to the curb a few blocks down. "Here's the bus stop."

He looked across the street to see a bench and a couple of people waiting beside it. He looked back at Eve. "I'm not getting out of this car until you tell me what's wrong."

She gripped the wheel. "Dixie's in the hospital. Somebody came after her."

"What? Who?"

"Vince and his goons."

"You're sure?"

She wiped at her eye and Adam wished he could reach out to her, but he knew she'd rebuff him. "Eve..."

"They beat her up, took the dogs. She's at St. Mary's."

"She's at church?"

Eve let out a frustrated breath. "No. The hospital."

Adam sat back and thought about it. "How did they even know she was your friend?"

Eve paused. "They must have asked around. Talked to the neighbors."

"They're trying to get to you, aren't they?"

"Yes. It's my fault." She bit her lip.

Adam didn't know what to say. "You know what they're doing, don't you? They're trying to find you through Dixie."

She nodded but didn't answer.

"You can't go to the hospital. They'll be waiting for you."

She looked over with watery eyes. "The bus will be here soon. You need to go."

"No. I can't leave like this." He reached over and took her hand. She pulled it away as if he'd shocked her. "I want to help."

"You can't help, Adam." She wiped at her face. "Vince wants to meet. I'm going to go."

"You can't do that, Eve. He'll kill you."

"I have to. I'm putting everyone at risk until I do."

"It's a death sentence."

"Get out of the car."

Adam held his breath. "Where are you going? You going to meet him in the hospital? Does Tony know?"

She shook her head. "No. Tony doesn't know anything. He thinks I'm going to turn myself in."

"Then how do you know where Vince is?"

She stared out the window. "Because I know where he wants to meet. Dixie told Tony that Vince took my dogs with him. He wanted to take them back to where they came from."

"You're not making any sense."

She shot a look at him. "I know where that is. That was a message to me." She sniffed. "Get out. I need to go."

"You can't go alone. Let me go with you."

"No. You've done enough."

"I can help. You know I can."

"No. You can't. He'll be ready this time. We got away before, but he won't let it happen again. He'll make sure of that." A bus pulled up at the corner. "You have to leave, Adam. Go home." Her eyes softened. "I..."

"You what?"

She swallowed. "Nothing. Never mind. Just please go." She wiped at another tear.

Adam's heart thumped again. He hated leaving her, but she wasn't going to let him stay. He opened the door but paused. "I'm sorry. I wish...I wish I'd handled things differently." He resisted the urge to reach out and touch her. "I wish you trusted me."

She made a strangled sound. "Don't." She paused. "Please."

Something twisted in his heart. Nodding, he pushed the door open and stepped out. As soon as he closed the door, she hit the gas and was gone.

He watched Mike's car disappear around the corner. Spying the bus, he made up his mind. He ran across the street and hopped on.

"Morning," said the driver.

Adam didn't waste time. "How do I get to St. Mary's hospital?"

Chapter Fourteen

Two hours later, Adam hopped out of a taxi and ran into the lobby of the hospital. It had taken two bus rides and a cab to get him here, but he'd made it. He approached the registration desk and asked for Dixie Royal's room. They sent him up to the fourth floor and the nurses there pointed him toward room 412.

On the way up in the elevator, he discarded the sling. His shoulder was sore, but he ignored the discomfort. His worry for Eve was far more painful. Finding Dixie's room, he knocked on the door and heard a quiet, "Come in." Pushing the door open, he saw Dixie lying in the bed. She had a black, swollen eye and her jaw was bruised. Despite her injuries, she sported a blonde wig swept up in a twist. Someone sat with her. It was a woman with jet black hair and heavy make-up, but on closer look, Adam knew this woman was like Dixie.

Seeing Adam, Dixie's jaw dropped, and the visitor stood. She wore a slim black dress and yellow high-heeled shoes and was as tall as Adam.

"Adam, honey? Is that you?" asked Dixie.

Adam came into the room. "Dixie? You okay?"

Dixie tried to raise herself, but she stopped and grimaced.

The woman put a hand on her shoulder. "What are you doing, Dix? You'll strain yourself."

Dixie waved her off. "I'm fine, Daisy. Stop fussing over me."

"You damn near had your head knocked off, girl. You need to be still."

Adam found the bed controls and raised the bed.

Dixie sat back with a heavy breath. "Thank you, honey. That's better." She patted Adam's hand. Daisy gave Adam a dubious look. "Daisy, this is Adam."

Daisy looked him over. "He your new beau?"

"Oh, heavens no, honey. He's with Evie." She looked behind him. "Is she here?"

"Evie always gets the pretty ones," said Daisy.

Adam didn't bother to correct her. "She's not with me."

Her eyes widened. "She isn't? Why not? What happened? Is she okay?" She gripped her side and winced. "Damn these ribs."

"Dixie, was it Vince? Did he do this?" asked Adam.

The pain seemed to subside, and Dixie relaxed. "Bastard took me by surprise. I never saw it coming. I came home last night after spending it with my handsome new suitor and they were there." She sighed. "I'm just glad I came up alone. I'd hate to think what they might have done to my man." She fanned her face. "It makes me sweat, and I don't like to sweat, unless I'm having fun at the same time."

"Dixie, where did Vince take Eve's dogs?"

Dixie scrunched her face. "The dogs?" She looked worried. "Is that what this is about? Eve and those dogs. She's wondering where they are." She looked back toward the door. "Is Eve afraid to come in? She's worried about Vince, isn't she?" Her face turned fearful. "Is he waiting for her? He's using me, isn't he?" She pushed up again. "He's looking for her and knows she'll come. Oh, sugar. I should have suspected. Poor Evie. You tell her to stay away."

"Listen. It's too late for that. Eve has gone to meet Vince."

"What?" Dixie held her ribs, but managed to pull up and grab Adam's wrist. "She can't do that. Vince is crazy. He'll kill her."

"I know that. That's why I need your help. You told Tony that Vince said he's going to take Eve's dogs home. What does that mean?"

Dixie's eyes narrowed. "The dogs? Why are we talking about the dogs? We have to call Tony and tell him."

"Tony can't help unless we know where to look. Eve said she knew what Vince meant, and that it was a message to her. That's where she's headed."

"Then why aren't you with her?"

"She wouldn't let me go. She went alone."

"Oh, Evie." She laid back on the pillow. "She's so damn headstrong."

"Where, Dixie?" He resisted the urge to yell because he knew he didn't have much time. "Do you know what Vince meant?"

Dixie shook her head. "I don't know where the dogs..." She stopped and stared off. "Wait a minute."

"What is it?"

Dixie's eyes shifted as she thought. "Eve told me once...something about where she got them."

"Where?"

"A few years back. Eve said she found them." She paused.

"Yes?"

"She was on a weekend trip. In the woods at a cabin. She was with a man. Said she heard barking and went outside. She saw the animals. Said it looked like they'd been on their own for a while, likely dumped on the side of the road. She took them in and she's had them ever since."

"Where is this cabin?"

"I...I don't know."

"Think. She must have told you."

Dixie paused. "In the woods. She said they were in the woods."

"I know that, but where?"

"Oh, sugar, I'm trying to think." She closed her eyes. "Wait." She opened them again. "There's a place her brother told her about. A place she could go to get away for a bit. I think that's where she was."

The mention of Eve's brother didn't intrigue Adam at all. Dixie could have told him Royce was in her closet and he wouldn't have cared. He just wanted to get to Eve before Vince did.

"Dixie, we don't have much time."

She held up a hand. "Pondera Forest."

"Pon...what?"

"It's not far from here. Up in the hills. In a wooded area. There are cabins. That's where. She invited me once, but honey, do I look like a woodsy gal?"

"How do I find it?"

"I don't know."

"I do."

They looked at Daisy, who studied a nail.

Dixie swatted at her. "Tell us. This is Evie we're talking about."

Daisy rubbed her arm where Dixie smacked her. "You don't have to be bitchy about it."

"Daisy...you want to borrow my red pumps again?"

Daisy raised a brow. "Fine. I stayed with Carl up there. Last year. It's about an hour north, off the main highway. You'll see the signs once you get close."

"How do I find out which cabin?" asked Adam.

"There's a main house where you go to register. I'm sure they can tell you, especially if she's been there more than once."

Dixie shifted in the bed. "I'm calling Tony."

"No," said Adam. "No Tony."

"What are you talking about?"

"Because..." Adam wasn't sure what to say. The last thing he wanted was for Tony to show up with the cavalry. Vince was a hothead, and he didn't want Eve getting caught in the crossfire. Plus, if Eve was right and the police couldn't be trusted, he wasn't exactly sure they would want her to escape alive, Tony or no Tony. Something told him he needed to go on his own, and once he got Evie out, then call for help. "Because he can't be trusted."

"Really?" asked Daisy.

"What? Of course he can," said Dixie.

"I'm not saying he'd hurt Eve, but he's the reason Vince found us at Mike's."

Dixie's painted brows rose. Apparently, a bruised face still warranted sculpted brows. "He'd never tell anyone where Eve was."

"They followed him. He didn't know it. His fondness for her blinds him to the risks."

"But it's Tony."

"I can take care of it. I've dealt with Vince a couple of times now. I'll make sure she's okay, but I have to go now."

"But it's just you."

"Exactly. I can sneak in and get the upper hand, plus I have a few surprises up my sleeve. You bring in Tony and a group of cops, Vince is likely to start shooting."

Dixie studied him. "How will you get there?"

"I..." He hadn't considered that. "Hell."

Dixie looked at Daisy. "Give him your car."

Daisy looked blankly at Dixie. "You're kidding. I will not."

Dixie swatted at her again. "You think I was bad before? Honey, you're about to see me in epic bitch mode. Now give him your keys, or I'll tell Carl all about your fetish for high-heeled shoes and what you did to Steve with them." She pointed. "Which you better not have done with my red pumps, or you owe me a pair of shoes."

Daisy's jaw dropped. "You wouldn't."

Dixie looked around. "Where's the phone?"

Daisy's face flattened. "Fine." She picked up her pink suede purse, dug around and pulled out a purple key chain. "Here. It's the red convertible out front."

Adam grabbed the keys and turned to leave. "It's got tacky animal print seats," said Dixie. Daisy frowned. "You can't miss it."

"Thanks," said Adam.

"You bring her back safe, Adam, or you'll deal with me."

"I will."

"I'll give you one hour, then I'm calling Tony."

Adam hoped that was enough time. "Deal." He ran out of the room.

· · • • • • • • · ·

Eve pulled up in front of the cabin. A black car with tinted windows was parked in the pebbled driveway. Stopping Mike's Caddy, she killed the engine and sat. It was quiet. A soft rain gave the woods a dull, misty look and the cloudy skies threatened more showers. From what she could see, no one was in the other car. She suspected Vince was waiting for her inside.

She'd made a few stops before arriving here. If she didn't make it out of this, then she needed to take care of a few things first. She'd wanted to talk to her family, but she knew that phone call would be too hard, so she'd written notes to explain everything. Then she'd written to Tony, telling him the details about what had happened since that fateful moment in Benny's office. If he could do anything to stop Vince, then Eve knew he would.

Sitting in the car, she considered her options. There weren't many. Going after Dixie was Vince's way of telling her that anyone Eve cared about was at risk. Her only plan was to go in and talk to him, maybe get him to see reason. But he'd already killed his father. So, killing an old girlfriend wouldn't be a big leap. The only leverage she might have would be the supposed papers and safe deposit box she'd told Benny about, but neither existed. It had only been her attempt to buy time and make Vince think twice.

She massaged her neck. Her story would not stand under scrutiny for long. If Vince demanded to know more and she had nothing to show for it, she'd be back to square one. Remembering something, she opened her purse, dug through a pocket, and pulled out a small gold key. It unlocked Dixie's storage unit. Dixie had asked her to keep a copy since she'd kept misplacing hers. Holding it in her hand, Eve wondered if it could work. Could she convince Vince there was some mysterious box? If they believed the deposit box existed, they'd want to take her to the bank to open it. Then what?

Eve was just going to have to trust fate. There was only so much she could do.

She closed her eyes and rubbed her hand. Despite everything, the tingle of energy from Adam's touch still lingered. Just thinking about it made her body react. She cursed Bindings and tried to think of something else.

An image of her dogs, Ginger and Fred, popped into her head. She focused in on them and knew they were inside. Vince would use them against her, but she had the upper hand there. Communicating with animals maybe wasn't as sexy as Gilli's intuition or Royce's telekinesis, but there were obvious advantages.

Dropping Dixie's key back into her purse, she said a quick prayer and opened the car door.

· · · · • · • · · ·

Adam hit the gas pedal and drove the convertible onto the highway. Time was running short. If he was too late, he'd walk in only to find Eve dead and Vince gone. He forced himself not to think of that scenario. It made his stomach lurch.

He wondered how he'd found himself rushing to help a woman he hardly knew. He'd never planned on falling in love, especially not with someone from another planet. In his experience, love only meant pain and betrayal. He told himself that this wasn't about love; he only wanted to ensure her safety before he left. He didn't need her blood on his hands because his soul was tormented enough. Once he took care of Vince, he would get Eve to Tony, and then he was gone.

Thinking of leaving, he wondered if it was still an option. He picked up his phone and dialed Tez again. If his friend had truly left, then Adam would be spending the rest of his days as a lonely Earth man. But he and Tez went way back. His friend had a temper and could be dramatic, but Adam hoped their long-standing friendship would be enough to keep Tez around.

It rang several times with no answer. Cursing and dodging traffic, Adam was about to hang up when he heard an audible click.

"Hello, Tez?"

There was a brief pause. "You better have good news for me. I hope I didn't hang around for nothing."

Adam breathed a sigh of relief. "You're still here. I knew it. Did you get my message?"

"Adam. Do you or do you not have Royce's location?"

Adam tried not to care that his friend had little concern for Adam's situation. "Listen. I need your help. Eve's in trouble."

"I don't care. Do you know—"

"Shut up, Tez. I'm telling you I need you. What are you here for if I can't count on you? You want to know where Royce is, then make yourself useful. Eve is going to meet Vince and is going to get herself killed. If that happens, then there will be zero opportunity to find her brother."

"Zero is a strong word. She has a sister."

Anger bubbled up. "We have invested too much time in this assignment to start over. You know that and so do I. So stop being part of the problem. You want to know how to find him? Saving Eve's life will go a long way toward greasing the wheels."

"I'm not too sure of that. And we're overdue by two weeks. I feel fairly sure our catastrophic failure is secure. I don't even know that we'll have anything to go back to."

"Stop being so final. How about we do something that makes us feel good for once?"

"That doesn't pay the bills."

Adam swerved around a car, whose driver blared its horn. "There will be other jobs."

"Not after this."

"You don't know that. And I don't have time to argue about it."

"Where are you? We need to leave. I should have left two days ago."

"I'm on my way to Pondera Forest. There are cabins there. Eve's on her way to meet Vince, who is going to kill her unless I can get there and stop it."

"You'll only get yourself killed, too. You need to turn around and come back."

"I'm not leaving until I know she's safe."

There was a pause. "I knew it. You've fallen for her."

Adam gritted his teeth. "I need you to get up here. You can use the ship. It's a wooded area, so it will be easy to hide."

Tez chuckled. "You want me to risk detection to save your girlfriend?"

Adam gripped the wheel. "How about to save me?"

Another pause. "You're not in danger, Adam. You walk in there, you do it alone. I gave you a second chance, but I'm not giving you a third. We came here to find Royce Fletcher. I don't care about Eve Fletcher, her boss, or her problems."

"What about me? Do you care about me?"

Adam heard a muffled curse. "One hour. You're either here or you're not. But either way, I'm gone." The line clicked and went dead.

"Tez?" Adam listened, but there was only silence. "Tez?"

Adam threw the phone into the passenger seat and stared at the road, passing another car. After a few quiet seconds, he punched the accelerator.

•••••••••

Eve approached the door. It was slightly ajar, and she didn't bother to knock. Pushing it open, she peered inside. The last time she'd been here had been two years earlier with Vince, shortly before she'd left him. On a walk, they'd found two dogs in the woods, obviously abandoned. Eve took them in. As she entered the front room, she heard yapping, and Fred and Ginger bounded toward her, their little legs moving fast.

Eve stooped to greet them, glad to see they were unharmed. Looking up, she saw the familiar living area with a worn brown leather couch and an old wooden coffee table. The kitchen remained unchanged with its yellow countertops and dull gray linoleum. The only sign that someone was there was a lighted candle on the nicked dining table.

The bedroom door opened and Vince stepped out into the room. He looked tired, as if he hadn't slept since this ordeal began, but his clothes were fresh and he was clean shaven. He was wiping his hands with a towel, and he threw it onto a dining chair.

"I see you got my message."

She tried to breathe steadily. "You didn't need to hurt Dixie."

"Would you be here if I hadn't?"

Eve didn't answer. She looked around. "You alone?"

Vince put his hands on his hips. "Are you?"

"I sent Adam away. He's not here."

"He left you to fend for yourself?" He chuckled. "You always did know how to pick 'em."

She clasped her fingers to keep them from shaking. "Present company included."

He held out his hands. "I never said I was a saint."

Before she could respond, Saul walked into the cabin behind her and shut the door. Her heart thumped faster.

"Looks like the gang's all here," said Vince. He walked to the dining table and pulled out a chair. Eve noticed there was a folder on the table with a pen next to it. "Have a seat."

Saul remained by the front door while Eve walked to the table. "What do you want, Vince?"

"I want you to sit. We need to talk."

She looked at Saul, but his face held no expression, and she sat at the table. Vince joined her. He dragged the folder and pushed it in front of her. "I need you to sign something for me."

Eve was confused. She didn't know what to expect when she entered the cabin, but it hadn't been this. "What is it?"

Vince glanced at Saul. "Turns out it's a good thing I didn't kill you a couple of days ago. I would have put myself in an awful bind." He patted the papers. "I talked to dad's attorney. After an hour of gentle coaxing, he told me something interesting."

Eve felt a shiver run through her. "What?"

Vince smiled, and the room felt heavy with anticipation. "Dad left the bar to you."

Eve dropped her jaw. "He did what?"

His smile evaporated. "My father left everything he had to you." He rubbed his chin. "Not me."

Eve shook her head. "He left it to me? That can't be true."

Vince leaned forward, his face flat. "You two must have been very close." He touched her arm. "Guess Dad and I were able to share something together."

Eve reared back. "Stop it. That's not true and you know it."

Vince relaxed. "To be honest, Eve, I don't really care. Right now, I'm just tired. Tired of this whole ordeal. Tired of chasing you and your boyfriend. Tired of worrying." He pointed at the folder. "All I want you to do is sign the damn papers. Then I'm going to shoot you and your dogs. And then I can live a happy life." He picked up the pen. "Here you go."

Eve stared at him. Her mind flipped through a myriad of possibilities of what to do, but none of them were effective. She stared at the pen. The only thing she could do was keep talking. "What am I signing?"

He sighed. "What does it matter? You'll be dead soon." When she didn't respond, he answered her. "Fine. You're signing the bar over to me."

She tried to understand. "But if I'm dead, won't you get it, anyway?"

His face flickered with anger. "Damn it. Can't you do anything without having to ask a million questions?"

"If I'm going to die because of this, the least you could do is humor me."

He tapped at the table. "Dad put in a loophole. If you were unable to assume control, then the bar goes to the sisters of St. Julian, where they can do with it what they will. Which means they'll sell it and take the money."

"What makes you think I wouldn't do that?"

The tapping became more rapid. "You don't seem to understand. I don't give a shit about the bar, but it belongs to me." He shot a thumb at himself. "Not you. And sure as hell not to a pack of nuns."

"They're women, not wolves."

He slammed his hand on the table, and Eve jumped. He stood from his seat and loomed over her. "That bar is mine. I need it." His face was pale, and she could see a sheen of sweat on his forehead. "So you're going to ensure that I get it. Whether you're dead or alive." He tipped his head. "But you'll be dead."

Her mind raced. She used the only thing she had. "What about the safe deposit box? I have the key, remember? It won't be much use if I'm dead."

Vince grinned and leaned low. "Nice try, sweetheart. There is no box. Dad's attorney knew nothing about it. So as far as I'm concerned, it doesn't exist. And with you gone, box or no box, it won't matter. All I need is your John Hancock." He tapped the folder and straightened.

Something didn't make sense. "This is about money?" She stared at him as his eyes narrowed at her. "What have you gotten yourself into?"

He laughed softly and ran a hand through his hair. "All you need to know is that I have debts and I intend to pay them." He grabbed the folder and shook it at her. "Now sign the damn papers." He patted his jacket pocket. "And don't even think about tearing them up because I've got a second copy, and if I have to use them, you'll be signing with broken fingers."

She glanced over at Saul, who still stood at the door with his hands clasped in front of him, looking as if he was waiting for a table at a restaurant. Eve thought of Benny. What would he want her to do? She looked back at Vince and set her shoulders. "No."

Vince glared, and a gust of energy erupted from him. Before she could react, he drew his hand back and slapped her across the face. Her head reared back with the impact. Her cheek went numb, and she blinked watery eyes. The dogs immediately started barking, but she sent out a silent message for them to be still. They sat but continued to watch. Holding her face, she watched Vince step back. He stared at her, his face stony.

"What did Dad call you? Spark?" He took hold of his fingers and cracked his knuckles. "That's fitting." He looked toward the door. "Saul?"

Still holding her now burning cheek, Eve watched Saul turn and walk out the front door. He came back carrying a jug. He popped the lid open.

Vince sighed. "That's gasoline. I'm going to douse you and the cabin. Then I'm going to light you up. But first," he looked over at Fred and Ginger, "I'm going to start with the dogs."

Eve widened her eyes in horror as Vince picked up the candle and took a step toward the animals. Saul walked closer, too, holding the jug out. "Wait!" she said.

Vince stopped and turned. "You sign now, I'll shoot you quick and easy and then we'll burn the place down. The mutts can head back into the woods for all I care. You give me a hard time, then you and the dogs burn first. But not in that order."

Eve stared at the man she'd once called her boyfriend. How had she never seen his madness? How could she have shared a bed with someone like this? "Vince..."

"You've got sixty seconds, *Spark*." He nodded at Saul, who began to pour the gasoline onto the floor. The dogs jumped and whined but remained in place.

Sweat trickled down her back. She tried to think. Either way, she was dead. There was no way out. She had known going into this that she would likely die, but she must have harbored some hope that Vince would spare her, or she'd find a way out. But that hope was dwindling.

Saul continued to sprinkle gas over the floor. Scanning the room, she saw Saul had left the front door ajar. Seeing an opportunity, she sent out a quick mental message and made it urgent. In response, the dogs jumped up and ran for the door. They darted through it and were gone before Vince barely had the chance to frown.

"The dogs! Damn it. Saul, get the dogs."

Nearing the kitchen, Saul straightened, dropped the jug, and ran out the door behind Fred and Ginger. The jug toppled and spilled, spraying gas. Eve jumped up, and Vince, avoiding the flammable liquid, stumbled back. The distraction was her only chance. Using the only thing she could find, she picked up the wooden dining chair and swung it at Vince. Vince saw it coming and raised his arms in defense. The chair hit him with a smack, knocking him backward into the wall. The chair crashed to the ground as Eve made a run for the exit.

Before she could get there, though, Vince caught her arm and yanked her back. Swinging out, she fought to get away and hit the candle Vince held dead on. It flew from his hand and hit the floor with a thud. There was a quick burst of ignition, and then the floor turned red with flames.

Chapter Fifteen

THE SHOCK OF THE fire bursting into life caused Vince to let go of her and leap back. Eve darted for the door, scampered down the porch steps, and dashed into the woods, grateful that the trees still held their leaves and would provide her with coverage. She didn't look behind her. If Vince was on her heels, it wouldn't make her run any faster.

She ran deep into the woods, dodging trees, roots, and shrubs. Using her hands, she swiped at the branches that whacked at her face. Breathing hard, she risked a quick glance behind her. No one was there. Holding her side, she jumped over a few more roots, found a healthy bush, and squatted behind it, catching her breath. Waiting, she watched.

Thinking of her dogs, she sent out a silent message, hoping they were okay. There was nothing at first, but then she received a weak communication. They weren't far. They'd found a small stream and were drinking water. Saul was not there.

Peering around the shrub, she listened as her breathing slowed and her heart began to return to a more normal rhythm. She debated her options when she heard a noise. There was a rustling, and then the sound of footfalls. Looking between the leaves, she held her breath when she saw Vince running through the trees. She froze. Her cover behind the shrub only partially concealed her, and if Vince looked her way, she would be seen.

Looking around, she hoped to find somewhere else to go, but saw no path that would conceal her. Hearing a noise, she glanced back and her heart rate zoomed upward when Vince ran up to a tree only three feet from her. He stopped and rested a hand against the trunk, his breathing rapid as he looked around.

Eve didn't move. She was squatted low. He was standing, looking at eye level.

Moving in a circle, he scanned the trees. Eve prayed when he turned in her direction, asking whatever spiritual being that might be in the area to hide her from his sight. He continued to look and then, shaking his head, found a nearby fallen log, sat, and rested his elbows on his knees.

Eve watched and wondered what to do. Wait him out? Run for it? Find a dead branch and knock him over the head? She swallowed and tried not to inhale or exhale, thinking he would hear. She jumped when Vince made a snort. Peering through the shrub, she saw him smiling. The smile became a chuckle and then became laughter. Holding his side, he looked straight toward her hiding place, reached under his jacket, pulled out a gun, and stopped laughing.

"You gonna come out, or do you want me to shoot you through the leaves?"

· · · • • • • • · ·

Adam drove down the pebbled drive at a frantic pace. The tires skidded but gripped again, and rocks hit the underside of the vehicle. He came to a stop next to Mike's car. There was another car parked beside it. His mind raced, but he didn't think for long. Dark smoke was drifting out of the cabin and into the sky, and looking closely, he could see orange flickers of light through the windows.

He jumped out of the car. "Eve!" He ran up to the porch. The front door was open, but fire enveloped the interior. There was no way he could access the house. He scanned the inside, but he saw no one. "Eve!" he yelled again. If she was in the cabin, then it was too late. There was no way he could get to her.

Refusing to believe the worst, he turned and looked around the area. He jumped off the porch but saw no one in the woods. Fear twisted his insides. *God, no*, he thought to himself. Seeing the dark car, though, he felt a ray of hope. Vince was still here. He hadn't left. Had Eve somehow escaped? Envisioning her running away, he checked the ground. A small part of his heart thumped when he saw footprints in the dirt leading into the woods. Small ones and larger ones. Without thinking, he ran into the trees, following the trail.

········

Eve's breath caught. Her prayers had gone unanswered. Moving slowly, she stood and moved out from the shrub. He chuckled again.

"Ah, Eve. Looks like your luck has finally run out." He stood with a groan and held the gun on her.

Despite her situation, she refused to back down. "I still haven't signed the papers."

His smile fell, and he took a couple of steps toward her. "Not yet." He reached into his jacket pocket and pulled out the folded sheets. "Dad always said to be prepared." He shook the paper at her. "Now you're going to sign them."

She bit her bottom lip. "Vince, listen. What about this? I sell the bar. I give you the money. Whatever you need. I don't care. I don't want it."

He frowned. "We've gone way past that. Right now, you're wanted for murder. Once you talk to the police, you'll implicate me. Either way, one of us is going down. And it's not going to be me."

She wrung her hands. "We can figure something out."

The side of his lip rose. "What are we going to figure out? Are you not going to turn me in? Are you going to go to jail for me?"

"Vince..."

"Are you going to blame your pretty boyfriend? Let him take the brunt?"

She shook her head.

"This is the only option. You sign. I get the bar. Then I have to kill you. Then I go my way. You get the blame for Dad, but it won't matter, because you'll be dead."

She shivered. "That won't work. They'll figure it out. Too much has happened. What about the cabin?"

He glanced back. "It's not a big deal. It looks suspicious, but it will only shed more doubt on you. Your car will be here. Not mine. Saul and I will be long gone."

"Tony will know."

He cocked his head. "Your other boyfriend? Come on. Who do you think you're dealing with? A few well-placed pieces of evidence could implicate him just as well. It wouldn't be hard to make it look like he was in on it with you."

Icy fear crawled up her spine. "You can't leave me dead out here. That alone will be suspicious. People know I came to meet you."

He fumbled in his jacket and found a pen. "People? You mean Dixie? She'll be defending her friend who she believes to be innocent. Big deal. Especially when you'll be found with the gun in your hand. The same gun that killed my father. It will look like a murder-suicide. Not so uncommon these days. Once that happens and they read the will, I'll produce the signed papers, and voila, the bar's all mine." He tipped his head. "It's a little more convoluted than I planned, but it still gets the same result."

She stepped back as he stepped closer. "How will you explain how you have the papers? That would imply you'd seen me."

He paused and thought about it. "You were despondent over Benny. You knew he'd left the bar to you, but your guilt wouldn't allow you to keep it. So before you offed yourself, you signed the bar over to me, the rightful heir, mailed the papers to me, and came to the cabin to end it. You doused it in gas, but chickened out and ran for it. Then you shot yourself out here." He smiled. "It's perfect."

Eve's mind raced. "I won't sign the papers. You may kill me, but you won't get the bar. I can do that much for Benny."

He grinned. "You want to play it that way? Fine. My first stop after I leave here is Dixie. Then what's your sister's name?" He raised a brow. "Gillian, isn't it? She's the next stop." He smiled when her eyes widened. "You take from me and I take from you."

At the mention of her sister, something unexplainable coursed through Eve. She had a temper, but Royce had always been known as the hot head. But with Vince's threats, a blinding rage sliced through her. She clenched her fists, and before she could think twice, raced forward and launched herself at Vince.

The move took him by surprise. He flinched and pulled the trigger. The gun discharged, and Eve swore she felt the ripple of air against her skin as the bullet passed her cheek. Before Vince could fire again, she tackled him to the ground. He fought, but anger fueled her. She punched and kicked at him, using everything she had to obliterate him. She wanted to decimate him, make him cower. All of her frustration, worry, and fear came out as she beat on him.

Flailing, Vince dropped the gun. He cursed and grabbed one of her arms. With her straddling him, he rolled and tried to pin her to the ground, but she bucked against him. The flat of her palm connected with his cheek. Letting go of her, he hit back. Eve deflected him until he grabbed her throat and squeezed. Her airway closed, and she clenched at his wrists as she kicked with her feet, but she couldn't get him off. Squeezing harder, he loomed over her, sweating and breathing hard.

"Damn it Eve. Why do you have to make this so difficult?"

Eve struggled but could not get away. Spots swam in her vision, and she fought to find air. Desperate, she accepted her fate. She would die in some forest where no one would find her body for months. Shoving against him, she fought, but he was too big. Her body weakened, and she clawed at his face, but it made no difference. Shutting her eyes and gasping, Eve prepared to die.

In the chaos, one sound penetrated her senses. It was the click of a gun and the sound of a voice. "Get off of her. Now."

Chapter Sixteen

EVE OPENED HER EYES and saw Adam pointing Vince's gun at Vince's head. Vince glanced back, but still held his grip.

Adam kicked out hard, connecting with Vince's midsection. Eve heard a deep grunt and then Vince was off of her. Beautiful, crisp, cool air filled Eve's lungs as she inhaled. She rolled away from Vince and managed to get to her knees and elbows, gasping and coughing.

Still holding the gun on Vince, Adam crouched beside her. "You okay?"

Eve nodded, sure she was pale as the chalky rocks in the dirt. She pushed up on shaky hands and tried to steady her breath, but leaning over, she continued to cough.

Glancing at Vince, she saw him in a similar position, only holding his gut. He tried to get his feet under him, but Adam stepped close and kicked him again. Vince let out a muffled curse and fell back onto the ground.

"How does it feel?" asked Adam. "Not too good, huh?" He kicked him again in the side. "Maybe you should pick on somebody else." Another kick and Vince rolled on his back and moaned. He attempted to push up, but Adam put his foot against Vince's throat. He pressed down, and Vince grabbed Adam's ankle and gagged. "I ought to shoot you right here."

Vince held out a hand. "No. Don't," he said weakly. He winced as Adam pushed harder with his foot.

"Why not?" asked Adam.

Eve sat back on her heels. "Adam."

Adam leaned over and put the muzzle against Vince's forehead. "Your brains will splatter all over the forest floor and the squirrels can eat them for dinner. Although I suspect they'll prefer your nuts. What do you think?"

Eve rubbed her throat. "Adam. Stop." Her voice was rough.

That seemed to penetrate. He straightened, taking the gun off Vince's head, but still pointing it at Vince. "He was going to kill you."

Eve tried to stand, but her legs were trembling. "But he didn't. We can take him to Tony. Turn him in."

"We can't trust him. He'll try to get away. And if he does, he'll come after you." He stared at Vince, who still held his foot. "He deserves to die."

Eve got on her feet and held on to a tree trunk for balance. "You can't do it because you're not like him. You don't kill people."

Adam grimaced, but continued to point the gun and hold Vince down. After a pause, he spoke. "How do you know I'm not?"

Eve cleared her throat, trying to speak. "Because I know you. Despite whatever our circumstances may be, you're a good man." She hesitated. "Don't become a bad one."

The gun wavered. Adam's face blanched, and Eve hoped she'd gotten through to him. No matter what Vince had done, or tried to do, she didn't want him to die at their hands. She knew it would haunt them for the rest of their lives. "Please."

Adam took his heel off of Vince's throat but kept the gun on him. Vince gasped as he sucked in air and grabbed his neck. Adam stepped back. "Dixie was going to call Tony. Tell him where we were." He stood beside Eve. "You sure you're okay?"

Eve nodded. It hurt to swallow, and she was sure she would sport a vibrant bruise on her neck, but she was breathing, which was all that mattered. "I'll live."

The cock of a gun sounded behind them and another voice spoke. "I'm not too sure about that."

Vince began to laugh.

· · • • • • • · ·

Adam turned, swiveling the gun, and saw Saul pointing a pistol at him.

Saul straightened his aim. "Drop it."

Adam hesitated, and Saul grinned. He pointed his weapon at Eve. "I'll shoot her first."

Adam didn't hesitate and tossed his gun into the shrubs. Vince got up, rubbing his neck, and picked it up. He shoved it into his waistband and stooped to pick up some papers that had fallen into the dirt. He brushed them off and found the pen next to a scrubby root. Standing with the items in one hand, he stepped closer.

Adam didn't move as Vince got close, sneered at him, and without speaking, punched him in the face. Adam stepped back, but didn't fall. White pain flared in his head, and he grabbed his nose, feeling warm liquid on his fingers.

"Vince," said Eve.

Vince stared hard at Adam. "Whose nuts are the squirrels gonna eat now, asshole?"

Adam stared back, nose bleeding, wishing he'd pulled the trigger. "At least they'll find mine. I suspect they'd have to do some searching to find yours."

Saul chuckled, and Vince's face fell. He pulled his gun out of his waistband and pointed it at Eve. "I don't think you're really in a position to make jokes right now."

Adam's blood went cold. It was the same feeling he'd had when he'd found Vince strangling Eve. Adam had been searching the woods, fearing the worst, when he'd heard a gun discharge. Running toward the sound and seeing the scuffle, he'd almost charged Vince when he'd seen the weapon on the ground. The same weapon that was now pointed at Eve.

He faced Vince. "Kill me. Not her. Let her go."

Vince shook his head. "Oh, I'll kill you all right. But first," he glanced at Eve, "she's got some signing to do."

Eve stared at the sheets Vince held out. She went even paler. "No."

Vince's brow furrowed, and his face went red. "I'm tired of messing around." He stepped toward Adam and kicked him in the back of the leg. Adam grunted and went down on his knees, and Vince cocked the gun against his head. "You're going to sign or I'm going to shoot him right in front of you."

Eve dropped her jaw. She locked eyes with Adam.

"Don't do it, Eve," said Adam.

Vince pushed the muzzle against Adam's head. Adam shut his eyes. He thought of his family and Tez, but the one who had broken his heart was Eve. He hated that he'd let her down. He opened his eyes again and watched her, willing her to understand.

Eve held his gaze, looking stricken, and raised her hand. "Give me the papers."

Adam shook his head. "Eve, no. He'll still kill us."

Vince handed the papers and pen to Eve. "Shut up, pretty boy."

Eve took them with shaky fingers. Her neck was showing the marks from Vince's fingers, and that made Adam seethe. He tried to think of anything he could do to get them out of this situation.

The wind picked up, and the branches swayed as the shrubs rustled. Adam looked around. So did the others. The wind grew in intensity, causing the trees to arch and bend. Leaves swirled, and Eve's hair blew back. Adam put up a hand to protect his face as the dirt got caught up in the wind.

Vince and Saul continued to hold their weapons, but they watched to see what was causing the sudden change in the weather.

The gun still pointed at his head, Adam was ready to tackle Vince when he realized what was occurring. Just feet from them, the woods splayed open as the wind intensity pushed back everything within a small circle.

Vince and Saul couldn't help but stare as a small, tubular, silver craft descended and landed in a rocky space.

Adam looked over to see Eve, Saul, and Vince, mouths open in surprise and squinting against the wind. He could have grabbed at Vince's gun, but Saul still had his. If the man reacted, Eve was still in the line of fire. Right now, the craft in front of them commanded everyone's attention, so Adam held back. He kept an eye on Saul and Vince and waited to see what would happen.

The wind decreased, and the only sound was the soft whirring of the ship. Saul and Vince kept staring, and Vince shifted his position so he could keep the gun on Adam and face the strange vehicle at the same time. Saul kept his gun on Eve, but all his attention was on the unexpected arrival.

The whirring stopped and everything went still. No birds chirped, and the wind died completely.

"What the hell?" asked Vince.

"What is that?" asked Saul.

Vince pushed harder with the gun on Adam's head. "Don't get any ideas."

"You think it's the cops?" asked Saul.

Vince smirked. "Since when do the cops land crafts in the middle of the woods?"

"Maybe it's a spacecraft," said Adam. He looked at Eve. She met his gaze, and he sent a silent message to her, hoping she'd get it. He didn't have much experience with telepathy, but he was finding under stressful circumstances, he could rise to the task. When she raised an eyebrow at him, he knew she'd received it.

Vince sneered at him. "Maybe I ought to shoot you right now."

Before anything could happen, they all turned when the side of the craft slid open and a ramp emerged and dropped to the ground.

Adam held his breath.

"What the...' asked Vince.

Saul took a step back. "Vince?"

Vince started to answer but stopped when a figure emerged. Adam widened his eyes when a creature with a large bald head, unnaturally long arms, and huge round eyes raced down the ramp toward the four of them.

Vince reacted first. He swiveled the gun and pointed it toward the strange being. Saul did the same. Adam lunged at Vince, taking him down to the ground. Vince's gun discharged into the air, but Adam got his hands on him and directed a blazing heat flare into Vince's side. Vince grunted and went still. Seeing Vince was unconscious, Adam turned just in time to see Saul step back, the weapon still trained on the visitor. He fired two shots that deflected off the creature. The being approached Saul, who tried to run, but tripped on a branch and fell backwards. As the being reached him, Saul screamed and scrambled back, but the being touched him, and Saul jerked and went limp.

Eve didn't move. She stared as the strange creature faced her. Adam got up and kicked Vince's gun away. Ensuring Vince and Saul were no longer a threat, he walked up to the stranger and looked him up and down.

"Where did you find that?" he asked.

The being raised his long arms, grabbed the side of its head, and lifted. The head came off with the sound of Velcro separating, and Tez stood there, looking sweaty with his dark hair askew. "I was going to bring it back with me. I find it funny that this is how they portray us." He held the head under his arm.

Adam shook his head. "Since when did you have time to shop?"

Tez frowned. "What exactly was I supposed to do while I was waiting for you? Watch birds and climb trees?"

Adam walked over and kicked Saul's gun away.

"Um," said Eve, looking pale. "You want to introduce me?"

Adam walked over to her. "Eve Fletcher. Meet my partner, Tez."

Tez nodded. He dropped the head on the ground and kicked off the rest of the costume. Once it was off, he balled it together and picked it up.

"I suppose I should thank you," said Eve.

Tez remained distant. "Thank him." He glanced at Adam.

"How'd you dodge the bullets?" asked Adam. "He aimed right at you."

"I used the ship's deflectors. Set them up so I had a range I could operate within before they could hit me."

"Smart."

"I thought so."

Eve looked between them and pointed. "You two came together?"

"We did," said Tez. He looked at Adam. "You get what we came for?"

A kernel of fear flickered in Adam's chest. "Tez..."

Tez's face dropped. "I'll take that as a no."

Adam could see Eve straighten.

"What's that?" she asked, looking at Adam. "Is this about Royce?"

Adam put a hand on Eve's elbow. The familiar electricity between them flickered, and she pulled back. "Eve..."

"Yes. It's about Royce," said Tez, ignoring Adam. "Your brother. We came here to find him."

"What for?"

"Tez..." Adam stepped forward, intent on speaking to his partner before he could say more.

"Because he's the High Child."

Eve flicked her eyes at Adam. "So, you know my family. And my father."

"Yes. We know," said Tez. "Roma sent us."

"Roma?"

"Your half-sister."

Eve's face flattened. "Why? What does she want with Royce?"

Adam stepped forward. "Tez...stop."

Tez continued. "She's High Leader now. And she wants it to stay that way."

Eve's eyes narrowed, and she swallowed. "Where's my father?"

"Ousted. He was voted out six months ago."

"Is he alive?"

"Yes," said Adam.

"Don't know," said Tez at the same time.

"You don't know he's dead," said Adam sharply.

"And you don't know he's alive. He hasn't been seen in public since his departure."

Eve's jaw jutted forward. "So Roma sent you to kill my brother."

"No, that's not true," said Adam.

"More or less," said Tez.

Adam shot a fiery glare at Tez. "Stop it. We weren't here to kill him and you know it."

Tez glared back. "What do you think Roma was planning to do with the information once she had it? Throw him a 'Welcome to Eudora' party?"

"You're thinking the worst."

"And you...as they say here...are burying your head in the dirt, or sand, or something. You know Roma and what she's capable of."

Eve shut her eyes.

Adam stepped forward. "Eve. Listen."

She opened her eyes. "You knew. All along you knew."

"Let me explain."

Her eyes went dark and before he could answer, she stepped close and slapped him across the face. She was breathing hard. "You told me you knew nothing. That you were only supposed to find Royce. But you knew who I was, who Royce was, who my father was. You knew everything."

He shook his head, feeling his whole body deflate. "You don't understand."

"I understand." She blinked watery eyes, and Adam's heart thumped. "You lied to me. Again."

"Eve—"

"Would you have killed him if you'd found him?"

"No."

She shook her head. "You're lying again."

"No, I'm not."

"I was wrong about you."

He tried to keep up. He wanted to say more, to explain, but the words wouldn't form. "Please listen..."

"I told you that you were a good man. But I was wrong. You're a bad man. You always were, weren't you?"

Adam's heart sank. The words were like daggers, maybe because he knew they were true. He set his jaw but didn't answer.

Tez sighed. "As much as I hate to interrupt this lover's tiff, I don't suppose you want to tell us where your brother is?"

Eve looked away from Adam. "Go to hell."

Tez nodded. "We're actually headed to Eudora, but close enough." He looked at Adam. "You ready?" He adjusted his hold on the alien costume. "I want to go home."

Adam caught Eve's eye. She stared back with angry eyes. There was so much he wanted to say, but knew it was pointless. There was only one thing that made sense. "I'm sorry."

She bit her bottom lip. "Go home, Adam." She wiped at a blurry eye as a tear spilled from the other. "And don't ever return."

They stared for a few quiet seconds before Eve turned, walked into the woods, and never looked back.

Chapter Seventeen

EVE WALKED BRISKLY, BRUSHING tears off her cheeks. *Damn*, she thought, *why am I crying*? She rarely cried over men. The last one had been Billy Thorton. He'd broken her heart when she was eighteen. After that, she swore she'd never let a man hurt her again. Yet here she was, crying over someone she'd known for two months, who'd lied to her and wasn't even from this planet. *Hell*, she thought. *I know how to pick 'em.*

Sniffing, she sent out a message to Fred and Ginger and was pleased to hear a bark. A few seconds later, they scurried out of the woods and Eve greeted them, happy to see they were okay.

As she neared the cabin, smoke drifted into the air, and she saw the flicker of colored lights. Wiping her eyes and nose with her shirt, she picked up her pace, and the dogs followed. As she got closer, a fire truck and police cars came into view. Firefighters were hosing down the cabin. Luckily, because of the misty weather, none of the surrounding trees had been affected.

"Eve!"

She turned and saw Tony in the pebbled driveway. He ran up to her. "Are you okay? We were just about to search the area." He saw her neck. "Jesus. What happened?" He looked down at the dogs, who jumped up on his ankles.

Eve touched her swollen skin. "I'm fine. So are Fred and Ginger." Her voice was still rough. "How'd you find me?"

"Dixie. She called. Said Adam showed at the hospital. He took her friend Daisy's car and came here." He looked behind her. "Where is he?"

Eve wasn't sure what to say. "He's gone."

"Gone? Gone where? What about Vince?" He looked at the cabin. "What happened to your neck? What went on here?"

Eve blinked. The day's events and its emotional toll were catching up to her. "Vince was here. He wanted me to sign papers. Apparently Benny left the bar to me. But Vince needs money and wants the bar. Only he didn't get it. So he wanted me to sign the bar over to him, and then he was going to burn the cabin down with me in it."

Tony rubbed a hand through his hair. "Shit. Did he do that to your neck?"

"Yes." She swallowed and her throat hurt. "I wouldn't sign, but I got away and ran into the woods. Vince caught up. He threatened my family, and I lost it. That's when he choked me." She considered how much to say. "He and his friend Saul were going to kill me but..."

"But what?"

Eve felt the emotion return, but she pushed it back. "Adam showed up. He took down both of them and I ran."

Tony stared at her as if she'd told him she'd stopped to pet the squirrels on her return. "Adam stopped Vince and his friend?"

"Yes. They're unconscious in the woods." She pointed. "That way."

"They armed?"

"Yes, but we kicked their guns into the brush."

He flagged down a nearby officer, who was also on the scene. "Henderson. Grab Billings. Check out the woods. Two men down, but use caution. Vincent Bonelli and Saul Trenton. Bring them in."

The two patrolmen jogged into the woods. Tony turned back toward Eve. "And Adam's gone?"

Eve nodded. "He didn't want to deal with the police."

Tony rubbed his eyes and sighed. "Eve, if you knew how many questions I have right now."

Eve got to the point. "Are you going to arrest me?"

Tony dropped his hand. "Of course not. There's been some developments. Benny was a smart man. We found a hidden camera in his office. It was triggered during the altercation. We got the whole thing on film. Vince and Saul killed him."

The tension in Eve's shoulders vanished. She felt like she'd dropped anchors of weight. Another swell of emotion threatened to emerge when she thought of Benny. All she could do was nod.

"Another thing," said Tony. "Vince is mixed up with the mob. He's racked up a hundred grand in debt. It's no wonder he was desperate to get the bar. It was his only way out."

Eve tried to shake off her sadness. "God. He killed his father for money." She rubbed her arms. "I hate this. Benny didn't deserve that."

"Vince was right, though. I talked to Benny's attorney. Benny left the Juke Joint to you. You're officially a bar owner."

"I didn't want the bar."

"Too bad. Looks like you got it. There's one thing, though. Whoever Vince owes money to may not go away so easy. That's a lot of change. If they think you were mixed up with Vince, I wouldn't put it past them to come after you to pay the debt."

Eve shut her eyes. "Great."

"I know." He paused. "Listen. I know you've been through a lot, but we need to talk. I need to get your statement. And I need to talk to Adam. Plus, I know one of those cars is Vince's, and the other belongs to Dixie's friend, but whose car is this?" He pointed at the white Cadillac.

Eve almost laughed from exhaustion. "It's Mike's."

"Who?"

Eve groaned. "I get it, Tony. You have a load of questions and I'm happy to answer all of them. But right now, I need to rest. I want to see Dixie. Make sure she's okay."

"They're springing her today. Should be home soon."

Eve nodded and wiped a watery eye. "Good. Can I get a reprieve? I promise. Tomorrow I'll show up at the station and let you know what I know."

Tony paused. "That's completely against regulation."

"Is that a yes or a no?"

"Where's Paul Newman? I need to talk to him, too."

Eve's chest constricted. "I don't know. He disappeared into the woods. If he shows, though, I'll let him know you want to talk to him."

"You be careful with him. I couldn't find any history on that guy. Something's up with him and I don't like it. He's hiding something."

Eve smiled softly. "Don't worry. He and I are done." She crossed her arms and looked away.

Tony reached out but didn't touch her. "You okay? If he hurt you, I'll kick his ass."

"I just want to go home."

"I think you should go to the hospital. Get your neck, and everything else, checked out."

"I'm fine. I just need to clean up and get some rest. I don't need a hospital."

Tony hesitated. "This is against my better judgment." Another patrol car had pulled up, and an officer stepped out. Tony glanced over. "Pemberton?" Tony waved, and the man approached. "I want you to take Miss Fletcher home. Make sure she gets there safely. Then park outside her apartment building and keep an eye on her until you're relieved. You got that?"

"Is that necessary?" asked Eve.

"Until we get this thing resolved and I know you're not in danger, then yes, it's necessary. And if you want to go home right now, then it's a requirement." He shot a finger at her. "But first thing tomorrow, I want you to see a doctor, and once he clears you, then you are at the precinct and we are going to talk. You got it?"

Eve held up a hand. "I got it." She glanced at the car. "What about Mike's car?"

"Consider it in custody right now. This Mike, and I'm afraid to ask who he is, will get it back eventually."

"He's a friend of Dixie's."

"Enough said. Dixie's friends are running out of cars." He shot out a thumb. "Pemberton. Take her home, please."

"Sure thing, sergeant." He stepped back. "Ma'am?"

The thought of going home, taking a hot shower, and sleeping for several hours almost made Eve collapse in gratitude. "Thanks, Tony."

He nodded. "Get out of here."

She smiled and headed toward the car.

· · • • · • • · ·

Ninety minutes later, Eve opened her front door. The dogs ran in and Officer Pemberton checked her apartment. Louis, Benny's cat, came out from the shadows, and Eve squatted to rub his neck. Dixie must have brought the cat over while Eve was gone. Confirming it was safe, Pemberton left to sit in his patrol car on the street. Eve had grabbed her things from Mike's car before leaving and had called Dixie on her way home. Dixie was thrilled to hear from her. She was in the process of being discharged and said she would be home soon. She insisted on seeing Eve, and Eve agreed to stop by once she got cleaned up.

Sitting on the couch, she watched Fred eat some of the dry food left in his bowl. Her thoughts turned to Adam. Had he left with his friend? Was he now a thousand miles away, already planning his next assignment? Berating herself for thinking or even caring about him, she stood and headed into the bathroom. Turning the water to as hot as she could stand it, she threw her clothes on the floor and stepped under the spray.

An hour later, clean, her hair dry, and in fresh clothes, Eve knocked on Dixie's door. She hoped her friend was home from the hospital because if she wasn't, Eve was going to collapse into bed. It had been a long few days and sleeping in her own room beckoned her.

The door opened, and Dixie greeted her in a purple feathered robe. Her make-up was on, but it only partially covered her black eye, and she wore a jaw length, bob-style blonde wig. Seeing Eve, her eyes filled, and she threw out her arms, pulling Eve into them.

"Evie, honey. It's so good to see you."

Eve hugged her back while feathers tickled her nose. She felt Dixie tense and pulled back. "Are you okay, Dix?"

Dixie let go and waved her off. "Just a few bruised ribs. Nothing a little vodka tonic won't fix." She fluffed her hair. "Come in, honey. Tell me everything."

Dixie ushered Eve in, and Eve sat on the couch. Eve was a little sore herself after her scuffle with Vince, and she moved slowly. Her throat still hurt, too. Without thinking, she touched her bruised neck.

Dixie gasped. "Oh, sweetie. What happened to you?" She touched Eve's swollen skin. "Looks like you could use a little vodka yourself."

Dixie straightened and moved through the living room into the kitchen, walking with ease, as if two mobsters had never attacked her.

"How do you do it, Dix?" asked Eve. "You just got out the hospital and you look as fresh as a daisy."

Dixie added vodka to two glasses and brought them into the room. She set them on the coffee table. Frowning, she said, "Oh, honey. Don't use that name around me. That Daisy. Do you know what she did? She gave her number to my new beau, Burke. Can you believe that? She can be such a bitch sometimes."

"She's the one who let Adam use her car?"

Dixie's face fell. "Well, I guess she did. But only after I threatened her."

Eve eyed the snow globe on the shelf. "Is this beau the man that gave you that?" She pointed toward the gift.

"Yes, it is." Dixie smiled. "Isn't he sweet? Most men give me gifts that are best kept in the bedroom, but not my Burke."

"I don't remember you telling me about him. When did you meet him?"

Dixie shook her head. "Oh no, you don't. We can talk about my fella later. Right now, I want to hear about you. What happened to your neck? What about Vinny? Where's Adam? Are Fred and Ginger all right?" She sat and took a sip of her drink.

Eve picked up her drink and held it, not even sure where to begin.

"Is it that bad? You look like you lost your best friend." She patted Eve on the knee. "Tell Dixie all about it."

The kind touch stirred Eve's emotions all over again and tears filled her eyes.

"Oh, sugar." Dixie grabbed a tissue from a side table. "Here."

Eve took it. "I'm fine." She dabbed her eyes.

"That's what they all say, honey."

Eve made a sad laugh.

"This is about Adam, isn't it?" Her eyes softened. "He's a special one, isn't he?"

Eve shook her head. "No. He's a liar."

Dixie frowned. "Are you sure we're not talking about Vince?"

"No. Vince wanted money. He killed Benny to pay off his debts. But at least he didn't lie about it."

"You think murder is more acceptable?"

"Of course not. Vince sunk to the lowest possible level. He deserves to rot in jail."

"Agreed. Jail is too good for him."

Eve sniffed and wiped her nose with the tissue.

"Take a sip of your drink, sweetie. You need it."

Eve did as she asked. The alcohol warmed her throat and helped take the edge off.

"So where is Adam?" asked Dixie. "Is he gone?"

Eve recalled her last words to him. "Yes. He left."

"That's too bad. He was so pretty."

"Dixie..."

"Sorry, but you know me. I say what I think. So I have to ask, and don't hate me, but haven't you ever lied before?"

Eve looked at her friend. "Of course I have. But this is different. There are certain things I can excuse, but not this."

"What could be so bad?"

Eve wished she could explain. "He wanted something from me. That's why he met me. All he wanted was to find my brother."

Dixie squinted. "Your brother? Royce? Whatever for?"

Eve took another drink and put her glass down. "It's a long story. Let's just say that Adam was hired to find Royce, and he used me to do it. And when I called him on it, I gave him the chance to explain himself, and he lied again. His intentions were far worse than he ever let on."

Dixie's jaw dropped. "What is he? Some sort of assassin?" She put a hand on Eve's elbow. "Wait. No. He's a government agent. Is that it? Oh, my, honey." She fanned herself. "How romantic."

Eve rolled her eyes. "Romantic? That's not what I'd call it. And he's not working for any..." She stopped herself when she considered what she was about to say. "He's not FBI, or CIA, or anything like that. This isn't a romance novel."

"Well, honey, still, it's intriguing. Don't you think? I mean, don't you want to know more?"

"He's a liar, Dix. I can't trust him to tell me anything."

Dixie looked off. "What if he's a double agent?" She glanced back. "What if he has to lie to keep you safe?"

Eve stared at her friend as if she'd told her that her next vacation would be to the moon. "What's in that drink? Did you add something extra that I need to hide from Tony?"

Dixie took another sip. "Sweetie. You know me. I like to see the good in things, not the bad. I saw the way he acted when he came to the hospital. That man was genuinely afraid for you. That look told me everything. And I see you now. You miss him. And you never miss men. I may have my shortcomings, and I'm not the smartest girl in the world, but I know love when I see it."

Eve stood. "Love?" She chuckled. "Love?" Eve stammered as she tried to think of what to say. "That's...that's ridiculous. I don't love him."

Dixie raised a brow but didn't answer.

"I mean, come on. I don't know him at all. Yes. There is an attraction. I mean...I find him attractive. And I think he finds me attractive. And the sex was great...actually phenomenal. But that doesn't mean its love. Love is..." She ran a hand through her hair. "Love is...is..."

"You had sex?"

Eve glared at her friend.

Dixie shook her head. "Sorry. We'll get back to that. Love is what?"

"Forget it."

"No. Love is what?"

Eve picked up her glass and took a healthy swallow. Dixie did the same. "Love is infuriating. It's complicated and messy and a pain in the ass, and I want no part of it."

Dixie waited, but when Eve didn't continue, she asked, "And?"

Eve put her glass down with a thud. She straightened and took a deep breath. "And damn it, I can't stop thinking about him." She pushed her hair off her face. "Hell."

Dixie smiled and raised her glass. "Welcome to the fire, honey. It happens to the best of us."

Eve walked to the mantel and leaned against it. "How is this happening? How do I get rid of it?"

"It's about as easy as getting make-up off a drag queen. And that's not easy."

Eve dropped her head. "I don't know what I'm worried about. He's long gone, anyway. I'll never see him again."

"Distance makes the heart grow fonder."

Eve glared again.

"Or so I've heard. It's probably not true." She leaned forward. "So tell me about the sex."

Eve sighed. "Dixie, really?"

"You know me. I want to know details."

Eve flashed back to their encounter in Mike's motel. Just the memory made her face flush and her body heat.

"That good, huh?"

Eve thought about the Binding and assumed it was over, but judging by how she was reacting just by thinking about Adam, it was taking its time to end. She sighed and rubbed her face. She wished she'd never met the man. "Can we talk about something else?"

Dixie sat back. "I'm not so sure that if he walked through that door right now, you wouldn't run into his arms."

Eve groaned. "I can't be with someone I can't trust. He doesn't want me, anyway. He wants to find my brother."

"Nonsense. That man wants you. I'd bet my lingerie on it."

"He just liked the sex."

Dixie finished her drink. "It's more than that. A man doesn't risk his life for sex." She paused. "Well, maybe they do for you. You incite odd behavior in men."

"Isn't that the truth?"

"My point is, he was ready to die for you, wasn't he?"

Eve sucked in a breath. She remembered Vince's gun at Adam's head. She closed her eyes, wishing she could forget. "He did. I'm not saying he isn't courageous. Or protective. Or even kind." She recalled her last words to him and her heart dropped. "But he wanted to hurt Royce." She turned and faced the mantel. A snow globe was in front of her, and she picked it up and shook it. White snow fluttered around a city landscape.

"And where is your brother, sweetie? Maybe with all this going on, you should talk to him. Maybe he can help."

Eve shook the globe again and watched the snow fall. "I can't get in touch with him."

"Why not?"

Eve turned back, still holding the globe. "It's complicated, Dix."

"Why is he so important?"

Thinking of Royce, Eve wanted to cry again. "He..." She shook her head. "I can't explain it. He disappeared. His heart was broken, and the woman who broke it may or may not be alive. And he was sort of in line to inherit something."

"An inheritance? Oh, my. Now this is getting interesting. Doesn't he want to inherit?"

"He tried. It didn't work out."

"Why not?"

"Because he was trying to protect me and Gillian. And everybody else."

"He sounds like a good man."

"The best man I know. Which is why I'll do anything to protect him."

"Is he in danger?" She sat up. "You don't think Adam meant to kill him, do you? Is that why you're so upset?"

Eve put the globe on the coffee table and sat on the floor beside the table. For some reason, the globe comforted her. She shook it again. "I don't suppose there's any reason to deny it. Yes. That's exactly why."

Dixie's eyes rounded. "So, you do think he's an assassin?" She sat with her mouth gaped open, and then chuckled. "Oh, honey. Adam couldn't kill anybody."

A memory of Adam kicking Vince and putting a gun to his head flickered. "You don't know that."

"I suppose it depends on what he's fighting for. Anybody can be pushed to their breaking point. Even you."

Tackling Vince came to mind. She touched her throat. "Why are you on his side?"

"Oh, honey. I'm on your side. I want you to be happy. Maybe there's more to this story. Are you sure you can't contact your brother? He probably could at least give you some advice."

"I can't do that."

She cocked her head. "Do you even know where he is?"

Thinking of her family and all they'd been through made her chest constrict. She looked up with teary eyes. "Yes. I do."

Dixie nodded. She stared at Eve, and Eve looked closer when Dixie's eyes seemed to swirl. Eve squinted. It was almost as if Dixie's eyes had changed color. "You okay, Dix? Maybe you shouldn't drink anymore."

Dixie stood, saying nothing. Her feathered robe fluttered. Eve was about to ask again when she noticed the globe in front of her. It began to glow. She looked back at her friend. "Dixie?"

Dixie turned, her body language changing as her back straightened and her arms dropped. "How about we end all the small talk?"

"Excuse me?"

Dixie dropped the robe. She stood in jeans and a black T-shirt. Then she pulled off her wig to reveal her short, dark hair beneath. She scratched at her scalp, as if annoyed. "Tell me where Royce is."

Chapter Eighteen

EVE SAT IN SHOCK. She couldn't move as she tried to understand what was happening. "Dixie? What's wrong?"

Dixie shook out her hair and threw the wig on the couch. "Your friend's gone away for a bit. But she'll be back. Provided I get what I came for."

Eve stood slowly and stared at the person in front of her. Dixie's mannerisms had vanished. Her voice had deepened, and her posture had changed. Eve's heart hammered. "Who are you?"

The man walked over and picked up the globe. Studying it, he shook it and the snow glowed against his fingers. "My name is Burke." Carrying the globe, he turned and walked into Dixie's bedroom.

Eve was stunned. She followed Dixie, or Burke, or whoever this person was. "Burke? Dixie's boyfriend?" Entering Dixie's room, she watched him put the globe on a shelf, go to the bathroom sink, and wash off Dixie's make-up.

Once his face was clean, he grabbed a towel and patted his skin dry. "Your friend has a creative look, but it's not my style." He threw the towel on the bed. "And yes. I posed as an interested suitor."

Eve squinted. "Who are you?"

"I told you. I'm Burke." He smiled. "I know. You're full of questions." He glanced in a mirror. "Much better. I feel more like myself." He looked back at Eve. "I met Dixie two weeks ago. She was my insurance, in case the first team failed."

Eve couldn't speak.

"Your lover, Adam, and his friend, Tez. Usually, they are a reliable pair, but I guess everyone fails at some point. Lucky for me, I don't let my emotions get in the way." He flicked a feather off his shirt. "So I got close to Dixie. She's your friend and the best way to get to you. Plus, she's vulnerable right now, which makes it easier for me."

"Vulnerable?"

"Her recent father's death, plus your escapades, then she's attacked. Add a little alcohol to the mix, and a new potential boyfriend," He threw out a hand. "And here I am."

"What happened to Dixie?"

"She's still here, but every moment I possess her, the weaker she becomes."

"Possess?"

"Yes. I understand the connotations that has on Earth. I saw your silly movie, *The Exorcist*. Very amusing how you depict the process. All spinning heads, bad skin, and vile language." He grinned. "I promise not to vomit on you. How unproductive."

"You're possessing Dixie?"

"For the time being. Until I get what I want. Then I'll let her go and she'll return. The sooner the better, though, for her sake. It can be very draining on the host. Which is why it's better you don't dawdle."

Eve tried to think. Nothing was making sense. Someone had taken over Dixie? How was it possible?

Burke smiled. "Still trying to wrap your brain around this?" He chuckled. "It must be the human in you. Let me help. I am from Eudora like your father. I have been sent to kill the High Child. When the first team failed to report back, I was sent as insurance. I became Dixie's suitor, which made it easier for me to possess her for a short time to get to you if Adam failed. I have no reservations in killing Dixie if you refuse to give me what I need." He stepped closer. "I don't have the sympathies for you that Adam did. I don't care about you, your family, your father, or your background. All I know is that it's my job to get rid of the High Child, and that's exactly what I plan to do. So tell me where he is. Then I'll release Dixie and go home. It's as simple as that. Refuse me, and I'll leave Dixie a mindless, drooling idiot. She'll be lucky if she can apply lipstick." He crossed his arms. "You said you know where Royce Fletcher is. Tell me where."

Eve felt bile rise in her throat. This man was threatening to kill her best friend and brother. Her mind raced as she tried to consider her options. "How do I know you won't kill Dixie, anyway?"

"You don't. Guess you'll have to take the risk."

"But why? Royce is not on your planet. He can't get there either."

"There's already been one attempt to retrieve him. Why risk another?"

"What the hell is happening on Eudora? Are you all crazy?"

"Nobody likes a threat to power."

"But he's the High Child. It's his rightful place."

He raised a palm. "Talk to the hand." He smiled. "That's one of the amusing gestures I learned from your friend. Now stop stalling and tell me what I want to know."

Eve tried to think. She had one more option. "Dixie? Are you in there? Can you hear me? I need you to fight this man. Push him out."

Burke grinned. "Another false premise. Your movies are dumb. She can't hear you. She doesn't even know this is happening. Once I let her go, provided I do, she won't remember a thing."

Eve grimaced. She considered fleeing, but she couldn't do that to Dixie.

Burke's patience was dwindling. He walked up to Eve, and Eve leaned back. "Don't think I'll stop with your friend. I'll keep going until I get what I want. You understand?"

Fear and anger swirled in Eve. She opened her mouth to speak when there was a knock on the door.

•••••••••

Adam banged harder. He'd been at Eve's apartment a moment ago, but no one had answered. He was breathless. After watching Eve walk away into the woods, her words had reverberated in his mind. She'd thought he was a bad man. Was he? After his upbringing, and all his past assignments, he'd done only what he'd needed to do to keep himself alive and fed. But his job here was not finished, and he planned to complete it. Despite what Eve may think of him or what it would cost him, he had to keep trying.

Tez was gone. Despite Adam's attempts to sway his friend, he'd watched Tez board the ship, start up the engines, and disappear into the sky. Adam felt the weight of being alone on a planet with no friends and no backup. His resources were limited. But he had to find Eve. If he explained everything to her, maybe she would listen. She may hate him forever, but at least his conscience would be clear.

He'd run through the woods, away from the cabin. Tony would be in the area, and Adam needed to avoid that confrontation. He'd made it to the road, flagged down a car, and hitched a ride back into the city. Now he was back, and he wasn't leaving until he got a chance to speak with her.

He pounded one more time on Dixie's door. Something told him Eve was there. If she knew it was him, maybe she was refusing to answer. He raised his hand one more time to knock when the door opened.

Eve poked her head through the crack of the door. Her eyes widened, and she looked pale. "What are you doing here?"

"I need to talk to you."

"You need to leave. Now."

He put a hand on the door. "I need to explain..."

"Please..."

The door flew open, and Eve jumped back.

Adam heard a male voice from inside the room. "By all means, let him in."

Adam's internal alarms triggered. Eve was rigid, and he heard her silent plea to run, but he ignored it. He stepped past her and into the apartment, and the door slammed shut.

Turning, he saw a man. Looking closely, he thought he recognized him. "Dixie?" he asked.

"Dixie's not here right now," said the stranger.

Adam continued to stare and study the man. "Who are you?"

The man shrugged. "We met once. A while back. The name's Burke."

Adam went cold. "Burke? Desmond Burke?"

"The very same."

"You know him?" asked Eve.

"Of course he does. We run in the same circles," said Burke.

"No, we don't," said Adam. He looked at Eve. "We met a while ago at a conference."

"Is that what you want to call it?"

"Who cares what I call it? We both know what it was."

Burke smirked. "As I recall, you left early."

"I had another commitment."

"Too bad that's not the case today." He glanced back at Eve. "Eve and I were getting acquainted. She was just about to tell me where her brother was."

Adam took a breath to steady himself. "What you're doing with Dixie? It's completely unsanctioned. The Council outlawed it years ago."

Burke shrugged. "Maybe they did on Eudora."

"It's not allowed anywhere. You know that. If they find out, they'll bring you before the Council. You'll be exiled."

"If I get what I came for, no one will care. Besides, who's going to tell them? You?"

"I will."

"You have to get back first. And that's uncertain now, isn't it? I take it your partner is gone?"

"I convinced him to stay. He's waiting to hear from me."

"You're a liar. Tez is long gone. He finally gave up on you. Just like everyone else."

His shock fading, Adam grew angry. "Maybe it's time for me to show my true colors."

Burke narrowed his eyes. "Your true colors have been visible since day one. You're a coward and a failure. Maybe Roma will see that now." He glanced at Eve. "Did your boyfriend tell you he's our High Leader's favorite errand boy? Rumor is they're a thing."

Adam straightened. "That's a lie."

"Is it? I've seen the way she looks at you. You sure you've never reciprocated?"

Adam set his jaw. "I've never been involved with her and never plan to be. She's my boss. That's as far as it goes."

Burke studied him. "Maybe you're a better liar than I think you are." He winked at Eve. "What do you think, sugar?" He mimicked Dixie's voice.

Eve stepped forward. "I don't trust either of you. As far as I'm concerned, you're both liars and cowards."

Burke raised a brow. "Oooh. Looks like I hit a nerve." He looked at Adam. "I think your girlfriend is getting angry."

"Leave her alone. Leave Dixie alone," said Adam. "Go home and kiss Roma's ring, or should I say ass. It's what you do best."

Burke went still. After a pause, his rigid shoulders relaxed. "I'm bored. Let's get to the point." He faced Eve. "Tell me where your brother is."

"Don't, Eve," said Adam. He stepped in between Eve and Burke.

"What's the problem?" asked Burke. "You want him too. Why don't we combine our efforts and bring him in together? We'll go back as heroes. You'll never want for another day in your life."

Adam held his ground. "I can't let you take him. Not like this." He looked around the room, searching, until he laid eyes on the snow globe on the end table beside the couch.

Burke noticed and picked it up. "Is this what you're looking for?"

Eve stepped around Adam. "What is that? It keeps glowing." She looked at Adam. "He's carrying it with him."

"It's his conduit to his ship. It allows him to connect to Dixie and maintain his energetic balance. He wouldn't be able to do this without it."

"My god," said Eve, staring at the globe. She thought back to stormy seas and a rickety pier when she and her sister had been at their uncle's mercy. Her injured brother-in-law, holding a glowing pipe, had confronted her uncle with unexpected strength. "I've seen this before."

Adam frowned. "What? When?"

"I'll explain later."

"Unlikely," said Burke. "At this point, there isn't going to be a later." He squeezed the globe, and the object flared white. "Where is Royce?"

Before Adam could get near Burke, a force hit him square in the chest. He was thrown backward and hit the counter of the bar that led to the kitchen. His side took the brunt, and a barstool toppled over. Adam ended up on his knees and held his ribs. He breathed in deeply and felt a flare of pain rip through his midsection.

"Stop it," said Eve. She kneeled next to Adam.

Burke walked up and placed a hand on Adam's back. Intense heat found his injury and there was an explosion of pain. Adam couldn't hold back a groan of agony. He fell over and brought his knees up to his chest.

"Don't!" Eve dropped next to him. "Adam?"

He sensed Eve's nearness and heard her voice, but couldn't respond. It hurt to breathe.

"Leave him alone," she said to Burke.

"That is completely up to you."

Adam cracked his eyes open and saw Burke reach for him again. He braced for the pain.

"Okay. I'll tell you," said Eve, standing. Burke pulled back. "Just don't hurt him."

"Where is he?"

Eve hesitated, and Burke reached again for Adam.

"I'll take you," she said, her face white. "I'll bring you to him."

Burke smiled. "See. That wasn't so hard."

Chapter Nineteen

"LET'S GO," SAID EVE. She walked to the door.

"He comes with us," said Burke, nudging Adam with his foot.

"What for? He has nothing to do with this."

"I find him to be an effective bargaining tool."

Eve wished Burke was wrong, but as hard as she wanted to hate Adam, she couldn't watch Burke continue to hurt him. The minute she'd seen Adam at the door, her heart had raced and she'd felt a glimmer of hope. Maybe she wasn't alone in all of this. Her mind warned her, though, not to trust him. But if she'd been able to, she would have done exactly what Dixie predicted—leapt into his arms.

She kneeled next to Adam and put her hand on his back. She did her best to send him soothing energy, but she felt his tension and pain. That familiar trickle of warmth returned, though, and spread through her. She leaned close. "Can you stand?"

He was sweating, but he nodded. "Eve," he whispered. "I'm sorry. I've caused you nothing but problems. I should have never come to this planet."

She squeezed his shoulder. "You're right." His energy rippled through her, and she wished she could understand her connection to this man. "But if anyone was going to turn my life upside down, it might as well be you."

He chuckled, but winced. "Do me a favor. Put your hand here." He took her hand and guided it to his ribs. "Focus."

She placed her palm flat against him. "What do you want me to do?"

"Just send me some energy." He sighed. "You make me feel better."

She closed her eyes at his words. What was happening to her? Why couldn't she hate him? Before she could overthink it, she did as he asked. She summoned up a well of peaceful, calm, and healing energy in her belly and sent it up through her chest and down into her hand. She opened her eyes and instantly felt him relax.

His breathing slowed and color returned to his face. "That's better," he said, breathing easier. "Thank you."

"How sweet," said Burke. He walked up and poked Adam's shoulder. "Get up."

Eve sent another wave of energy before taking his arm and helping him sit up. He grunted and his skin paled, but he got his feet under him. Wavering, he grabbed the countertop, still holding his ribs.

Eve put her arm around him to support him. "You good?"

He nodded.

"Let's go," said Burke. He waved a hand at Eve. "Ladies first."

With a reassuring glance at Adam, Eve let him go and walked to the front door and opened it. Adam followed slowly behind, holding his side, and Burke took the rear, holding the globe.

Walking to the stairs, she heard her name and turned. Pemberton, the officer Tony had assigned to watch her, stood in the hallway. She tried not to react.

"Ma'am?" He stood outside her apartment and glanced at the two men behind her.

Eve froze, a smile on her face. "Officer Pemberton. You need something?"

His posture tensed. "I wanted to check in on you. This man," he gestured at Adam, "matches the description of someone my sergeant wanted to talk to."

Eve and Adam exchanged glances. "His name is Adam," said Eve. "But he's been cleared of all wrongdoing. There's no need for questioning."

Pemberton held on to his belt buckle, his hand near his gun. He narrowed his eyes at Burke. "Everything okay, Miss Fletcher?"

Burke said nothing, but Eve saw him reach out and touch Adam's back. Adam sucked in a breath.

Eve held up her hand. "Everything's fine. We were just going for a cup of coffee. It's been a long day."

Pemberton studied the group.

"You all right, sir?" he asked Adam. "You look a little pale."

Adam nodded. "I'm great. Just a little under the weather."

Pemberton nodded, then looked at Burke. "You mind if I ask who your other friend is?"

Eve held her breath. It was taking everything she had to stay calm. "That's my neighbor. His name's Burke."

Burke stared at Pemberton. "Can I help you, officer?" He looked back at Eve. "I'm just so happy to see Eve alive and well. She's been through such an ordeal."

Pemberton didn't answer Burke but glanced back at Eve. "It would be better if you stayed inside for a while, ma'am. You know there are still some risks. My sergeant wants me to keep an eye on you until we get all this figured out."

Eve's heart pounded. "I completely understand, but Tony, your sergeant, worries too much. I'm perfectly fine. Besides," she nodded at Adam and Burke, "I have two strong men with me. I doubt anyone will bother us while we're having coffee."

"We'll be just down the street," said Adam. "I promise. We'll take good care of her."

Pemberton eyed Adam. "We'd still like to talk to you."

Adam nodded. "I'm happy to set up some time to have that conversation, but right now, I'm feeling a bit ill. I'd like to get some fresh air. Why don't you have your people call my people?"

Pemberton paused, looking over the three of them. His eyes traveled to Burke. "What did you say your name was again?"

Burke huffed. "For hell's sake..." He rolled his eyes. "I don't have time for this." Dixie's door slammed open on its own as Pemberton was thrown against the wall. The officer grunted and then fell to the floor and went limp.

Eve rushed forward. "Don't kill him."

"He's fine," said Burke. Eve stepped back as Pemberton slid across the floor and into Dixie's room. The door slammed shut. "He'll wake up in a few hours with a huge headache and a hell of a story to tell." He shoved Adam. "Now let's go."

Eve stared at the closed door, but there was nothing she could do. Pemberton was out of commission, and she and Adam were no match for Burke's abilities. Their only chance was to take the snow globe and smash it, destroying the link between Burke and Dixie, but Burke was holding it close. Eve met Adam's gaze. She would have to take them to Royce.

Glancing down the stairs and holding back tears, she began the walk to the ground floor.

·•••••••·

Eve hailed a taxi and gave the cabbie directions. They sat in the back with Adam in the middle. His side still ached, and he wanted to take Eve's hand as she stared out the window. He wished he knew what she was thinking. He thought about all she'd endured and wondered why he hadn't given this assignment to someone else. If he'd done that, though, then he would have never met her. Conflicted, he closed his eyes, hoping for guidance, but none came. As usual, he was on his own.

The cab drove outside the city, passed a local park, a small suburban neighborhood, and then down a long two-lane road before it turned into a wooded, narrow driveway. A black wrought iron-gate stretched across the asphalt, but it was open. A black metal archway hung above the road. Etched across it were the words "Hillside Angels Cemetery." The car drove under it. The trees grew sparse as an open field came into view. It was dotted with gravestones lined up evenly in rows of thick green grass. Several of them had flowers placed in front of them.

Adam glanced over at Eve, who sat quietly.

"What is this?" asked Burke.

The cab pulled to a stop in front of a row of headstones. Eve opened the door and stepped out. She paid the cabbie as Burke and Adam exited the car.

Adam felt a little stronger and walked over to her. "Where are we?"

"It's a cemetery."

He scowled. "I can see that, but why are we here?"

The cab drove away. "You wanted to see Royce."

Burke approached her. "This better not be a trick."

Eve shook her head. "No tricks."

She started walking, and Adam and Burke followed. They passed two rows of stones and turned toward a large leafy tree in the middle of the grounds. Eve walked beneath it and stopped in front of a headstone.

Adam narrowed his eyes and looked down. Burke did the same.

Adam read the stone. *Royce Fletcher.* And beneath it, *Beloved son and brother.* The dates of his birth and death were listed below. He'd been dead almost six months.

Adam wasn't sure what to say. He saw a tear trickle down Eve's cheek, and she wiped it away.

"Eve?" he asked.

"He's dead?" asked Burke.

Eve nodded. "Yes." More tears fell.

Adam shook his head. "What? How?"

Eve bit her lip and took a deep breath. "It was hard for him..." She paused. "After..." She stopped and composed herself. "There was someone special, and she left, and he blamed himself." She sniffed, dug around in her pocket, and found a tissue. "It's a long story."

"This has to do with the first attempt at retrieval?" asked Burke.

"I'm surprised you don't have all the juicy details." Eve dabbed her nostrils.

"I heard a few things," said Burke, "but nothing that would cause this." He cocked his head at Eve. "How did he die?"

Adam turned on Burke. "Why don't you leave her alone? Her brother's dead. You got what you came for. Give her some peace."

Burke shoved him back, but Adam stayed upright. "I'm done when I'm satisfied with her answers."

Adam stood still, but stared at the globe. If Burke loosened his grip...

"He disappeared for a while," said Eve, "after she left. He bounced from place to place. Never settling anywhere for very long. I'd occasionally get an email from him, telling me he was okay and not to worry. So would my sister and mother. He kept in touch with a friend who would let us know when he'd heard from Royce." She stopped and blew her nose. "Then I got a phone call one day."

Her eyes filled, and she bit her lip. Adam put an arm on her back, but she shrugged him off. She cleared her throat. "He'd been hit by a car."

"A car?" asked Adam. "How?"

Eve blotted her cheeks with the balled up tissue. "He'd stopped to help a stranded motorist. It was a windy road. He was changing a tire. Apparently, the driver had a child who'd strayed onto the road. Another car came around and Royce pulled the child to safety but was hit. He was thrown several feet and died in the ambulance on the way to the hospital."

Fresh tears ran down her face. Adam couldn't help but reach out for her, and this time, she let him. He put his arm around her as she put her head in his neck. "I'm sorry, Eve. I didn't know." He held her close.

She allowed him to comfort her for a few seconds, and then pulled back, wiping her cheeks and sniffing. "I'm okay. I'm fine."

Burke stood there, watching her. "How do I know you're telling the truth?"

Eve smiled softly, her eyes red. "Yes. You caught me. I faked my brother's death and put up a false headstone. Just in case two idiots from another planet came searching for him. Even though it was just as possible that his lover might return as well. Which is all he ever wanted. That makes total sense."

"He was the High Child. You would protect him," said Burke.

Eve shook her head in defiance. "He never cared about being the stupid High Child. All he wanted was to be left alone. If you'd known him, you would have realized that the most important things to Royce were his family and their safety. If that meant staying where he was, then he would have done that. He was doing that."

Burke glanced at the headstone. "This woman he loved. Tell me about her."

"Come on, Burke. You got what you came for," said Adam. "It's time for you to go home."

Eve crossed her arms. "What does it matter? He fell in love, she left, and he was devastated."

"Who was she?" asked Burke.

Eve hesitated. "I don't want to tell you because I don't trust you."

"Eve, dear, you seem to forget who's in charge here." Burke held out the globe. "The sooner you let me know, the better. For Dixie's sake, as well as your own."

"You might go after this woman. Hurt her."

"Why would I do that?"

"Because I know what you're thinking. If she were pregnant with Royce's child, then there would be a new High Child."

Burke smirked. "You're a smart one, aren't you?"

Adam eyed the globe. If Burke was distracted, then he might be able to reach for it.

Burke's face dropped. "Tell me her name."

"Why don't you know? I thought you had Roma's ear?"

"What I know and don't know is not your concern. It may very well be that we already have her in custody, but it doesn't hurt to be sure." He glanced at Adam, who felt a twinge in his side. "So don't make poor Adam suffer. He's got one broken rib. Don't make me break more."

"Don't do anything for me," said Adam. "I deserve what I get." The twinge flared and something popped in his side. An agonizing pain ripped through him. He bit back a scream and fell to his knees.

Eve rushed forward. "Desde," she said, grabbing Adam's shoulder. "Her name's Desde."

Adam tried to breathe. He held his side, grimacing.

Burke studied Eve, his face unreadable. After a moment's pause, his mouth turned up, and a chuckle escaped him. The chuckle grew. "Desde? Are you serious?"

Eve nodded. "That's her name."

Burke's smile disappeared. "Now you're the liar."

Eve's hand was still on Adam's shoulder, and despite his injury, Adam felt something flare within her. Ignoring his pain, he sent her a message and hoped Burke wouldn't pick it up. The man was powerful, but he was distracted, and Adam's connection to Eve would aid in the delivery.

Eve straightened, but her hand remained on Adam. "I'm a liar?" She pursed her lips. "Look at you standing there, acting like you're important, when I suspect you're just one of Roma's lackeys. Sure, you're gifted with ability. You can threaten with the best of them. But in the end, you're no more important than the pillow she sleeps on at night." She squeezed

Adam's shoulder. "You said Roma likes Adam. Does that make you jealous? Maybe you'd rather she liked you instead?"

Burke glowered.

"Maybe you want her attention? But she doesn't see you, does she? Doesn't even notice you exist?"

Adam, confident Eve was picking up his signals, listened and waited. By the feel of it, she was just getting started. Holding his ribs, he waited for an opportunity and prayed it wouldn't backfire.

"You want her, don't you?" asked Eve. "If she Binded with you, you'd be the High Leader's significant other, entitled to all the rights and honors that position must bring. Sad you won't ever have it."

"Shut up," said Burke.

Adam sent her more information.

Eve kept up the onslaught. "You're pathetic. What happened to you as a child? Mommy and Daddy didn't want you either? Did they discard you? Leave you to fight to survive? And you did, didn't you? You did whatever it took to push your way up the ranks to get where you are today. But you crave more. You want it all. You want the power, and the esteem, but you can't seem to get it."

The globe brightened and turned an ugly red. Burke's face looked a similar color.

"What you don't understand is that power requires respect, and you don't have that. You may be able to break ribs, but you don't have the ability to heal them. That's where true power lies."

Burke squeezed the globe. "You stupid bitch. You have no idea who you're talking to."

"Don't I?" asked Eve. "I know a useless, unimportant, arrogant, and wasted use of a life when I see one. You should too, since you look in the mirror every day."

A wave of hatred bubbled out of Burke and popped into the air. Adam winced when he felt it.

Burke took a step forward. "I'm going to kill you, and I'm going to have so much fun doing it."

Eve's chin jutted out, and Adam admired her courage. "That's just what a coward would say. My brother was a better man than you will ever be. And I think you knew that, which is why you wanted to kill him."

Burke growled in his throat and launched himself at Eve. But before he could reach her, Adam rose up and met Burke's advance. His ribs flared, but Adam ignored the pain as he tackled Burke to the ground. They hit with a thud on the hard earth and the impact sucked the breath out of Adam. He reached for the globe, but Burke touched Adam's side with his free hand. Adam cried out, but not before he placed his own hand against Burke and pushed outward. Burke muffled a curse. Adam felt him recoil briefly. They continued to struggle as Adam fought to capture the globe, but Burke got the fingers of one hand around Adam's throat and Adam's airway closed. Adam shoved against Burke, but his fight for oxygen drained him. Burke rolled, getting on top of Adam. Adam kicked out, but with his ribs grinding and his throat closed, he had little leverage. He searched for Eve.

Spots swirled in his vision and he blinked as he tried to hold Burke back. With one last push, he struggled to free himself, but the effort failed. His energy rapidly deteriorating, he sent out one last message to Eve, telling her how he felt, when Burke's eyes suddenly rolled back. He went limp and fell against Adam's chest.

Adam sucked in a giant lungful of air as the grip on his throat released. He coughed through a burning throat. Groaning, but thankfully breathing, he relaxed, went slack against the hard ground and closed his eyes.

Thinking of Eve, he opened his eyes again and looked for her. He saw her beside Royce's grave. Chunks and shards of the snow globe lay in the grass and the tombstone was wet and dripping. She sat quietly for a moment, before standing and coming to Adam's side. She kneeled beside him.

"You okay?" She was breathless.

He groaned. "I'm great." He looked back at the smashed globe. "You got it away from him?"

"I kicked it out of his hand. Smashed it against the stone."

"Nice job."

She took his wrist. "Can you get up?"

He found her hand and took it in his. Her energy instantly flowed through him. "Maybe once I get this two-hundred-pound man off me."

Eve touched Dixie's arm. "Dixie? Can you hear me?" She shook Dixie's shoulder. "She'll be okay, won't she?"

At Eve's words, Adam felt the man on top of him stir. There was movement, and then Dixie's head raised. She blinked her eyes, looked around, and settled her gaze on him.

"Well, sugar," she said, "you're a kinky one, aren't you?"

"Dixie?" asked Eve. "Is it you?"

Dixie attempted to push up, and Adam groaned. "Sorry, hon," she said. "I tend to have that effect on men." She sat up, looked at Adam and then at Eve. Her face fell. "Oh, sweetie. This isn't what it looks like." She rubbed her head and winced. "On second thought, what does this look like? Where am I?" Feeling her hair, her eyes opened wide. "Where's my hair?"

"Dixie," said Eve. "It's me, Eve. Can you stand?"

"Honey, I know it's you. I'm not that crazy. Not yet, at least." She poked Adam in the ribs, and he bit back a moan. "You better not be cheating on my Evie. Especially with me. She loves you, you know."

"Okay, Dix," said Eve. "Come on. Let me help you." Eve got her arm under her friend and assisted Dixie as they both stood.

A chill pulsed through Adam. Did Eve love him? Eve avoided his gaze as he tried to sit up, but his ribs protested.

Eve helped a shaky Dixie to a nearby bench and sat her down. Then she returned to Adam, who tried again to sit up, but the pain was excruciating. "Here," said Eve. "Let me help." She put her hand on Adam's side, and Adam felt immediate relief. It allowed him enough respite to get upright without crying. Eve walked him to the bench and, feeling a little nauseated, he took a seat next to Dixie.

Dixie took a look at him. "Was it as good for you as it was for me?"

Adam shook his head. "You have no idea."

"Judging by how you look, sugar, I didn't disappoint."

Adam couldn't help but smile. "You never do, Dix."

Dixie rubbed her temples. "Eve, honey, would I be mortified if I looked into a mirror right now?"

Eve patted Dixie's knee. "I'd say it's best to wait."

Dixie sighed. "It must have been a hell of a party. Sad I can't remember it." She blinked tired eyes at Eve. "Why is that always the case?"

Eve smiled softly. "Don't worry about it."

Dixie nodded and stared off, still in a partial daze.

"How are you?" asked Adam to Eve.

Eve regarded him, but something shifted in her and she stood. "I'm fine." She pulled out her cell. "I'll call a cab. We should check on Pemberton."

Dixie shook her head and rubbed her scalp. "I hate not having my hair."

Chapter Twenty

ONCE BACK AT THE apartment complex, they'd found Pemberton still on the floor at Dixie's. Rousing him, they'd helped him up and found an ice pack for his head.

Eve and Adam explained how they'd returned from their coffee to find him collapsed. They had no explanation as to why he was at Dixie's or how he'd gotten inside.

The confused officer had rubbed his head, looking lost.

Dixie had been prepared before their arrival that Pemberton would know her as Burke, and she handled his doubtful looks with ease. Despite her own confusion, she played along, explaining that she was only preparing for an upcoming role in a musical theater production, and she apologized if she'd come across as ill-mannered.

She'd made the man tea, given him some aspirin, and before he'd left, had made him promise to come see her sing at the nightclub, his wife included. The man had left smiling and reminding Eve again to stay close to home and telling Adam that Tony would want to talk to him. Adam made no argument.

After he left, Eve put an exhausted Dixie to bed, ensuring she would do her best to answer her friend's questions after she rested. Dixie had argued, but had fallen asleep within minutes.

Leaving the bedroom, Eve shut the door behind her.

"How is she?" asked Adam.

Eve rubbed her stiff neck. "She's okay." She walked into the living area. "She won't have any lasting effects from this, will she? Burke can't come back, right?"

Adam held his ribs, still looking pale. "No. He can't come back. A connection like that takes time to create. The snow globe is smashed along with his connection to her. Plus, he'll be just as exhausted from the experience. He got what he came for anyway, so why return?"

Eve nodded. "He wanted to know who the woman was."

"You told him."

"He didn't act convinced. Do you think he'll go after her, too?"

Adam studied her. "You worried he will?"

Eve shrugged. She sat on the couch and rubbed the bridge of her nose. "I don't know. I'm so worn out, I don't know what to think."

He walked over to stand beside her. "Well, there's not much you can do about it either way. Whoever this woman is will have to take care of herself. She's not on this planet, anyway."

Eve sighed. "I just don't want to endanger anyone. Royce..."

Adam sat beside her with a groan. "You are not responsible. There's nothing you did or said to put anyone in danger, other than this Desde." He paused. "Which, judging by your demeanor, is not the woman he loves."

Eve tried to think. Adam's nearness was affecting her, and she wanted to pull back but didn't do it. "I don't want to talk about it."

He nodded and shifted on the couch, wincing. "I understand. You don't trust me either. I don't blame you."

"Why are you even here? Aren't you supposed to be a million miles away by now?"

He cleared his throat. "Well, let's just say I couldn't leave things the way they were."

"Why not?"

He looked at her with sad eyes, and Eve's heart, despite her wishes, thumped harder. "Because..." he played with a feathery pillow on the couch. "I couldn't leave you. Not that way. I didn't want you to think..."

Eve's anger flared, and she used it to combat her attraction to him. "Think what? That you were a liar? When you were? That you didn't want Royce the way Burke did?"

"Eve...listen."

Eve stood. "No. You listen. I'm done. I can't do this anymore."

Holding his side, Adam pushed off the couch and slowly stood. "Let me explain..."

"I don't need to hear it. Besides, any explanation from you means nothing. If your friend Tez is gone, then you should have gone with him." She crossed her arms. "Or is he still here? Waiting to hear from you to see if you've bedded the lonely Eve again and found her brother? Well, nice job. You know where Royce is now. You can report back the good news. My brother is dead."

Tears sprang to her eyes, and she turned away, not wanting to cry. She had so many mixed emotions, she didn't know what she felt. She just wanted Adam to leave so she could get back to her life.

"I don't mean to upset you, but I have to ask. Why didn't you tell me he was dead when you learned who I was?"

She sniffed and rubbed her neck. "In hindsight, I should have. Then all of this could have been avoided. But I was angry. What business was it of yours? What right did you have to go home and high-five everyone, taking credit for his demise with others like Burke? It sickened me. It still does. I hate this, and I hate you. And I miss my brother." Her throat constricted, and she bit her lip.

There was a tug on her arm, and she pulled away, but the tug grew. She turned to see Adam standing beside her. She backed up, but he followed, until she bumped up against Dixie's door.

Adam stood over her, and she resisted the desire to touch him.

"Listen to me," he said. He was breathless, and Eve suspected he was feeling similar emotions. "I know you're mad at me. I've given you every reason to hate me. But Burke and I are not the same. I would have never hurt Royce."

"You would have just directed men like Burke to find him."

He held up a finger. "That's not true. I..."

"You what?"

He grimaced. "Damn it, Eve. I didn't come here to hurt anyone. I simply had a job to do, like anyone else. I wasn't sure who Royce was and certainly didn't know you. It was a chance for me. An opportunity to leave my planet and come here. It was the biggest assignment of my life, and Roma entrusted it to me."

Eve pushed back against the door. "Apparently, there's a reason for that. Maybe Burke's right. You messing with Roma, too, to get what you want?"

His eyes widened. "Stop it. That's not true and never will be. I'm not interested in Roma."

"Why not? She sounds like someone who could bring you everything you want."

He laid his hand against the door beside her head. "She's not." He hesitated. "You are."

Her heart swelled, and she fought her emotions. "Don't be ridiculous."

"I'm not, and I suspect you feel the same way."

She shook her head. "I don't."

He loomed over her. "Yes, you do. And you hate it. Hate that you love me."

She laughed. "Love you? I don't love you."

He nodded. "I think you do, because, like it or not, you and I have a connection. Our feelings mirror each other's. And I know how you feel about me, because I know how I feel about you." He leaned closer, his lips almost touching hers. "I love you, Eve. I love you so much it hurts, worse than these damn ribs."

Eve couldn't think. She wanted to run, but her heart wouldn't let her. It was like some tendril of electricity had reached out from her chest, wrapped around Adam, and was pulling tighter. Staring at his lips, her desire grew greater than her doubt, and before she could stop herself, she shifted against him and lifted her lips to his. He responded without hesitation and pulled her into his arms. His mouth opened over hers, and she kissed him hungrily. His rib injury did little to prevent him from wrapping his arms around her waist. He kissed her like a starving man with his first taste of food. Eve couldn't get close enough to him. She moved her fingers into his hair and felt his hands slide down her back and cup her backside. She ground against him. Breathless, he kissed her harder, moaning as he moved his hands lower and picked her up. Eve wrapped her legs around him, and he showed no sign of pain. She wondered if their shared attraction was somehow healing his ribs, because the more they touched, the less discomfort he seemed to be in.

Holding her, he pulled back from the door. Fumbling, he found the knob and opened it. Still kissing him, Eve let him carry her outside. Using his foot, he closed Dixie's door behind him. He got Eve to her apartment, fumbled again with the knob, and, cursing against her lips, got her inside. The dogs ran to greet them, but Eve barely heard them. Adam let go of her and she slid down his legs, feeling every inch of him against her. By now, the fire burned so hot that Eve could barely breathe. Standing again, Eve pushed him backwards into her room. He bumped into a wall, and she became the aggressor. Sliding her hands down his chest, she moved her lips to his neck, tasting and sucking his skin. She lifted his shirt and pulled it off, revealing his muscular chest. The butterflies in her belly danced and fluttered. All her attempts to hate him vanished. Exploring his chest, she grazed her fingertips over his injury. He stilled, and she lowered herself to kiss the area where his ribs were bruised. He groaned with delight. She continued to tease him with her lips until she felt his hands in her hair. He gently guided her back to his lips, where he captured her mouth with his again. They parted briefly when he found the edge of her shirt and pulled it up and off of her. The kiss resumed, and wrapping her arms around his neck, she let him tease her tongue with his own. The fire in her belly flamed brighter, and she felt the burn travel down into her toes.

Pushing her back from the wall, Adam guided her until the edge of the bed bumped against her legs and she fell back against it. He stared at her briefly, as if taking her in and relishing her, then he joined her on the bed, kneeling over her and slowly lowering himself against her.

She put her hand behind his neck and pulled him in. For a moment, she felt a twinge of guilt. Was it right to be bedding a man who'd lied to her and posed a threat to her family? For a moment, it seemed so, but then his lips descended over hers, his fingers found her breast, and all her worries vanished.

·········

Adam blinked. There was a dull light in the room, and he opened his eyes fully. He saw the empty pillow beside him and pushed the sheets back. Sitting up, he rubbed his eyes, seeing his discarded jeans on the floor and Eve's beside them.

He wondered what time it was. He and Eve had spent an active afternoon together and fallen asleep in each other's arms. Thinking of her, his body reacted. Eve had muttered the word "Binding" days ago, although it felt like years, and now he had to admit that she was probably right. Female Red-Lines had a powerful sexual urge when they found a mate, and apparently that urge was no different for the mate.

Leaning over, he picked up his jeans and slid them on, then left the bedroom.

Entering the kitchen, the dogs trotted over and sniffed his feet. Patting their heads, he saw the half-filled coffeepot, but no Eve. Poking his head into the living area, he saw only Louis, the cat, sleeping on the sofa, but an envelope on the coffee table caught his eye. Something cold twisted in his chest as he walked over and picked it up. *Adam* was written in Eve's scrawl on the front. Holding his breath, he opened it.

Adam,

I'll make this short and sweet.

You're right. I'm falling for you, and we are in the middle of a full fledge Binding. But there's a problem. We can't Bind. I know you will argue, which is why I've left this letter.

Truthfully, I believe you're only in love with the idea of me. And I'm in love with the idea of you. But none of it's true. Binding or not, it will fade. Then you'll want to go home. You'll miss your life, your planet. I'll get restless and resent you. It's better if we end this now.

I know none of this makes sense, but too much has happened. I still don't know if I can trust you. You could still be a threat. I don't know if I'll wake up one morning and you'll be gone. Or if you still have ulterior motives. Maybe you want to know who Royce's lover is. Maybe you're still using me. These are questions I'll never know the answers to.

This is why it's better you and I part ways now, while we're still...less Binded. There's no future for us. I'll never sleep well at night wondering if you'll betray me again.

I'm asking you to leave now before I return. I'm not good at messy goodbyes. So please get your things and go. I think once we put some distance between us, you'll come to see that this is for the best.

If you truly care for me, you will understand and honor my wishes.

Eve

Adam stood like a limbless tree in the room. His heart thumping, he crumpled the letter in his hand. He didn't know whether to be angry or heartbroken. There were so many things left unsaid, and she'd given him no opportunity to explain.

Several scenarios played through his mind. Go find her? Wait for her to return? The thought of never seeing her again was almost too difficult to comprehend. But the last line of her letter got to him. Did he love her enough to let her go?

Tossing the balled-up letter next to Louis, he returned to the bedroom, finished dressing, gathered his things, and headed toward the front door. Looking back for a moment, he swallowed, remembering their night together. Thinking of her soft smile and their magnetic connection, he almost changed his mind. But she'd asked him to honor her wishes, and if she needed the space, he would give it to her. Maybe in the not-so-distant future, she might change her mind and give him the chance he so desperately wanted. But until that time, he would have to wait. Shaking his head and with one last sigh, he opened the door and left.

· · · · ●· ● ● · · ·

Eve sipped her coffee and stared into space. Rain drops dotted Dixie's window, but Eve barely noticed. But as thunder rumbled, the rain picked up and turned into a downpour. Eve couldn't help but think of Adam. She'd thrown him out into a downpour, with nothing but a letter to say goodbye. Trying not to think about it, she closed her eyes and rubbed her temples.

"You want some more coffee, sugar?" Dixie walked over with the coffeepot. She looked at Eve's cup. "You've barely touched the cup I gave you." She put the pot down and sat next to Eve, putting her elbows on the table. "You ready to talk about it?"

Eve played with the rim of her mug. "Talk about what?"

Dixie pushed Eve's cup away. "Don't play dumb with me, honey. You show up on my doorstep waking me from a perfectly sound beauty sleep, which I need, by the way, in your robe, looking like you're about to cry, and there's nothing to talk about? That's like telling me the dinosaur in the room is only Freddie trying to look tough." She reached over and patted Eve's wrist. "Now tell me."

Eve sniffed. "I broke it off with Adam. I left a letter for him in my apartment this morning telling him to be gone when I got back."

Dixie sighed. "Oh, sugar. I'm sorry."

Eve cleared her throat. "It's no big deal."

Dixie smiled softly. "I can tell. You're not bothered at all." She grabbed a tissue and handed it to Eve. "Wipe your nose, dear. You must have allergies."

Eve shot a sideways glance at her friend and took the tissue. "I'm fine. He was just a temporary distraction."

"Uh-huh."

"I mean, we aren't suited for each other."

"Not in the least."

"I can't trust him."

"Certainly not."

"He lied to me."

"That bastard."

Eve didn't know if it was her emotional turmoil, her fatigue, or just the craziness of her particular situation, but she chuckled. Dixie smiled and chuckled, too, and before Eve knew it, the chuckle became laughter. Dixie joined her until they were both crying from humor instead of sadness.

Eve dabbed her eyes, grateful for the respite. "Oh, Dixie." She giggled again. "I'm such a mess."

Dixie grinned. "But you're a cute mess. Most girls can't say that."

Eve smiled. "You're lying through your teeth, but thank you."

Dixie rested her chin in her palm. "You already know what I think about all this. I know you have your reasons and I'll respect your decision, but honey, I'll say it one more time, then I'll shut my mouth. I think he's the one."

Eve shook her head. "It doesn't matter."

"Don't you think it should? Whatever is making you push him away, can't it be resolved?"

"I don't think so."

"Why not? How complicated can it be?"

"You'd be surprised."

"You sure? Maybe Dixie can help."

Eve sighed. "Honestly, I just want to talk about something else."

Dixie sat back. "Okay, we can do that. What do you want to talk about?"

Eve pondered. "Well, I guess I'm a bar owner."

Dixie's eyes brightened. "Really? Benny's? He left it to you?"

Eve nodded. "Apparently so." Eve made a mental note to contact Benny's attorney. The man had left a voicemail on her machine and Eve had heard it that morning. "Although what am I going to do with a bar?"

Dixie leaned forward with her arms outstretched. "Why, run it, of course. You'd be a great owner. You'll have that place hopping in no time."

Eve shrugged. "I don't know. It feels so...permanent."

"What's wrong with that?"

"I guess I just like the feeling of being able to pick up and go when I want to. I've always been more of a floater instead of a sinker."

"Sinker?" Dixie thought about it. "That's one way to put it. But it doesn't have to be that way. You can try it. If you don't like it, sell it. Take the money and run, sugar."

"That's another thing. The money."

"What about it? Is the bar in the red?"

"I have no idea. But Vince is."

"Vince? What does he have to do with this? Isn't he in jail?"

"He is now. But he's got a hundred grand in gambling debt to the mob, and they want their money. And they're not going to get it with Vince in jail. Tony warned me to be careful."

Dixie's eyes widened. "Careful? What for? You didn't do anything. It's not your debt to pay."

Eve shifted in her seat. "You're right, but the mob may not see it that way. Vince and I have a history."

"So do you and Tony, but you don't see his superiors blaming you for his inability to catch the flasher in the neighborhood."

"There's a flasher in the neighborhood?"

"Fun, isn't it? I keep hoping to run into him. See what all the fuss is about."

Eve held her head. "Maybe you're right. I'm probably overthinking it. Surely they can get their money elsewhere."

"Of course. Men like that know how to get what they want."

Eve stared at her friend, who was adjusting her hair in the reflection of the coffee pot, and realized how true Dixie's words were. If Vince was no longer able to pay his debt, the next logical conclusion was Benny's bar. And Eve was sure Vince would tell anyone who came asking the same thing. He'd probably go so far as to blame Eve. Eve sat back. She didn't voice her fears because Dixie would worry, and her friend had been through enough, but she made a mental to note to talk to Tony. As far as she knew, Pemberton, or Pemberton's replacement, was still parked outside her apartment building, but that would not be a serious deterrent to anyone who might want to get to her.

Satisfied with her appearance, Dixie stood. "Enough talk about men and mobsters, sweetie. How about you and I bite into a scrumptious raspberry danish? I can watch my waistline another day."

Eve's stomach grumbled. She'd had little to eat in the past few days. "Sounds great, Dix."

Chapter Twenty-One

ADAM WALKED DOWN THE quiet alley and kicked an empty soda can. It skittered against the pavement and came to rest next to a large, brown dumpster. Passing the trash receptacle, Adam turned at the smell of rotting food and headed toward the street. Once there, he hooked a left and kept walking. The rainy days had finally given way to sunlight, and Adam was happy for the warmth. It had been three days since he'd left Eve's. Confused and angry, he'd returned to the apartment he'd rented for a few months. His lease was up in four days and he either needed to pay for another month or move out. Short on funds, he knew another month of rent was not an option, so he would have to leave.

He'd attempted to contact Tez several times with no success. Adam was on his own. The credentials he'd used to get the job at Benny's were suspicious at best, and he knew if anyone dug deep enough, they would learn they were false. His success with Benny had resulted from the amount of research that had gone into preparing. He'd studied Benny and the bar and had a thorough plan as to how he would win Benny over. But things were different now, and he still wasn't on level ground. He could barely focus after leaving Eve. Sleep was elusive, as was forming a coherent thought. His body ached, and his head hurt. It was as if losing her was its own disease. He wished he knew the cure. Her letter continued to play in his head, and he wondered if she was right. Was it better to break it off? If Tez were here, would it have been better to return and leave her behind?

The questions hammered him, but in the end, it didn't matter. Eve had made up her mind. She'd made no effort to contact him, and although he knew she cared for him, she wasn't going to let that get in the way. Something was holding her back. Granted, they'd had a rocky start, but he'd thought they'd moved past it. Apparently, that wasn't true.

Adam continued to walk, passing a coffee shop, a retail store, and a restaurant. He was going to have to think of something soon because his options were dwindling. Thinking of Eve, he put his hands in his pockets and kept moving. After a few more minutes, his building came into view. It was a low rent area in the seedier part of town, but his presence attracted little interest and people didn't ask questions. Wanting to avoid the landlord who would ask him about next month's rent, he took the back alley, planning on entering through the emergency exit. He knew if you jimmied it just the right way, it would open. Trash and graffiti littered the narrow passage, and he dodged a few puddles left over from the rain.

At the back door, he turned the creaky knob. Sometimes it opened on its own, but it didn't budge. He searched for the small screwdriver he'd hidden behind a pile of discarded boxes beside the door. Reaching for the tool, he heard footsteps from behind.

Before he could turn to look, something hard came down on his head and his knees buckled. He had enough time to see two men standing over him before he was hit again and collapsed into a pile of boxes.

· · · · · · · · · ·

Eve stepped through the threshold of Benny's bar. The quiet unnerved her. The usual vibrant pace and bustling activity of drunk and disorderly customers was absent. The stage sat in darkness, lonely for a performer to hop up and begin their song. Her argument with Jerry, her conversation with Adam on the roof, and her last moments with Benny played in her head. It was almost too much for her to handle, and she pushed back the emotion that threatened to erupt.

She'd left the attorney's office earlier, where he'd informed her of Benny's wishes and presented her with a key to the bar. It was a melancholy moment. If she could have chosen, she would have wished Benny back in a heartbeat. She missed him. And she would have liked to have asked him about Adam. She wondered what advice he would have given her. Hearing Benny's voice in her head, she realized she already knew. He would have told her to get over whatever was eating at her and go for it. Love didn't grow on trees.

She walked past the empty stage and into the back hall. Benny's office was on the left. Crime scene tape hung from the door frame. Bolstering herself, she walked up and pushed the door in. It swung open, and Eve bit back a sob.

She could still see Benny lying on the floor, blood soaking through his shirt, as she held his hand. She remembered his last words. "I did it all for you." She wondered then if he'd meant leaving the bar to her. She couldn't be sure. Closing her eyes, she took a deep breath and straightened. Now was not the time to fall apart. She had work to do.

Shoving aside the memories, she walked in and sat at Benny's desk. The light was murky from the small window, and she flipped on a desk lamp. Sitting back, she looked around. Benny's office was a mess. He'd always had a chaotic way of organizing things, but combined with the police investigation, it looked like a bulldozer had traveled through. Files were scattered over the desk and floor. Furniture was overturned, paper littered the ground, and a fine layer of dust coated everything. Benny was never one for housekeeping.

Spying a clock on the desk, Eve picked it up. Tony had said that Benny had placed a camera in the office, and Eve wondered where he'd hidden it. She'd never known about it, and she wondered how long he'd been using it. Had he always suspected his son could be dangerous? Had he known Vince was in trouble? Studying the timepiece, she saw nothing unusual about it and put it down.

Realizing the amount of work it was going to take to get this place back up and running, she doubted her decision. The last few days, in her effort to forget about Adam, she'd taken the time to consider her life as a bar owner. Was it something she wanted to do? Did she want the headaches of management? She'd gone back and forth, at one point deciding she would sell the bar and move on, then changing her mind, thinking she was ready to take on a new challenge. The last few days had been tortuous for her. She'd barely slept, and her appetite had disappeared. Her energy levels were so low, she could barely make the effort to go to the bathroom. She wanted to blame her lethargy on the decision she had to make, but she knew it was more than that.

As much as she hated to admit it, she knew Adam was the cause. Their Binding had been well on its way to completion, and she knew from her sister's experience that breaking that energy mid-connection could be detrimental to both Binders. She knew now what her sister had gone through, and it was not fun. Mustering the energy to dress and get herself over to the attorney's office had taken all the energy she'd had. Stepping into Benny's had offered her a momentary respite, but now that she was sitting down and reflecting, she felt the exhaustion return.

She thought about Vince. He was in the county jail, his bond set at a hundred thousand dollars. She thought that was ironic, since that was what he owed his debtors. Playing with a loose leaf of paper, she recalled her conversation with Tony the previous day. The police protection he'd ordered had been rescinded, to Tony's dismay. The department couldn't afford to keep an officer outside her door based on a supposed threat. Tony had asked her to disappear for a while, until he could get more information from his sources, but she had refused. She couldn't hide forever.

Sighing, she picked up an upended trash can and began to go through the papers on Benny's desk. Staring at an old receipt, she thought she heard footsteps. Was someone in the bar?

Standing, she stared through the open door, her heart picking up its pace. "Hello?" she asked. "Somebody there?"

The steps encroached, and two men appeared in the hallway. One was tall and the other slightly shorter. They wore dark suits with colorful ties and both had dark, short, cropped hair and olive skin. A third man was with them, only his head was covered and his hands bound. Before Eve could react, the suited men entered the office and shoved the bound man to the floor, who fell with a grunt.

Eve stood in shock. The taller man spoke.

"Hello, Miss Fletcher." He adjusted his tie. "My name is Sam, and this is my associate, Billy." He nodded to the shorter man. Billy said nothing but maintained a dull stare.

Eve stared at the men, and then at the man on the floor. His energy was familiar, and fear made her belly flip-flop. "Who are you? What do you want?"

Sam walked over and yanked the hood off the fallen man. Eve sucked in a breath when she saw Adam, hair disheveled and face red. He blinked and squinted, but saw her. "Eve?"

She stopped herself from rushing to his side. "Adam."

Sam tossed the hood aside. "Miss Fletcher, my associates and I do not want to take much of your time. We just need some help. You and your friend here have caused us quite a bit of trouble. One of our other associates, I believe you know him, is behind in his payments and he owes us money. He came to you for help but failed to gain your cooperation. Now I know his problems are not your fault, but we also know that your connection to this man is our only way to pay his debt."

Eve gripped a pen on the desk. "I have nothing to do with Vince or his debts."

Sam shrugged. "Nevertheless, you are still involved. Vince knew there was money to be found and now we want you to get it for us."

"I don't have any money," said Eve.

Sam held up a finger. "Oh, but you do." He waved a hand. "You've just become the proud owner of this fine establishment. That sounds like a windfall to me."

"This place belonged to Benny. He is not responsible for his son's debts."

Sam frowned. "I feel for you, Miss Fletcher. Really, I do. But that's not my problem. My boss wants his money, and that's all that matters."

Adam tried to sit up. "Leave her be. Get your money somewhere else."

Sam glanced at Adam and then nodded at Billy, who walked over and kicked Adam in the stomach. Adam made a breathless grunt and rolled to his side. It took everything Eve had not to react.

"When I want your opinion, I'll ask for it." Sam looked back at Eve. "Now, as I was saying, we want our money." Eve started to speak, but he stopped her. "Before you argue with me, let me finish." He traced a finger over a dusty file cabinet. "You can either sell the bar to us, or there is a key."

"A key?" she asked.

"We have some friends in law enforcement. They keep us informed of pertinent facts. Apparently, your policeman friend found a key in this office during his search. It is apparently a safe deposit box key. Despite their investigation, no one has determined what bank this key is from, but there is a lot of curiosity as to what your friend Benito may have kept in the box. I'd like to know myself."

Eve's mind raced. A safe deposit box? She'd used that as a ploy to distract Vincent, but she had no knowledge of one actually existing. She thought back to her conversations with Benny. Had he mentioned one to her?

"So, if you'd prefer that option, you can roll the dice and see what you find."

Eve squinted. "What do you mean?"

He wiped the dust off his fingers. "Pretty simple. Get the key, find the box, and pray there's money in it. If there is, then," he gestured to the air, "this can be all yours. If not, well then, time to sell. And I know an excellent buyer. My boss will buy this place for the tidy sum of one hundred thousand dollars."

"It's worth more than that."

"Maybe to you it is."

Eve tried to think. Adam slowly got to his knees. "What if I say no?" asked Eve.

He smiled and looked at Billy, who grinned back. "My friend Billy here is excellent at persuasion. He can use the most rudimentary equipment to achieve a most satisfying result." He picked up a paperclip. "Something as simple as this can be most effective. Matches, pliers, simple things are so helpful...you get the point."

Eve held her breath. "You'd torture Adam?"

"Him?" Sam shook his head. "No. Not him." He pointed at Eve. "You. Your friend will get to watch while you scream. A few minutes of that and you'll be begging to sell. And he'll be begging you to do it."

Bile rose in the back of her throat, and Eve swallowed it back. She met Adam's gaze and felt his anger. "I think I prefer another option."

"Most do."

She took a deep breath and centered herself. "Where is this key?"

"Evidence locker, at your friend's precinct."

"How do I get it?"

"That's your problem. Not mine."

She widened her eyes. "How am I supposed to get a key out of an evidence locker in the middle of a police station?"

He made a face. "I don't know. Magic? Prayer? Inside help? Maybe your friend Tony would assist for a little cut of the action." He looked her over. "I'm sure you can be just as persuasive as my friend here, only your tools are much prettier to look at." He put his hands in his pockets. "Whatever you decide, you have twenty-four hours."

"Twenty-four hours? How am I supposed to get that key, find the bank, and access the box in twenty-four hours?"

He shrugged. "You can always sell now. I have the papers in the car."

She held up a hand. "No. I'll figure it out."

He smiled. "I'm sure you will." He glanced at Adam. "I'm sure between the two of you, you'll do just fine." He walked to the door, and Billy followed. "We'll be in touch. And please don't run. I don't like to chase people. You disappear, and so does a family member. You understand?"

Eve nodded. "I do."

"Excellent. Have a nice day." He nodded at Billy, and they left.

Adam struggled to pull himself up. She went to his side, untied his hands, and helped him to sit on the couch. He fell back against the cushions with a curse. "How do we keep ending up like this?"

Eve wondered the same thing. "I don't know. It seems we have a dark cloud following us."

He rubbed his belly. "I'm getting tired of being a punching bag."

She stifled the urge to reach out. "Guess you're beginning to regret knowing me."

He raised a brow. "You'd think."

Warmth flooded her, and she inwardly cursed. Just when she thought she was getting back on her feet, she found herself back on shaky ground. She stood from the couch. "You don't have to stay. I can figure this out on my own."

"You know I can't do that. You're worth every bump and bruise. Besides, you heard him. We can't disappear."

"He just wants the money. If I get it to him, he won't care about you."

"You don't know that. He's using me as leverage. And if he thinks that's gone, he'll either come after me again, or someone else you lo—care about."

She wrung her hands and figured he was right. "Once this is over, we still go our separate ways. This doesn't mean we're together."

He raised his palms. "I promise to keep my hands to myself. But feel free to use yours whenever you wish."

"This isn't funny, Adam."

"No, it isn't." He stood, holding his stomach, and faced her. "I promise you this. I won't touch you again unless you ask me to. And if you do, just know that I'll never let you go."

A vivid memory surfaced of his tongue flicking over her belly while his fingers explored her body. Her face flushed. She could never let her guard down around him. "Fine. I accept those terms."

"Good." He was a little flush himself as he looked around the room and then at her. "Now, how do we get that key?"

Chapter Twenty-Two

"BEFORE WE CONSIDER THE key," she said, "maybe we ought to consider the box first. If we can't find that, then there's no point in getting the key."

"Benny never mentioned a box to you? Didn't you tell Vince that you had a key?"

"I did, but it was made up. I used it to buy time. Benny never said anything to me about having a key or a safe deposit box."

"So, who would he mention it to? Does he have a significant other? A wife or girlfriend?"

Eve glanced at the picture on the wall of Benny and his wife, Maggie, on their wedding day. "His wife passed. There's no girlfriend I'm aware of."

"Who was he closest to? And why have a box, other than to protect something?"

Eve rubbed her head. "I don't know."

"Any other kids?"

Eve looked up. "Just me."

"He didn't confide in you?"

"He did, but not about things he didn't want me to worry about. Those things he kept to himself."

"But he would want you to know what to do after his death, wouldn't he? Otherwise, why have it? What did he say before he died? That he did it all for you? What did he mean?"

"I don't know."

"Maybe he died before he could tell you. Or maybe he tried to tell you, but you didn't realize it."

"He didn't tell me anything."

"How do you know? Maybe you missed it."

"I think I would know if he told me about a box."

"What about another way? Did he leave a voicemail, send you a letter?"

Eve began to argue, but stopped. She thought of her apartment. She'd listened to her voicemails and there was nothing from Benny, but there was the large stack of unopened mail on her dining table. Could Benny have mailed her something?

"What?" asked Adam.

She picked up her purse. "Come on. Let's go.

"Where?"

"To my apartment."

· · · · ● · ● · · ·

Twenty minutes later, Eve opened her front door and Adam followed her inside. The dogs ran up to greet her, and she gave them a quick pet before sitting at the dining table. Benny's cat, Louis, rubbed against Adam's leg before disappearing back into Eve's bedroom.

Adam observed the messy table and the pile of unopened letters. "Jeez. When's the last time you checked your mail?"

"I pull out the bills and leave the rest."

He sat down beside her and began checking the envelopes, looking for anything that might be from Benny. He reached for a letter that had fallen on the floor and drew back when something crawled out from under it. A roach scurried across the floor, and Adam jumped out of his seat.

Eve discarded a letter. "What's the matter?"

He pointed at the black bug. "It's a roach." Freddie ran over and sniffed it, and the roach ran under the table. Adam stepped back, and the dog trotted away, uninterested.

Eve narrowed her eyes. "Don't tell me you're scared of it. Don't you have bugs on Eudora?"

"Bugs. Not creatures. I hate those things."

"I don't like them either, but it's not going to hurt you."

"You sure about that? That thing looks like it's from that island in King Kong."

Eve chuckled. "I can't believe you're scared of bugs when you've been chased and attacked by mobsters and aliens."

"If I'd known that thing was in here, I would have never been able to have a relationship with you." He picked up a discarded catalogue.

"I'll keep that in mind. What are you doing with that?"

Adam rolled up the magazine. "I'm going to kill it."

She stood. "No, you're not. Give me that." She took the catalogue and threw it back into the trash pile.

Adam stared in disbelief as she squatted down, put her head below the table, and held out her hand.

"What are you doing?"

Eve moved closer to the insect, and Adam stared in horror as the bug crawled toward her and walked onto her fingers. The blood drained from his face. "I think I'm going to puke."

Eve came out from under the table and stood. "Don't be such a baby. Look. It's harmless." She reached out, and Adam darted back and almost jumped on the couch. He managed to maintain a small amount of composure though and kept his feet on the ground.

"Keep that thing away from me."

With the roach crawling over her fingers, Eve walked to the window. She cracked the pane, put her hand down, and the roach walked off. It took a few steps as it sensed its new surroundings and then flew away.

Adam dropped his jaw. "It flies?" He put his hand on his chest. "Why didn't you tell me that?"

Eve shut the window. "I didn't want you to leap out the window first." She looked outside. "He'll find a new home now." She went to the kitchen sink, washed her hands, returned to the table, and sat. "Now help me go through this pile."

Adam eyed her, trying to assess her level of sanity. After a few seconds, though, his heart rate recovered, and he sat back next to Eve. But he kept a wary eye out for other creatures.

For the next few minutes, they checked every letter, throwing away the junk mail and opening anything that looked of interest.

Opening the last letter, Eve sighed and threw it away. "Nothing from Benny." She sat back in her seat.

Adam was about to throw away another stray retail catalogue when he saw what looked like the corner of an envelope poking out from the side of it. He pulled it out. "Eve, look."

Eve took the letter and read the front. *Spark* was written in tidy letters on the front. There was no postage and no return address. "Oh my god."

"Isn't that what he called you?"

She nodded. "Yes." With shaky fingers, she opened the envelope and pulled out a sheet of paper. Her face paled.

"What is it?"

She showed the paper to him. There was one sentence on it.

Metropolitan National Bank, #423

He dropped his jaw and fell back in his seat. "Oh, hell."

Chapter Twenty-Three

"I can't believe it." She dropped the letter on the table and stared at it. "I wonder when it was sent? Did Benny deliver it before he died, or did someone do it for him?"

"Either way, we now know where the box is. Question is, what next?"

Eve tapped the letter. "We have to open the box. Obviously, there's something there he wants me to have."

"Why be so cryptic about it?"

Eve sighed. "Knowing Benny, he's trying to protect me. He wants to be sure I'm the only one with access."

"That's going to be hard without the key. It would have been helpful if he'd included it in the envelope."

"I know. It doesn't make sense. Maybe Vince interrupted his plans. Benny may have prepared to give me the key at some point. Or maybe he instructed his attorney to take care of it if something happened. Only the police found the key first." She stood and began to pace. "There's no way to know. All we can do now is work with what we have. Which means we have to get to the key."

Adam turned in his seat. "How do you propose we do that? Unless you plan to ask Tony to help."

Eve frowned. "No. I can't involve him. It would risk his career. Plus, it's better he not know what's going on."

"Why not? Maybe he can help."

"I know Tony. He'll get himself killed trying to protect me. No. We have to figure this out on our own."

Adam chuckled. "How do you think we're going to get into the evidence locker in a police station? You have some hidden talents I'm not aware of?"

A knock on the door made them jump. "You expecting someone?" asked Adam.

"No." She walked over and peeked out the peephole. "What in the..." She opened the door. "Declan?"

A tall man with sandy blonde hair and a lean physique stepped inside.

Eve closed the door. "Is everything all right?"

Declan stood in the living room and eyed Adam.

"Looks like you've fully recovered," said Declan.

Adam moved his arm. "Good as new, thanks to your friend." He recalled Sarah's healing touch. "How is everyone?" He didn't know what else to say. This man and his friends had good reasons to distrust him.

"We're fine," said Declan. He glanced at Eve. "We were actually concerned about you. We've been trying to reach you the last few days, with no result. I called your sister and got your address. I thought I'd check in." He looked between the two of them, and Adam sensed his energetic inquiry. Declan was more capable than he let on.

"You called Gilli?" asked Eve.

"Don't worry. She doesn't know. Said we wanted to send you a thank-you card. How are things?"

"We're okay," said Eve.

"We've got a problem," said Adam at the same time. Eve scowled at him.

Declan paused. "Sadly, I believe him."

Eve didn't argue. "I'm sorry I didn't get back to you and Sarah. I got the voicemails. I've just been busy with everything that's happened. But I'm fine and so is Adam."

Adam stepped closer. "You tell him about Burke? You tell him about the mob?"

A message from Eve best not spoken aloud rang in Adam's head.

Declan's brow raised, and he took off his jacket and threw it on the sofa. He looked at Eve. "You want to fill me in?"

Still glaring at Adam, Eve walked into the living area and crossed her arms. "There's nothing to tell. Adam is exaggerating. It's nothing we can't handle."

"We?" asked Declan. "I expected you to have kicked Adam out the minute you left the house. I'm surprised to see him here."

Eve opened her mouth to speak, but hesitated.

"She did kick me out," said Adam. "A couple of times. But we've had a few hiccups since we left."

"Getting rid of him isn't so easy," said Eve.

Declan nodded. "Interesting."

"Not really," said Eve.

Declan appeared to smile before stopping himself. "So, fill me in. I heard you were cleared of all charges in your friend's death."

"We were," said Eve. "I inherited Benny's bar."

"Is that good?"

"It's great. I'm just figuring out what's next."

Declan stared at her, obviously expecting more. When Eve didn't say anything, he looked at Adam. "You want to tell me what she's leaving out?"

Despite Eve's warning frown, Adam didn't hesitate. "How about how Benny's son is in debt to the mob for a hundred grand and now they expect Eve to pay up. Or how a man named Burke from Eudora came looking for Eve's brother. He projected himself into Dixie's body, threatened me, and forced Eve to take him to Royce."

Declan's eyes widened. "Excuse me?" He shook his head. "Who's this Dixie?"

"Eve's best friend. She lives next door. Burke befriended her. He's a powerful Red-Line who's capable of projection. It's outlawed on our planet, but he was able to possess her for a short time, enabling him to get close to

Eve. He threatened Eve, using me and Dixie as leverage. Eve had no choice but to take us to Royce."

Declan stared at Eve, who looked away. "You took him to Royce?"

Eve paused, her eyes shiny. "Yes. They saw the tombstone." She blinked watery eyes.

"You know he's dead?" asked Adam.

"Yes. We were at the funeral." Declan watched Eve. "What happened after that?"

"Adam attacked Burke," said Eve. "It allowed me the opportunity to break the connection that held Burke to Dixie. Burke disappeared, and Dixie returned. She's okay and thankfully doesn't remember a thing."

"Where's Burke?"

"Probably on his way home," said Declan. "He got what he came for. Royce is no longer a threat to the throne."

Declan nodded. "I hope it stays that way. And why does the mob expect Eve to pay Vince's debt?"

"Because Eve inherited the bar. They want her to sell it for the amount of the debt. But we may have another option."

Eve sighed. "Adam, please. We don't need to involve him. He's done enough."

Declan frowned. "Tell me."

Adam picked up the letter. "Apparently, there's a key to a safe deposit box. The police found it when they searched Benny's office. But they can't figure out what bank the key's from. But Benny told Eve." He handed the letter to Declan. "We have twenty-four hours to see if we can get into the box. Problem is, the key is in an evidence room down at the police station. We have no way of getting it."

Declan read the letter. "Once you get the key, you think the bank will give you access? They have strict rules about who can open a box."

"I'll be able to," said Eve. "Benny sent me the information. I think he means for me to open it."

Declan gave the letter back to Declan. "And what happens if you get there and there's nothing in the box but old photos and a few letters?"

Eve cocked her head. "I guess I'll be selling the bar at a major discount. It's not worth people's lives."

Declan stood quietly, appearing to think. "You should have asked for help, Eve."

"This isn't yours, or anyone else's, problem. I can take care of myself."

"Your brother said the same thing. You know if he were here, he would advise you otherwise."

Eve straightened. "But he's not here, is he?"

Declan didn't answer. Eve pushed the hair off her face and sat on the couch.

Adam sensed the tension between the two, but was unable to discern the reason behind it. "So, what do you think?" he asked Declan.

Declan looked away from Eve. "Twenty-four hours?"

"Well, more like twenty-three now."

Declan checked his watch. "Where's this key?

"Down at the local precinct. Not sure which one. Her friend Tony is the sergeant on the case."

Declan nodded. "Okay. Sit tight. You two stay here until you hear from me."

Eve looked up. "What are you going to do?"

"You let me worry about that."

"Declan..."

"Eve," he said sternly. "I said let me worry about it."

Adam sensed again some underlying issue.

Eve crossed her arms but didn't say a word. Declan spoke to Adam. "You stay with her. She does something stupid, you call me." He pulled a card out of his pocket and handed it to him. "If you don't hear from me within twenty-two hours, call that number."

Adam took the card, and with one last glance at Eve, Declan picked up his jacket, opened the door, and left.

Chapter Twenty-Four

THE NEXT SEVERAL HOURS were slow-moving, weary ones. Dixie, once hearing Adam was back, had invited them to dinner. Eve was grateful for the distraction. The attraction between her and Adam would not abate. She was sure Adam felt the same. He avoided sitting too close. She recalled his promise: that he would not touch her until she touched him first. She was grateful. Despite her desire for him, she kept her distance. Once this was over, he would be out of her life for good.

Dixie, to her credit, made no mention of the two of them being together, and Eve told her that Adam was there only to help with opening Benny's bar. Dixie had raised a brow at her, but said nothing more.

That night, Eve made up the couch for Adam and went to sleep in her room. But despite her fatigue, she slept little. She tossed and turned and woke in the morning feeling like she wore a weighted robe. Seeing Adam at the coffee table, she knew he'd also had a terrible night. An empty coffee cup was in front of him and the pot was half empty. Eve helped herself to a cup.

Adam yawned. He had a bad case of bed head, and Eve found herself wanting to run her fingers through it.

"How'd you sleep?" he asked.

She glared at him.

"That well, huh?"

She sat across from him and drank from her mug. The brew was luke-warm, but she couldn't summon the energy to heat it. Just sitting across from him, she could feel the pull of energy between them. It felt like it was sucking the life out of her. But she refused to back down. Binding to this man was not an option.

"What do you want to do today?" he asked.

She rubbed her tired eyes. "Shoot myself."

He sipped his coffee. "Besides that."

"Shoot you."

He chuckled. "I can always rely on you for interesting conversation."

"I aim to please."

"I wish."

She glowered again.

He scanned the room. "You got any games? Puzzles?"

"Are you serious?"

"I can't sit in this room all day and try not to think about you. It was murder yesterday, and last night was intolerable. So either we think of something to occupy our time or I might take you up on that offer of shooting me. At least that would take me out of my misery." He paused. "Or if you'd like, we could talk about that letter you left me."

Eve thought of a variety of responses, but none that were helpful. "Top drawer. On the TV stand."

"I figured." Adam walked over and opened the drawer. He pulled out a puzzle box with a picture of a gray kitten on a gray background, swatting at a gray ball of yarn. It was a thousand pieces. "Perfect." He brought the box over, sat, and opened it.

For the next two hours, Eve helped Adam put it together. They took a break and had some breakfast before resuming the puzzle. They continued to drink coffee, and by the time they'd finished, it was late morning and Eve was jumpy with caffeine overload. If Adam had challenged her, she would have raced him around the block and probably jumped a few cars along the way. Jittery, she went to take a shower. Using cold water helped, and when she was done, Adam went in after her. He emerged looking more refreshed but still heavy-lidded.

Eve checked her watch. It was close to twenty hours since they'd talked to Declan.

"Should we call him?" asked Adam.

"He said twenty-two hours. He's got a couple hours left."

"This is cutting it close."

Eve sighed. "Yes, it is."

Adam sat on the couch and leaned back. "So, since we have a little time, what's the story behind your friends?"

"Story?"

"Yes. How does a group of Grays and one potent female Red-Line end up on Earth?"

Eve sat at the coffee table, away from Adam. "It's a long story. But the short version is that their group has been here a long time. In your planet's history, there was a time when exploration was welcomed, even expected. Communities sprouted up on a multitude of planets. From what I understand, it was considered a rite of passage to travel and live among other species. But when things changed on Eudora and travel was stopped, those communities were left to fend for themselves. All communication ended between home and the host planets. The communities still exist, though, despite the division. This group is one of them."

"Why only one Red-Line? Where are the others?"

"That's a little confusing to me, too. When Eudora stopped communicating several years ago, the Red-Lines here died out. Their sensitivities could not sustain Earth's harsh environment without help from home. Sarah is different, though. She is the product of Red-Line and human DNA like me, which enables her to survive, while still using her unique gifts."

"I've never seen, or felt, anything like her."

"She's special. Her healing abilities have come in handy."

"Declan has some gifts, too. He's a pretty powerful Gray."

She studied him. "You're not too shabby yourself."

"I have my moments."

"You shut that door at the motel. Few Grays can do that. Plus, you project your thoughts pretty easily."

"I suspect that has more to do with you than anything else."

Heat rippled through her, and she shifted on her chair. "Maybe."

Adam rubbed his temples, and Eve knew he was feeling the same discomfort.

"How long have you spoken to animals?"

Eve straightened. "You know I speak to animals? How long have you known that?"

"Since you commanded Louis to attack Vince in Benny's office. And that whole roach thing was a big clue."

"I didn't realize I was that obvious."

"You are to me."

Her heart thumped. She needed to keep talking. "What would happen if your people learned about Sarah and her group?"

"You keep saying 'your' people, but they're our people. You're part of them too, you know?"

She wasn't sure how to respond to that. "Yes, well, I suppose. But I'm not quite ready to claim them yet."

"Your dad is one of them, and he's a good man."

"So you do know him?"

"I know of him. I've never met him. He was a good leader, though. Well respected and kind."

She hesitated. "Is he still alive?"

"Why would you ask that? Why wouldn't he be?"

"I heard he was ill."

"Ill?" He looked off. "Is that why he was voted out?" He looked back. "I had no idea. In his last weeks as our leader, he was less seen in public, but I never thought much about it."

"But you would know, right? If something had happened?"

"If a former High Leader had died? Yes, we would know. It would be announced, and he would have a public ceremony."

Eve nodded.

"Why do you think he was sick?"

Eve considered how much to say, but her brain was so muddled it was hard to think. "Our half-brother, Jasper, visited. He and Royce met. Jasper told him that our father was mysteriously ill and no one could find the cause."

Adam's eyes rounded. "Jasper visited? He came to Earth?"

Eve had no idea if she was saying too much or not. "Yes. Over a year ago. Do you know Jasper?"

Adam's face fogged over, and Eve suspected his brain wasn't working any better than hers. "I met him once. At a gathering."

"Really?"

"He was a giving a speech. He's an intense guy and passionate in his beliefs."

"What was he speaking about?"

"Your dad. He was trying to rally the vote to keep him in office. Unfortunately, it didn't help. The Council still replaced your father."

Eve rested her head in her hand. "I wish I knew where Dad was, and if he was okay."

"When's the last time you saw him?

Eve had to think about it. "Four years, I think?"

Adam nodded. "That's a long time."

Eve recalled their conversation at the motel. "When's the last time you saw your parents?"

Adam's face dropped, as if he disliked having to think about it. "I don't know. Ten years, maybe?"

"Ten years? That long?"

"I saw my sister two years ago. That counts for something, doesn't it?"

Eve thought four years was hard enough, but ten years? She prayed it wouldn't be that long before she saw her dad again, provided he was alive. "Who exactly do you have to go home to?"

He stood and walked to the window. "I do just fine on my own."

The urge to comfort him almost made her forget her plan to avoid him, but she held strong. "How long have you known your friend, Tez?"

"Since we were kids. We had a similar upbringing. He's not much closer to his family, although he did marry."

Eve nodded, unsure of what to say next. "What will you do if he doesn't come back?"

He looked over. "That's a great question. I don't suppose you know anyone who can take in an unemployed, broke Eudoran, do you?"

They held the look, and before Eve could answer, there was a knock on the door.

She startled in her seat, and Adam jumped. "I hope that's him."

Eve stood and walked over to look out the peephole. There was a tall man wearing a baseball cap standing at her entry. She didn't recognize him. "Who is it?" she asked. Adam stepped up beside her.

A voice spoke from outside. "Eve Fletcher? I have a delivery from a mutual friend."

Adam leaned in and looked out the peephole. "What mutual friend?" he asked.

"One who has a penchant for keys," said the man.

Adam paused and cracked the door open. The man handed an envelope to Adam.

"Have a nice day," was all the visitor said before he disappeared from view.

Adam closed the door and gave the envelope to Eve. She took it and quickly slid it open. Turning it upside down, she was astonished when a small copper key fell into her hand.

Chapter Twenty-Five

THE CAB PULLED UP to the steps that led to a large building surfaced with dark paneled glass. Situated in the grass in large steel letters were the words *Metropolitan National Bank*. Adam stepped out, and Eve joined him. They stared up at the tall skyscraper. "This is it?" asked Adam. "That's a huge bank."

"I think it's only on two floors. Come on."

Eve took the steps up to the entrance. She'd changed clothes, and her red, full skirt blew in the wind. Adam wore khaki pants and a long-sleeved collared navy shirt. Between her and Dixie, they'd found something a bit more suitable for him to wear. His worn jeans and stained t-shirt made him look like a college kid during spring break.

"You sure they're going to let you in?" he asked. Reaching the stop of the stairs, they paused at the entrance.

"I guess we'll find out. How much time do we have before Sam expects us?"

He glanced at his watch. "About two and a half hours."

Eve nodded. "You ready?"

"I'm not exactly sure what I'm ready for. There's not much for me to do, except sit there and look cute."

She smiled and had to admit she was glad he was there. Doing this alone would have been difficult. "It's what you do best."

The corner of his mouth rose. "I think there might be a few other things I do better."

Her face heated. "That topic is best not discussed right now."

"When would you like to discuss it?"

She didn't look at him. "How about we open this box first, and make sure we're still alive in three hours? Then we'll consider opening that other box."

"I'll hold you to that."

"I'm sure you will." They entered the building. Inside was a large lobby with a row of elevators. Men and women in suits and briefcases came and went. Next to the elevators was a large, metallic front desk with a computer and a man in a brown suit and tie was seated and typing on a keyboard.

Eve approached him. "Metropolitan Bank?"

The man stared at the screen, and Eve noticed he was looking at security monitors. People arriving and leaving through various doors could be seen in the footage. "Floors two and three."

"Thank you."

She and Adam took the elevators and arrived on the second floor. When the doors opened, a woman sitting at a desk greeted them. Only her desk was black, and the floors were carpeted. Her blonde hair was pulled up and looked as smooth as the glass wall behind her. Eve could see desks and cubicles in the area behind the woman.

They approached the front desk. "How can I help you?" asked the woman.

"We need to open a safe deposit box," said Eve.

"Sign here, please." The woman slid a sheet of paper toward her, and Eve signed her name.

"One moment." The woman picked up the phone and dialed a number. Looking at the sheet, she gave Eve's name, had a brief conversation, and hung up. "Terrance will be out in a second. Why don't you have a seat? Can I get you something to drink?"

Eve shook her head. "No, thanks." Adam declined as well. Turning, Eve saw a comfortable leather couch and two upholstered chairs with a coffee table in the middle, sporting various magazines. She sat in one of the chairs.

Adam sat in the other. "I had no idea banks were so formal."

"Me either." She felt out of place, as if at any moment, one of the employees would come out of his cubicle, see her, yell "imposter!" and security would arrive and throw her out. She settled back in her chair and tried to relax.

"Is this normal?" asked Adam.

"I have no idea."

Adam flipped through a magazine.

A man approached. He was slender, with thinning hair and a blue suit. "Eve Fletcher?" He spoke as if he were in a library.

"Yes. That's me." She stood, and so did Adam.

"I'm Terrance. I'm happy to help you today. Please follow me."

They followed Terrance past a row of cubicles. Faint talking and the occasional boisterous laugh came out. Terrance led them to a desk. It was uncluttered and tidy; the only thing on it was a paperweight and a folder. Terrance sat behind it, and Eve and Adam took the chairs in front.

Terrance opened the folder. "So you're here to open a deposit box?" he asked.

Eve shifted in her seat. "Yes."

"What number?"

"Four thirty-two."

"May I see your identification?"

Eve pulled out her driver's license and handed it to him. He looked it over and made a few notes on a piece of paper in his folder.

"You have the key?" Eve nodded and pulled the key from her purse.

He handed her license back. "Thank you." He pulled out a sheet of paper and a pen and handed it to her. "Can you fill this out, please?"

Eve took the paper and looked it over. It was basic questions, so she filled it out as Terrance produced a laptop from a drawer, opened it, and began to type.

Eve completed the form and handed it back to Terrance as he continued to read the screen. Eve glanced at Adam as they waited. He winked at her, and she realized how tense she was. She took a deep breath and made herself relax.

Terrance raised a brow at the screen. "Interesting," he said. He punched a button and a printer beside the desk whirred to life.

"What?" asked Eve. "Something wrong?"

"This box was opened by a man named Benito Bonelli."

"Yes. I know."

Terrance glanced back at the screen. "Apparently, he's rather cautious. You are the only one who has access to the box."

Eve nodded.

"So?" asked Adam.

"There are a series of questions he wants you to answer before I give you access. Failure to answer any of them will result in me denying you entry. I guess he wants to be sure it's you."

Eve gripped the arms of the chair. "But it is me."

Terrance pulled a paper off the printer and made a few notes on it, then put it in the folder. "Well, we're about to find out."

Adam reached over and took her hand. His touch sent shivers through her, but she found his skin against hers calming. "It's fine," he said. "He just wants to be sure, so don't worry. You'll know all the answers."

She squeezed his hand in return and nodded. Looking back at Terrance, she said, "Okay. Shoot."

Terrance eyed the screen. "What is his nickname for you?"

Eve relaxed her shoulders. "That's easy. Spark."

Terrance clicked his mouse. "What was Benito's best day?"

Eve smiled. "The day he married Maggie."

Terrance clicked the mouse again. "Who is his cat named after, and why?"

Eve breathed easier. This was simple. "Louis Armstrong. Benny's favorite song is 'It's a Beautiful World.'"

Another click on the mouse. Adam squeezed her fingers reassuringly.

"What type of man does he want you to meet?"

Eve hesitated. She and Benny had spoken many times about her taste in men. Had he given her one piece of advice? Sweat popped out on her skin, but the answer quickly appeared. She held her breath, hoping it was correct. "He wanted me to meet someone who made me laugh."

The mouse clicked again, and Eve swallowed.

"Really?" asked Adam.

She didn't answer him.

Terrance continued. "Why did he give you the nickname 'Spark'?"

Eve thought back and almost laughed. "It was the first day we met. I came in to audition. His son Vince set it up. I was singing on stage when suddenly all the lights went out in the bar. Benny started cursing and yelling at someone in the back." She paused as she reflected back on that day. "I remember I saw a cord crossing the stage floor. I followed it and saw that the plug was lying on the ground beside an outlet. Just out of curiosity, I plugged it in. There was this big pop, the outlet sparked, and all the lights came on." She smiled softly. "Benny stared in shock. He walked over to the cord and saw that it only led to a vacuum cleaner. The cleaning crew had left it and it had no connection to the electrical system. There was no reason for the lights to be affected when I plugged it in." She remembered clearly standing on stage with Benny, looking at her as if she were a ghost. "He looked at me and said, 'You provide one hell of a spark. Maybe this is what this place needs.' He had me sing one more song and then he hired me. He called me Spark ever since."

Terrance glanced at the screen and clicked the mouse. "Last question. What would Benny want you to do right now?"

Eve went blank. "Excuse me?"

Terrance repeated the question, and Eve tried to think. What in the world did Benny mean?

"Eve?" asked Adam.

She frowned. "I don't know."

Adam leaned in. "It's probably so obvious you're missing it. Don't overthink it."

She squeezed his hand in worry. "I don't recall anything specific. I'm not sure." She thought back over her conversations with Benny. Was there something he'd mentioned that she'd missed? Did he want her to be specific and say open the box? Or did he mean something more general, like get married and have kids? She shook her head. None of that made sense. Their last conversation played in her head. Had he said it then?

"Just relax." Adam leaned toward her. She looked at him for reassurance, and his soothing energy traveled from his hand into hers. "Take your time. It'll come to you."

Nodding, she took a deep breath and closed her eyes. Benny's face appeared clearly in her mind. She knew she had to calm down. Her mind was in overdrive. Making herself go still, she shut out the surrounding distractions. Focusing on Benny, she saw him smile at her, and she knew he was trying to tell her something. She waited patiently. After a few seconds, he spoke. It was a phrase. Something so casual that she'd never thought twice about it. His voice soothing her, she relaxed, opened her eyes and answered.

"He'd want me to show 'em who's boss."

Terrance paused for a moment, clicked the mouse, and stood. "This way, Miss Fletcher."

• • • • • • • • • •

Terrance escorted her to a set of doors off the main hallway. Adam stayed behind because only she was allowed access. Once out of the main area, Terrance came to another set of doors. He punched in an access code. After a beep, he opened the door and walked into a smaller room. A woman sat at a desk, and at first glance, it looked like she was working a crossword puzzle. Seeing new arrivals, she put the paper down.

"Terrance?"

"Sheila. This is Miss Eve Fletcher. She has access to four thirty-two. Can you help her out?"

"Yes. Of course."

Terrance turned to leave. "I'll meet you back outside when you're finished."

"Thank you, Terrance."

Terrance returned from where they'd entered, and Sheila rose from the desk and smiled at Eve. "Right this way, Miss Fletcher."

Eve followed Sheila down a short hall and to another door. Sheila punched in another code and gained access to another room. Stepping inside, Eve saw numerous small, shiny, narrow boxes. Sheila guided her to box four hundred thirty-two. "You have your key?"

"Yes." Eve pulled it out.

"Insert it into the lock on the right."

Eve did as she was asked. Sheila presented another key that hung from her neck and inserted it into the other lock. "One, two, three, turn."

Eve turned her key at the same time and the small door opened. Inside was a shiny container. Sheila pulled it out and took it to a small room off the main area. "Here you are. Take your time. Just put the box back when you're done."

Sheila left and shut the door behind her. The small room was as silent as the empty bar and just as unsettling. Eve touched the metallic box and realized her fingers were shaking. She clasped her hands together and then shook them out. She was so nervous. What had Benny wanted her to have? What was so secretive that it required this level of protection to keep it safe?

There was only one way to find out. Raising the lid, she looked inside. She saw a bulky manila envelope and a smaller white envelope on top of it. *Spark* was written in plain letters on the front of the white envelope.

Closing her eyes, she took a deep breath and pulled out the white envelope. Fingers still shaking, she opened it, removed a sheet of paper, and saw Benny's familiar scrawl on the page. Feeling her chest tighten, she began to read.

Hi Spark.

Well, kid, if you're reading this, then my greatest fear and my biggest hope has come to pass. I'm dead, and you own the bar.

I had hoped it wouldn't work out this way, but sometimes we don't always get what we want. I suspect it was Vince. I've known for a long time that he was in trouble. I've saved him many times from his debtors, but his gambling debts continue to grow. I've reached a point where I can no longer protect him. I know he is growing desperate, but he will have to figure his way out without me. My sweet Maggie told me many times that I was overprotective, and God love her, she was right.

I refuse to pay Vince's latest debt. He's in the hole now for a hundred grand. If you're here, then I figure he ran out of options. He knows, and I know, that the men he's in debt to will not be kind. They want their money, and they will ultimately get it.

I'm not stupid, Spark. I know the bar is an attractive way to get some easy green. Vince knows it too. There's a showdown coming, and I'm expecting it soon. But I have no plans to sell to Vince. Never did, actually. Now, I love my kid, but he's not a businessman. Never was. Can't hold on to a dime to save his life. And this place is not meant to pay his bills.

So, I decided a while ago that this place belongs to you. You're the one that keeps it alive anyway, so you might as well have it. You can do with it what you like. I know you'll do what's best. My only request is that you NOT sell it to pay Vince's debt. This is your baby, not his.

Now, I know you may be in a tight spot right now. I've prepared for that. I'm not gonna leave you hanging. I've made sure that you, and only you, have access to this box and the key. I hope it wasn't too complicated. I can only plan ahead so much. The rest must be left to fate.

But you're here, so destiny wins again. Please use what you need to deal with any problems and take the rest for yourself. The bar is yours, as is my unending gratitude.

I've told you many times that I love you like my own. My Maggie would have loved you, too. You are the daughter we never had. I thanked the Big Guy upstairs many times for that day when you walked into my bar and lit up the place (literally). I know you have your own father, but I hope you don't mind if I enjoy a small part of that credit as well.

I can't be there now to give you any more of my famous advice, but I will say this: Go live your life, Spark. Stop being so safe. I know you like to think you're this brave wild child who fiercely fights the demons, but I see the fear in you. The fear to let go and let yourself be loved by someone. To let them help when you need it. No one's an island in this world, kid. And if they are, it's a lonely life.

Find someone who makes you laugh. Keep or sell the bar. I don't care. Use what's in the envelope. Just be happy. Take risks, love dangerously, and don't be scared. It's the only way to live.

And one more thing—go show 'em who's boss.

I love ya.

Benny

The tears flowed so hard and fast the Eve had to stop and start the letter many times before she could finally get through it. Finally finishing, she sniffed and wiped the tears off her cheeks. She was thankful for the privacy. There was a box of tissues on the table, and she grabbed a few of them. After blowing her nose and wiping her face, she finally pulled it together.

She folded the letter, put it back in the envelope, and placed it in her purse. Another round of tears threatened, and she bit her lip and dabbed at her eyes. Taking a few deep breaths, she steadied herself and pulled out the manila envelope. It was thick with whatever was inside of it. She undid the clasps and turned it upside down. Several short stacks of money fell out.

Eve gasped. Looking closer, she could see they were bundles of one hundred-dollar bills. She did a quick count and realized what Benny had left her. It was two hundred thousand dollars.

Chapter Twenty-Six

ADAM SAT UNCOMFORTABLY IN his chair across from Terrance's desk. Terrance worked on the computer and completed the paperwork while Adam fidgeted.

"You sure I can't get you something?" asked Terrance. "Coffee? A magazine?"

Adam waved him off. "No. I'm fine." He stared out the window at the neighboring buildings. He was too nervous to read anything, and the last thing he needed was coffee. He thought of Eve and wondered what was happening. What had Benny left her?

He glanced at his watch. It was now down to less than two hours before the Sam and Billy show came looking for their money. Trying not to squirm in his seat, he pulled out his communicator/phone. He flipped through the various screens, trying to keep busy, but paid little attention. What would happen after this drama played out? Would Eve want him to stay or ask him to leave? And what would he do either way? He knew in his gut that they were meant to be together, but he also realized he hadn't told her everything. What was his obligation at this point?

Tapping his foot, he traced his fingers along the seams in the leather chair. Staring back at the door that Eve had disappeared through, he jumped when the phone in his hand buzzed.

Surprised, Adam looked at the screen. A message was coming through with no number attached. Adam went still. The only one who could send him a message like that was Tez. Anxiously, he opened the screen, unsure of what to expect.

Adam.

I will return tomorrow at noon at the drop off point. If you're ready to go home, be there. I'll wait ten minutes. After that, I leave.

Tez

Adam stared at the message, then closed the screen. Just then, the door off the hallway opened and Eve emerged. Adam put his phone away and stood. Terrance stood, also.

"Everything okay, Miss Fletcher? Anything else we can do for you?"

Eve looked a little pale and her eyes were red, but there was an extra perk in her step she hadn't had going in.

"No thanks, Terrance. I'm good."

She walked up to Adam and winked at him. His heart warmed, and he took her hand. She didn't pull away. "You ready?" she asked.

"You bet," said Adam.

Terrance walked them to the elevators. The doors closed, and Adam couldn't stand it any longer. "Well?"

Eve patted her purse. "Benny took care of everything."

"He did?"

"Yes. How much time do we have?"

"About ninety minutes."

"Let's head to the bar. I'm guessing that's where they'll show."

The elevator stopped. "Eve, what was in the box?"

The doors opened, and a couple stepped in. Eve leaned in and spoke into his ear. "Money. And plenty of it."

Her breath against his skin drove his body temperature up a notch, making him want to pull her into his arms and kiss her senseless, couple or no couple. Remembering his promise, he pulled back. "You serious? How much?"

She shook her head at him and nodded toward the couple, signaling that it would be best to discuss later. Putting his hand in his pocket, he felt his phone and recalled Tez's message, still unanswered. If what Eve said was true, and they were finally going to find their way out of this mess, then Adam had a choice to make. Was it time to go home?

· · · · ●· ● · · · ·

Thirty minutes later, they were at the bar. The cab dropped them off, and they headed into Benny's office. Eve shut the door behind them.

"Okay. I can't stand this anymore. How much was in the box?" asked Adam. Eve had stayed silent on the cab ride over, as if saying the amount would make it magically disappear. She kept telling him to wait until they got to Benny's.

Eve put her purse down and glanced at the clock. They had about an hour left. She opened her bag and dumped the contents onto the desk. Several stacks of money fell out, along with a white envelope.

Adam approached, his heart thumping. "How much is that?"

"Two hundred thousand dollars."

Adam didn't know what to say.

"I know, right?" said Eve. "I couldn't believe it."

The door to the office opened. "I can," said a familiar voice.

Adam turned and his stomach dropped.

"I thought you were in jail," said Eve.

Vince stood in the doorway and grinned. "It's called bail, sweetheart. I'm out." He walked in and shut the door behind him. He opened his jacket and pulled a gun from his waistband. "Good 'ole dad. Leave it to him to hide his money from me. Greedy bastard."

"That's not your money," said Adam.

"It is now."

"How did you know I was here?" asked Eve.

He cocked his head. "Come on. I'm not as stupid as pretty boy here looks. I had you followed. As soon as you pulled up to the bank, I got a phone call. And looky, looky what you found."

"We're paying the debt. Not you," said Eve.

He aimed the gun at Eve. "That's kind of you, but I'll be paying it. Now get out from behind the desk and join your boyfriend."

Eve hesitated.

"Now," said Vince, cocking the gun. "My patience is long gone, so move."

"Come on, Eve," said Adam. Vince's demeanor convinced Adam that he could pull the trigger at any moment.

Eve reluctantly walked away from the money and stood next to Adam. Vince went to the desk, and with his free hand, counted the piles of cash. He whistled. "Two hundred grand. Nice." He put the stacks in his pockets.

"What are you going to do?" asked Eve.

"I'm going to pay my debt. Then I think it's time for me to relocate. Find a little beach somewhere and hunker down for a while." He shrugged. "Or what the hell? Maybe I'll just go to the track."

"Vince, you can pay off your debt. But the rest of the cash was given to me," said Eve.

"Like I give a rat's ass." Vince turned. "I'm Benny's son. You're just some trashy singer dad had the hots for. You're easy on the eyes, babe, put you've been a thorn in my backside."

Seeing Vince take Benny's hard-earned money made Eve squirm. "You leave here, and my first call is to Tony," she said. "You'll be picked up before you reach the end of the block."

Vince stuffed the last stack of bills into a back pocket. He straightened his aim.

"What are you doing?" asked Adam.

"I've had about enough of you two as I can stand. I can't let you contact the police. Or anyone else."

Adam stepped in front of Eve. "Don't be stupid, Vince."

"Think about what you're doing," Eve said.

Vince stepped away from the desk. "I'm already accused of shooting my dad. I've got nothing to lose. Besides, I'm not sticking around for any trial."

"Just take the money and leave," said Adam. "We're no threat to you."

Vince sneered and waved the gun at Adam. "I need time to take care of business. I can't risk that. I going to pay my debts and then get out of town. With no cops on my tail."

"You kill us and there'll be a statewide manhunt for you. You won't get past the border."

"Only if they find you." Vince paused and looked up. "We'll go to the roof. I'll take care of you up there. With a little luck, no one will discover you until you start to stink, and by then, with a little help from my friends, I'll be out of the country."

"What friends?" asked Eve. "You think your mobster cronies are going to do that for you?"

"Why not?" Vince stepped closer. "All I need to do is pay the debt. I can still be of value to them. They have operations overseas, too."

Adam held up his hand. "Think this through. This is not as easy as you think. You're a loose end, Vince. There's nowhere for you to go."

Vince frowned. "You don't know shit about me." He pointed the gun at Adam. "I think I'll shoot you first."

"No, don't..." Eve pushed forward but stopped when the door opened. Vince swung the gun as Billy and Sam walked into the office.

"Well, well, well," said Sam, looking dapper in a gray suit and white tie. "Look who's here. It's Vincent."

Billy stood at the door and made no acknowledgement. Vince's face fell, and he lowered the gun. "Sam. Billy. I was just coming to see you." He put the gun in his waistband and pulled out a couple of wads of cash. "I've got the money. It's all yours."

"She got the money, not him," said Adam, pointing at Eve.

Sam looked between Vince and Eve. "It doesn't really matter, does it? We just want what's due." He focused on Vince. "I'm surprised to see you out. You must have a mysterious benefactor."

Vinny shrugged. "I'm lucky, I guess."

Sam nodded, and Adam picked up on something else from the man. He glanced at Eve, who looked back with wide eyes.

Sam approached the desk. "Get the money, Billy."

Billy walked up, and Vincent pulled money out of his pockets and counted one hundred thousand of it. Billy pulled a bundled, small plastic bag from a pocket, opened it, and put the money inside. Then he stepped back.

Adam wondered what to do next. Should they mention the extra cash?

"Funny thing about luck," said Sam, tapping on the desk. Adam saw Vince swallow. "I don't believe in it."

Adam instinctively moved back, and Eve did the same.

Vince held up a hand. "What do you mean? I got the cash. I was gonna bring it to you guys. Debt paid. Everything's good."

Sam studied a nail. "Maybe. Maybe not."

Despite the tension in the room, Adam felt compelled to speak. "He's got more money in his pockets. It was Benny's gift to Eve. But he took it."

Sam's head turned, but he kept his eyes on Vince. "Is that true, Vincent?"

Vince's face turned red. "It's my dad's money. It belongs to me."

"And he was going to kill us," said Adam.

Sam sighed. "You've never been good at problem solving, have you?" He took a step toward Vince. "Empty your pockets."

Vince froze. He opened his mouth to speak, but stopped. Looking between Sam and Billy, he slowly pulled out the hidden cash and dropped it on the table. "I don't know what the big deal is. I was just going to hang on to it. Use it for a rainy day." The money on the table, he pointed at Sam. "Hey, maybe the boss could use it? Maybe in return, he could let me in on a little action? I'm free at the moment. I could use a job or two to keep me busy."

Sam studied the cash, then glanced back at Billy, who said nothing. "I don't think so." He picked up a stack, and then tossed it back. "Problem is, we don't trust you. I mean..." He smiled, and Vince paled. "You're in jail with a hundred-thousand-dollar bail and suddenly you're out? I find that suspicious. Who's going to put up a hundred grand for you?"

Vince seemed to take offense. "I got friends."

"Who? Hookers and gamblers? No." He sighed. "I think your friends wear badges. I think maybe you agreed to rat on us and they let you out so you could get the goods on the boss. Am I right?"

Vince shook his head so fast Adam wondered if it would pop off. "No, Sammy. There's no way. I'd never do that."

Sam smirked. "All right. We'll see about that. Why don't you come with us?"

The terror coming off Vince almost made Adam want to flee. "What for?" asked Vince.

"We're going to go see the boss. Get his take on it." He stuck out a thumb. "Let's go."

Vince's jaw dropped, and he pointed at the spare cash. "But...but the money."

"Ah, Vincent. Where you're going, you won't need it." He nodded at Billy, who walked forward.

Vince raised his palms. "This is just a big misunderstanding. You guys have got it all wrong." Seeing Billy advance, Vince took a few steps. "Fine. I'll go. I can explain everything."

"I'm sure you can, Vincent. I'm sure you can."

Vince passed Billy and made his way out of the office, with Billy behind him. Before he left, Vince glared at Eve. "I'll be back."

Billy gave him a shove, and then he was gone. Eve and Adam didn't move as Sam walked to the door. Eve glanced at the desk. "What about the cash?"

Sam paused. "We've got our money, Miss Fletcher." He gestured toward the table. "And it appears you have yours."

Adam had to ask. "What about Vince?"

Sam put his hands in his pockets. "Don't ask questions you don't want the answers to." He stepped out into the hall and without looking back said, "Have a nice day."

Chapter Twenty-Seven

EVE STARED OUT INTO the empty hallway. "We should call Tony."

"Leave it," said Adam. "He got himself into this mess. Let him get himself out of it."

"He's in trouble."

"And there's little we can do to save him. Even if you called in the cavalry, it will only delay the inevitable. Besides, we don't know what they're going to do."

She shot a look at him. "You said you saw *The Godfather* movies, didn't you?"

His face dropped. "Like I said, it's out of our hands. The man was going to kill us."

She knew he was right. Reluctantly, she walked to the door and closed it, trying not to think about Vince's fate, but praying for him just the same. "Knowing Vince, he'll find some way to wiggle his way out of it." She shook her restless hands.

"You okay?" asked Adam. He curled his fingers with tension, and Eve realized he was just as shaky as her.

Eve nodded, feeling her heart race. "You think he would have killed us?"

"I think Vince is on the edge of a complete breakdown. I think he's capable of anything."

Eve closed her eyes and shook her head. "What happened to him?"

"He's lost everything. It can make a man desperate."

Eve opened her eyes. She wanted to fall into Adam's arms and hold him, but she remembered their deal. "I suppose so."

Adam walked to the pile of cash. "So, you've got the bar, a pile of money, and the mob off your back." He picked up a stack of cash.

Eve joined him at the desk. "Hard to believe." She rubbed her neck and felt the onset of a brewing headache.

"I'll ask the obvious. What next?" he asked.

"What do you mean?"

He dropped the cash on the desk. "You know what I mean."

She turned away. Their attraction had not receded, and if anything, had only gained strength. The more she tried to avoid him, the more she wanted him. She hated that. She didn't want to have to rely on anyone for her happiness. Just standing here now, she imagined having her way with him on Benny's couch. But she knew if she did, she'd never break free from his hold. Besides, she had other things to consider. She had to ensure his presence in her life wasn't a threat. And the truth was, she couldn't be sure of that.

She sat back against the desk. "I already told you. After this mess was over, you would go your way and I would go mine. That hasn't changed." Saying the words was harder than she expected, and she played with the edge of the desk. Benny's letter was in view, and his words played in her head.

Adam paused. "Eve, are you seriously telling me we don't have a future? There's no room for me in your life?"

"I have a lot to deal with right now. We've been through an ordeal. We had a moment, but don't forget why you're here. You came to find Royce. Then there's that whole issue with Burke."

"What about Burke?"

She stood. "He just happens to show up right after you and your friend do? I find that rather suspicious. How do I know you three weren't working together?"

He blanched. "How can you say that?"

"How did he find Dixie? How did he know to use her? I've been wondering all along how suddenly three men from Eudora all show up looking for Royce. You want to know what I think? I think Burke was your back-up plan. You came after me first but got caught up in Benny's murder instead. Your plan went off the rails, so Tez called in the big guns."

He stared at her as if measuring his response. "I'll be honest. I don't know if that's true or not. Maybe Tez called him, maybe he didn't. I had no control over that. I know I haven't been completely honest with you, but there's a reason for that."

Adam's phone buzzed, but he ignored it.

"Please Adam. It doesn't matter what you say. Because I won't be able to believe you either way."

"Just listen..." His phone buzzed again, and he cursed and pulled it out of his pocket and turned it off.

"Who is that?" asked Eve. "It's been doing that since we left the bank."

"It's nothing. Just an unanswered message."

Eve doubted that. "Who's trying to reach you? The only people you know on this planet are basically me and Dixie." She cocked a brow. "It's Tez, isn't it?"

"It doesn't matter."

"I thought you said he was gone? That you were broke and alone."

"He was gone. And I am broke."

She walked behind the desk and began to separate the cash.

"What are you doing?"

"I'll make this easy on you." She broke open a bundle, counted it, and put half in one pile and half in another. Now she had two even piles, and she slid one toward Adam. "Here. This is your share."

He put his phone away. "I don't want that."

"It's yours. It's only fair. You risked your life and you should have it."

"That's not what this is about."

She sat at the desk, feeling exhausted. "I don't know what anything is about anymore. You said your friend is gone, but now he's back? How can I not question your honesty?"

Adam sat on the chair across from the desk. He rubbed his face in his own gesture of fatigue. "He's making one last swing by before he heads home for good. Says he can pick me up tomorrow."

Eve nodded. Her stomach twisted at the thought of his absence, but she ignored it. "That's good."

"I don't want to go."

"Yes, you do. You just think you don't."

"I want to stay with you."

"But you can't. Either you go home and get back to your life, whatever that is, or you take the cash and use it to start a life here. I can't stop you if that's what you want. But I can't be a part of it."

"I still don't understand. Why not?" He stood in frustration. "I mean, come on. We're perfect together. We both have hard edges that the other one can soften. We need each other."

She stood. "I don't need anyone." She opened a drawer and found a manila envelope. She dropped Adam's share of the money into it. "Here. Take it. It's yours. If you decide to leave, donate it to charity."

He eyed the envelope. "It doesn't matter what I say, does it? You're never going to believe me. And even if you did, you're not going to allow yourself to be loved. Because I do love you, and I know you love me."

"Love and lust are two different things."

He smiled sadly. Sighing, he reached out and took the bag. His smile dropped. "Okay, Eve. You win."

Something in her heart broke, but she kept a straight face and shut down as best she could. She didn't want him to know how much it hurt to say goodbye. "I know you don't believe me, but this is for the best."

He held her gaze. "I know that's what you think, but the truth is, I think you're scared."

Benny's words pulsed in her head, along with her heartbeat. Her headache was in full swing now. "Maybe you're right. But that's my cross to bear." She crossed her arms. "Have a nice trip."

He held the envelope. He was making no effort to cloak his misery, and she could feel every jab to his heart. "I'll send you a postcard."

Her emotions in a swirl, she swallowed back tears. "That's a lot of postage."

He raised the cash. "I've got the funds."

Her body felt like wood. Her heart was thudding and some part of her ached to tell him to stop, to not leave. But her head wouldn't let her do it.

He turned away from the desk and walked to the door. Putting his hand on the knob, he looked back. "Goodbye, Eve."

She didn't answer, and with one last nod, he was gone.

Eve stared at the empty doorway, hearing only the distant sounds of the street. She opened the top drawer of Benny's desk, shoved the rest of the cash into it, and closed it. Sitting at the desk, she listened to the sounds of loneliness and allowed the tears to fall.

· · · · • · • · · · ·

The ship hovered over the ground as the tree limbs swayed and the leaves blew.

Adam waited until it gradually descended and touched the ground. The engines slowed, and the whirring stopped. After a few seconds, there was a popping sound, the door slid open, a ramp rolled out, and Tez walked off the craft.

Adam adjusted the pack on his back. It held everything he owned, save for the fifty thousand dollars. He'd left that on the front desk of the homeless shelter near his apartment. Judging by the people who came and went from there, they needed it.

Standing there, he thought of Eve. Everything in his gut told him he was supposed to be with her, but what else could he do? She didn't trust him, and without that, there was nothing to build on.

Tez skirted past a shrub and approached. "I'm glad to see you came to your senses." Adam shoved his pack into Tez's arms. Tez almost dropped it, but secured his hold. "Somebody's in a bad mood."

"Let's just go."

Tez followed him onto the ship and dropped the pack onto the metallic floor. Adam walked into the cockpit and sat in the passenger seat.

"So I heard Royce is dead."

Adam sat up. "How'd you know about that?"

"I talked to Burke."

"You what? When?" He stood and got in Tez's face. "Did you call him in?"

Tez shoved him back. "Don't get pissy with me. I told you what would happen if we didn't get results."

"He projected himself. He used a human's body. Did you know that?"

Tez paused. "No, I didn't. Did it work?"

Adam had to staunch the impulse to grab his friend by the throat. "That is completely unsanctioned and you know it. That's grounds for exile."

Tez stepped forward. "Exile? I'll take that any day over imprisonment, which we could face if Roma makes examples of us. So don't get mad at me. I told you Eve was no good. And we lost out on a big pay day because of her. I hope the sex was good because that was one expensive tryst."

Adam grabbed a handful of Tez's shirt and pulled him forward. "What is the matter with you? Not everything is about money."

Tez shoved him back, and Adam let go. "It is when I don't have a bed to sleep in or a roof over my head. At the rate we're going, I'll be lucky if I can buy my wife a decent meal."

Breathing hard, Adam ran a hand through his hair. "Damn it." It was all he could think to say.

Tez turned and took a seat at the pilot's chair. "We can fight about this later. We're sitting in the middle of the forest. We need to go." He hit a few buttons, and Adam heard the ramp slide up and the door close. "Take a seat. Strap yourself in."

Adam tried to pull it together. He was missing Eve, his mind was a jumble, and he couldn't think straight.

"Or I can leave you in the woods. You could go back to your beloved and have her kick you in the balls again." He flipped a switch. "It's your choice."

Adam cursed, but then reluctantly relaxed into the passenger chair. "I hate you."

Tez turned a dial, and the craft began to vibrate. "I hate you too. Now buckle up."

Chapter Twenty-Eight

Eve drove down the street. She passed several homes with large trees and long driveways, but paid little attention.

"The stop sign!"

Eve hit the brakes. She stopped the car just beyond the sign as another car honked and crossed the road.

"Earth to Eve," said her sister Gillian, who sat in the passenger seat. "Should I drive?"

"Sorry." Eve sighed. She had picked her sister up at the airport thirty minutes ago, but had barely spoken to her since.

"What's up with you? I've had better conversations with Max."

Eve recalled her brother-in-law's dog. "How is Max? Grayson still feeding him what I suggested?"

"Of course. That dog lives well. But don't change the subject. Tell me what's going on with you. I know about Benny's tragic death and how you've inherited the bar, but when are you going to tell me more about this Adam person?"

Eve bit back a groan. This was the last thing she wanted to discuss. It had been a week since Adam had left, but it still felt like he'd just walked out the door. Sleep was elusive, her mind wouldn't turn off, and she couldn't go an hour without thinking about him. Blinking with fatigue, she wondered when this Binding thing would finally break its hold on her.

"There's nothing to tell."

"Uh-huh."

Eve could feel her sister's scrutiny and tried to close up, but it was hard to do. Her sister knew her too well.

"Wow. He really means something to you, doesn't he?"

"No, he doesn't."

"Look at you. You're the only woman I know who can make puffy eyes and pale skin look good. And quite obviously, you're trying hard just to drive straight. Declan told me about him. I know what he came here to do. What I don't know is what happened between you two after you left Sarah's." She paused, but Eve didn't respond. "It must have been something, because I've never seen you like this. He must have made quite an..." Her eyes widened and she her jaw dropped. "Wait a minute. Did you *Bind* with him?"

Eve hit the brakes and pulled the car to the side of the road. Driving was hard enough, but this conversation was going to require more focus, and Eve didn't trust herself to keep the car on the road. "I did not Bind with him."

Gillian scrutinized her. "Yes, you did."

"I *almost* Binded with him. There's a difference."

"No, there isn't. And don't tell me I don't know what I'm talking about, because I do. You know I do."

"You and Grayson are different. What you two went through was different."

Gillian narrowed her eyes. "The circumstances don't matter. What matters is the connection. And judging by your demeanor, it was strong. So why isn't he here?"

Eve grunted. "Did we forget who he is? He lied to me. He came here to find Royce, and he used me to do it. I can't trust him."

"So why did you Bind with him then?"

Eve wanted to jump out of the car, run down the street, and never come back. "Do you think I know?" She laid her head back. "My taste in men has never been the best. I suspect that hasn't changed."

"Nonsense. You've just been having fun until now. There's nothing wrong with that. But maybe you're being forced to look at your life differently. Maybe he showed up the way he did because you wouldn't have given him a second glance otherwise." She took off her seatbelt and shifted in her seat. "You don't just Bind with anyone, Evie. There's a reason he's the one. I know it's scary. There's a lot to consider. If you let him in, your whole life will change."

Eve gripped the steering wheel. "I just wish I knew the truth."

"Did you give him a chance to explain?"

"It wouldn't matter. I wouldn't know if he was being honest."

"Excuse me? Your spidey sense is almost as good as mine. I don't know why you don't trust it."

Eve put her head on the steering wheel. Her body ached, and she wished she could lay across the seat and sleep. "I hate my life."

"Let me guess. Your whole body hurts. You haven't slept. You're not eating, and you feel like there's a snowstorm in your brain."

Eve could barely summon a response. "More like a hurricane."

Gillian opened her door. "Okay. Switch. I'm driving."

Eve didn't argue. She unbuckled, and when Gillian opened the driver's door, she made herself get out and move to the passenger side.

Once situated, Gillian pulled back out onto the road.

"You remember where to go?" asked Eve.

"Just lean back and get some shuteye. I'll let you know when we're there." She pointed. "But we are not done with this conversation."

Eve closed her eyes. "It doesn't matter. He's gone, and he's not coming back."

Gillian may have responded, but Eve never heard it, because the next thing she knew, Gillian was jostling her shoulder.

"Eve. Hey. We're here."

Eve blinked. "What? Already?"

"You've been out the entire time."

"I have? Really?" She wiped the sleep from her eyes and was relieved to feel slightly less weary. She wanted to shriek in excitement.

"Feel better?"

"Yes."

"You feel much lighter to me now. Before it felt like there was a dead body in the car."

"Gee. Thanks."

"At least you don't look like a dead body. Although this is the closest you've ever come to it."

Eve narrowed her eyes. "Why did I bring you along?"

"Because you love me."

"You're lucky I do."

They got out of the car and Eve saw the familiar house. The tarp was still up in the back where the recent addition was being added, and it gently blew in the breeze. Gillian had parked in front because there was a delivery van in the driveway. The words *Jerry's Hardware and Landscape* were emblazoned along the side panel of the truck, along with the words *We dig your business.*

At the entry, Eve knocked, and the door opened.

"Hey, Sarah," said Eve.

Sarah Ramsey smiled. "Gillian. Eve. I'm so glad you're here. Come in."

They entered, and Sarah gave them each a hug. "How was your flight, Gillian?"

"Pretty standard. At least it was on time." She looked around. "Where are the kids?"

"They're at their grandmother's, but they'll be back for dinner."

"Good. I can't wait to see them. I bet they've grown a lot since the last time I was here."

"They have. I feel like I'm constantly buying them new clothes."

Eve walked into the house. "Where is everybody else?"

Sarah took Gillian's jacket and hung it in the front closet. "John and Declan are in the back. They're talking to the man from the hardware store."

Eve nodded and sat on the couch. "Everything okay with the new room?" asked Gillian.

Sarah sat next to Gillian. "Everything's fine," she said. "That addition to the house is just taking more time and effort than we thought. John needed more lumber, so the store dropped some off. Now I guess they're back there talking 'man' stuff."

"Sounds like fun," said Eve, rubbing her eyes.

"How are you?" asked Sarah.

"She's a mess," said Gillian.

Eve dropped her hand. "I am not a mess."

Gillian ignored her. "She Binded with Adam. Did you know that?"

Sarah raised a brow at Eve. "He's still around?"

"No. He's gone." Eve leaned back on the couch. "Almost a week now."

"You couldn't tell," said Gillian.

Eve rolled her eyes. "It's not that bad."

"No. You just look like you've been run through a grinder."

"It'll pass."

"Where is he?" asked Sarah.

"He went home."

"You ever find out what he wanted with Royce?" asked Sarah.

"I met Tez. He said they were going to kill Royce to prevent him from becoming the High Child."

"Adam was going to kill Royce?" asked Sarah. Her face scrunched. "That's not what I felt from him."

Eve recalled the encounter in the woods. "Adam denied it. Said it wasn't true. But he knew who Royce was the whole time."

Gilli leaned forward. "So maybe you don't know everything. Maybe Adam didn't either."

Eve sat up. "Why are you defending him? You've never even met him."

"Because you are in *love* with him. Surely he has some admirable qualities."

Eve began to speak but stopped at the sound of approaching male voices.

Gillian pointed at her. "We are not done with this conversation."

Sarah smiled and rose from the couch.

Eve held her head. "God help me."

John Ramsey walked into the room, followed by Declan and a man Eve guessed was from the hardware store. He was tall and lanky with dark hair pulled back in a ponytail. He wore a red work shirt with an embroidered name, *Curtis*, above the pocket.

"Come on in, Curtis," said Ramsey. "I'll get you that water." He waved at Eve and Gillian. "I'll be right back."

"Curtis?" asked Sarah. "Where's Jerry?"

"Jerry had a conference call at the store," said Declan. "He sent Curtis to make the delivery."

Curtis held a clipboard and had a pen behind his ear. "Sorry, ma'am. Don't mean to interrupt. I was just hoping for some water for the road."

Sarah waved him off. "Don't worry about it."

"Hi, Eve," said Declan, stepping forward. Gillian stood and gave him a quick hug. "How are you, Gillian?"

"I'm great," said Gillian. "Where's Hannah?"

"My lovely wife is working. She should be on her way soon."

"Good. I look forward to seeing her. Maybe she can help talk some sense into my sister." She glanced at Eve. "I'm worried about her."

Eve stood as well. "I'm fine. There's no need to worry about me."

Declan nodded. "She's had an interesting couple of weeks."

Eve spoke to Declan. "I still want to know how you got that key."

Ramsey returned, holding a water bottle. "Here you go, Curtis. Nice and cold."

"Thank you, Mr. Ramsey," said Curtis, taking the bottle.

"Please. Just Ramsey. And thanks for bringing the lumber. Maybe now Declan and I can get that room finished."

Curtis opened the bottle. "Like I said, I'm happy to help. Just let me know if you need an extra hand."

Ramsey smiled. "We appreciate it. I may take you up on that. Declan here likes to take too many breaks."

Declan made a face. "So stop buying the beer."

"You could both use an incentive," said Sarah. "That room was supposed to be done a month ago. Curtis, maybe you could challenge them to get some work done."

Curtis held up a hand. "I don't know about that. If there's beer, then I doubt I'd offer much in the way of help."

"Sounds like we need to switch to lemonade," said Ramsey.

"I'll bring the lemons," said Declan.

"Well, you let me know. You can get a hold of me through Jerry." Curtis put his clipboard under his arm. "I won't keep you. Thanks for the water."

Ramsey walked him to the door. "Thanks. Tell Jerry we'll see him later. Hopefully by then I'll have a room to show him."

"Great. Will do. Have a nice day."

Curtis left and Ramsey closed the door. "Sorry about that." He came back into the room. "Gillian. Eve. Good to see you." They exchanged hugs. He regarded Eve. "How are you? Everything okay? Declan told me about your issues with the mob."

Gillian swiveled. "Mob? What mob? You didn't tell me about a mob."

Ramsey's face dropped. "Sorry. Didn't mean to spill the beans."

Declan clapped Ramsey on the back. "You do it so well, though."

Eve sat on the couch, and Gillian sat across from her. "It's a long story," said Eve. "But it's all fine. Everything worked out."

"Was Adam involved with this, too?" asked Gillian.

Eve closed her eyes. "Why does the conversation keep coming back to Adam? Can't we talk about something else?"

"Because I'm your sister. Was your life at risk?"

Eve looked at the group, who were all looking at her. "We didn't come here to talk about me."

"I know why we came here," said Gillian. "And you know this will all come up anyway, so why not talk about it now?"

Eve shook her head but offered no answers.

Gillian stood and regarded Declan. "You know what happened, don't you? What do you know about this Adam person?"

Declan stared blankly. "Honestly, I don't think I'm the best person to answer that question."

Eve stood. "Gillian, we'll talk about it later. Like you said, it's going to come up, anyway. So, in the meantime, please stop pestering these poor people and let's talk about something...anything else. Please. Adam has taken a big enough toll on me, so let's not ruin this little reunion by bringing him up. I just want some peace."

Everyone paused, and Eve was sure they thought she'd gone over the edge. Shaking her head, she sat again, not sure what else to do.

The doorbell rang.

"Saved by the bell," said Ramsey. "I'll get it."

Gillian pointed at Eve. "You win, for now. But..."

Eve mimicked her sister and pointed back. "We are not done with this conversation."

There was a pause before Eve heard Ramsey say, "Son-of-a..." She glanced over and saw him standing at the door, mouth open.

Sarah turned. "Who is it?"

Ramsey looked back. "That peace you wanted? It may just have to wait." He opened the door wider and Eve saw who stood there.

Adam took a step inside. "Hi, Eve."

· · · · ●● · ● · · · ·

Adam locked eyes with her. Her face paled, but she didn't look away. Adam was aware of the other people in the room, but he didn't pay attention. All he wanted to do was talk to Eve. It had been a long week, and he didn't want to delay any further.

Another woman stepped in between them. She was similar to Eve in appearance, but just as striking. She was shorter and her hair was darker and more wavy than curly.

She looked him up and down. "Is that him?"

Eve looked away.

"That's him," said the woman he remembered as Sarah. "Come in, Adam."

John Ramsey closed the door. "I'd say it's good to see you, but I don't know if that's true."

Adam nodded. "I understand. I know this is a shock. I apologize for showing up unannounced."

Eve pushed her hair back, and Adam thought he heard her groan. He took another step forward. "I need to talk to you."

Eve shook her head.

The other woman stepped forward. "I'm Gillian. Eve's sister." She held out her hand.

Adam hesitated, but then accepted the handshake. Gillian held the grasp for a few seconds, and Adam felt her reading him. He recalled Eve telling him about Gillian's intuitive abilities.

Eve finally spoke. "What are you doing here? I thought you went home."

Gillian released his hand. "You should talk to him." She shook out her hand and let out a rush of air. "Whew. I can see why you like him."

Eve threw out her hands. "I don't like him!"

Adam saw Declan in the room and nodded. Declan tipped his head in return. "You're a brave man."

"That or incredibly stupid."

"There's that too," said Declan, who stepped back.

Gillian crossed her arms and spoke to Eve. "You like him. You just don't want to like him."

Eve glared at her sister. "Gilli, would you mind staying out of this? This is none of your business."

Gillian was unfazed. "He came here to talk to you. So let him talk. Then, if you still want to throw him out, I won't argue with you."

"Eve, please," said Adam. "Just give me a few minutes. That's all I want."

"Where's Tez? Where's the ship? Why aren't you on it?"

Adam glanced around. Everyone was staring at the two of them, but they all knew who he was, so he answered. "The ship broke down."

"What?" asked Eve.

"Where?" asked Declan.

"In the woods. Don't worry. It's well concealed. We had to set down and do some repairs. It took a few days, but we finally got it up and running."

"Is the ship still here?" asked Ramsey.

"No. Tez left yesterday," said Adam.

"What?" asked Eve. "He left?"

"Yes, without me," said Adam. "I had to stay." He stepped closer. "I can't stop thinking about you. You're in my thoughts during the day and in my dreams at night. I can't sleep. I can't eat." He held a backpack and dropped it on the floor. "There's a reason the ship broke down. It's because I'm not meant to return."

Eve shook her head at him. "It doesn't mean anything. Can you still reach him? Can you call him back?"

"I'm not going to do that." Adam was aware he was being scrutinized, and if he gave anyone a reason to doubt him, he knew they would call him out. But he wasn't there to hide. He was there to tell the truth.

"Well, you should," said Eve. "You're going to be very lonely here on Earth."

"I don't care. As long as I can tell you what I came to say, then I'll live with whatever you decide."

"It doesn't matter what you have to say. We've had our shot, and it's done. There's no future for us."

"Let him speak his piece, Eve," said Gillian.

"Maybe we should leave the room," said Ramsey. "Give you two some privacy."

"I agree," said Sarah. She, Declan, and John started to walk away.

"No," said Eve. "Don't go. This is your house. We should step out."

"Nobody needs to leave," said Adam. "This won't take long. And everyone needs to hear it."

Sarah, Declan, and Ramsey stopped. "Well, now I'm intrigued," said Ramsey.

Adam paused, trying to focus. He'd been thinking about this speech for the past five days, and now that he was here, he struggled to begin. "I haven't been honest with all of you."

Eve straightened. "Tell me something I don't know."

"I know you think I met you in order to find your brother, and that's true. I got a job at Benny's with the sole purpose of meeting you. What I didn't expect was to get caught up in Benny's death and find us running for our lives."

Gillian gasped. "I knew it! You didn't tell me everything, did you?"

Eve rolled her eyes.

"But that time allowed me to get to know you. I learned so much about you and you got to know me. I found myself falling for you. And I know you felt the same."

"It was one night."

Gillian clasped her hands together, a dreamy look on her face.

"No. It was more than that. We had moments." He thought back. "You sitting with me on the bed when I was injured. The night on Benny's roof. The night and day I stayed at your place. The puzzle we did together. We talked about our lives, our families, and our pasts. I've never done that with anyone else. And if I leave here, I doubt I'll ever do it again."

"You're being melodramatic," said Eve.

"I don't think so. I think you feel the same."

"It doesn't matter. Why can't you understand that?"

"Because it does matter. You're pushing me away because you say you don't trust me. You think you know why I'm here, and you don't."

Eve stomped around Gillian and encroached on him, making him almost step back. "What are going to tell me, Adam? That you were here on some sort of benevolent mission? That you had nothing but good intentions? That's ridiculous, because if that were true, you could have told me up front. What would be the point of hiding? So, you see, none of it matters. Because not everything is about you. I have my own reasons why we can't be together. So I wish you would listen to me when I tell you there can be nothing between us. There never could."

Flustered, she stepped back, breathing hard.

Adam took a moment to collect himself. He hadn't expected that revelation, and he had to absorb it. This whole time, he'd thought it was him. "Eve. That can't be it. What is it that's stopping you? I'm trying to be honest here. Can't you be honest with me?"

Eve's face was red, and she bit her lip. She took a deep breath and let it out.

Gillian stepped forward. "Eve...is it...?"

Eve shook her head at her sister, and Gillian quieted.

Adam moved closer and tried to take her hand, but she pulled away. "Whatever it is, we can figure it out."

"There's nothing to figure out. You just need to leave."

Adam opened his mouth to speak, but no words emerged. The thought that he'd lost Eve, no matter what he did or said, was hard to comprehend. Was he really going to do as she asked? Distraught, Adam's heart thumped, and slumping his shoulders, he turned to leave, but then reconsidered.

He'd come here for a reason and he would follow through. Eve had to know everything, even if it changed nothing. Facing Eve, he started to speak when he saw something out of the corner of his eye. A strange energy began to fill the room, and he paused. Perplexed, he looked around, half expecting to see another presence, because for a moment, it was as if someone was standing beside him. As soon as he felt it, though, the energy moved, but it remained in the room.

Sarah and Gillian noticed it too, because they began to look around.

Eve stilled, then looked to her right, and Gillian glanced in the same direction.

"What is it?" asked Ramsey, looking in the corner.

Adam stared in shock as the air shimmered and took shape. Unbelievably, the image of a man began to appear out of nowhere. It slowly became solid, and Adam saw him clearly. He was huge, standing easily six feet, five inches or more. His arms were crossed and his muscles bulged despite his long-sleeved, loose-fitting shirt. He had short cropped light hair, and he was glowering, making him look like some sort of angry god about to call down a thunderstorm.

"I'll be damned," said Declan.

"Wow," said Sarah.

"How long have you been standing there?" asked Ramsey.

The man stepped forward. "Long enough."

Gillian and Eve stared. "Were you spying on us?" asked Eve.

"Of course he was," said Gillian.

Then Adam realized who they were talking to. It was Royce Fletcher.

Chapter Twenty-Nine

ADAM WAS SPEECHLESS. THE man he'd been sent to find was now standing right in front of him.

"You know, you're taking unfair advantage of this whole cloaking thing," said Eve.

Royce didn't even look at her, but kept staring at Adam. "I use it when it's necessary. And it comes in handy, because apparently, I've been out of the loop."

"I wish I knew how you did that," said Ramsey. "Think of all the things I could do." He smiled at Sarah. "All the housework I could get out of."

"Royce, what are you doing here?" asked Gillian. "We weren't expecting you until tonight."

Royce briefly glanced at her before returning his gaze to Adam. "Hi, Gilli. How's that husband of yours? He treating you right?"

"His name is Grayson. And of course he is."

Royce grunted, and Gilli rolled her eyes.

"What brings you here so early?" asked Declan. "You know it's better to travel at night."

Royce glowered some more. "I know how to keep out of sight, Declan. I just walked in here without anyone knowing."

Declan shrugged. "Point taken."

Adam finally came out of his stupor long enough to understand what was going on. "I saw your grave. You're supposed to be dead." He looked around the room, but nobody said anything. The only reaction was Royce rolling his eyes. Apparently, all the Fletcher's did it.

"The tombstone was Declan's idea," said Royce. "And Eve and Gilli went along with it. Who was I to argue?"

"It's supposed to keep you safe," said Eve. "After what happened to you last year. And what happened with Gillian, it made sense."

"If it made sense," said Royce, "then we should all be in hiding."

"You're the High Child," said Gillian. "They came looking for you before, and guess what?" She pointed at Adam. "They came looking for you again."

He finally stopped scowling at Adam, and Adam took a deep breath.

"That doesn't mean you and Eve are safe."

Gillian stepped closer, undaunted by her brother's anger. "I can't go into hiding, Royce. I'm married. Makes it a little hard on the relationship."

"Steele's not good enough for you. Never was."

Gillian straightened. "Nobody ever will be in your eyes. So, can we get past that?"

"You're the one at most risk," said Sarah. "We can keep an eye on Eve and Gillian."

"And I appreciate that," said Royce. "But I still consider them my responsibility."

"You can't protect everyone," said Eve. "You've been through a lot. You needed some time. This scenario gave it to you. Besides, it worked."

Royce's left eyebrow raised and a wave of intense energy flared from him. Adam half expected the roof to crack open. Royce threw out a thumb. "You mean with him?" Royce looked back at Adam, and Adam swallowed as Royce stepped close and got in Adam's face.

The man loomed over him. "You want to tell me what your business is with me? And why you would use *my sister* to find me?"

Adam could only stare.

"Oh, boy," said Declan.

"If this gets bad," said Ramsey, leaning in toward Declan, "you want to pull him off or me?"

"He's all yours," said Declan.

"I'm also curious," Royce continued, "how you managed to nearly get my sister killed by mobsters." He got closer, and Adam could smell a hint of aftershave. "Because I'd really like to know."

"How do you know about that?" asked Eve. She looked at Declan. "Wait a minute. Is that how you got the key? You used Royce?"

Declan shrugged. "It seemed like the obvious choice."

Eve dropped her jaw. "You didn't. Did you cloak yourself and walk into a police station?"

"I did what I had to do. It got you what you needed," said Royce.

Eve stuttered. "Well...that is...the most stupid thing."

Royce straightened. "Would you have rather faced the mob with nothing but this guy?" He cocked his head at Adam, who still said nothing. He figured that was the smartest thing to do. Nobody else spoke either.

"What happened with the mob was not his fault," said Eve. "But you going into a station, when at any moment you could be seen. And then stealing evidence...that's crazy."

Royce frowned. "When it comes to my family, I'll do whatever it takes. You know that. So don't question me. It worked, so stop yelling at me."

"I have to agree. Maybe it was for the best," said Gillian.

"The both of you are nuts," said Eve.

"How about you stay out of this," said Royce. "I'm still trying to get a word out of your boyfriend here." He set his sights back on Adam.

Adam tried to search for a word, but his mouth wouldn't move. All he could do was stare.

"What is he? Mute?" asked Royce.

"He's not my boyfriend, and maybe if you toned down the giant ogre act, he might answer," said Eve.

Something fired in Adam's head, and he recalled his mission. The whole reason he was on Earth was standing in front of him. His body took over, and without thinking, he kneeled in front of Royce.

He heard Royce speak. "What are you doing?"

Adam bowed his head. "Paying my respects to the High Leader." He stayed in that position for a few seconds before Royce answered.

"Get the hell up. I'm not your leader."

Adam rose and finally found his voice. "I beg to differ. Your father has stepped down, which makes you head of the Grand Council. Thus, the High Leader."

Royce looked at the others, who didn't have much to say.

"Must be nice," offered Ramsey.

Royce glowered again. "How is my father?"

"As far as I know, he is fine. But I'm not privy to any more than that," said Adam, beginning to feel more confident.

"What exactly are you privy to? And why are you here?"

Adam didn't hesitate. "Jasper sent me."

Royce froze, and some of the color left his face. "Jasper?"

Eve and Gillian stepped closer. "Our half-brother?"

"Yes." He spoke to Eve. "I was sworn to secrecy. I was to tell no one of my mission other than Royce. Jasper made me promise."

"How do you know Jasper?" asked Royce.

"I met him after a rally where he spoke. We became friends after realizing that we were on the same side. I've been disillusioned with our government for some time now, but didn't know what to do about it until I met Jasper. Since then, we've been working together. I use my connections on the inside to help him with his activities. My superiors have no idea of my involvement in the activist movement."

"So, you're like a double agent?" asked Gillian.

Adam nodded, looking at Eve. "You could say that."

"This is getting more interesting," said Declan.

"Now I really like him," said Gillian.

Eve didn't say anything.

"And why did he send you?" asked Royce, looking slightly less intimidating. "How do I know you're telling the truth?"

Adam reached for his pocket and pulled out his communicator. He clicked a button and a side panel slid open. Inside it was a letter. He pulled it out and gave it to Royce. "This is for you. I was to give it only to you and no one else. In the event I couldn't deliver it, I was to destroy it."

Royce stared at the envelope. Nothing was written on the outside, giving no sign as to who it might be from. Now pale, Royce reached for it.

"Is it from Jasper?" he asked quietly.

"I have no idea," said Adam.

Gillian and Eve watched with wide eyes as Royce took the letter. Adam noticed an almost imperceptible shake in Royce's fingers.

"You okay, Royce?" asked Eve.

Royce turned the letter over in his hands, as if he tried to sense who it was from. He looked up. "I'll let you know after I read it." He continued to stand, unmoving.

"This isn't going to be some sort of trap, is it?" asked Eve. "There's nothing in that letter that would hurt him?"

Adam shook his head. "Jasper gave it to me. That's all I know."

Eve stuck out her jaw. "If you know Jasper so well, then how come you don't know the condition of our father?"

"Jasper doesn't speak about him, and I don't ask. I figure if I needed to know, he would tell me."

Eve seemed to relax a little. Royce continued to study the letter, his face unreadable.

Sarah stepped into the hallway and opened a closed door. "Here. You can use this bedroom. Take your time."

Royce stood silently, but after a few seconds, he nodded and, holding the letter, stepped slowly into the room. "Thanks," he said and closed the door behind him.

Chapter Thirty

"WHY DIDN'T YOU TELL me who you were?" asked Eve.

Adam deflated. "I couldn't tell you. I promised to only reveal myself to your brother."

"Even after you thought he was dead?"

"Would you have believed me? Like you said, what would it matter?"

Eve crossed her arms. "You could have showed me the letter."

Adam sighed. "No. That letter is for Royce's eyes only. I promised."

Gillian stepped up. "But we're his sisters."

Eve nodded. "Exactly."

"I didn't ask questions. I only did as Jasper asked. Besides, you don't know what's in the letter. Neither do I. If it was meant for any of us, Jasper would have stated that, but he didn't."

"So you came all this way, just to deliver a letter?" asked Declan.

"Yes," said Adam. "It was the only way to communicate with him. Plus, it was an opportunity to meet the High Child. It's a great honor."

"That remains to be seen," said Ramsey. "It's proving difficult for him to assume the position."

"What happens now?" asked Sarah. "Now that you know he's alive, and you've given him the letter, what's your role?"

Eve considered something. "What about Tez? What role does he play in all of this?"

"Who's Tez?" asked Gillian.

"I traveled here with him," said Adam. "We've worked together on various missions for Roma. Tez has no idea I'm working for Jasper. Our job was only to come here, find Royce, and report back."

"And what were you going to tell them if you found him?" asked Eve.

Adam rubbed his brow. "You mind if I have a seat? It's been a long week, and I haven't slept much."

Eve studied him. She'd spent so much energy rebuffing him that now she was finding it hard to let her guard down. Standing there, she realized everyone was staring at her, and she stepped back. "Fine."

"Maybe we should all sit," said Sarah. "It's been quite a day. Can I get anyone some coffee?"

Everyone nodded. "I'll help you," said Ramsey.

"Me too," said Declan.

The three disappeared into the kitchen as Eve, Gillian, and Adam sat in the living room. Eve made it a point to sit across, and not next to Adam.

Adam sat and hung his head.

"You okay?" asked Gillian.

His face was pale. "Now that I've done what I came here to do, I feel exhausted."

Gillian eyed Eve, but Eve didn't say anything.

"So," said Gillian, "You've accomplished your mission. But what about Eve's question? Were you going to report back about Royce's whereabouts?"

"That area was a little murky, but since I was the one down here, I could say whatever I wanted. Tez wouldn't know the difference. I figured I'd either tell him a phony location, or tell them he was dead, which is what ultimately happened." He tipped his head. "It was smart to fake his death."

"You think it worked?" asked Eve. "You think they bought it?"

"Of course they did."

"Who's they?" asked Gillian. "What are you two talking about?"

Eve paused. "There was someone else looking for Royce. His name is Burke. He showed up when Adam didn't report back. He's the one I took to the grave."

Gillian's jaw dropped. "I can't believe you didn't tell me this."

"I haven't seen you," said Eve. "What am I supposed to do, pick up the phone and say, 'Hey, Gilli. Guess what? Some bad guy is threatening us and looking for Royce and, by the way, the mob wants a hundred grand.'"

"Threatening you? A hundred grand?" Gillian's eyes widened. "Yes. I think that warrants a phone call."

Eve returned to the subject. Dealing with Adam no longer seemed so bad. "Is that it? Tez is gone. He thinks you've fallen for the High Child's sister and the High Child is dead?"

Adam stilled. "I have fallen for the High Child's sister. And, yes, Tez is gone."

That familiar heat bloomed. Adam's cheeks flushed, revealing that he felt the same. She could see her sister glance at each of their faces. "You know," said Gillian, "let me see if Sarah needs help with that coffee." She stood and walked behind the couch. Before she left, though, she spoke soundlessly to Eve behind Adam's back. Eve could make out the words "Talk to him" before Gillian smiled, did a thumbs up, and left the room.

Eve made no reaction but sat quietly across from Adam.

Several seconds passed as Eve fidgeted and Adam stared at everything but Eve.

"So," said Adam.

"So," said Eve.

"Now that we've cleared the air, and you know everything, what do you think?" asked Adam.

Eve scratched her head. Her stomach was in knots. A big part of her wanted to throw herself in his arms, but there was that nugget of doubt and fear that kept her in her seat. "I don't know what I think. We've been through so much. I've spent all this time pushing you away, but now..."

"That's why you held back, isn't it? Because Royce was still alive and you were protecting him."

"Yes. I couldn't risk it. As much as I wanted to trust you." She paused. "It's hard enough for me to trust anyone, period."

He sat forward. "I know. It's hard for me too. We've both been relying on ourselves for a long time and it's not easy sharing the burden with someone else. Sometimes I think letting go is more difficult than holding on."

Eve nodded. "For such a long time, it's been me and my brother and sister relying on each other, but now Gillian's married and Royce, well, one day he'll be leading another planet." She fiddled with a couch pillow. "So that leaves me."

"Yes, it does."

"What about you? You've left your home. Your family. Don't you miss it?"

He chuckled. "What am I missing? A planet that treats me as a subordinate. Parents and a sister I barely speak to? You've been kinder to me than they ever have, and I get more respect here than there. At home, I'm just a hired hand."

"But you could help Jasper. It sounds like he needs a few patriots."

"Jasper can use me right here. I can keep an eye on Royce, now that I know he's alive. And when the time comes for him to leave, I can make sure he's ready for what's coming. I'd be honored to stay and be here for you and your family."

Eve bit her lip. Adam was saying all the right things, and the only thing left for her to do was open her heart.

Adam reached over and touched her hand. "I love you, Eve. And the other reasons are valid, but I only want to stay because of you."

Electric heat shot up Eve's arm as she struggled to decide what to do next. She hesitated and tried to think past the fog in her brain. "Adam..."

The doorbell rang.

Eve pulled her hand back, and Adam dropped his head and sighed. The kitchen door opened, and Eve caught sight of Gillian, Sarah, and Declan against the door as Ramsey stepped out.

"Sorry about that," said Ramsey, hurrying. "Let me get it."

Apparently, they had an audience. Eve shook her head as Gillian and Sarah came into the living room, sipping their coffee.

Ramsey opened up the entry. "Hey. You're early."

A tall, muscled, dark-skinned man with a shaved head entered behind an older woman. She was tall and slim and dressed in a stylish black and white pantsuit. Her silver hair was swept up into a smooth chignon, and she walked in like she was royalty.

"No reason not to come now," said the woman. "I know how much you enjoy my company."

Ramsey huffed. "A pleasure, as always, Morgana."

"Hi, Sherlock," said the man. "Everybody here?"

"Hey, Leroy." Ramsey shut the door. "For the most part. Hannah will be here in about an hour. The kids and mom will be here by dinnertime."

"Great," said Leroy. He and Morgana greeted Declan and Sarah.

"You must be Eve and Gillian," said Leroy. "It's nice to finally meet."

The sisters stepped up and shook hands with the big man.

"This is Leroy Sampson," said Ramsey. "He runs the Protector program." He motioned toward the woman. "And this is Morgana. She is the leader of our Council." He gestured toward Adam. "This is Adam. He just arrived from Eudora and he's full of exciting news."

Leroy's and Morgana's eyes widened. "Is that so?" asked Morgana.

"I thought you might like that," said Ramsey. "I'm sure he'd love to talk to you."

Adam shook hands with Leroy and Morgana. "What's the Protector program?"

"It's a program that assists our people who are shifting, to ensure the process goes smoothly and there are no issues with discovery," said Leroy.

"I've heard some things about your visit. I trust everything has been reconciled?"

"You worry too much, Leroy," said Morgana. "I've been looking forward to meeting the Fletcher's, but you are an unexpected bonus." She put her bag down and unwrapped the scarf around her neck. "The Council would love to meet you."

"You have a Council here?" asked Adam.

"We do. There are currently ten of us, although I'd like it to be eleven." She glanced at Sarah, who smiled softly.

"I've been trying to talk her into it," said Ramsey. "She's just not into all those fancy robes."

"You wear fancy robes?" asked Eve.

Morgana frowned. "Certainly not. Ramsey here finds himself amusing, although it's rare for anyone else to."

"Perhaps you ought to consider the robes. Those meetings could use a little excitement," said Ramsey.

Leroy chuckled. "I'll remind you of that next time you visit. I'd like to see you in a robe, Sherlock."

Ramsey waved a hand. "Forget I said anything."

"Sherlock?" asked Gillian.

"He insists on calling me by my middle name. He's been doing it since we met. Most everyone else calls me Ramsey."

"Sherlock's a good name. It suits you," said Leroy.

"Can I get anyone something to drink?" asked Sarah. "I was just making some coffee."

"I'd love a cup," said Leroy.

"What about Royce Fletcher?" asked Morgana. "Is he here yet?"

"They know about Royce?" asked Eve.

"They do," said Declan. "It was actually Morgana's idea to fake Royce's death."

"Really?" asked Gillian.

"She's smarter than she looks," said John.

"Too bad we can't say the same for you," Morgana said coolly. She sat at the dining table. "I'd love to sit and speak with you ladies when you get a chance. There's so much I'd like to ask. You too, Adam."

Glancing at the full room, Eve tugged on Adam's arm. "Actually, Adam and I need to talk for a minute. We'll be outside." She pulled him toward a sliding glass door that led to the backyard.

"Take your time," said Sarah. "Morgana, can I get you some tea?"

Chapter Thirty-One

ROYCE SAT ON THE sofa beside two narrow beds that occupied the room. His fingers were shaky, but after taking several deep breaths, he opened the flap of the envelope. He slid out the papers inside. They were white, and Royce could see the handwriting in black ink on the page.

His heart rate quickened, and he closed his eyes, telling himself to stay calm.

Settling, he opened his eyes, opened the letter, and began to read.

Dearest Royce,

It's me, Sarna.

Royce released a long-held breath. *Sarna.* She was alive. He squeezed his eyes closed, recalling their last moments together as she clung to life. He hadn't known if she'd survived the return home, but now he did. He sighed and gave silent thanks.

His hands and breathing still unsteady, Royce blinked back tears, refocused, and kept reading.

I hope this letter finds its way to you. I have written and rewritten it, imagining what you are doing and what you are going through. Jasper told me what happened and why you stayed. I was heartbroken to not have you here. But I can't deny who you are and why I love you. You are the fiercest protector with the gentlest spirit, and because of that, I know you did what you had to do.

I can't imagine what you must be dealing with, not to know my fate, but I am fine. Jasper got me immediate care when I arrived home. It took some time, but I am now back on my feet and just as feisty as before.

I don't know when this letter will find you, but as of this writing, your father is alive. He was voted out of his position and Roma took power in his place. He is now at home and in general good health. The reason for his strange illness has not been discovered, but Jasper and I have our suspicions.

Your father has learned of our visit to you, and although outwardly he disapproved of the risks we took, he is also grateful that we met. He misses your family a great deal and has asked me many questions about my visit. Now that I've gotten to know him, I can see where you get your deep love and affection for your friends and loved ones. You two are very much alike.

Since your father has stepped down, Jasper has taken a more active role against the Dark Reds, much to Roma's dislike. When we returned to Eudora, Jasper was briefly imprisoned but was released when your father insisted. Roma complied, but I know in my heart that she is angry with Jasper. Right now, he is an annoyance, but as his following grows, he could become more of a problem for her. Roma and Jasper rarely speak, and I fear that if she feels threatened, she will retaliate. I have voiced my concerns to Jasper, but he rarely listens. I pray he doesn't end up as my brother did, but there is little I can do about it. Like you, he is stubborn and obstinate. And now, because of what is happening, he is mad.

I feel I must tell you about someone else that I suspect you are wondering about. Jasper explained what Desde did to you, and I cannot express my outrage enough. The woman is vile and unscrupulous, and she made it back, but she did not *have your child.*

Royce lowered the letter and hung his head. The revelation that Desde was not raising his offspring took a great weight off his shoulders. He took a deep breath and let it out.

Relieved, but his heart still thumping, he rubbed his face and kept reading.

She is still dangerous, though, and Jasper keeps his distance from her and her mother. They have made it their mission to befriend Roma and to stay as close to power as possible, although I think Roma suffers them only because it annoys Jasper. Desde has her claws into a powerful Council member who is no doubt swayed by her charms. I stay away from her and have seen her only once since our return, but the look on her face alone convinced me of her hatred toward me. She is a formidable enemy, but I think she realizes I am formidable as well. She's not the only one with powerful allies.

Which brings me to my next subject. I can only imagine what you have been going through, wondering what happened to me. Please don't worry. I am well and in good health. I keep out of the spotlight and keep a low profile. Jasper checks in on me frequently, as if he knows that's what you would expect from him. He is the dutiful younger brother. I have moved away from the city and stay out of the political arena. This may surprise you, since you know I am not one to keep my thoughts to myself. But there is a reason for this. I am protecting myself...and your daughter.

Royce stopped. He reread the last sentence, not sure he understood. He kept reading.

That's right. You read this correctly. You are a father. I gave birth to a beautiful little girl I named Greta, and as of this writing, she is three months old.

Royce could barely see straight as tears clouded his eyes. A daughter. He had a daughter? He leaned forward and held his head. The relief he felt that Sarna was still alive was eclipsed by the knowledge that she'd given birth to his child. His composure threatened to crumble. How was it possible? Sarna had been near death when she'd left, and her injuries should have ended any potential pregnancy. He shook his head, trying to take in air. He was a dad?

He wiped his eyes. Sniffing, he continued to read.

She is gorgeous, like her daddy. She inherited your light hair and bronze skin, and she is an angel. That part she got from me.

Because of who she is though, I must keep her a secret. No one knows of her other than Jasper and your father. If Roma were to learn of her existence, I'm not sure what she would do. Since you fathered her, Greta is the next High Child. That puts her at great risk, and although she is just a baby, I fear for her. At some point, word will get out. I cannot keep this secret forever. I can only hope that since your existence is still unknown to the public, then that is some small protection for Greta. But if what I fear is true and Roma is sending soldiers to remove you as a threat, it would logically mean that Greta could be next.

If that happens, I will do whatever it takes to protect her. Jasper has suggested repeatedly that if he has the opportunity, he will find a way to get me back to Earth. But since our previous excursion, he is watched constantly, and since your father no longer holds the sway he once did, his reach is limited too. Roma knows what we want, and she is doing all she can to prevent us from contacting you.

Because of that, I must warn you to please be careful. Jasper has a few trusted friends that he believes can get this letter to you. And if you're reading this, then take caution. Roma fears you. She knows who you are and knows your plans to take your rightful place. She is aware of your sisters, too, but you are the bigger threat. Since she is not aware of Greta, she believes Eve and Gillian, in the event of your death, would be the next in line to become High Child, so they must be careful. My fear is if they succeed in removing you, Eve will be next. Gillian is less of a worry because she is married and is unlikely to leave Earth, but she is still in d anger.

I tell you these things not because I want to scare you. I hope I am overreacting, but Roma will protect herself, even it means killing her half-brother and sisters.

As for me, I will continue to stay where I am, attracting as little attention to myself as possible. I will raise Greta to know what a wonderful father she has and how much he loves and misses her. The picture I have of you sits by her crib, and I show it to her every night. I pray that one day you will be there in person and will kiss her yourself and wish her goodnight.

I want that for myself too. I miss you every day. When I go to sleep, I imagine you wrapped around me, holding me close. Sometimes, the pain of not having you here is almost too much to bear, but then I think of our daughter, and I realize how much responsibility I have. I am raising the next High Child, and I cannot take that lightly.

I love you, Royce. I refuse to believe that I will never see you again. My heart breaks to consider it, so I don't. One day, we will find our way back to each other, and until that day, I will hold strong. It's what you're doing, and I will do the same.

Until then, I have given you something to remember us. Put it by your bed, and when you're ready to sleep, please think of us, and maybe, if we're lucky, we'll be looking at your picture at the same time and doing the same thing.

I love you, and Greta sends you kisses.

Sarna.

Through teary eyes, Royce checked the letter. There was nothing else. He picked up the envelope, looked inside, and saw a picture. Fingers trembling, he pulled it out and turned it over. It was a picture of Sarna, smiling and holding an infant. The baby had chubby cheeks and her eyes were open. There was a thin layer of blonde hair on her head, and she was wrapped loosely in a blanket. Sarna wore an open-collared shirt, and she wore the necklace he'd given to her the night she'd left.

He stared at the picture, touching and studying everything in it. Sarna's beautiful face; Greta's tiny fingers that gripped Sarna's pinky. It was everything he'd ever wanted. The baby blanket was a soft shade of blue and was dotted with various animals, although Royce couldn't be sure what kind—they looked like bears. Sarna's smile was happy, although behind her eyes, he detected a layer of sadness.

Holding the picture, his composure crumbled. Setting the letter aside, he allowed himself a moment of respite, and missing Sarna and his daughter, he stared at the photo and wept.

Chapter Thirty-Two

Eve opened the patio door. Adam followed her out. Everything went silent, and she took a moment to enjoy it. She thought of the people inside. "You sure you want to stay here?"

He smiled. "It seems you have a lot of family and friends looking out for you. Why wouldn't I? They seem like a tight-knit group."

Eve nodded. They were on a deck with two irons chairs and a table beneath an overhang. An empty blue baby swing sat beside the chairs. Eve sat in one of the seats, and Adam took the other.

"They are close," said Eve. "John and Sarah have been very kind, and you've seen what they've done for Royce."

Adam nodded. "You think they trust me enough to join the family?"

She picked at the arm of the chair. "It seems that way."

"Then all the more reason to stay." He paused. "Except, of course, if you don't want me to."

The urge to reach out and touch him was almost too hard to ignore. "Adam, I want you to stay. I just..."

"What?"

"I'm just not sure about us. My track record with men is not great. I like my 'me' time. I can be self-absorbed, cranky, and I frequently speak before I think. It's not the most accommodating trait. I've always lived alone, so I don't know what I'd be like as a roommate. Probably awful. I'm a terrible housekeeper."

He grinned. "I've seen how you handle your mail."

She smiled.

"Are you saying you're willing to give it a try? I know this won't be easy. I'm not the perfect guy, either, as I'm sure you've noticed."

Eve hung her head. Her mind was a jumble. But she knew she had to decide. Take him in and risk losing him, or play it safe and protect her heart? Despite the fact she knew Adam was different and that they'd begun to Bind for a reason, her past failures reminded her that nothing was certain. Before she could answer, Benny's image popped into her head and she heard his voice clearly. *This is not the time to play it safe, kid. It's time to lighten up and laugh a little.*

A buzzing sound made Eve look up. It came from a large leafy bush planted beside the patio.

"What's that?" asked Adam, eyes narrowing.

"I don't know."

The buzzing got louder, and Eve watched the shrub. "Sounds like a bug."

Adam sat up. "What kind of bug sounds like that?"

A large, green, flying insect flew from the bush and landed on the porch rail. Its body was fat and round. Its wings fluttered.

Adam froze.

Eve raised a palm. "Just relax. It's a cicada. I'm surprised to see one this time of year. It's late."

Adam's eyes were round. "It's huge. What kind of food do the bugs eat around here?"

"Just stay still. He'll fly away."

The bug twitched its wings. Eve attempted to convince the creature to head back from where it came when it suddenly took flight. It shot forward and headed straight at Adam. There was a distinct 'thump' when it contacted Adam's chest. The reaction was instantaneous. Adam stood and flailed like a swarm of bees were on him. Yanking at his shirt, he struggled to pull it over his head. His shirt blinding him, he staggered into the baby swing and got his foot tangled up in it. There was a ripping sound as Adam pulled on the fabric, and it came off. He tried to run, but his stuck foot dragged the swing behind him. Still waving his arms, he tripped and fell to the ground, breathing hard and throwing his shirt into the dirt. The cicada was nowhere to be found.

Eve watched it all in shock. Seeing him on the ground, shirtless, with the swing caught around his ankles, she giggled.

Adam wiped his face and did a once over of his body. "Is it gone?"

Giggles turned to laughter. She held her stomach.

"It's not funny. That thing came after me." He looked around and retrieved his shirt cautiously. He sat up, careful of his surroundings, shook out the shirt, and held it up. It was ripped in two places.

Eve doubled over. Tears ran down her cheeks. She managed to sputter two words. "You okay?"

Adam checked the shirt again and put it on despite the damage. He disentangled his foot from the swing. The leg he'd tripped on was dented, and when he sat the swing up, it listed to the side.

Eve could barely speak. She pointed. "You broke the swing." It was hard to breathe, and she snorted.

Adam finger-combed his disheveled hair. "That thing was Godzilla's grandchild. I think it targeted me. I'm pretty sure it had lasers for eyes."

Eve wiped at her tears. She took a breath and thought she had it under control, but another image of Adam flailing and tripping made her start all over. Her stomach ached from laughing.

He put the baby swing back, although the seat no longer moved back and forth. "I'll fix it." His breathing was returning to normal, but his shirt was ripped at the shoulder and at the neck. He watched Eve as she shook. "It's good to see you laugh."

Eve caught her breath. Still holding her belly, she thought of Benny again and she wondered. Had he sent her a message?

Wiping her face, she chuckled. She was going to enjoy the image of Adam flailing like a wild man for a long time. She thought about that. A long time. She would be with him for a long time. Was that so bad? Standing there, all her worries and fears vanished, and without thinking, she stepped forward and walked into his arms.

He wrapped himself around her and held her close. She felt his breath against her ear. Her body warmed and her breath quickened, and everything seemed so obvious.

She pulled back but still held him close. "I love you too, Adam. I think I have since our moment on the roof."

He brushed a lock of hair off her face. "You're the best thing that's ever happened to me." He touched his forehead to hers. "We're going to have a great love story."

"Promise?" she asked. She brushed her lips against his.

He held her with one arm and stroked her face with his hand. "Promise," he said huskily, and he lowered his lips against hers.

Eve tried to breathe as everything fired at once. His mouth and tongue moved over hers, and she moved against him. She kissed him senseless, and he returned the favor. His hands slid down her body and pulled her in, and Eve explored his chest when she realized where they were.

Breathless, she pulled back. "We have to stop. We're in the Ramsey's backyard."

He groaned. "You think they'd mind?"

She pinched him. "We can't embarrass ourselves."

He loosened his grip. "How long are we here for?"

"Dinner." She took a deep breath and tried to collect herself. "We have to get through dinner."

"Hell. This is going to be a painful meal."

Eve gasped. "No. Wait. Gillian. She's staying with me tonight."

"Not anymore, she isn't." He tried to pull her back in, but she pushed back.

"I can't kick her out."

The sliding glass door opened, and they turned and went still. Gillian poked her head out. "You two okay out here?"

Eve nodded, breathless. "We're great. Just great."

"Sarah wants to take me in to town tomorrow, so I thought I'd spend the night here tonight. That okay with you?" She smiled.

Adam pinched Eve from behind and she felt her face color. Her sister was using those telepathic powers again. "That's fine."

Gillian grinned. "Sarah's got some snacks out. Come join us."

"We'll be right there."

Gilli waved and went back inside. Eve turned, and before she could speak, Adam pulled her in for another passionate kiss.

· · · · ● · ● · · · ·

"He's been in there almost thirty minutes." Gillian took a couple of cashews from a bowl on the table and popped one in her mouth.

"You sure he's still in the room?" asked Leroy.

"Well, as far as I know, the man can't walk through walls. Not yet, at least," said Ramsey.

"How much time should we give him?" asked Declan.

"We don't know what's in the letter," said Sarah. "If it's personal, and we know it might be, he'll need some time."

Leroy took a swig of his coffee. "So, Adam came to deliver a letter? We're confident of that?"

"He's telling the truth," said Sarah.

"Definitely," said Gillian. "He's sensitive and compassionate. I'm surprised Eve didn't feel that herself."

"Romantic entanglements often lead to confusion. It's easy to doubt your own instincts," said Morgana.

"Ain't that the truth," said Ramsey. He waved his fingers. "I don't know why we're drinking coffee and tea. Anybody want anything stronger?"

Everybody's hand went up.

He glanced at Morgana. "One of our rare moments of agreement."

"Sometimes the fates align," she answered as she placed a piece of cheese on a cracker. She eyed the back patio door. "You think the happy couple will return?"

Ramsey stood from the table. "I hope they're not desecrating my backyard. What will the shrubs think?"

Declan chuckled. "Something makes me think they've seen it before. They're not the first Binding couple in this house."

Sarah colored. "The shrubs will be fine."

Ramsey smiled at his wife. "They're not dead yet." He headed into the kitchen.

"I'll help you, Sherlock," said Leroy.

Gillian watched the bedroom door. "I'm giving him ten minutes, then I'm going to check on him."

· · • • • • • • · ·

Eve slid the back door open, and she and Adam stepped inside.

"Welcome back," said Morgana.

Eve closed the door and held hands with Adam. "When's dinner?" asked Eve.

Gillian smiled. "Actually," she glanced at Sarah, who tilted her head, "dinner is postponed."

Sarah paused, and then nodded. "Yes. It's a pity. I bought the wrong ingredients." She huffed. "Can you imagine?"

Morgana looked between the two of them.

"You know," said Gillian, "I think we should all make our own plans for dinner. Don't you? We can all get together tomorrow."

"That's probably for the best," said Sarah.

"Nonsense," said Morgana. "I'm sure Eve and Adam would love to stay and converse. I can't imagine what else they'd rather do." Eve caught Sarah hiding a sly smile.

"You know," said Adam. "I think Eve and I will head out. There's no need for Sarah to worry about dinner tonight."

Eve had to force herself to stay composed when all she wanted to do was drag Adam out of the house. "What about Royce?" Eve asked.

"I'll explain. I'm sure he won't mind the change in plans," said Gillian, although Eve expected her brother may not agree.

Eve nodded, trying not to look flustered, but knowing she was failing. "Okay. I guess we'll plan on coming tomorrow then." She tugged on Adam's arm, and they walked to the door. "We'll go now. Adam's really hungry."

"Starving," said Adam.

Sarah rose from the table. "We'll see you tomorrow."

Declan, who'd been on the phone, ended his call. "What is this about dinner?"

Eve wasted no time in grabbing her keys. Adam reached for the door but stopped when the door swung open forcefully on its own, and Adam jumped back.

Curtis stood in the doorway. His clipboard was gone, and he held a blank stare on his face.

Sarah walked out from behind the table. "Curtis?"

He didn't move.

"Can I help you?" asked Adam. He put an arm in front of Eve.

Curtis continued to stand at the entrance. His empty stare gave Eve the chills, and she knew something wasn't right.

Declan put himself between Curtis and Gillian. "What's wrong, Curtis?"

"John?" called Sarah.

Curtis studied the people in the room, and Eve noticed something glowing from beneath his shirt. It looked like a necklace.

Adam apparently noticed it, too. He pushed Eve behind him. "Get back," he said, stepping away from the door.

Gillian stood. So did Morgana.

"What's going on?" asked Morgana.

Ramsey and Leroy came into the room. "Yes?" Ramsey saw Curtis at the door. "Curtis? You forget something?"

Curtis smiled, and the kind face and gentle manner Eve recalled from before was gone.

"It's not Curtis," said Adam, stepping back farther as he kept himself in front of Eve.

"Who is it?" asked Leroy.

Curtis finally spoke. "Excellent question." He stepped inside and the door closed by itself behind him. His walk and mannerisms did not resemble his earlier ones. Whatever he wore around his neck glowed brighter.

"Burke," said Adam.

"No," said Eve.

"Burke?" asked Declan, remaining where he was.

"He came looking for Royce," said Eve. She glanced at Gillian, and her sister's face told Eve everything. Gillian knew they were in trouble. "He's using Curtis's body," said Adam. "That stone around his neck. It's a conduit of energy which allows Burke to project himself into Curtis."

"Is this what he did to your friend?" Morgana asked. "How is this possible?"

Burke-Curtis moved farther into the room. "All sorts of things are possible." He cocked his head. "Morgana, is it?"

Ramsey moved into the room and stepped in front of Sarah. "What are you doing in my house?"

Burke stopped. "Interesting group you have here." He stared at Sarah. "Very interesting."

Ramsey pulled Sarah behind him.

Declan stood his ground. "You didn't answer the question."

Burke studied Declan. "You're a Gray." He glanced at Ramsey. "Several of you are."

"You must have gotten all As in school," said Ramsey.

Burke's lip raised into a sneer. "You're bold for a Gray. Where I come from, your disrespect would not be tolerated."

"Things don't work that way here," said Declan.

"We're a bold group. Have been for some time," said Ramsey. Sarah took his arm. "And we don't like outsiders."

"I'm not an outsider. I'm your fellow Eudoran. We have much in common."

"The only thing we have in common is two arms, two legs, and two eyes. Now that we've moved past the introductions, you need to leave," said Ramsey.

"Typical of a Gray," said Burke. He spoke to Sarah. "He's your mate? You're a Red. You could've done so much better." He grinned. "Too bad I wasn't around at the time."

Ramsey took a step closer, but Sarah held his elbow.

"What do you want?" asked Morgana. She stepped around Declan and squared her shoulders. Eve admired her courage and realized the woman was diffusing a heated situation. "You didn't come for conversation."

Burke-Curtis held a hard stare at Ramsey before speaking to Morgana. "Correct. I came to complete my assignment. Kill the High Child."

Eve sucked in a breath. Did this man know that Royce was still alive? The door off the hallway stayed shut. Royce was still in there, but Eve suspected Royce would be wondering what was going on. He'd been in there a long time. She closed her eyes and prayed.

"The High Child is dead," said Morgana.

"No, she's not," said Burke. He looked at Eve. "The next in line is the second oldest."

"Stay away from her," said Adam.

"I have no interest in the position," said Eve.

"I'm sure your brother thought the same at first," said Burke.

"This is insane," said Declan. "You plan to come in here and kill Eve?"

"I have to kill them both. Once Eve's gone, I can't have her little sister get in the way."

Eve and Gillian's eyes met.

"We're not going to just stand here while you attack two of our own," said Ramsey.

Eve watched the bedroom door.

Burke stepped forward again. Declan and Morgana moved back. "You have a choice. Let me do what I came to do or risk your own lives. I will kill anyone who stands in my way."

His back was now to the hall. Eve held her breath when she saw the door silently open. She looked at her sister and knew Gillian had seen it, too.

"I can see now why you use another man to do your dirty work. You don't have the courage to face us on your own. You're a coward," said Ramsey.

The necklace glowed. The door opened wider.

Burke glared. A mug from the table flew up and hit Ramsey in the head, knocking him sideways.

"John!" said Sarah.

Ramsey winced and held his head. Blood flowed from between his fingers.

"Stop it," said Sarah.

"I'm okay," said Ramsey, pushing her back behind him.

"You know," said Burke to Sarah. "I could get rid of him and you could join me on Eudora. Half-human, half-Red. You'd be all the rage."

"Get out of here," said Leroy. "Neither Eve nor Gillian have any interest in becoming High Child. You can leave them here and make up any story you want. No one would know the difference."

"You must be Leroy," said Burke. "At least I'll know everyone who's going to die."

"Nobody's going to die," said Adam, "because you're going to leave."

Burke narrowed his eyes. "You got lucky once. It won't happen again." He touched the necklace. "This won't be so easy to access." He pointed. "Now step back from her, unless you want to be a victim, too."

The door of the hallway was fully open. Eve's heart was beating so fast, she worried it would warn Burke.

Adam didn't move. "I won't let you hurt her."

Burke's face went flat. "Very well." He swiped out his hand, and a wave of force hit Eve straight in the stomach. Everyone in the room was knocked backwards. Gillian, Declan, and Morgana fell on the floor, and Adam was forced back into Eve and then onto the carpet. Ramsey, Sarah, and Leroy fell into the dining table.

Before Eve could react, she felt something pull on her foot, and she started to slide over the floor. She saw Gillian sliding as well. It was as if a rope had slid around her ankle and was dragging her. She grabbed for leverage but couldn't find anything.

Adam grabbed at her, but she was still being dragged. As Gillian passed Declan, he reached for her and took her hand, but it didn't stop Gillian's momentum. Burke was pulling them closer and there was nothing they could do.

Gillian and Eve were within a foot of Burke when there was a loud bellow. Burke flew off his feet, and he hit the ground hard. The force released, and Eve stopped moving. So did Gillian, and Adam scrambled forward and pulled Eve back as Declan reached for Gillian.

Burke struggled as his hands shoved against an invisible burden and then went to his throat, where he gagged and clawed at unseen hands. Items flew through the house. A plate raised off the table and crashed into the wall. A chair toppled over, and a glass framed picture slid off the mantel and shattered on the floor.

"His necklace," yelled Adam. "Take his necklace."

Burke continued to fight, his face now turning blue as he tried to breathe. He took one of his hands and shoved it hard against the air. There was a brief grunt, but the force against Burke did not release. But now the form of a man was taking shape over Burke.

Declan sat up. "Curtis. You're killing Curtis."

Adam did a fast crawl, dodging a flying cheese tray. He reached the gasping Curtis and pulled at his shirt. The glowing necklace was dimming, but still alight. As a now fully visible Royce continued to straddle and strangle the man, Adam gripped the stone and yanked. The cord snapped, and Adam got up, ran across the room, opened the back door, and threw the stone.

Curtis went limp.

"Stop," said Declan. He reached over and grabbed Royce's arm.

"Stop, Royce," said Gillian. "He's gone. Burke is gone."

Royce eased up and let go. He slumped backward, breathing hard and grimacing.

Eve raced forward and squatted next to her brother. "Are you okay?"

Declan checked Curtis's pulse, and Sarah ran up. "How is he?"

"He's alive."

Ramsey kneeled next to Declan. "Is it safe? Is Burke gone?"

Adam answered, looking pale. "He's gone."

"Where did he go?" asked an unruffled Morgana. She stood and straightened her clothes.

"Hopefully to hell, where he belongs," said Royce. He sat back and cursed, holding his side.

"What is it?" asked Gillian. "You're hurt."

"It's nothing. He zapped me, but I'm fine."

Eve studied him. "No, you're not. Let me see."

"We need to get Curtis some help. He's not looking too good," said Declan.

"Get him on the couch," said Sarah.

Leroy and Ramsey lifted Curtis by the arms and pulled him upright. They got him to the sofa and laid him down.

"Let me see, Royce," said Gillian. She reached for his shirt and lifted the hem. An angry red welt was blistered up and covered a wide area on his skin.

"God," said Eve. "He burned you."

"I'm fine," said Royce. "Help me up."

Eve and Gillian took Royce's arms as he stood on shaky legs.

"You need to take a seat. You look like you're about to faint," said Gillian.

"Stop mothering me. I said I'm all right," said Royce. He sat on a dining chair. "You should have let me kill him."

"He is not the man you want," said Morgana. "Apparently, this man was in the wrong place at the wrong time."

Declan shook Curtis, trying to rouse him, but the man didn't stir. "I'm worried about his neck. If it swells enough, he could have difficulty breathing."

Sarah sat beside Curtis on the couch. She put her hands on his chest and closed her eyes.

"You're sure Burke is gone?" asked Ramsey.

"I am," said Adam. "Without a conduit, he can't project. He's back on his ship."

"How did he find this place?" asked Leroy. "How did he know to come here? How did he know our names?"

"And who Sarah was?" asked Ramsey.

Adam stared off. "Hell." He looked at the front door, walked over, and opened it.

"What?" asked Eve. "Did he follow us?"

Adam looked up and down the street, then closed the door. "Tez. It's the only explanation."

"Your friend?" asked Gillian.

"He had to have been watching. He saw Curtis and targeted him. He led Burke here." He paused. "Tez knows about this house. I told him about your group. How there was a community of Gray's, and how Sarah healed me. I never suspected..." He closed his eyes as he tried to comprehend what had just happened. "I'm sorry. This is my fault."

"How could you have known?" asked Eve.

"It should have been an easy deduction. He can track me with this." He pulled out his phone. "I didn't expect him to collude with Burke, though. We've always hated the man."

"Destroy that thing," said Royce, holding his side.

"There's not much point," said Ramsey. Leroy had found a towel in the kitchen, put ice in it, and given it to Ramsey, who held it against his head. "He already knows where we are."

Adam hit a button on the device. "He can't detect me now."

Sarah placed her hands lightly on Curtis's throat. Eve watched her work. "Should we call an ambulance?"

Before anyone could answer, Curtis's eyes fluttered. Sarah opened her own and sat back. She lightly shook his shoulder. "Curtis? Can you hear me?"

Eve took a step closer to see Curtis open his eyes clearly. His skin tone was back to normal and the early signs of bruising on his neck had faded.

He blinked and looked around. "Where am I?"

Everyone looked at each other, unsure of what to say.

Sarah answered. "You're at the Ramsey's. You fainted on the porch, and we brought you inside. Do you remember?"

Ramsey moved to Sarah's side. "Yeah. You gave us a scare. You've been out for a few minutes. We almost called an ambulance."

Curtis held his head. "I fainted?" He sat up slowly. "I don't remember."

"How do you feel?" asked Sarah.

"A little woozy, and I have a headache." He glanced up at Ramsey. "What happened to your head?"

Ramsey stared at the bloody towel in his hand. "What, this? I hit my head on..." He stared blankly.

"A cheese tray," said Declan, picking up the item from the floor. "I was being stupid and threw it."

Curtis squinted, and Declan shrugged at Ramsey.

"You want us to call someone to get you?" asked Sarah.

Curtis checked his watch. "Is that the time? Man, I'm late. I have another delivery." He stood carefully.

"You should take it easy," said Declan.

Curtis waved him off. "No. I'm fine. It's probably that stupid diet I'm doing. My girlfriend's eating only lettuce for twenty-four hours. I told her I'd do it with her."

"Perhaps you should eat some protein," said Morgana. She began to pick up the broken cutlery off the floor.

Ramsey stepped over a puddle of coffee and a piece of a broken mug. "Don't mind the mess, Curtis. My friend here has a temper." He nodded at Leroy.

Leroy didn't hesitate. "You know I prefer cheddar over swiss. How many times do I have to tell you?"

Curtis held his head. "Sorry about worrying you." He walked to the door.

Declan followed. "You sure you're okay?"

"Just fine. My head's already better. Thank you." He opened the door and stepped out.

"You're welcome. Maybe you should go home instead of making that delivery. I'm sure Jerry would understand," said Declan.

"Nah, I'm fine." He waved and was gone. Declan shut the door.

Everyone let out a collective sigh.

"You think he bought it?" asked Adam.

"I think so," said Declan.

"I don't think the whole 'I was possessed by an alien' reason will occur to him," said Ramsey.

"He won't remember," said Adam. "He'll be tired and weak, but I suppose Sarah's mojo will help with that."

"I still think you should have let me kill him," said Royce.

"It wasn't his fault," said Leroy.

"Maybe not, but I'd feel better." He grunted and winced.

Sarah stood. "Let me look at your injury."

"I'm fine," said Royce.

"Let her help," said Gillian. "You're in pain."

Royce glowered at her, but when Sarah neared, he let her gently raise his shirt. His skin was raw and red and to Eve, it looked like the blister had grown.

"He got you, didn't he?" said Declan.

"Not before I got to him first." Royce gritted his teeth as Sarah touched his side.

"Sorry," she said before closing her eyes and going quiet again.

Gillian returned an overturned dining chair to its rightful place. Morgana had picked up most of the debris and deposited it in the trash. Leroy picked up another overturned chair and sat while Adam took Eve's hand. Ramsey sat beside Leroy and dabbed at his injured head.

Royce's wound slowly healed. The angry red turned a bright pink and then faded away until his skin returned to normal. Sarah dropped her hands, took a breath, and opened her eyes. "Better?"

Royce stared, wide-eyed. "Like new." He dropped his shirt. "Thank you."

Sarah shook out her hands and went to sit beside her husband, who took her fingers in his own. She looked at Ramsey's head. "You okay?"

He nodded. "I'm fine. You can work on me later." He glanced around the room. "Right now, we have a bigger concern."

Royce swiveled in his seat to face the table. Gillian pulled out a chair as Adam and Eve joined them. Morgana didn't sit, but stood beside Declan, who crossed his arms. "You mean what happens next?" he asked.

"That's exactly what I mean." Ramsey addressed Adam. "He'll come back, won't he?"

Adam's shoulders dropped. "Yes. He'll come back. He knows Royce is alive and now so will Roma."

"How much time do we have?" asked Declan.

Adam paused. "Some. Burke has made two projections. It's a powerful weapon, but it comes at a cost. The host is not the only one affected. It saps the projector's strength too. It takes time to recover. He's likely low on supplies, energy, and fuel. So is Tez. They'll have no choice but to return and report back."

"And what happens after that?" asked Leroy.

"Roma will decide, but I know Burke. He'll make it his personal mission to finish the job. Roma knows that and will use it. She'll foster his hatred and direct it for her own benefit." He paused. "Which means the Fletcher family is not the only one at risk."

Ramsey nodded, accepting the news.

"What are you saying?" asked Gillian.

"He's saying we're all in danger now, correct?" asked Morgana.

"Correct," said Adam. "A community of Gray's has just handed Burke a defeat. He won't like that."

"He returns, and I'll make him wish he'd never heard the word 'Earth,'" said Royce.

"He won't come back alone," said Adam. "Roma will send reinforcements. She won't make the same mistake twice."

The room went quiet. Declan rubbed his head. "So what now?"

Eve didn't know what to say, and apparently, neither did anyone else.

Morgana broke the silence. "We do what we always do. It's not the first time we've faced adversaries." She eyed Ramsey, who nodded back.

"And what would that be?" asked Adam.

Morgana aimed a steely gaze at him. "We haven't survived on this planet for as long as we have by being meek. We are not defenseless, but they think we are. That gives us an advantage. So we prepare, and when they return..." Her gray eyes sparkled in the waning light of the window and Eve realized why this woman was on the Council. "We'll be ready."

What Happens Next?

Find out what happens when the Fletcher and Ramsey families join forces to battle their enemies in *Forged Lines*. They'll confront a foe prepared to destroy the ones they love, and they won't give up until the enemy is vanquished, but will the cost be too great?

Enjoy an excerpt below.

Want more from J. T. Bishop?

Sign up for her newsletter at jtbishopauthor.com to get the short story, *Red-Line: Prelude to The Shift,* plus a novella, future books, missing scenes, excerpts, and fun promos for **free**.

Follow J.T. on her Amazon author page to be notified of new releases.

How did it all begin with the Red-Lines?

Discover the *Red-Line Trilogy*, which started the Red-Line story. Sarah Randolph holds the key to the survival of a secret community. But first she must survive her "Shift." Her protector, John Ramsey, is assigned to keep her alive, but falling for her was never in his plans. When a powerful adversary reveals himself and his intentions for Sarah, her unique destiny may be their only hope.

The Red-Line Trilogy includes *Red-Line: The Shift, Red-Line: Mirrors,* and *Red-Line: Trust Destiny*. A boxed set is available, too!

What's next after the Fletcher Family Saga?

Do you like mystery thrillers with a touch of the paranormal? Then check out the *Family or Foe* saga featuring Detectives Daniels and Remalla. A killer with strange abilities is on the loose and he's targeting the family he believes wronged him. Can Daniels and Remalla catch him before he seeks his revenge and kills them all?

Detectives Daniels and Remalla get their own series.

After *The Family or Foe Saga*, the two charismatic and affable detectives battle psychopaths, unexplained evil and unsolved cases.

In *Haunted River*, book one in the series, the ghost of a woman haunts a small town where she lived and died. When a second woman's body turns up twenty-five years later, Daniels and Remalla become suspects, and the next targets.

Or pick up the omnibus *Shadows and Secrets*, which contains *Haunted River, Of Breath and Blood*, and *Of Body and Bone* (books one through three) of the paranormal thriller series.

A Note From J.T.

I love to hear from my readers about their experiences with my books, and I'd love to know what you thought about *Spark*. Eve's story was trickier to write because she's such an independent character and I had to wonder about the type of guy Eve would fall for. Gillian and Royce, while protective of who they gave their heart to, were less cynical and were ready for love. Eve, though, was a tougher nut to crack. She needed someone who had his own rough shell and Adam fit the bill. His struggles with his difficult past created his own unique issues. His pain, along with Eve's, made them a compelling couple and provided a path for each of them to find each other. I think that's why they became an irresistible love story.

The story isn't over yet though. *Forged Lines* will tie up loose ends and answer lingering questions. The Ramseys and Fletchers aren't out of the woods, and unfortunately, it's going to get worse before it gets better. So, hang on for the ride. It's going to have its ups and downs, but I think you're going to like it.

Reviews are a huge plus and big help for a writer, and potential readers. I would love it if you could please take a couple of minutes to leave a review for *Spark*. And if you'd like, please leave a few comments, too.

As always, thank you for your time and readership. It is deeply valued and appreciated.

Now, on to the next book!

Books in Chronological Order

Although recommended but not required, in case you prefer to read in order...

Red-Line: Prelude to The Shift, a short story (subscribers only)
Red-Line: The Shift
Red-Line: Mirrors
Red-Line: Trust Destiny
Curse Breaker
High Child
Spark
Forged Lines
**

The Girl and the Gunshot, a novella (subscribers only)
A Hamburger Christmas, a novella
The Magic of Murder, a novella (subscribers only)
First Cut
Second Slice
Third Blow
Fourth Strike
Murder Unveiled
Haunted River
Of Breath and Blood

Lost Souls
Of Body and Bone
Lost Dreams
Of Mind and Madness
Lost Chances
Of Power and Pain
Lost Hope
Of Love and Loss
Lost Lives
Dominion
Lost Time
Illusions
Lost Love
Vendetta
Black Bird

Acknowledgements

IT IS IMPOSSIBLE TO thank everyone who helped me to get to this point. There are no words. Publishing book six with number seven on the way does not happen without support.

To my amazing family and friends, your love takes me through all of this and carries me on. None of this exists without you. (I know I keep saying that, but it's true.) Every time I think twice about continuing this, you convince me otherwise, and I am eternally grateful.

To Amie, who does my covers, edits my books, and proofs the final version, thank you for all your help. Sharing this workload makes it infinitely easier.

Thank you to Mayza Clark for taking such lovely author photos. Your talent helped me look my very best.

To those whose kind words and thoughtful feedback have made my writing stronger and better, thank you for your guidance.

And to those who stand by my side in the unseen, I know you are there, and I feel your love. Your support is every bit as powerful and welcomed.

About the Author

Award-winning author, J.T. Bishop, is a writer of mystery thrillers with a paranormal edge. Growing up, she read Stephen King, Mary Higgins Clark, and Dean Koontz, devoured every episode of the X-files and watched plenty of TV shows with great partnerships that leave you wanting more. She loves tangled relationships, unexpected twists and turns, heart-stopping love stories and the complications that come with all the above. Throw in a little supernatural fun and she's hooked. Her evil plan is to hook you, too.

She's the author of The Red-Line Trilogy and its sister series, The Fletcher Family Saga, which features touches of urban fantasy, light sci-fi, and paranormal romance. She's also happily writing mystery thrillers featuring two charismatic detectives who may occasionally encounter a supernatural villain or two, and a crossover series which follows the exploits of a gifted, but troubled, paranormal P.I. and his spunky sister.

All the above keeps her busy, but in her spare time, she loves good movies, tasty food, an unfortunate sugar addiction, and traveling.

Enjoy an excerpt from book four in The Fletcher Family Saga, Forged Lines

VEE WALKED THROUGH THE heavy brush, pushing back tree branches and scanning the dense forest. She'd attempted to explore the area the previous night, but Larry had been right. It was too dark, and a flashlight was not adequate.

It was a warm evening, and she unzipped her jacket. Having gone to work that morning, she still wore her police officer's uniform. If she'd taken the time to go home and change, she'd have lost valuable light.

Remembering the previous night, Vee felt confident she was in the correct area. The ship, or whatever it was, had gone down somewhere near here. It was an area thickly populated with trees, but not people, making it an ideal area to hide something big.

Continuing to walk, she scanned the brush, looking for anything out of the ordinary. Her mind briefly wandered back to her workday, and she wondered if her coworkers and Larry were right. Was she crazy? She could live with being called "VT." She knew it came with the territory when you revealed to people that you were a lifelong MUFON member and your dream one day was to find proof that alien life existed. She'd dreamed about it since she was young and she and her dad would sit out on the porch, watching the night sky. They used to compete to see who could count the most shooting stars until one night when they'd seen much more.

It had been chilly, and she'd been wrapped in a blanket, holding a hot chocolate, when something very bright appeared in the sky. It was too slow to be a meteor and too fast and bright to be a satellite and as she and her dad continued to stare, the object moved closer and became brighter. It almost seemed to be scanning the area. She hadn't spoken, and neither had her dad, but they continued to watch as the object slowed, hovered, and then moved at a right angle over the trees, before it suddenly ascended, shot up and away, and was gone. Mouths open, she and her dad had sat in shocked silence.

Ever since that night, Vee couldn't learn enough about UFOs. She'd searched with her father the area where the ship had hovered, but had found nothing. They'd continued to watch the night sky in hopes it would return, but it never had. Veronica had not stopped looking, though. One day, she knew she would find the answers she sought.

She pushed back a bushy shrub and stepped into a small clearing. The golden-brown dried grass was uniform except for two small patches of dark circles. Vee walked over to them and studied the ground. From her view, it looked as if the stalks were burned. She kneeled and touched the area, then smelled the ground. It definitely smelled as if someone had lit the grass on fire. She looked up and surveyed. Standing, she saw an area of trampled foliage and disturbed dirt. Looking closer, she realized it was human footprints. Someone had been walking through here. A drop of rusty brown liquid dotted a leaf, and she touched it. Rubbing her fingers together, she realized it was blood. They'd been injured. She followed the footprints back into the brush and was about to step into another clearing when the radio on her shoulder squawked to life. She was off duty now, and she reached to turn it off when she heard the call.

"All units, respond. We have ten-eighty on 5967 Maple. People trapped inside. Fire department is responding. All units respond. Over."

Vee heard the address. She stepped away and jogged through the clearing and back out beyond the trees. In the distance, she saw the thick, black smoke drifting out of a wooded neighborhood a few miles away. Judging by the amount, there would likely be casualties.

She would have to save this hike for later and reached for the radio. "Ten-four, control. Officer Chappell responding. Over." It was going to take her at least twenty minutes to get to her car, but if she ran, she could try to get there faster. Jogging and dodging loose rocks, she flew down the trail.